ALL
THAT'S
LOST

Black Shuck Books
www.blackshuckbooks.co.uk

First published in Great Britain in 2022 by
Black Shuck Books
Kent, UK

Versions of the following stories have previously appeared in print:
'Adrenaline Junkies' in *The Porcupine Boy and Other Anthological Oddities*
(Macabre Ink, 2019)
'Mary, Mary' in *The Spectral Book of Horror Stories 2* (Spectral Press, 2015)
'In the Wake of My Father' in *Black Static #75* (2020)
'6/6' as a 66-copy limited edition chapbook (Black Shuck Books, 2019)
'Sideways' in *Interzone #266* (2016)
'Child of Thorns' in *Black Static #50* (2016)
'Painted Wolves' in *In Dog We Trust* (Black Shuck Books, 2018)
'Steel Bodies' in *New Fears 2* (Titan Books, 2018)
'The Swans' in *Black Static #60* (2017)
'Trapper's Valley' in *Crimewave #13* (2018)
'The Castellmarch Man' in *Great British Horror 1: Green and Pleasant Land*
(Black Shuck Books, 2016)
'The Whalers Song' in *The Devil and the Deep* (Night Shade Books, 2018)

Set in Caslon
Titles set in Caxton Book
Cover art and interior design © WHITEspace, 2022
www.white-space.uk

978-1-913038-76-2

All
That's
Lost

by

Ray Cluley

BLACK
SHUCK
BOOKS

This one's for three very special women:
Marie Bowdidge
Stephanie Rose
Jess Jordan

I'd be all the more lost without you.

| Contents |

~

They Might Have Mouths, They Might Have Eyes

An Introduction to Ray Cluley

by Stephen Volk

What do you want from a horror writer?

Someone who will churn out the usual Stephen King tropes, perhaps in a sub-Stephen King milieu, with set pieces reminiscent of that last horror film you saw that bored you with endless jump scares and bad CGI?

Yawn.

Or do you want something truly original? Something honest-to-God, don't-put-out-the-light scary?

For me, no contest.

Rest assured, as you read the following pages, your heart will beat a little bit faster, with fear, but also with glee.

Mine did. And I've read most of these stories a second time. I'll happily read them a third. In fact, I'd say at least half of them I'd put in a list of Stephen Volk's Favourite Horror Stories of All Time. And that's not just blowing smoke up the author's ass.

I have no need to. See, we're already friends.

Ray and I first met several full moons ago at some FantasyCon or other. I think I complimented him on "Shark! Shark!" and, happily, I've been complimenting him ever since. (No hard task.)

We've even – full disclosure – spent writing weekends together, with redoubtable fellow scribes Lockley and Lewis, in the wilds of Gwent. Where a selfie in the woods subsequently posted on Facebook gets a grizzly bear added by a wag with Photoshop. Where every stroll seemed (to us) to reveal signs of a potential serial killer's abode. Where, in a rustic farmhouse, Ray would secrete himself with his laptop in an upstairs room, applying himself to his word count or googling far-flung lands, while I'd sit downstairs, watching DVDs and fretting over a movie outline.

But it's from his writing I know Ray Cluley best.

Even before I knew him, I loved that he got the hell out of the way of the stories and stayed there, as if saying: "Here it is. This is what happened. Weird, huh?" He never shouts from the rooftops. Far from it.

In so doing, he allows the reader to sink into the story with no life jacket, no loud hailer through which to cry for help. No map except the scant directions he chooses to provide. You are alone, and he's got you.

To my mind, the extraordinary results he achieves on a regular basis come from pin-sharp observation, a cunning lack of artifice, and a command of language that reels you in like a tuna, tugging you from your natural environment to a scary new world of unknowns where there's no place to hide.

Another quality I'm in awe of in his work is the wide diversity of settings he chooses – evidential of a great, generous, and enquiring mind. I happen to know (because he has told me) that research is one of the things he enjoys most about the process of storytelling. But there's an element of fear involved in yanking yourself out of the normal world that surrounds you, and a thrill that goes with controlling it and using it to effect. Ray genuinely owns each leap into alien-ness and it's never just window dressing.

Within these pages you'll flirt with extremes in mid-air over Mexican ruins; be present at Martha's Vineyard as a famous movie is shot; accompany a television crew in a national park in Africa; experience Burma under an authoritarian regime; explore a ghostly, deserted shipyard in Bangladesh.

Every location as perfectly realised as the last.

To me, they represent, gathered together as they are in this collection, fearful glances – prying glances, even – into the darkest corners of the globe, striving to point out that even the places you thought you knew can have a veil lifted to reveal an unpleasant or revelatory truth.

This is one thing that sets Ray Cluley apart. Not for him the Ray Cluley Universe in which all stories are part of a vast, intersecting (and therefore strangely reassuring) whole. His subject matter ranges far and wide, however the theme is arguably a constant; nowhere, and nobody, is safe. That, of course, is what horror is all about – that, and so much more. Trauma. Memory. The consequences of harm. The fear that it will be visited again. The things that don't go away.

Ray achieves this, often, by the use of stunning, poetic images that sometimes evade logic but cling and suppurate within us long after the covers of the book are closed. It's in these unforgettable word pictures that he truly excels:

"The baby voiced its first cry. The sound was a series of broken sticks, like a small tree falling."

Human attraction as the painful embrace of thorns… A boy made of mud… The freedom of falling, only to be cut horrifically short… The dream of other dimensions, a step away from grief and distress… The resonant symbolism of a lightning-struck tree.

You will also find sly comments on contemporary culture in these tales – and specifically genre culture, in various forms:

A starchy academic treatise on a found footage phenomenon which out-chills *Blair Witch*… A return to an unsafe resort long after the artificial shark is gone… A test pilot's weird experience way beyond *The Twilight Zone*… A wistful and intensely moving coda to a video nasty.

Clearly, Ray is unashamed of his influences, but he does not go for the all-too-easy option of pastiche. In each case he utilises key texts in his own unique way to illustrate, often by contrast, the emotionally real. Sometimes the emotionally devastating.

What I value too, at his best, is the way he turns a thought, a line – often the *last line* – to stop you in your tracks:

"Hell is the things I heard with my eyes closed."

Wow.

In creating such exquisite moments, Ray allows you the space to join the dots, to fill in the gaps. The way he pulls the rug from under you being yet another way in which he proves himself an absolute master.

And so, as I come to the end of this introduction – having consigned my previous draft to the wastepaper bin ("Good filing," to quote Mel Brooks) – a last bit of smoke-blowing seems inevitable. Forgive me.

"The Final Girl's Daughter" is sheer perfection. I'm sorry. It sucked me in and spat me out, weeping like a baby. "The Swans", similarly, knocked me for six – even on second fucking reading. "Child of Thorns" should be acknowledged as an absolute classic of the fantastic, while "In the Wake of My Father" (possibly my favourite here: tough choice) is haunted by vivid characterisation, again with the use of poetic imagery that sears the mind with no requirement for elaboration.

So, go. Start reading. I'm holding you back.

Enjoy these superlative tales. They are without doubt the best that horror can give you right now. Some of the best horror has *ever* given.

I treasure them as endlessly rewarding examples of the best the short story form can deliver, allowing us to flirt with extremes, touch or feel the invisible, commune with troubled souls, experience otherness, and, in so doing, feel (as we all desperately need more than ever) a connection to what makes us human:

"It hurts," Jessie said. "Hurts plenty. But love does, don't it?"

Without further ado, turn the page, set off on the path in front of you, and don't be surprised if something goes wrong, something scares you, or there's a bear in that selfie.

You are in safe hands.

Stephen Volk
Bradford on Avon
February 2022

|Adrenaline Junkies|

~

"Carpe the fucking diem."

~

I'm thinking about Suki when Cate pats my arm and gives me the thumb-to-forefinger okay. For a moment I think she means we're ready to jump but the door's still closed and everybody else in the plane is triple-checking their harnesses and packs, pockets, cameras. She means the sign as a question, I realise. I don't want her to think I'm worried about the jump – I'm not – so I smile, and return the sign with a nod. She gives me a thumbs up, grinning. She's excited, adrenaline already working its magic. This is her first freefall, no static line, and I can't be looking sad when I know she's probably as nervous as she is excited. She doesn't know much about Suki yet, just the little she's heard from the others and maybe a tiny bit more from a well-meaning Kit. I'll give her my version after we've landed. Or tonight. I'll tell her tonight.

"You okay, pretty lady?" Todd shouts. We're flying in a tiny prop and the cabin is loud with its noise. I have no okay sign or thumbs up for him, just a middle finger, and he laughs. He's called me 'pretty lady' ever since Quintana Roo where one of the barmen kept trying his luck, complimenting my dress, my hair, no gaydar whatsoever. Cate had joked I should kiss her so he'd get the hint and a few tequilas later I did, but it wasn't for the barman's benefit. I'm not sure what I was trying to prove. Or who I was trying to prove it to.

There'd been tequilas last night as well, and a morning wake-up so early that we may as well have not gone to bed. It had left most of us silent at breakfast, even though it was jump day. For the other stuff, the climbing and kayaking, we'd fill up on oatmeal and protein snacks, but a jump day breakfast was whatever you wanted it to be. I opted for brown toast, scrambled egg, and half an avocado because that was what Suki used to have. Todd noticed, I could tell, so I stole a spoonful of baked beans from his fried breakfast and spread it over mine and he'd laughed, pretending to protest, and everything was okay.

"Come on, come on," Måns urges, sweeping his arms to bunch us together for a pre-jump selfie. He's got his phone on the end of a selfie-stick. He actually owns a selfie-stick. Maybe it's a Swedish thing. He leans into us, arm outstretched, and Todd rubs at Måns' bald head as the picture's taken. "Makes me more aerodynamic," Måns says, and although it's an old joke, we all laugh. We're all excited. Pumped.

Måns retrieves his phone. He's taken a good picture. Four of us huddled close, Måns in our laps. Cate where Suki used to be, right beside me. She's made rabbit ears behind my head, fingers sprouting from my helmet. A sign for two. A sign for peace.

I wonder if the others feel Suki's absence as strongly as I do. There's a quiet moment after the picture when everyone's lost in their own thoughts, and I like to think they're all remembering her. But maybe they're not. Maybe they're just suffering what's left of their hangovers, or thinking about the jump, running through a mental list of everything they've done in preparation.

Måns is flicking through the pictures on his phone. They're old ones. He stops at one of him and Suki; she's in profile, a curve of glitter garish around one eye, planting a big kiss on his painted cheek as he grins at the camera. A club in Rio, almost two years ago. Måns notices I'm looking and turns the phone so I can see better and I smile at both of them.

"Okay," says Todd. "Okay, okay, this is it. We ready?"

"Yeah!"

"I said, are we ready?"

"*Yeah!*"

"Wieslander. Helmet."

Måns reaches to Kit and she slings it to him. He straps it on, knocks the top of it with one fist, and Kit copies. We all copy. Even Cate, who hasn't been told, realises the ritual of it and does the same. I catch her exhale a few hard breaths, looking at the door, then Todd yanks it open and the wind tears in.

Nothing wakes you up or blows away a hangover like squatting in the back of a light aircraft with the slipstream rushing in around you. I do my best to take slow, deep breaths. Kit crouches in the opening. She's flexing her knees, rocking on the spot, pulling and pushing at the doorway, back and forth, back and forth. Todd crouches beside her, looking down, then he pats her on the shoulder three times – go-go-go – and she's gone.

Måns is next. He stands long enough to put his head to Todd's and they bump, then he squats and rolls forward out of the plane in one quick movement.

"Cate."

Todd beckons her and she shuffles to him, squatting. I follow her. She glances up at where she would normally hook onto a static line and then she looks at me. I sign the okay, nodding. She puffs out another breath then Todd's patting her, go-go-go, and she's gone.

It's a good clean exit. We've timed the jump especially for dawn and the light is breaking out over the jungle below. I can see her as she falls. She's holding a stable position, her body open like a giant starfish, arching into the force of the wind.

"She's all right," Todd yells.

I can't see anything of his expression behind his face shield, but I can see his eyes and they are like mine. I know what he really means and yeah. She's all right.

"You ready?"

I give him a nod. He gives it back to me.

I bend my knees to crouch lower. Hold the sides of the door. The wind tugs at me from the front, pushes at me from the back, and passing below is the vast green carpet of jungle canopy. Between me and that is 13,000 feet of sky.

"Carpe the fucking diem!" Todd shouts, then he's slapping at my shoulder: go-go-go!

And I'm gone. Plucked out into a sky Suki never got to see.

I first saw Suki in a waiting room. Not my practice, a colleague's. And as important as that meeting was, as striking as she'd been, sitting there in one of those god-awful plastic chairs, the memory that always comes first when I think of how we met, my preferred memory, is of her walking a slackline at Malham Cove. We were meeting there to climb Upper Terrace but I was late thanks to some unavoidable overtime and when I'd arrived at the site there was something of a low-key party already in progress. Nothing too wild; a night of drinking before jumping out of a plane isn't genius but the night before a climb it's a definite no-no, even if the climb is supposed to be an easy one. Low-key party meant only a couple of drinks, a bit of a smoke (courtesy of Kit), and some music (courtesy of Måns). Someone had strung up a rope between two trees. Suki was barefoot, toes scrunched around the line as she walked a metre above the ground, arms out for balance. She had a line of stars tattooed on her foot, I noticed, and she'd changed her hair since I'd last seen her, her head shaved on one side while the rest of her hair swept over in a deep purple wave. This is how I always see her first when I remember her, balanced between a beginning and an end. Laughing, and giving Todd shit about something he'd said. My heart had expanded into a feeling far more intense than the attraction I'd felt in the waiting room, turning into something far more powerful and needy. I wanted to be with her, and belong to her, and all of that happened right there and then while she balanced on a taut tightrope.

"You'll never make it," Todd said. He turned to Kit and said, "She'll never make it." He called over to Måns, "What do you think, Wieslander?"

Suki raised one leg out to the side, oh so carefully, and brought it around slowly to the front. She did the same again with the other leg.

Without looking up from his guitar, Måns said, "She'll never make it."

Suki had her arms out to balance, but she made fists of her hands and turned them to raise a middle finger both sides, moving slowly forwards as the others laughed. That was when Måns looked up from his guitar and noticed me. He stopped playing to raise a hand in hello and the others noticed me too. They were quiet, taking me in. Kit nodded hi and looked to Todd, smiling. Suki must have picked up on the mood change, or maybe just the new quiet, because she looked up from the rope to glance at them, left quick, right quick, and then at me. "Hey."

"I love your hair."

She wobbled on the rope, "Fuck," and adjusted her balance as the others made dramatic noises. She stepped quickly now, rushing to beat her fall, but even I could tell she'd never make it, much as I wanted to believe otherwise. She was moving too fast. She slipped from the rope about a metre away from the opposite tree.

The others laughed and clapped and cheered, and Todd declared, "Told you," to all who would listen, saving his grin for Suki who told him to fuck himself, she'd done better than anyone else.

"So far," said Kit, stepping up onto the rope and immediately stumbling off again on the other side, much to everyone's amusement. "That doesn't count!"

Suki came over to me and I had a moment of, oh shit, how do we do this, a hug, a handshake, what? She swept her hair back and exaggerated tossing it, a shampoo model, and said, "Part of my 'alternative' phase. You like it, then?"

"I love it."

I love.

"Sorry about that just now," I said. "I distracted you."

She put her hands on my arms, just below my shoulders. She looked at me for a moment, then came in to kiss me on each cheek. Afterwards she opened her arms to the group at the rope. "These are my friends," she said. "And Todd."

Todd smiled like she'd complimented him. "You must be the hot doctor lady."

I've often wondered what Suki'd said about me prior to that meeting, and Todd probably would've told me if I'd asked, but I never did.

"Yeah, Todd," said Suki, "thanks for that." But she barely looked embarrassed at all. "Come on, I'll introduce you properly."

She took my hand to lead me to her friends and she held it the whole time we exchanged hellos and little bits of background. She smiled with me, and laughed with me, and by the end of that night I was hers forever.

You don't jump out of a plane: you drop. You hold the doorway and somehow you convince your brain that it's okay to let go, to pull yourself out of a perfectly good, fully functional airplane. You tuck in tight. You plummet. There's no better word for it. You might even experience a few moments of sensory overload while the mind tries to figure out what the fuck has just happened, sorting through all these new sensations while the whine of the plane fades and wind rushes up and all around you. Some people even black out for a moment. But your brain figures it out soon enough and maybe you scream because you're scared or because it's fun, maybe both. The wind pushes at your clothes and at your face and if your mouth's open then it rushes into there as well and flaps your cheeks. Your thoughts roar with the sound of your falling.

I'm falling in silence this time, feeling the fullness of the rush downward and thinking it's apt, thinking this is how I've been feeling for nearly a year now. I'm waiting to stabilise so the chute can get a good clean wind when I open up, but I don't know if I'll ever stabilise. Don't know if I'll ever open up again.

Below me: Kit, Måns, Cate. Kit's rolling, knees tucked to her chest to spin around her own axis, head over heels. Måns is spread wide, looking left and right. He has a GoPro mounted on his helmet and he's catching as much of the experience as he can because memories are all anybody ever has, something I wish I'd realised a lot sooner. And there's Cate, her arms and legs open wide in an X that marks the spot. Somewhere safe to land, maybe. Or maybe she's just a shooting star, bright and brief like all of us are. Not much more than a kiss in a jumpsuit.

I could lean, if I wanted to. Could tilt forward, streamlining myself, and choose to fall faster. I could urge the winds to take me closer.

Instead, I pull the cord to release my chute and force a greater distance between us.

"So there I am, bungee-jumping over crocodile-infested waters—"

"They weren't crocodile-infested."

Todd was standing to tell his story, *grand*standing, you could say, for the benefit of the new group we'd joined for the night. He was lit from below by the campfire that cast classic eerie shadows up his face. We all saw him scowl at the interruption, though.

"They bloody well were crocodile-infested, mate."

Måns shook his head. He exhaled smoke and said, "The crocodiles live there."

"Like I said."

Kit passed the joint up to Todd as if to calm him. "He means if they live there then it's not infested."

Todd puffed once, twice, and said, "Whatever," with a tight voice. "Smart-arse."

Of all of us, Todd had travelled the most. He had a world map outlined on his back, and he added a flag to the tattoo for every place he visited. There were a lot of flags. He'd done it all, and done it almost everywhere, and he had plenty of stories to prove it. I think that's one of the things Suki loved so much about him. His eagerness to cram as much as he could into life. Carpe the fucking diem, as she put it to him once. They'd kayaked the Congo River together, at the turbulent low end, and they'd gone BASE-jumping in Hong Kong, leaping illegally from the International Finance Centre. The Grand Canyon was the one big one Todd still hadn't done, the flag he most wanted to add to that atlas on his back, but he was caught between desperately wanting to thru-hike the canyon to completely avoiding it as too touristy. Never mind that more people have walked on the moon than have thru-hiked the GC.

"So there I am, bungee jumping over this, fucking, crocodile *residential area*, right? Fucking, croc central…"

I'd heard the story before, so I tuned it out to focus on Suki. She was looking into the flames of the campfire and I doubted she heard Todd's story either.

"You okay?"

Suki smiled. It was one of the gentle ones I'd grown to hate, a token gesture rather than one of her typically vibrant smiles. The fire was bright in her eyes, but it was only reflected there. Used to be they lit up with a light all of their own. They drew you to her, those eyes. Pulled you along for whatever wild ride she had planned next. Before meeting her, the craziest thing I'd done was go trampolining with my nephew, but since Suki there'd been plenty, starting with that first climb at Malham Cove. There'd been abseiling, zip wires, hang-gliding, skydiving, an awful attempt at surfing, and the whole time I felt like

I was trying to catch up. It was exhilarating. *She* was exhilarating. Or she used to be. Those days near the end, she spent a lot more time in her own head, and I couldn't blame her for that, though I still did. Just a little.

"You remember the first time I came back to yours?" I asked her quietly while the others listened to Todd. It worked; I saw a proper Suki Smile. She leaned into me. Nudged me.

"*Yeah* I do."

She was referring to the sex, but for me it had been a much bigger step than that. No adrenaline rush has ever come close to what I felt that night, stepping into that private space where she lived. There had been ropes everywhere, loops of it draped over furniture or coiled on the floor, with metal clasps and carabiners and hooks. I made some terrible joke about her being kinky. Then I saw the mountain bike held on a wall mount, the collapsed sail of a windsurf board leaning beside it like a bright limp shark fin. There were skis, and a snowboard. In the ceiling, sitting across the beams, was a kayak and paddle. She was a cooped-up city girl in a tiny flat surrounded by all the things she enjoyed going elsewhere to use. It was overwhelming, seeing so much of her so clearly on display, and not in some pretentious way for others to appreciate: this was what she loved. What was familiar to her, the equilibrium she moved about in, was to me an exciting presentation of her personality, and it brought with it a lightness to my stomach, a shortness of breath.

She took my hand and led me to her bedroom. There was a helmet on the dresser next to her vanity mirror, a headlamp attached. She draped a vest over it and switched the headlamp on, then went back to the other room to turn the main light off.

"Sorry about all the mess," she said. "Romantic, hey?"

It its own way, it really was. The light shone back out from the mirror at an angle that diffused it. The décor here, if you ignored the safety gear and the wetsuit draped over a chair, was a nod to her Indian culture that she otherwise ignored. And the bed looked very comfortable.

"It's very comfortable," she said. I laughed at her mind-reading, and with nervousness, and because I had clearly been staring and waiting, expecting. She laughed with me and pulled me to the bed, and to her.

Afterwards, hearts pounding, we'd talked about adrenaline.

Todd was trying to do the same now, in a roundabout way, but Todd's adrenaline-fuelled stories were always about Todd. Where he'd been, what he'd done, what he'd dared. Stories were what he told so he had something to hide behind.

"Look, do the crocodiles eat you in the end, or not?" someone asked.

"Hey, if you want stories about being eaten, you—"

"Don't you go there," Suki warned, and people laughed. I tried to, but I'd just seen my attempt to cheer her up surpassed by a crude joke.

Todd held up a hand to accept the warning. "Okay, where was I?"

"Heart hammering, blood pumping, something melodramatic like that."

Adrenaline does lead to an increased heart rate. There's an increase in blood pressure, too, thanks to the kidneys producing more renin, and the blood is redistributed to the muscles, increasing the power for muscular contraction and altering the body's metabolism to maximise glucose levels, all of it happening very quickly in anticipation of fight or flight. I remembered, when Suki and I had talked about it in bed, that I explained how fear was healthy in its own way, thinking I was being clever and talking about us, the excitement of a new relationship, but having no fucking clue what she was going through at the time and how scared she must have been.

"A lot of people think adrenaline is a kind of fear," she'd said, "like there's a good kind of fear, right? But the adrenaline is what you get when you say 'fuck you' to fear. That's what it is for me, anyway."

She used to say fear was subjective, that you could choose whether to be scared or not, but thinking back, I realise she was scared all the time and did whatever she could to shift it elsewhere. Fight or flight. You couldn't fight what she had, not really, and there's no running from it either, though she tried for a while. Not so much flight as falling at high speed.

"You okay?"

She wasn't, but it would be a long time before she told me. In the meantime, she would distract me.

"Are *you* scared?" she asked.

"What?"

"It's just... How did you put it? The airways to the lungs expand." She leaned closer, quickened her hand. "Or, to put it in normal language, you're breathing heavy."

I smiled. "Because of what you're doing right now."

"And your pupils have dilated."

"Because you're so fucking beautiful."

"Yeah," she said, slipping away from me, further down the bed, "keep saying things like that..."

I did. I said things like that all the time, through all of that night and all the others after. It's just that, as it turned out, there weren't as many of them as either of us would have liked.

Nylon and rope spews behind me, unravelling above, and suddenly the chute is forced full. On TV you'll see the body jerk upwards as if yanked by the parachute, but that's bullshit. I've seen it myself in some of Måns's films, but it's just the camera falling faster than what it's seeing. The slider slows the opening of the chute, and you get an intense deceleration, but that's it. A jolt. It's a little abrupt, but not severe.

Below me, one, two chutes blossom open. Three.

On TV, you also see people suspended gently beneath their parachutes, floating like fucking dandelion seeds in a breeze, but the truth is you're still falling and you're falling fast. You've got more control, and you're able to guide yourself by pulling on the toggles left and right, snaking long Ss in the sky, but you're still buffeted and tossed about by the wind. The lush green canopy of the jungle might look like some giant moth-eaten green blanket plumped up thick and soft, but it won't be. It'll be hard and sharp if we haven't timed this right, and we'll hit it with force. If we miss the clearing, we'll be shredded by the trees or jerked dead with a sudden neck-snap crack. We might all look pretty from down there, flowers falling slowly, but thousands of feet up it's a different story, and that's fine by all of us. That's the rush. The adrenaline. The reason why we do it. One of the reasons, anyway.

I can see a gap in the trees. And there, taking up most of the clearing, is a vast sinkhole. A cenote. Godzilla, we've been calling it, but it's Zotzil-aha or Zot-hilza, or something like that. Aligned with it, the ruins of a Mayan temple, a relatively new discovery far off the tourist trail. We'd all been to Chichen-Itza and marvelled at it, glad we'd missed the equinox when tourists descend on the place to watch the light snake its way down the pyramid, but it had still been a little too crowded for us. Godzilla was ideal. We'd look around the site then abseil down into the cenote. Todd had wanted to drop right into it, wipe away our primary sense for a moment, namely our sight, and plunge into sudden night for that extra rush. But there was daring and there was stupidity. We'd hit water in the dark and our next adrenaline rush would be trying not to drown in a tangle of parachute ropes.

I glance at Cate below, wondering how she'd liked her first proper freefall. At this altitude we had a whole 60 seconds of it. How's she feeling?

Is this how Suki used to feel, watching me?

The wind I'm falling in changes abruptly and a sharp riffle of the canopy overhead has me yanking hard left to compensate. Then the canopy flaps wildly as the wind suddenly drops and I plummet twenty feet faster than a moment ago before lurching into a steadier stream.

Todd falls past me. He twists around onto his back as he passes. His face shield is gone and he's so stricken with terror that I think I know what's happened, I'm sure I know: his chute has failed. And for a moment I see it's tangled around him somehow, and I'm thinking ditch it, cut it loose, pull your reserve, come on Todd. Except it's not his chute at all. Whatever it is wrapped around his legs, his waist, it slithers up and around him in a quick tight coil and a wing, a fucking *wing*, long and leathery and brightly feathered, unfurls from behind him briefly before snapping shut again against the wind.

"Todd!"

The wind snatches that away.

A head appears behind Todd, at the nape of his neck. I see only the squat shape of it, only for an instant. The dark colour. The open mouth. It snaps at him. Then a splash of something hot is on my face and I shut my eyes, twisting away. I wipe the blood away with my forearm as best as I can. Blink my eyes clear. I've arced away in my S shape but hurry to twist back and look behind, look down, look for where Todd falls. Something that's not his parachute unfolds around him, a mottled rainbow of colours spanning left and right, and just like that he's carried away out of sight on beating wings.

What the fuck? What the *fuck?* What the actual *FUCK?*

Coming in from the right, something too snake-like to be a bird, too bird-like to be a snake. It dives right into where Måns hangs suspended. Folds its wings away a moment before impact and strikes him like some scaly torpedo, disappearing beneath the canopy of his chute and snapping it sideways.

"Måns!"

He's carried away somewhere out of my sight. His chute has whipped free, some of the ropes severed, and drags behind him like a bright streamer.

There's no way he'll hear me, but I scream for him anyway.

Måns collected trinkets wherever we went. Kit collected postcards, sending them home to herself as mementos, Todd collected tattoos, and Suki would pick up a rock, or some sand, or a shell, something like that. She had jars filled with these bits and pieces. We all had our things. For Måns, it was the trinkets, and the local stories.

Two nights ago, we'd been sitting around the fire, listening to it pop and crackle, while behind it, somewhere in the dark, the sea hushed up the sand and away. Måns had pulled a pendant out from under his shirt. He held it up to us, as much as the length of cord would allow, and said, "Look at this, eh?" before ducking out of the loop to pass the necklace around.

It was a wooden carving, impressively intricate, about the size of a pen. A nearly-naked man stood in front of a column or cylinder. He was wearing what I thought was a feathered headdress, wonderfully detailed, and part of it had a long beak coming down over the head. But I noticed, too, talons at either side of the figure's waist and turning the pendant saw a scaled tail running down from the head and snaking around the column. A very elaborate headdress, then, I thought. Or some weird lizard-bird thing standing behind him. In which case the beak wasn't decorative at all. It was coming down to scrape at the face and throat of the man, talons ready to rip at the stomach.

"What the hell, Måns?"

"Grim, huh? Bit weird."

"Just a bit." I passed it on.

"There were these Mayan heroes—"

"Oh, here we go," said Todd, settling back into the sand. "Story time."

"They were twins," Måns said. "These heroes. And they were put in a cave filled with bats."

"Why?"

Måns shrugged. "Punishment for something, probably."

"What were their names?" Cate asked. She was already pretty good with the banter. For some reason I liked her a little less for that. Or maybe I liked everyone else a little less for letting her fit in so easily. I don't know.

"Come on, guys, just let me tell it."

We pretended like we were doing him a favour, but the truth was if it wasn't for Måns our only local knowledge would be geographical and alcoholic, nothing cultural. He was the one told us about Chaak and other gods, the Quetzalcoatl, the ancient Aztec sacrifices. All the fun stuff.

"These two brothers," he said, turning to Cate to add, "whose names I've forgotten because they're probably unpronounceable with lots of Qs and Xs and Zs, they were put in a cave with these creatures called Camazotz and—"

"I thought you said bats?"

"These are like bats. Camazotz are, like, bat creatures. Or bat-gods, or something."

"You remember that name, then?" Todd said.

Cate laughed. Måns gave them both the finger.

"They have these noses, these long snouts, like blades. Like a beak. And these giant leathery feathery wings. They're like birds and bats mixed together. Flying around in the dark of the cave."

Måns lunged at us all in turn around the fire and we humoured him with shrieks and flinches. I clutched playfully at Cate in mock-fright, and perhaps lingered longer than I should have afterwards. She felt good.

"So to get away from these Camazotz, the bat-things, these brothers hid inside their blowguns—"

"But—"

Måns silenced Todd with a warning glare, exaggerated into cartoon proportions. "They hid," he said again. "Inside their blowguns." He waited, but there were no more interruptions. "And the whole time, these creatures tried to attack them while they hid inside, all through the night, until, at dawn… nothing. Not a sound. So one of the brothers looked to see if it was safe."

Cate said, "I'm guessing it wasn't."

"As soon as he poked his head out…" Måns looked around, choosing someone, and lunged at me suddenly, clapping his hand together at my face. "No more head!"

"Well that *does* sound terrible."

Cate grinned at me. I smiled back, politely. Quick and then gone. I've never been very good at flirting, except with Suki. Suki was the queen of flirting, pursuing it with the same eagerness for new experience as she did her shots of adrenaline. It made me worry about losing her, the same way I worried about slipping off a cliff face and smashing myself on rocks, or the way I worried about drowning upside down in a capsized kayak. Which is to say, I was always careful to pay attention, just like she taught me. Never become blasé, because complacency could end everything. It was how accidents happened. "Always be, like, super aware of where you are and what you're doing at all times. Live in the moment," she told me, "be right there, in it, all the time." So that's what I did with her. Seized every moment I could until suddenly she was never there at all.

"It's hollow," said Kit. She was holding the pendant horizontally to the fire. She put it to her mouth.

"It's a whistle," Måns said.

"It's a blowgun." Kit mimed shooting it at him and he collapsed back into the sand.

"They've got a lot of bats here," Todd said. Kit feigned a blowgun shot at him as well and he clasped it to his chest with a groan of pain. "Makes sense that they'll tell stories about them. Southern Mexico, Bolivia, Brazil, Paraguay even, and Argentina. All these bats."

"Vampires?"

"Meat-eaters."

"When the fuck did you suddenly become David Attenborough?" It was the sort of thing Suki would've said, and I was glad to have said it because of how he laughed.

"I got talking to some guy and he said as soon as the sun goes down, the whole sky around the Yucatán Peninsula comes alive with bats. Regular ones, vampire ones, these meat-eater ones. All of them out to feed. He was probably exaggerating, trying to sound smart or scary or something. He was probably coming on to me. But yeah. Lots of bats."

Måns had his pendant back. He gave it a long look and said, "Pretty fucked up bat," and ducked into the loop of its leather cord, tucking the carving back under his shirt.

"Hey," said Kit, rummaging in her bag, "I've got one for you. Why did the Mexican push his wife off the cliff?" She produced a bottle for her punchline and we all cried, "Tequila!" and cheered.

"Okay, I have a story," Cate said.

Everybody settled into quiet for her because, well, she was new. There was no getting around that fact, although we all did a pretty good job of pretending otherwise. I saw Kit and Todd share a look and I thought, don't fuck this up Cate. You've just volunteered for an early make-or-break moment, created an audition for yourself, and the spotlight is bright on you right now. We're all looking, and we're all listening. Don't try too hard, but do try.

"I got this from some tourist in—"

"Tourist? There are no tourists out this way, just people like us." Todd glanced at me and I knew right then he was judging her as hard as I was, and testing her a bit, but mainly hoping she'd pass. I think.

"Those are the tourists I mean. The extreme sports kind. Anyway, out here, tourist is just another word for foreigner, right?"

There was some agreement.

"Well, some of these people, they disappear. Nothing all that unusual, I suppose, when many of them are a little off the radar anyway, and doing crazy shit like jumping out of airplanes or swimming with crocodiles or whatever. People fall, they drown, get eaten."

"This is one of those cheery stories, yeah?" Kit said, passing the bottle.

"I can add kittens and lollipops if you like?"

She was doing well.

"Anyway, if they just disappeared, that would be one thing. But sometimes they'd turn up again in crazy places. The bodies of white-water rafters found in the treetops, miles from the river they disappeared from. Skydivers found years later in cenotes, their chutes still packed. Things like that. This one group, they were climbing, although fuck knows what because there aren't many mountains around here, maybe it was one of the ruins or something? Whatever. Three of them were climbing, one of them wasn't. The climbers all vanished. The one on the ground, he heard them scream but that was all. By the time he got to where they'd secured their lines, there was nothing, not even rope. They had a guide with them, some local boy, but all he could do was say, '¡Lo vi! ¡Lo vi!' I saw it! I saw it! Pointing up. But there was nothing. No one. They were all there one minute, and the next minute –" She clicked her fingers. "– gone. Just like that."

I knew exactly what she meant.

"There was a full-on search, but nobody found them for days. When the bodies eventually did turn up, they were ten miles away. And all of them were cut open."

"Cut open," Todd said.

Cate nodded. She made a slashing motion across her abdomen. "Same for all the others that turned up, the kayakers and the skydivers. Their kidneys, gone."

There was some groaning at this, a collective sigh of exhalation.

"The black-market thing? Selling organs?" said Kit. "Basic urban myth stuff."

"I know, I know," Cate said, "but these weren't clean excisions or anything. More brutal. Ragged." She settled back, a little deflated. "From what I heard."

"Wieslander's bats got 'em," Todd said, and Måns swooped at her, screeching while we laughed.

"It's interesting," I said. "The kidneys are where you'll find the adrenal glands."

I suddenly had their full attention. They liked it when I went doctor on them. Sometimes because of the gruesome stories, sometimes for the more exotic ones, like how the parasite *toxoplasma gondi* can make its host take greater risks, they loved that one. Humans can catch it from cats, but cats pass it to each other through rats – an infected rat becomes reckless, daring, gets caught and eaten and that's that: toxo-cat. A cautionary tale if ever I heard one. They also liked to be reminded that as a doctor I could patch them up pretty good if I had to (and I often had to). But I wasn't looking to reassure them right now.

"Yeah," I said. "The adrenal medulla. And from the sounds of it, the victims all had one thing in common – apart from the missing kidneys…" I paused just enough to make it dramatic. "They were adrenaline junkies. Like us."

I watched as each glanced at the other, Todd eventually making an ominous "*oooh*" noise. Cate smiled her gratitude at me, but I hadn't really done anything. Whatever fixing her story needed had been achieved by Todd and Måns joking about bats. She was part of the group now, and she was smiling at me, and I was okay with that.

Below me, Cate is spinning. Whatever's happened to her, I missed it, but her chute is tattered and her body swings around beneath it. An occasional flash of colour suggests one of the things is on her, too, or close by; she doesn't seem to be entwined yet, but there's an irregularity to her spinning that suggests something more than momentum has her moving like that. One of the creature's wings is beating while the other is held upright, caught in the ropes of her partially ruined parachute. Some sort of tail lashes around as if to balance or steer and—

I'm hit hard in the chest. It knocks me swinging in a direction that defies that of my falling. I feel a sharp line of pain in my thigh as something clawed takes hold there, and suddenly I'm wrapped about the leg. A muscular pulse and the coils spread upward, enveloping my abdomen. A head rises to look up at me from there. It is both snake-like and bat, squat-faced but with fangs, sabre-toothed and red-fleshed where its mouth opens. The fangs are so close together as to be almost one tooth, like a curve of beak. It tilts its head in an effort to sink these into the softest part of my body, uncoiling slightly to allow it more movement.

Somehow, I get my hands under its jaw. The flesh is scaled but it feels leathery, with ridges to hold onto as I try to redirect its attack, shoving its face away from my body. Two monstrous wings unfold and beat... beat... beat, controlling our descent. I flail with the sudden shift in direction and speed. With one leg still free, I kick at the creature wrapped around my other. With my elbow I smash at its puckered snout before grabbing at what I can find of the nearest wing. I slap at it, push at muscle and pull at scales, at feathers, but it constricts tighter. The wings fold around me with the smell of something wet and dark, and something snags at my back, yanks at the pack I wear.

This close to its body, I can smell meat, alley-meat, something spoiled. I'm too close to strike it now, arms crushed to my chest. But I can reach the cut-away. I yank at the handle on my harness and detach the main chute. I'm not thinking of how it might help, only that it has to.

And it does.

Whether it's caught in the fabric, or simply surprised by the sudden change of circumstances, the creature parts from me at the same instant I jettison the main parachute, one claw raking a line of pain across my abdomen. I see the thing only in snatched glimpses as I spin, falling. Its wings are open at full span to arrest or maybe steer its descent as I plummet. My chute flutters away above us both.

I turn from the sight. Lean myself into a headfirst vertical arrow, streamlining my fall to get away. To get to Cate.

I can see someone else below me. Whoever it is, they're being tossed from one creature to another like a toy, parachute nothing more than a tangle of torn colours pulled after them. They spin spread-eagled, and even from this distance I see, or imagine I see, lashes of blood thrown out from the body. Because that's all they are, now. A body. That, or they've passed out.

I think it's Måns.

It is Måns. I recognise the colours of his jumpsuit.

The flying snake things with the bat faces, they're strikingly colourful from above. The wings are a combination of blue, red, orange, like twin skies at twilight. They're not beautiful, I've seen too much to think that, and the length of body that whips around denies them the majesty of birds. The sound they make is a high-pitched screech but short, like the quick scrape cutlery can make on a plate, only louder.

I don't dare look above to the one that had me moments ago. I've no doubt that it pursues, or readies itself to, spiralling in or diving on my fall. I'm flooded with adrenaline – seeing Todd, the attacks, falling without my chute – and I keep thinking of that story, that stupid fucking story, and I'm thinking that'll make me a tasty breakfast for them, all that adrenaline, and I'm thinking that's what we'll all be now, nameless victims in a tale told with beers around a fire, and I'm thinking I'm going to die, we're all going to die. Even as my heart tells me not yet, not right now.

I've got a reserve chute. I can control this descent.

I'm gaining on Cate. I am controlling this descent.

Above me, behind, something makes a series of shrill sounds. A shriek of noise. A stuttered *reek-reek-reek-reek*, each syllable louder than the last.

I'm not going to fucking die. I can't die. Not yet.

"You hear a lot of near-death experience stories doing the adrenaline junkie stuff," Suki told me once. We were in bed, which was where we spent a lot of our time when we weren't pursuing some sort of outdoor adventure. Not always for the sex, you understand, but the intimacy. It was our private place, our safest space, where the rest of the world disappeared and there was only us.

"I bet," I said. "Near-death experience stories, and actual real-death experience stories, too, no doubt."

"Fair enough. That's true. But I'm talking about the whole, 'life flashing before your eyes' moment. You believe in those?"

"I'm not sure. You?"

For a moment, I had forgotten about her cancer. I was thinking of rock climbing and freefalling and BASE jumping and all the other crazy shit she'd done and continued to do. She could tell I'd forgotten, or rather she could tell as soon as I remembered – which was almost immediately – because she kissed my shoulder. "It's okay," she said.

"Suki."

She kissed my neck and then leaned over to kiss my mouth. She'd told me about the cancer a month or so prior to this conversation, but any time I tried to talk about it she kissed me to close the subject before it could begin. We were only allowed to talk about it on her terms, which had seemed fair at first but less so as time went by.

"When the doctor first told me," she said, "I had something like one of those near-death things, only instead of seeing my life so far flash before me in a series of snapshots or whatever, it was more like a flash forward. I saw every little thing I hadn't done yet, it felt like. Every part of the life I had left to live, if only I could've lived it. The things I could've done if I'd been brave enough. When I realised I was thinking in the past tense, like my life was over already, I decided, fuck it. I'll do it all."

"Carpe the fucking diem."

She nodded against me. "Damn right. Carpe the fucking diem. I started taking greater risks, travelling further abroad to try things, racking up the credit card bills. But it changed the nature of it for me. I thought it would be like, I dunno, more of a fuck you to death or something, right? But it was weird. First time I jumped out of a plane after getting the shitty news, I kept thinking of that Tom Petty song. Fucking, 'Free Fallin'.' Just the chorus, over and over."

"I don't know it."

She sang, dramatically grabbing at the air above us and pulling it down to her face with, "Because I'm freeeeeee... Free fallllling."

I laughed a lot at the abruptness of that. The kind of laugh that leaves you breathless. She watched me, smiling.

"You know, that one."

"No, I don't know, you'll have to sing it again."

She pushed me lightly. "I felt it, you know? Free. Rushing towards something that would kill me, i.e. the ground, but having control enough to stop that from happening, right? Like, I'm the one that says, that's enough now, let's slow it down and live for a bit longer. Up in the clouds. Yank the cord and all is well." Her lip trembled. Her chin. "Except when I land I'll still have cancer."

"Baby."

"The ultimate fucking c-word, right?" she said, and she was crying now. "What a cunt of a disease."

"Baby, hey. I'm here."

"I *know*, and that makes it even worse, because now I've got so much more I want to live for, and it's not *fair*. I've only just met you."

I held her for a long time, and wiped away tears, kissed away others.

Eventually she settled, and the first thing she said was, "You know, it's fucked up, but if it wasn't for that c-word bitch fucker, I never would've even met you."

I was stroking her hair by this point, her beautiful now-blue hair, but I stopped at that.

"Yeah," she said, and sniffed. "Exactly. Fucked up, right?"

"God, then I wish you'd never met me."

She sat up then, suddenly, and said, "No. No fucking way, don't wish that. Not ever."

"Are you angry?"

"Yes I'm fucking angry. You're too fucking perfect for me to ever wish I never met you, okay? I'm so stupidly happy."

"I thought you were angry."

"Fuck off."

"I can't take your anger seriously when you're naked."

"Shut up, I'm trying to be serious. And you know what else? You're too perfect to be wasted on just me, so when I'm gone—"

"That's it, this conversation is over."

"No. When I'm gone—"

"Come here."

I tried to kiss her, pulling myself up to her, pulling her down to me, but she shook me off.

"I'm going to be gone, that's just medical fact, doc, and you need to find someone else quick before your beautiful body gets all old and decrepit."

"Suki—"

"I mean it." She relaxed, and she touched my cheek, and she said again, "I mean it. You're too good to go to waste. Someone else should get to experience you like I have. Fall for you. And you for her. Promise me."

"Suki, I'm not—"

"If you don't promise, I'll end things right now."

"No you won't."

She didn't say anything. She just held my stare. And I realised, with absolute certainty, that she wasn't kidding.

"All right. I promise."

"Okay," she said. "Okay. Good." She laid back down beside me. "That's good." She nestled close, resting one arm across my chest, and kissed my shoulder. My neck. My ear. "If she's too pretty, I'll haunt you."

I wanted to make her promise, but all I did was kiss her.

I'm hurtling towards Cate. It isn't going to be graceful, like with a team jump, gliding towards each other to hold hands. I don't even know if Cate's done one of those, and she won't have seen me coming anyway, so she can't prepare for it. Her chute's open, but only partially effective, damaged as it is. I'm heading right for her.

For all I know, there's something heading right for me, as well.

Closer, I can see the creature on Cate is as much caught around the ropes of her parachute as it is around her. One wing buffets them both back and forth, the other tugs and drags at the chute, claws it with talons.

Cate's conscious. She's kicking at the length of tail or scaled body that curls first one way and then the other, whipping around her as the thing struggles to free itself.

I tilt into a more horizontal position. Doing it slowly. I even sweep at the air like I'm swimming, for all the good that does. I'm only going to get one shot at this, and after that we're both on our own.

"Cate!"

It's pointless, but I scream it anyway.

She's still moving erratically, but for a moment it looks like I'm going to fall clear of her chute and manage to latch onto her. It doesn't go that way. I strike a taut edge of her canopy and am engulfed by it. Briefly. It whips over me with burning speed as I fall past, though I've collapsed it enough that Cate drops quicker for a moment. A suspension line slices the inside of my wrist and face but then I hit her and grab her, and grab something of the creature, too. I yank them with me before Cate's parachute takes a fuller shape again and by then I'm holding her suit, her harness, I think a handful of her skin as well. The creature slips away from her body, tearing as it goes. She screams. She tries to buck me off, too, still screaming, and panicked.

"It's me! It's me!"

Above, still caught in her ropes, shaking us around like marionettes, the fucking Camazotz or Quetzalcoatl or whatever the hell is fighting to free its wing.

I grab at Cate's helmet, not too softly, and pull her to face me. "The cut-away!"

She screams again, this time in surprise, in recognition. Her eyes are cartoon-wide, pupils so dilated there's almost no colour, only blackness.

"Your cut-away! Pull it!"

She nods.

I tighten my already white-knuckled grip on her.

She pulls the cut-away and clutches at me simultaneously. The lines fly free of her, seem to whip up above us. I look up after them to see the creature become more tangled in its attempts to escape. But there's no joy to be felt in that: another is bearing down on us in a dive. Its serpentine body is straight. Its wings are folded back like dart-flights. It comes at us with its mouth open wide, twin fangs bared.

"Hold on to me!"

She's got handfuls of my clothing and harness like we're about to fight. I wrap my legs around her like we're about to do something else. "Don't let go!"

I pull my reserve chute. Immediately as it deploys, I'm freeing my hook-knife. I've never had to use it before. I pray it's sharp enough to do the job quickly; a reserve chute doesn't have a cut-away.

I slash at the lines just as the chute puffs full, setting it free to envelope the fucker coming at us. The thing streams past us like a fiery comet, a bulk of red nylon and a thrashing tail.

Cate and I are freefalling again. I'm holding onto her like my life depends on it because it really fucking does.

"You need to pull your reserve," I tell Cate, yelling into her ear, "but not yet."

She nods and reaches for it.

"Not yet!"

She nods again, just holds her hand ready. Her other is holding onto me. She's wrapped some of my harness into her fist. I still have my legs around her. I've got one arm around her, too, wedged between her back and her pack. The other I've forced under the harness at her front so that the straps cross my forearm and I'm able to hold a handful of her clothing. I can't be separated from her. Cate's reserve is all we have.

But she can't release it too soon. We're turning, rolling. She can't release the chute until we can hold a decent position. Also, releasing it will slow us down, make us easy targets. We'll need to alter our course, too, if we're going to make the clearing and not smash ourselves into the trees. That'll slow us down, as well. She needs to wait as late as possible.

I worry about the AAD; the Automatic Activation Device automatically opens the reserve chute at a pre-set altitude if the descent rate exceeds a certain pre-set speed. We must be nearing those parameters.

I catch glimpses all around us. Shapes in the air. Colours that are the bat-snake things, colours that are torn chutes and limp jumpsuits. My friends. Below, the lush green carpet of jungle, coming up at fast. The clearing, with its ancient stone. I want to point it out to Cate but with no chute of my own I'm too scared to let go for that kind of movement.

"As soon as we land, run for the rainforest!"

I can't tell if she's heard me.

"We'll get cover from the rainforest!"

The wind is trying to wrench us apart, whipping our hair around, ruffling our clothes, sharp and loud. Cate's hand, the one pressed closed to her chest for the release pull, finds mine and grips it hard without forcing it away from where it clutches at her. She nods at me.

Even hurtling towards the ground with weird monsters in pursuit, the world turning topsy-turvy around us, it's a strangely intimate moment. I think, yeah. I can do this again. I'm sorry, Suki. And thank you, Suki.

Then there's a beep-beep-beep and a sudden unravelling and Cate's reserve chute releases.

"Hold on!"

I'm not sure which of us yells it. I think maybe we both do.

Above, the parachute billows open and fills. It's a good, clean deployment. We're blind to any dangers directly above us, though.

Can't think about that.

Cate begins to guide us. No long snaking S moves, but quick pulls that correct and re-correct our course in short circles. I can't tell if it's calculated or panicked. Sometimes there are trees beneath our feet. Sometimes the ruins. A short distance away I can see another gap in the trees and the dark open pit of the cenote.

Drifting across the jungle canopy, caught in a breeze, are the ragged remains of someone's parachute. It's snagged on something, or it's still tethered to someone, and before I can help myself I'm straining to see who, turning my head each time Cate changes our course, moving to see around her without lessening my grip. If there's a body, it's caught in the lower branches somewhere.

Above, the shrieking screech of one of the creatures coming at us from a blind spot. There's a moment I think I see it in silhouette through the chute.

The ruins are right there. Right fucking there.

The creature hits our parachute, claws it into a bunch of nylon and lines, and pulls us away with it. Yanks us off course at the latest moment.

Cate gives a short scream. I'm wrenched along with her.

For an awful moment it looks like our legs are going to get dragged through the treetops, but they're not as close as that and suddenly the trees are gone altogether. We're still dropping fast.

"Oh shit!"

We pass across the gaping hole of the cenote, then swing down into it. Collide into the side of the opening. Cate takes the brunt of it across her shoulders and grunts with the impact. We smash our heads together with the force of it, too, and I'm shaken loose. Thrown from Cate to grab at the ground's edge, at air, at nothing.

I'm falling again, this time into the dark of the cavern. Cate's legs kick for a moment and are gone, dragged out of the light above, out of my sight.

Looking up, I tumble into icy water back first. The sudden cold dark closes over me and pulls me down, further down, settling over and around me and closing out everything else and this, I realise, is what death feels like.

~

We were going to go to China. That was the plan. A last trip together, climbing and caving, mostly.

"I'll show you Crown Cave, which is all handrails and elevators, now, probably, but after that we'll see some proper caves."

Suki had been excited about the trip. She'd been several times already, but she loved the place. China has a huge concentration of karst, which makes a decent playground of rock columns and sinkholes and rivers that just disappear into nothing, swallowed up by the ground. She wanted to show me The Stone Forest, a vast area of limestone eroded into a variety of column formations with beautiful names like 'stone singing praise to the sun' and 'tiger roaring at hawks', things like that. Geographical poetry.

"Karst areas hold loads of chi," Suki had told me. "You know, life energy."

Suki loved all that spiritual stuff. A lot of travellers do, I've noticed. Maybe they're more open to other possibilities, having seen more of the world and accepted their own very small part in it. Near the end, as the cancer took a firmer hold on her, tightening its skeletal grip around her organs, so she grasped harder at a range of religious beliefs. Some she'd been brought up with, others she'd picked up on her travels the same way Todd collected tattoos. She liked to point out that there was plenty of weird shit out there that no one knew or noticed, whatever my science might say. *My* science. She pulled away from me at the end, you see. Only a little, but it hurt. I understood it, though. I represented those who couldn't help her. And she didn't want me diagnosing her, seeing her only as someone to be cured. She didn't like that I would know how hopeless it all was, or that I would pretend otherwise for both of our sakes.

But China, with its wonderful caves and all its life force, all its glorious chi, never happened.

You know what they worship in Mexico? Death.

I see a light. A tunnel of dark, and a circle of light. I reach for it, pull at it. Chop my legs back and forth and sweep my arms to get to it. I pull. I kick. And with a sudden gasp of air, I'm there. Inhaling lungfuls of breath, sucking up my own echo, head back and arms splashing to stay above water.

The cenote is deep. The few I'd seen already were tourist spots, with steps carved into them, or laid with wooden boards and rope rails. This one, though, is natural and untampered. Above – far above – is a circle of morning light surrounded by stalactites. The walls around me are twisted thick with the roots of the surrounding rainforest.

I swim for them. I unclasp my harness and refasten it around one of the lower roots, freeing my hands so I can pat down my body, checking for injuries. The lacerations on my wrist and face are minor, but the gash across my abdomen feels serious. I fumble for my headlamp; the LED light will give me about 150 feet of clear sight. Only it doesn't work. I can feel that the helmet is cracked right through, too, probably from when Cate and I hit each other. I leave it on, though. If nothing else, it will help keep my hair out of the way.

I feel lightheaded, as if simply acknowledging the possibility of a head injury has created one, made me aware of a concussion.

I want to rest. Sleep.

"Can't, baby. You've gotta climb."

"Suki."

She's treading water, looking around at the walls. Looking for decent handholds. Suki used to free solo, climbing with nothing but rock shoes and a bag of chalk, daring the world to kill her. Something like this would be easy for her. I'd seen her dancing across rock faces, leaping from one outcrop to another likes she's playing fucking hopscotch.

Not me, though.

"They used to throw people into these as sacrifices," I tell her.

"That's nice."

She turns a circle, looking for the easiest route.

"Cenotes were home to the ancient Mayan rain god, Chaak. Or Chuck, or someone. He was very important to the Mayan people because he was a rain god. He poured the rain from jars he smashed to make thunder. I don't know how I know this."

"Måns told you."

"Mm. That's right. He also told me that cenotes are entrances to the underworld."

She glances at me, but that's all.

"Yeah. An open mouth that devours the living, that was how he put it. And you know what else he said? He said, sometimes it spits out the dead."

"You believe that?"

I sigh. "There's some weird shit out there."

"Karstic rock, doc. It sucks the rain down to groundwater level. Cenotes are where the Mayans got their drinking water, that's all."

"Karstic. Like, with all the chi?"

"Exactly. Now come on, climb."

Sunlight angles in from above. It holds Suki like a spotlight.

"I just want to rest for a minute."

"You can't." She slicks her hair back in the water. "Come on. Jam your hand into whatever crack you can find."

I smile, remembering how she'd made that into an innuendo before. She doesn't smile back, though, not this time. She points up, and I remember the guy in the story, '*¡Lo vi! ¡Lo vi!* I saw it! I saw it!'

"You're not here. I'm seeing you, but you're not here. You left me."

"Did I?"

I've hit my head. That's what this is.

"Cate's up there, and she needs you."

But I'm already unclipping my harness from the root that had been supporting me. I pull myself upward with one arm and reach with the other. Taking hold.

"Yes. You can do it."

I look up at where the sunlight of a new day forms a circle far above me and I think, carpe diem. Carpe the fucking diem. I try not to remember what happened when one of the twins poked their head out of the blowpipe.

And suddenly there's Suki, leaning out of the light, offering her hand.

Below me, the water of the cenote is empty, but I hear her voice down there. "She's pretty."

From above comes my name, and I look again to see it's not Suki silhouetted against the daylight but Cate. She's lowering the lines from her parachute.

I grab for handhold after handhold, eager to reach her. Eager to climb out of the dark.

|Mary, Mary|

~

Mary was tending the sweet peas in her front garden when the new neighbours arrived. Or rather, she was *supposed* to be tending the sweet peas. She was *supposed* to be pinching out the tips to encourage branching because bushier plants gave more flowers, especially if she picked them regularly. She had a particular fondness for her sweet peas because they produced a delicious scent (she always went for the annual sweet peas rather than the everlasting because the shorter-lived flowers had the stronger smell) and usually she was very focussed on her garden tasks, but this morning she was distracted by the dirt at her knees.

There had been a brief but heavy shower in the early hours of the morning and the soil was still alive with writhing worms, called to the surface by the rain to wriggle in the freshly turned earth or squirm their way across the lawn. She wondered if the rain sounded like drums to the worms in their subterranean homes, a constant tom-tom rhythm that called them up despite the risks of birds or the unmerciful tread of human feet. A couple of worms were attempting to cross the pavement, as if the grass verge on the other side was somehow more desirable. Greener, perhaps, Mary thought with a smile. She wondered if they knew the dangers but came up from the safety of the soil anyway, compelled by forces beyond their control.

It was the rattling up of the removal van's back door that pulled Mary back from those thoughts to distract her with new ones. She had been so engrossed in the activity of the worms that she hadn't heard the vehicle arrive, but that rat-a-tat-tat-tat-tat-tat of the door rolling up was impossible to miss. U-Drive. She was glad to see the new neighbours had driven the van themselves rather than hire someone. She thought it admirable, such independence, especially these days when everybody seemed happy to pay somebody else to do something for them. She was also glad to see the new people were black. She might be of an older generation, but shame on anyone who thought that was an excuse to be racist. No, she was glad some people of ethnic origin, or whatever the polite term was for them these days, had decided to move into her street. Added a little… Ha! Colour.

The man at the back of the van handed a box to his teenage daughter, a beautiful girl with long braided hair who said something to him and laughed as she took the box. A girl, that was good. Before Mary could complete her smile, though, a young boy leapt down from the van and, *oh*, he was beautiful too. He gave his father a bright smile and, oh *my*, he had such an energetic body, impatient to be somewhere else, running around enthusiastically and pretending to pull at his hair as his father laughed and kept a box high out of reach. The boy bounced on the spot and made grabbing motions for the package. "*Pleease!*"

Mary struggled up from her knees for a better look. It was more of a struggle than she liked to admit, and she needed to use the nearby lawnmower for support. If she was honest with herself, and she always tried to be, she had brought the lawn mower out with that very purpose in mind, for the grass would probably be too wet to cut until the late afternoon.

The boy had his box and set about unpacking it straight away, there on the street. His enthusiasm for the task was delightful, and Mary enjoyed watching the way his face lit up as he retrieved a car from inside and set it on the pavement. Next came a handheld control and then the street was a little less quiet, the vehicle whining its way up and down and around as the boy followed. The child liked to play. That was good.

"Peter, go and help your mother."

Peter.

Mary hadn't seen the mother yet, but here was a car parking behind the van and, yes, there was a black woman inside. She had short cropped hair but the same figure, amazingly, as her daughter. When she saw Mary looking she waved. Brief, but polite, delivered with a quick smile. Mary returned it. Her hands were still gloved and caked in soil, palms darker than those of the woman she waved at.

Peter was standing at the roadside, the gadget in his hands pointing at the car that weaved around his mother's feet. She stepped over the toy several times with a practised ease that was almost supernatural, barely glancing at it as she headed towards her family.

"Hello, Mary."

The voice startled her, but she resisted putting a hand to her chest.

"James, hello, good morning. How are you?"

James smiled and showed her some letters he'd brought out to post. He was an elderly gentleman around Mary's own age. "Just being nosy, really," he said, nodding towards the new neighbours. "Good to have some new people in that house."

Mary smiled and said, "Yes," though it hadn't been empty long.

"Especially children again."

She didn't know if it was because he used to be a priest or because they couldn't physically have them, but James and his wife Claire didn't have any children. They had several cats, though. Surrogate children, she supposed. Mary had needed to speak to both James and Claire on different occasions about their animals digging up her flowerbeds.

James pointed to where Mary's trowel lay in the dirt. "Weeding?"

"No, no, I was just turning the soil. Helping it drain. It's important, though really sweet peas are the easiest things in the world to grow. I'll probably do some weeding later, it's getting out of hand. Nature can be difficult to tame."

Why did she always prattle on so with men? But James was barely listening, so she supposed it didn't matter. Across the street the girl had come out of the house with cups of something for her parents. That first box must have been the kettle and tea things.

"Pretty," James said.

Mary nodded. The boy chased his car up and down the drive.

"Well, these aren't going to post themselves," James said, shaking the envelopes in his hand. "Good luck with the weeding."

Mary gave him a tight smile but allowed it to broaden into something more genuine when the boy across the road saw her and waved. He directed the car towards her front garden but turned it in a tight circle before it could reach the kerb. Then he did the same circle in reverse before driving the car back to his feet. A boy's hello.

"Little Lewis Hamilton," James said. Mary had no idea what he meant but he was already heading towards the post box at the end of the street so she was able to avoid any embarrassment by asking.

She eased herself back down to the ground, kneeling on a padded mat. She bowed her head towards the soil and tried to focus on the task at hand but found another worm, twisting upon itself in some strange rapture. With a quick thrust of her trowel she cut it in half. It would be all right, she thought. Half of it, anyway. As a child she used to think that both bits grew into new worms but really only one part survived. And it didn't grow back anything. It just survived, that was all.

Mary didn't believe in god with a capital G. She used to. She used to believe in the very same God James preached about once upon a time, though she never went to his church. For Mary, the only god, or god*dess*, was Mother Nature. A goddess so old that She resided at the Earth's core, having gathered the world around Her when the planet was mere pieces in space and time, pushing and pulling the tectonic plates into new shapes the same way Mary fidgeted sheets around herself in bed. Mary's goddess was protected by the world's crust and warmed by the world's magma. Mary's goddess was the soil's heart, beating in a series of seismic shifts, and worms carried Her pulse through a network of arteries they made themselves. No turn of Mary's shovel could hurt Her. Nature's heart was a hot molten rock that beat in earthquakes and rushes of ocean. The bones of Mary's goddess were the bones of people who thought they were returning to the clay from which they were made but really only fed it. The bones of Mary's goddess were those pressed into chalk over millennia. Her skeleton was stone. Mountains were Her vertebrae. Volcanoes spewed such exhalations that She could, if She desired, block the sun, and the world would know a darkness it had only seen when young.

Mary had known darkness but she buried it. Sometimes what she buried turned into something that gave her strength because even the foulest of things could flower. Mother Nature produced plenty of poisons but She also provided the remedies. Sometimes they even grew side by side. Sometimes the only difference between one and the other was the dosage. Plants were like people that way, Mary thought, standing straight and wiping sweat from her brow.

She was up to her waist in a hole she'd been digging for three days. Since the Turners had moved in: Elijah and his improbably named wife, Pixie, plus their daughter Jasmine. And Peter. She'd had a wonderful chat with Peter. About digging.

Occasionally a well-intentioned neighbour would tell Mary she was getting too old for some of her gardening work but she could never stop doing something she enjoyed so much. She felt particularly at peace when digging. The rasp of the spade in gravelly ground or the heavy scoop of sod levered by her foot or turn of wrist. It was hot work though, especially cooped up like she was in the garden shed. She had removed the floorboards some time ago, gaining access to the soil beneath, and now, shovelling load after load of the dirt into an ever-growing heap, she really felt the dusty heat, close and stifling. Almost the entirety of the shed's floor space had been dug away with just a small area left for the mounting dirt. She would dig until she felt better, however long that took, and then she would refill the hole and tread the soil down flat once more. She'd long since given up replacing the floorboards – had burned them, in fact, on one November fifth or another – because eventually she would dig again. Sometimes the soil would still be freshly turned when she needed to and the going was easy (too easy, actually) but usually she managed months before the need returned.

She took a sip of iced tea. It wasn't some awful shop-bought concoction. No, this was lemon iced tea she made herself (the secret lay in letting it steep with lemon peel rather than using the juice, and adding a great deal of sugar). The glass had lost a lot of its coolness but the drink was still refreshing and the sugar perked her up for the work she still had to do.

She took a final sip of her tea, set the glass back down on a shelf of empty plant pots, and wiped her forehead with a sleeve grimed with dirt and sweat. It was already going to need a good wash but, safe in the privacy of her modified garden shed, she began unfastening the buttons.

When she'd seen Peter digging, he'd been grubby with mud all up his front. In his lap, clods of dirt had gathered like tiny earth-babies nuzzling for comfort.

Mary arched her shoulders back to remove her clothing and mopped her brow a final time with the bunched up blouse before hanging it on the handle of the shed door. She contemplated taking off her bra as well, not liking the way the straps rubbed or how the sweat built under the cups, but the way she'd sag and swing without it depressed her more and more these days. She was no Charlie Dimmock, not anymore. There was something to be said, though, for the freedom of being without it. If she was honest with herself, and she always tried to be, there was a wonderful frisson to be had in being so exposed amongst the earth. It gave her pleasure, being so intimately close to Nature. Even thinking about it gave her a shivered thrill that was more than the coolness of the soil seeping into her skin.

Mary retrieved the spade and stabbed it at the ground, treading the blade into the soil to lever up a fresh heap of dirt and stone. Her grip was firm. She felt no pain in her back or knees. She took strength from the ground she stood in, letting the labour keep her mind from other things.

"Good morning, Peter," Mary had said. "That's your name, isn't it?"

She'd smiled. She had crossed the road to pass the Turner place, taking inspiration from her neighbour James in that she carried a handful of letters to post (she liked to enter competitions, and there were letters she sent to gardening magazines – one of those had once been 'letter of the week', winning her a £50 voucher to spend at the garden centre). She had planned to post them at the weekend on her way to the shops but when she'd seen Peter in the front garden, turning soil with the sort of spade best used at the beach, she'd changed her mind.

"My name's Peter Lewis Turner," he'd said. "We just moved here." He'd been bringing the plastic spade towards himself in a series of pulls, dirt flicking up his t-shirt as he scraped a shallow trench. A matching bucket sat nearby as if he was going to make mud castles.

"I see you enjoy getting dirty," Mary had said with a soft chuckle. She'd pointed at his t-shirt and the small mound of earth building in his lap.

"I'm looking for treasure."

"Well, there's lots of that in the ground."

Peter had looked up, clearly delighted. "Is there?" And Mary had smiled.

"Of course. All the nutrients plants need to grow, for starters. And all sorts of precious metals and pretty gem stones. People dig them up all the time, though personally I think they're supposed to stay there. I think they're in the ground for a special reason."

"What for?"

"I don't know, dear. I just don't think Mother Nature would put anything in the ground that wasn't meant to be there."

"I like stones. I've got seven with holes in them but I found those at the beach. Dad says they're lucky."

"If you like stones, you should see my fossil collection. I have them in my garden, bordering the lawn and standing in some of the flower beds. Sort of like garden gnomes, but much prettier."

"Fossils are like stone dinosaurs, aren't they?"

"Sort of. They're special rocks that show you something that died, years and years and years ago."

"Coal's a special rock that burns," Peter had said. He'd said it like it was something he'd learned recently, new knowledge, shiny and fresh, that he wanted to show off.

"You're absolutely right," Mary had said. "Did you know, there's a place where anthracite, which is a type of coal, is burning *right now*? Lots and lots of it, all underground, burning and burning. It's been burning for over fifty years, nobody can put it out. Imagine that."

Peter had looked around as if it might be right underneath him. His expression had been part excitement, part fear.

"It's in America somewhere," Mary had assured him.

"What about the people who live there?"

"Nobody lives there, it's too dangerous. The land is really hot and the fumes are really poisonous. It seeps up out of the ground."

"There's poison in the ground?"

"Sometimes."

"What else is in the ground?"

The boy had stopped digging. Cross-legged, spade held across his lap, he'd sat looking up at Mary.

"Well," she'd said, "buried treasure, as you know."

Peter had grinned.

"But also things that lay forgotten, waiting to be rediscovered."

"Like a bone? Our dog used to bury bones but then forget where she'd put them."

"Yes, like bones, I suppose. I didn't know you had a dog."

"She died."

"Oh."

"She was killed. She ate something bad." He'd frowned, bringing his hand up to his eyes. Mary had thought he was about to cry and she'd panicked but it was only that the clouds had moved and Peter was saluting to shield his eyes, squinting a little into the sun.

Mary had wondered what on earth to say next but then there'd been a creak and screech from the side gate and Peter's mother had appeared. She'd been surprised by Mary but only for a moment. She'd smiled. "Hello."

"Hello." Mary had introduced herself, pointing across the road. "Number 42, if ever you need anything."

The woman greeted her again. "Hi, Mary, I'm Pixie." She'd brought her hands up as if to ward off a blow. "I know, I know. Awful, isn't it? I sound like someone from Harry Potter or something."

Mary had smiled. "I think it's a wonderful name. Magical."

Pixie had smiled in return. "My husband, Elijah, says the same thing."

"You have a daughter, too, don't you?"

The woman had nodded. "Jasmine. And this little one-" Here she'd crossed her arms and scowled at her son. "Peter Lewis Turner, look at the mess you've made!" It had been pretend anger, though, the woman suddenly sweeping in low, arms outstretched, to scoop the boy up for tickles. He must have been rather heavy at his age but maybe mothers didn't notice that kind of thing.

"We were talking about buried treasure and fires and bones," Peter had said between laughing and trying to breathe. A beautiful sound.

"That sounds lovely, but you've got to come in now and get ready for lunch." Then, to Mary, "It was nice meeting you."

Mary had watched as the woman ushered her child inside. When she swatted playfully at his behind to hurry him along Mary had looked away.

In the ground at her feet, a small hole, a narrow trench, had gaped vacant, a plastic spade protruding from one end like the headstone of a grave, or an invitation to keep digging.

~

In the shed, in the hole, Mary scooped heaps of ground from around her feet and tossed them aside at a near frantic pace without caring that most of the dirt fell back into the opening she had made. She was sweating profusely now (or rather she was perspiring – she was a lady) and she could feel it running down her sides from her armpits. She could feel it at the nape of her neck where curls of grey hair were sticking to her skin. She was wearing comfortable trousers but even so they were damp around the elasticated waist and crotch. She couldn't tell if it was the physical activity or the exertions of her mind that made her feel this way. Still, she levered up more earth, raised it, and tossed it away.

Abruptly, her spade bit into something softer than soil. She stopped and angled the blade carefully to see…

Yes.

"Hello Adam."

When she dug this deep, Mary always found Adam. The first time it happened had panicked her and she'd wondered if somehow she'd forgotten where she'd put him. She soon discovered, though, that it didn't matter where she put the blade of her spade or shovel, Adam would always be unearthed. Sometimes the other children followed – not always, only sometimes – but Adam was always there for her. His eyes were clogged with soil but he saw everything.

"What are you going to do?" he asked, his throat choked with dirt. His teeth were black with soil and clumps fell from his mouth as he spoke. His was a voice that bubbled beetles, and things that burrowed moved his tongue, itself a writhing twist and turn of worms that dropped in tangles with each of his words.

"Go away," Mary said. She plunged the spade into the boy's face and he crumbled into sodden clods, all muddy blood and stones for bones. He fell apart into a fleshy compost that Mary tossed aside with an enthusiastic swing of her arms.

"I don't *know*," she said. "I don't know what I'm going to do."

She spoke it to the ground beneath her feet, and to all the dark that had gathered there as the light outside faded.

"Yes you do," it said.

~

A chill had descended as day faded into early evening. Mary didn't feel it until she left the shed and it made her wish she'd brought a cardigan out with her. Often, especially when digging, she lost track of time. In the shed, that was. In the hole. Sitting at the flower beds, trowel in hand, transferring potted plants to the great outdoors or picking at weeds, she was fine.

The light had diminished a great deal with the onset of evening, more so than was usual for the hour, because low-lying cloud, dense with rain, had settled over the neighbourhood. Mary took the opportunity while it was still dry to transfer her rubbish from the bin to the kerb. She only had to do it once a fortnight because with all the recycling, and the amount of household waste she used for compost, she had very little to dispose of these days.

Each of her neighbours had already put their rubbish out, slumped sacks lining the street like squat little sentinels, and she realised it must be even later than she'd initially thought. The streetlamps were on, heavy rain clouds reflecting the light so that the road seemed to simmer in a sulphurous sodium glow. It made Mary think of how the Earth's volcanic sky must have looked, back when the planet was young and still forming, cloud-filled and lava-lit, all aglow with fire.

She deposited her rubbish and was about to return to the house when a mobile phone beeped twice, loud in the quiet of the evening. It made her pause.

The new girl across the street, Jasmine, was lingering at her gate with a young man. There was another double bleat, the technological heartbeat that seemed to keep teenagers alive these days, but Mary saw that neither of the two made any effort to check their phones. They were too engrossed in each other, their hands on each other's waist. They looked as if they were about to kiss, or had recently been kissing.

"Careful," Mary said quietly. "Boys are bad for your heart."

She glanced away and down at the plants in her front garden, uncomfortable watching the couple in their private moment but too curious to go inside just yet. She focussed her attention on the gladioli she had growing at either side of the front gate where they'd catch the sun. Gladioli were great for bringing colour to a garden, a bright array of simple flowers hardy enough to use year after year, if the winter was a mild one. That said, and it was difficult to tell in the poor light, it looked like the leaves of these were mottled. She bent to look closer rather than kneel, wincing at the crack in her back, and took a few of the leaves into her hand. They were certainly wilting a little. She'd check in tomorrow's daylight but she thought (hoping she was wrong) it was perhaps greenfly.

Across the road, the two shadowy forms at the gate melted into each other as they kissed. Mary thought of the young brother, and what he might think of it. She thought about the hole she had made in the back garden, in the shed, and that maybe she should fill it in again already.

When the outside light came on at number 45 the teenagers pulled away from their embrace. The front door opened and there was the father. "Jasmine, time to let the boy go. School tomorrow."

Mary thought that as far as reprimands went, Jasmine had been lucky. Mary's own father had been a far sterner sort. He had made boys afraid of him, and her afraid of men, and she thought it no exaggeration to say that as a result of such a strict upbringing she had become the seventy-year-old spinster she was today.

She watched as her new neighbour retreated inside to allow his daughter a final moment of privacy, though he left the front door open to emphasise his point about curfew. Mary waited in case she caught a glimpse of Peter but the boy was probably watching television or maybe even in bed. Then the door was closed and Mary was alone again except for a teenage boy walking away, face lit eerie green by the light of his phone.

A movement to her right caught Mary's eye and she turned in time to see the curtains of 44 twitching closed. James or Claire had been watching as well, it seemed, but the show was over.

Mary retreated to the warmth of her own home for a much-needed drink.

Mary had not been much of a drinker until recent years. Oh, she used to enjoy the occasional tipple on special occasions, and once or twice she maybe had a glass of wine in the bath, but otherwise she was very much a tea-drinker. Tonight, though, she needed something a little stronger. And for Mary, that meant whisky. Just a wee dram.

Her hands were sore from clutching the handle of the spade so fiercely and for so long. The skin of her palms had been rubbed raw and it hurt to straighten her fingers. She looked, in fact, like she had been stricken with the arthritis she had so far been lucky enough to avoid, her hands curled into fleshy claws. Still, she managed to twist the bottle open easily enough. Only a supermarket own-brand (on her pension, it had to be) but it would do. She half-filled a cup and took it through to the living room where she could put the electric heater on for a few minutes, just to take the evening chill from her bones.

The island of Islay produced a wonderful whisky, she'd heard. It had a delicious smoky flavour, apparently, thanks to how the malt was dried over a peat-heated fire, the barley infused with the flavours of the smoke.

Peat-heated fire, she thought. Pete-heated.

Peter.

Peter: the stone, the rock. From the Greek, *petro*. Mary had looked it up.

Peat was similar to coal in that it came from plants but it burned down more quickly, delivering a lot of heat but only for a short period of time. Coal took a lot longer to form, but it burned for longer.

She put the whisky down on the drop-leaf table beside her but her hand remained bent into the shape that had held it. Or rather, the shape that had pushed and raised and turned a spade for the last few hours. Like petrified wood, her hand looked like it always had but was locked in place the same way trees would transition into stone as minerals replaced organic matter. Fossils were mere impressions in rock, a trace of what was, but petrified wood had its own three-dimensional shape, not simply a trace of what once was but a stronger version of what it used to be. Solid, not hollow. It had substance, albeit one that lacked any kind of life. Like the Tollund Man, wonderfully preserved in a peat bog for centuries. Curled up like a child in the belly of Mother Nature.

Mary took another drink, a petrified fossil trying to forget what had made her.

~

Mary was in her front garden picking at mottled leaves when Mr Turner came over to say hello. She hadn't noticed him at first, examining the plants which were just as damaged as she'd feared. She turned each leaf to check the underside because often a problem lay underneath, unseen, and yes. Greenfly. She wasn't sure how that had happened – she'd been spraying the garden regularly – but here was the proof. The leaves had curled and browned and she knew the combination of toxic greenfly-saliva and the plant's lack of sap would prove to be its downfall if she didn't act quickly.

"Good morning."

Mr Turner had a very deep voice, loud even from across the road. He was approaching her garden, smiling politely. "Problem with your flowers?"

"Good morning, yes, gladioli, Mr Turner. I mean, it is a good morning, yes, Mr Turner, and the flowers are gladioli. It's a—"

He was holding up his hand and Mary worried about her babbling – he'd clearly heard enough – but he simply said, "Elijah, please. Mr Turner makes me feel like I'm in trouble for something." He smiled.

"Elijah." Mary said it quietly.

"Actually, I suppose I am sort of in trouble. Thought I'd come to ask you for some help."

"Is it the forsythia? It can get out of hand if left for a while like yours has been. I mean, that's not your fault, of course, the property's been empty, but you should prune it just after it's bloomed. If you—"

"No, no, it's not the… forsythia? I'm not too sure what that even is, actually. It's just that-"

"It's that beautiful yellow shrub. Sunrise forsythia. The one you have tangling with the hydrangea, in that corner bed by your front door."

"Is it? Thank you. I'll take a look at that, see if I can sort it out. Mrs, Miss…?"

"Oh, just Mary."

"Mary. Hi, Mary. My wife said you two had met, and that's the closest I've come to meeting anyone yet, and I was wondering if you knew someone around here who babysits? Maybe there's a teenage girl, like my Jasmine, only one who doesn't disappear with her boyfriend at the last minute and conveniently forgets her own little brother?"

He smiled again, but it looked a little strained to Mary. She thought his attempt to joke actually had its roots in a more serious concern about his daughter. That was what happened, though, and it was a shame: children grew up. And whatever they grew into was often the parents' fault.

"I only ask because we're desperate, you see. My wife and I, Pixie, we're supposed to go to this—"

"I could look after him for a few hours."

The first expression on Mr Turner's face was a mixture of relief and happiness but he recovered enough to shake his head, saying, "No, I couldn't ask you to do that. I didn't come over to ask that."

Mary thought he had come over with at least the hope, if not the expectation, that she would look after Peter, but she simply said, "Nonsense. It would be a pleasure. I haven't seen my grandchildren in a while. It'll be good to have some lively young blood in the house again."

Grandchildren? Oh, why had she said *that*? Now he'll want to know their names, and their ages, and all sorts of other things.

"Grandkids, eh? How old? How many?"

"Just the two, and not so young now. The eldest is about the same age as your daughter and the youngest is eight. Both boys."

Mr Turner was nodding. It was the nod of a man not really listening but rather agreeing with his own thoughts. Mary thought they probably went something along the lines of *she's got grandchildren, they're boys, she'll be fine.* "Thing is," he said, "it's rather short notice, too. As in, tonight."

Mary waved that away as the trivial detail it was. What would she be doing that couldn't be put off for another day? How did any of her days or evenings differ anyway? "That's okay, he'll save me from the horrors of *Coronation Street*."

"Petey said you two spoke the other day," Mr Turner said, more at ease.

"Yes, that's right. About digging, and fossils. I said I'd show him some of mine. I have a few fossils in the back garden, you see, ammonites mostly, all in a row bordering—"

"Sounds wonderful. Just his cup of tea. If you really don't mind?"

"Not at all. It would be my pleasure."

They arranged a suitable time and said their goodbyes, Mr Turner offering a final compliment before he went. "I love your garden. So full of colour."

When he'd gone, Mary looked again at her gladioli. Aphids were the most destructive of pests in any garden and last year her sweet peas had succumbed, becoming sickly and dangerous themselves so that she'd had to destroy them. Greenfly reproduced asexually, the offspring an exact replica of the parent, and they would spread quickly throughout the entire garden if she didn't act quickly. Nip it in the bud, so to speak.

She went to the shed.

Mary thrust the shovel into the thick wet earth, grunting with the effort.

The babysitting had not gone well.

Peter's parents had given him dinner before bringing him over but Mary had fed him fuller still with biscuits and cakes she had made especially for his visit. They had played a board game in the conservatory, surrounded by cacti and draping ferns, snug beneath hanging red stars and purple petunias. They'd played Snakes and Ladders. Mary only had old games, and certainly nothing like a computer, but that hadn't seemed to bother Peter, unless he was just very polite.

"I *like* snakes," he'd said, moving his piece down one of the colourful serpents. "Do you like snakes?"

"If I'm honest, and I always try to be, I find them a bit frightening," Mary had admitted. "I'm all right with slow worms, though."

Peter had looked at her with a frown and so she'd explained. "They look a lot like snakes but actually they're lizards. You wouldn't know it, though. I find them in my garden occasionally, near the compost heap where the grass is longer. They're quite harmless." She'd smiled, adding, "Unless you're a slug or a worm."

"Can we look for some?"

"Slow worms? Of course we can."

Peter had leapt up, knocking the board but only scattering the pieces a few squares backwards. "Can I keep it if I find one?"

"We can't look *now*. It's too dark, and quite chilly."

"I've got my hoodie."

"It's still dark."

"I've got a torch at home, I can get it."

"They're probably sleeping now anyway, underground. We can look in the day time. Let's finish our game. It's your go."

He had sat on the settee again without sulking or complaining, correcting the knocked pieces on the board, and Mary had thought, *such a nice boy*. Such a nice young man. So well behaved. Then he'd started shaking the dice for his next turn, his fist pumping up and down, back and forth in his lap, like something obscene.

"All right, come on, let's look for snakes," Mary had said, just to make it stop.

"Yes!"

"Slow worms, I mean. I've got a torch. And I'll show you those fossils."

In the hole, in the shed, Mary attacked the mound of soil with renewed vigour, shovelling all she'd unearthed back into the dark hole she'd made. One hard horizontal thrust buried the shovel blade right up to the shaft, and when she tried to lever it there was a loud crack and the handle broke so suddenly that she fell.

Nothing else broke, nothing in Mary. Nothing dislocated. That was a small miracle at her age. It was going to be tricky getting up again but for now she sat staring at the length of wood she held in her hands. "Bloody thing," she said, and dropped it into her lap where she saw that the handle was indeed bloody. She checked her hands and found them wet with it. Sticky where it had mixed with her sweat. It hurt to straighten her fingers but she would not cry. She would not. The skin was pink, seeping in places and bleeding in others where blisters had burst. Dirt lined each of her wrinkles, emphasising them with a brown colour not her own. She was herself a fossil, hollowed and cracked.

"He has such beautiful smooth skin," she said. "Dark like soil. Like wet earth."

She brought her hands close to inhale the pungent damp smell of the dirt but smelled only her own sweat and the tinge of blood.

Peter had smelled of sunshine, as if all the heat of the day had been trapped in his skin. They'd gone to the compost heap, sweeping at the long grass with sticks, small lengths of cane that she used to support young plants. Sweeping at the long grass with torchlight, looking for slow worms.

"Ugh, *gross*," Peter had said, "what is that *smell?*"

"That's the compost. Look, there." She'd pointed to a dark heap in the gap between the shed and back fence, hidden behind the water barrel that collected rain from the shed's guttering. Peter had shone the torch over it, covering his nose and mouth with his free hand. Mary had become used to the odour but Peter's reaction had her smelling it as if for the first time. A sour smell, like spoiled milk, yet sickly sweet, too, with grass cuttings and the stems of decaying flowers as well as potato skins and egg shells, the rotting refuse of her past meals. Draped across the top, loose bouquets of pulled weeds and pruned branches, and beneath it all the rank smell of damp manure. The pile had greyed up one side with a fur of mould, and some nettles had sprouted. A warmth emanated from the waste, the compost snug in the heat of its own decay.

"It's so gross," Peter had said again, pretending to vomit.

"Well, maybe it's *you*," Mary'd said, daring a joke. "When did you last have a bath?" She had scooped him close and breathed deep, her nose pressed to the nape of his neck, and that was when she'd discovered his sunshine. Mary was too old to lift him for tickles as his mother had, but she pressed her fingers to his armpits. Peter had tried to pull away.

"Stop it!"

Mary had released him immediately. "Sorry," she'd said. "I thought you liked tickles."

"That hurt. You pinched me."

"Sorry."

Peter had swept at the long grass, making a show of one final check. "No snakes," he'd said.

"No snakes," Mary said again, sitting in the vast hole she'd excavated. She pressed her palms to the cool damp soil and it soothed her raw skin. She clutched the soil in tiny fragile fists and turned her hands to see what she'd been given, opening her fists to find muddy shapes, ridged by the squeeze of her fingers. "He has such beautiful skin," she said again. She dropped the two clods of earth and plunged her hands deep into the pile of dirt beside the hole, scooping it towards herself and tossing cupped handfuls over her shoulder, trying not to sob as somewhere behind her Adam told her what it was she wanted to do.

He had emerged early in the digging this time, his head appearing on a shovelful of dirt. She'd cast it aside, heard it land and roll, only to see him rise again from the earth with the next shovel of soil. She'd cast this one aside too and it rolled to where the other had been only moments before. She'd bury it with the next load. She'd bury all of them, again, as many times as she had to.

She was hot, even at this late hour. Using the broken handle to help, Mary eventually, carefully, stood. She stripped away her clothes, undressing down to her underwear, throwing her garments to the door where they wouldn't be buried. She felt as heavy as the soil beneath her feet, slow and sagging, a repulsive filthy old woman, but still she swept handfuls, armfuls, from the dug up heap back into the hole, sweating in the fury of her activity. She thought of the world's earliest years, when continents crashed together and spewed volcanic clouds to fill the skies, raising the temperature so that life had a chance to form and flourish. The world heating and cooling, breathing, so that new life might bloom or, sometimes, end abruptly.

"I bet he tastes like soil, too," Adam said. "I bet he tastes of life. You'd taste all the nutrients of the world in the sap of that darksoil."

Mary shuddered but still she shovelled, using both hands to fill the hole. She thought of things not Peter. She thought of the titanic heaves and descents of plate tectonics, rocks (Peter, *petro*, the stone, the rock) taken down into the Earth's depths before being shoved up again filled with new nutrients, convulsions of earth shaping the surface of the world anew with mountains and valleys, an up-down wave of stone and soil forced into shape by the churning of the world's hot rocks. It was the same movement that created the world's magnetic field, the irresistible push and pull that made Mary think of her own impulses. If she didn't let such shifts affect her, who would she be? What was her Nature if not this?

No. Nature could be contained, controlled – her own garden was the beautiful proof. But the weeding, the pruning, the constant landscaping, it was so exhausting. If she was honest with herself...

The next handful of earth she brought to her face, relishing its coolness on her cheeks and brow, the moist aroma of it. She plunged her tongue into the dirt she held and tasted an acidic sourness, a metallic sharpness, sweet alkaline. Kneeling in the earth, half-buried in it, tasting it on her skin, she prayed to her Nature, a monster goddess she could worship but never hide from. She confessed her deeds and desires until the entire pit she had made was gone, full again, sated with its own soil.

~

Mary didn't leave the house for a few days except to dig or refill the hole in the garden shed. Digging deep, but all for nothing: she sat in the conservatory, waiting, warmed by the sunlight and drowsy in the scent of contained flowers. Sometimes one of the Adams sat with her.

"You could blame the priest," he said to her. "Next door. You know they always like to—"

"Shut up."

She said it quietly, staring at the floor. Sometimes it worked. Other times it would only make the Adam more cruel and he'd sit with her through the entire night, forbidding sleep or chasing her into it with dreams that were mostly memories. Desires she thought had died, only to find they'd fossilised deep inside, heavy weights in a heart which was itself only a trace of what it used to be.

"Play with me."

"No," she said. But she looked up.

The child's naked body was entirely caked in clay, face besmeared and hair pasted flat with mud. He was every bit the dirty little boy she'd said he was, all those years ago. Show Mary an acorn and she could see the tree, or so she liked to say.

"Come on, play with me," the mudboy said again, eyeing the Snakes and Ladders board still set up on the table. He mimed shaking the dice but he did it low in his naked lap and what he threw was a scattering of soil that buried both of the playing pieces.

Mary looked away, back at the floor again, though in her peripheral vision she could see that others had come. Her foundations made topsoil through some psychological seismic shift. Dead boys given new life in being dredged up from the earth they were buried in, just as they had given new life to that earth as they slumped into soft pieces, oozing juices that fed the soil and everything that lived within it.

There was a knock at the front door.

Mary struggled to stand, her limbs and joints stiff and painful with all the work she'd busied herself with, but stand she did.

"I'll wait here," the Adam said.

"Don't bother. There's no need."

It took her a while to get to the door and in all that time there was no second knock or impatient ringing of the doorbell. He was a good boy. Considerate, the way only children could be. Or maybe he'd gone home again. Yes, and maybe that was for the best.

He hadn't gone home.

"Wow," Peter said. "What happened to you?"

Mary glanced down at herself. She was filthy, grimed with everything she'd taken out and put back again.

"There's a snake," she said. "A slow worm. In my garden."

"Really? Can I see it?"

Mary stepped back from the door and as Peter passed her she said, "I made some more of those cakes you like."

She felt a brief draught as the back door opened behind her in the conservatory and the children waiting there retreated into the garden. Into the soil. She looked left and she looked right and she saw the street empty both times, the neighbourhood quiet. She closed the door firmly on the world outside.

Mary had set a ladder in the pit. Peter went first and she followed. She had dug one of the edges away into a narrow opening and the ground beyond sloped further down. The wind whispered from it, short phrases in gusts that cooled the skin, a low hush of voices that came and went like the repeated chorus of some strange soil-spoken song.

"A tunnel," Peter said. "Is this where the snake went?"

The shadows seemed to writhe away from Mary's torchlight as they descended deeper into the dank, dark earth, outcrops of rock and fossilised curves, stone spirals, casting shapes that were snake-like themselves across the walls of the tunnel and the sloping ground beneath their feet.

"How far do we have to go?" Peter asked.

"All the way," Mary told him, pressing close.

The earth angled down at a steep gradient. The heavy humming of fattened bluebottles thickened the air, a droning buzz rising around them as they moved lower, lower, into the earth, and underneath that sound came the steady tom-tom beat of a powerful heart.

"I feel strange," Peter said. "I'm sick."

"Me too."

"I think I had too many cakes. I don't feel good."

"You'll feel fine in a minute," Mary said. "You'll feel wonderful. We're going to play a game." She took Peter's hand and he let her. The only sign of any fear or trepidation was in his backwards glance up to the surface where the outline of Mary's garden shed, a rectangle of light, diminished with every step, shrinking away above them. "Let's see the snake," she said.

Peter's expression was part excitement, part fear. He tried to say something but when he opened his mouth to speak he only dribbled clods of mud, his throat choked with dirt and stones that burned and burned and burned as they dropped from him, hot as coals.

"Come with me," Mary said, and she pulled him into the ground with her, an earthen mermaid swimming down into the sunless soils of the world.

|In the Wake of My Father|

~

I was surprised by how many people visited my father in hospital. I shouldn't have been; he was popular enough, in his own way, despite the distance he maintained between himself and others. He'd buy as many rounds as he was bought, no matter how tight money might have been, and he never said no to a job that was offered to him. Bringing the sheep down from the fells, dipping, shearing, working the market, helping at the auctions; my father could always be relied upon whenever an extra man was needed. He had no close friends, but he was known, and if he wasn't especially well-liked in the most social sense, he was at least respected.

I came back to the fells to spend some time with him at the end, though I didn't stay at the old place. There's a room above the Folly, my father's local, so when I wasn't at the hospital I was there, or in the pub itself where a picture of my Da and several other men with sheep behind them hung askew and faded on the beam across the bar. As a child, keeping quiet and eating my crisps, I used to imagine that my mother had taken that picture, though I'd never been given any reason to think so. I never asked, either. I understood, even then, that sometimes what I want to believe is better than what is true.

People in the pub recognised me, despite the years. They shook my hand and they said the expected things about how I'd grown, upwards and outwards, and they said kind things about my father. Most testaments about his character used words like private, and quiet, and hard-working. They would have said he was stoic, had they known the word. A few of them, once they'd taken enough drink, said it was a shame he never found himself a good woman after my mother left, but I didn't know if I agreed with that or not. The most drunk among them tried to tell me things about him they thought I didn't know, but the same ale that loosened their tongues made their speech difficult to follow and all I did was nod during the pauses. They seemed keen for a story from me, too, but I had nothing for them. Nothing I wanted to share. There's a tiny gap between the stories we tell ourselves and those we tell others and that's where you'll find the truth. I wasn't ready to create that gap yet. One of my fondest memories of him wouldn't have satisfied them anyway. A day spent helping build a dry-stone wall was only a chore to these people, and most had turned their own hands to it more than once.

So I kept my story to myself.

I was twelve, and waiting forever to become a teenager. The weather was turning, the sun bright but without much heat, not yet. A cool breeze that chilled us in the morning would be refreshing in the afternoon, once the work had warmed us both. Come lunch time we were stripped down to our jeans, my father's upper body the well-muscled physique you get from years of hard work, and mine all ribs and elbows back then as I scrambled about for suitable stones. My responsibility that day was mostly to backfill, stopping up gaps with smaller stones in the wake of my father. I enjoyed the slow, considered process of it, finding the right stones and carefully placing them so that the plain side, the ugly side, was hidden while the more pleasing side became part of the wall's face. My father's job was to place or reposition the through-stones, stones that would hold the wall firm over the years (unless someone drove into it, as had happened with the stretch we were repairing). We worked in silence, but it was a comfortable one, the only sounds an occasional grunt of effort or the scrape of stone against stone as we made a waist-high line of them at the roadside. Sometimes a shrill whistle carried down to us from the fells as someone worked a dog to gather sheep. Otherwise it was a clear and quiet day, one that I remember with a sort of sheen over it, a varnish of memory-light that preserves its perfection.

Many of my favourite memories from back then are held in this kind of hazy sunlight. The sun dictates much of what can be done on a farm. With fewer hours of light, winter could be a stressful time, but come the hazy days of spring there was plenty of work to be done and

I would help whenever I could. My father paid me pocket money, but it felt like I was earning more than just that. I often wished we had sheep of our own, but instead my father worked all sort of odd jobs for other people, cash in hand. He'd do anything. As a child, I'd taken a certain amount of pride in that, seeing him as an efficient man, a jack-of-all-trades. Only as I became older did I realise that a jack-of-all-trades was a master of none, and that some of the work that came my father's way was sympathy work. The community doing its bit to look after one of its own.

"Jake."

I looked up, stone in hand, to see my father a short way along the wall. He was looking down at the ground beyond it. He glanced at me then beckoned.

"What is it?"

"Come see."

It was a dead ewe. It had taken shelter where the land dipped into a ditch, a curve of rock making a shallow ghyll where a beck had long since run dry. When it was hot, sheep sought cool nooks exactly like this one, and the wall would have offered it further shade. As good as this spot was, though, it was also steep on one side. The poor thing must have fallen and broken something, become trapped. Maybe it died right then. Maybe it took some time.

It had certainly been there a while, quietly rotting, its soft meat slumping into the soil in slow disintegration. It sat seeping fluids, leaking into the land and feeding the grass it had once eaten in life.

"Why are you showing me this?"

I'd seen dead sheep before. On the fells, working the farms, you see plenty of dead things. Unless there was going to be a lesson here, I didn't understand why my father had taken the time from his labour to show me.

"I thought you might draw it," he said.

I loved to draw, back then. Still do, and it's kept me sane during some long, lonely periods of my life. I even studied it at college for a while, though that never went anywhere. My father thought it was all a waste of time. It wasn't proper work, as far as he was concerned. Proper work meant using your whole body. He admitted I might sell a few landscapes to the in-comers, but in the same breath noted they wouldn't pay much. We'd argued about it, briefly, prior to this day at the wall, which is to say he'd voiced his view and I had sulked. Yet here he was, showing me something I might draw. Years later, watching TV, I'd learn about how Leonardo da Vinci dissected corpses to get his drawings right, and later that evening I'd phoned my father to exchange a few simple sentences about how we were both doing. There was little left to bind us beyond blood by then, and though I wanted to remind him of that dead sheep, and the crow that came after, I was worried he'd have forgotten. I wanted to go on thinking he remembered the day just as well as I did, so I said nothing. What I wanted to believe being better than what might be true.

"Is it breathing?"

"What? No, Jake. Look at it."

I could see right inside. See its bones, and the soft darkness behind them. But...

"It looks like it's moving. Just a bit. Like it's breathing."

It couldn't have been, of course. It was all rotten meat and ruptures, barely held together. Yet my father stepped over what there was of the wall and gestured for me to come closer, too. He pointed. The animal's cavities seethed with insects and their larvae. They crawled over each other or writhed in tangles, dropping into piles of themselves before moving again, back into the corpse-home that sustained them. "Maggots," he said. "See?"

"Gross."

My father smiled. "Natural. Same thing as will happen to us, one day." He crouched and stretched a leg into the ditch to nudge the dead animal.

The body erupted into a dark explosion of noise and feathers. My father fell onto his back and I yelled in surprise as a startled crow took flight from somewhere behind or within the body. I ducked and covered my head with my arms; my father swung wildly with his while the bird beat at the air around us, rawk-rawk-rawking its anger before rising away.

My father laughed. I remember that very well because he didn't do it very often. He followed the crow's progress, looking up at the sky with one hand shielding his eyes and the other on his chest. I took some strange comfort in knowing he'd been startled too.

"Bloody hell," he said.

"Yeah," I agreed. Then I risked my own, "Bloody hell."

The dead sheep had toppled, pushed away by my father and abandoned by the crow that had been feeding inside. It had fallen in such a way that it seemed to look right at us, though its face was mostly only bone and gaping absence. The meat had been eaten, plucked by beak and scratched by claw, and much of the fleece had been picked away, too. The body would be spread far and wide across the fells, carried and devoured and shit out again, or dropped, lining nests and cosying dens with its bones and wool. No choice but to give all of itself to the land.

A cloud of flies had dispersed with the crow's exit but they quickly returned, buzzing sharp frantic shapes around the corpse as they settled again.

"Well?" my father asked. "Any good for drawing?"

I wasn't sure, but I nodded anyway.

"We'll take a break, then."

I always carried my sketchpad, rolled into a tube and stuffed inside my jacket. My father must've known, or guessed as much. I fetched the jacket from where it draped the wall and sat down to draw.

Had I known how that corpse would come to haunt me, I never would have committed it to paper. Never would have sat, and stared, and replicated. That very night I had the first of many nightmares that would wake me over the years into a cold fear I could never shake until the morning light brightened my bedroom. I would dream of shadows breathing, and of a darkness that seeped out from the ground to claim any and all that touched it. In the worst of them, I saw my father eclipsed and gone before I could call any kind of warning. Sometimes I tried, but all that came from my throat was a weak exhalation that seemed to empty me and I'd collapse into an absence of myself. Other times I fled without trying to save him at all. Every nightmare left me with the feeling that in drawing the rotting body of that sheep, I had drawn something else as well. Drawn something to me, or drawn something out.

But I didn't know that at the time. I only saw the darkness rise once night had fallen. Until then, the day was as perfect as so few others ever would be, and so I sat to draw.

It was difficult at first because I could feel my father watching. He was leaning on the wall, rolling a cigarette, but I could tell his attention was on me. I fidgeted to block my work, trying not to make it obvious. Behind me, my father's lighter scratched into flame and he moved away to smoke.

Looking at it, sketching it, I wondered again how the creature had died. I remembered one of the ewes I'd seen last year, how her body had bloated because she was carrying a dead lamb. She'd become infected by the corpse she carried. It happened like that sometimes, my father had said. Death can get you from inside. I sketched, and I thought about the crow again, hidden within and startling us. I considered adding it but in the end decided there was little need. In its own way, it was already there, drawn into the picture. Every shade of my pencil was another stroke of its dark feathers, whether I intended it to be or not.

My father grunted, and I turned to see he was behind me again, looking over my shoulder. Without thinking, I covered the drawing with my arm and hunched over it. He retreated.

"It's good," he said. "I could never draw like that. Don't have the right hands for it."

I was suddenly embarrassed. He had only complimented me once before that I could remember, and that had been to say I had good teeth. Shepherds assessed the quality of their livestock that way, but I'd still treasured the remark, and remembered it whenever I went to the dentist.

The teeth of the dead sheep looked longer than normal because the gums were mostly gone. I sketched them as crooked slabs, drawing dark shadows in between.

When I was shading the empty eye sockets, I heard an engine. From where I sat I couldn't see over the wall, but my father turned toward the sound. He stubbed out his cigarette on the drystone and pocketed what was left before raising one hand to wave. I could see the blue roof of Bill's truck as it pulled in. My father leaned to talk with the man through the driver's window. I could tell, after a few moments, by the way he lowered his voice and shifted so his back was to me, that he was discussing some work. Not all of the work he did for people was legal. If I knew that then, as a child, then I didn't think about it much. As an adult, I can understand it better.

I'd seen him fight, once. It had been with a man I didn't know. An awkward exchange of blows, clumsy but violent, but only one man bloody by the end of it. We were at an auction. It never crossed my mind how painful it must have been for my father to attend those auctions, to see men and women bartering for sheep or showing them off for rosettes. To hear them discussing the strengths and weaknesses of stock, hear them taking pride in their bloodlines and making a success of good breeding. He'd had his own sheep once, before foot and mouth took them from him and some fine print – or lack of it – denied him compensation. He never bought any more. Instead, he looked after other people's, or made deliveries, or carried out repairs. At the time of the fight, I'd wondered if the violence had grown out of some sort of frustration, it had seemed so unprovoked and undeserved. After the fight, though, Mr Pritchard from the lower fields had given my father some money and patted him several times on the back. My father barely looked at him. Just pocketed the money and examined his swollen hands. It hadn't crossed my mind, back then, that the money might have been for something other than the usual manual labour.

We didn't go to many auctions after that fight, which was a shame. The auctions and the fairs kept farmers from becoming too isolated, kept us from becoming as divided as the allotments. They brought people together and made a community of families who were otherwise held apart by the hedges and fences and walls that separated their scattered parcels of land.

At the wall, my father patted the roof of Bill's truck and it drove away with a friendly touch of the horn. My father waved it gone.

"All right," he said. "Let's get back to work."

I made a few final lines, darkened some more shadow, and flipped my sketchpad closed. I clambered out of the ditch.

"Our friend's back," my father said, helping me up. I looked to where he nodded.

The crow was settling itself on the wall further down, stepping sideways, left and right. It croaked at me when it saw me looking, beak wide open and head thrusting forwards as if something was stuck in its throat. Maybe some meat from its disturbed feast that it needed to dislodge. I pretended to throw my pencil, intending to startle it away again, but it only moved back a few hops and cawked. There were things to eat here. Soft, rotten things, and flies, and fat wriggling flies-to-be. It didn't care about a boy and his pencil.

My father's hands were busy at the rockpile. He had large, hard hands, my father, and his knuckles were scraped from the work of positioning the through-stones where they'd be strongest. I joined him at the pile and selected smaller stones of my own.

The first time I was arrested, I was sixteen. I'd broken into Bill's place a few days after he'd died. I didn't know he had any family because he never spoke of them, not once, and you hear a lot sitting in a pub, eating crisps, and staring at photographs you wished your mother had taken. He had a son, though, and it was him who found me slumped in the old man's armchair, an empty bottle of something in my lap. That alcohol was the only thing I stole, and I hadn't much liked it back then. I hadn't intended to steal anything at all, just wanted to see how the man lived. Wanted to see what it might be like to be someone other than myself or my father, as if he might have an outward face that hid something altogether very different. I walked the rooms, and I opened drawers, and I looked at the pictures on the wall, but the house had nothing new to show me. Bill was a farmer, and something of an alcoholic, but I knew both of those things already. So I sat, and I drank a little to taste a little of what his life might have been like, and I thought about how my own life might turn out different. It was what I always did when I broke in somewhere. I haunted other people's houses. I looked around, took in the details, and I compared our lives, but I never took anything because there'd never been a need.

It was the son who'd come to take things, loading up a van with all that was left of his father. He found me sleeping and called the police without waking me for an explanation.

My father was disappointed, of course. Embarrassed. I was released with only a caution and never knew if it was due to my age or something to do with my father, but when I was home again I found out just how hard his hands could be. It was the only time he ever hit me. My punishment was brief, and never repeated, but the only lesson I learnt from the whole experience was that when I drank myself to sleep I didn't dream. I wondered if that was why my father drank, why all the men drank, but I never asked. It was reason enough for me to do it, and that was all that mattered.

It took me a long time to learn how difficult my father's life must have been. To recognise his role as a through-stone in my life while I focussed on selfish pursuits. There were more break-ins, and I started taking things that didn't belong to me but felt like they should. I only broke into places death had visited, only stole from those who no longer needed the things I took – no longer needed anything at all – and I spent the money I made on whatever would keep the dreams away until it was me that went away instead. My father visited when he could. His jailbird son. He'd tell me about the work that kept him busy and I'd listen, looking at my hands flat on the table and thinking about his. He only ever asked me once why I did it, why I'd break in and take from those I'd grown up living with, and I told him, "Because of you."

He didn't understand the full extent of what I meant by that, how could he? How could he know that I did it to find out who he was, and who these people were, who they *really* were, because there was a good chance I was going to be the same as all of them. Following tradition into some unknown mundane death. That frightened me more than any seeping dark I might dream about. But I couldn't tell him all of that. There's a gap between the stories we tell ourselves and those we tell other people and I wasn't ready. I showed him anger instead, and hid within its shadow. All he learnt from his visits was how I could hurt him, so eventually he stopped coming. All I learnt from them was what I'd left behind.

Long periods of silence between me and my father kept us more divided than any bars or physical distance between us. It took him falling sick for us to talk again with any frequency. It took him becoming really sick for me to visit. And only when he was dying did I return home.

∼

I look at him now, withered in his bed, and I think of his lungs, black as a crow's wingspan inside him. I look at him and I see his hands, reduced to something skeletal, clutching at the bedsheets either side as he sleeps. The skin is spotted like I've only ever seen on old men. But I remember when they had been large, and strong, those hands. I remember how he'd shifted hundreds of heavy stones, picked them up, put them down. Proper work that used his whole body. I remember all the times he'd pointed, guided, as I worked in his wake, slotting rocks into gaps. The sun had been shining, and the land had held us in its green folds as we sweated together in our quiet labours. We've built many walls between us since that day, but back then we'd been repairing something.

"Da?"

He doesn't stir. The bedsheet has been folded down and I can see the thin gown they have him in. It shows how the mottled skin at his neck sags. I step closer to the bed to see if there's a pulse beating there.

"It's me, Da. My turn to visit you for a change."

Something in his chest hitches. I'd been watching its tiny rise and fall to make sure he was breathing but now it speeds through some wild, erratic rhythm. His back arches, and those hands of his, those once-strong hands, they grip the bedsheets as if trying to tear them down the middle. I rush over, reaching first for him and then for the button that calls a nurse, but before I can decide which should get priority he pushes at the sheets, pushes them aside, and hooks his hands into the collarless scoop of his gown to yank it down. His neck is tight, corded with muscle and veins. Below, his chest expands, filling to a preposterous size, and then the gown is tearing, a ripping split of fabric that frees a mass of tar-black feathers. They rise from him and open wide, finally filling the room, and in a sudden flurry of dark flapping, a crow vacates the body it had hidden within for so long. I turn my face away from it and shelter myself with a raised hand, waving my other to fend it away, but I'm still looking as this wet black thing shakes itself free and is gone. The air beats with its passing but already it's no longer there.

My father slumps, softer than the bed he rests upon. He relaxes the grip on his gown, fists loose, and he sees me. His eyes are open and they're as clear as I have always seen them, though wrinkles at the corners mark all the days he's squinted at the sun.

"You," he says.

"Me, Da. I came back."

Though I'm unable to fill the gaps he'll leave behind.

He gives me a smile or grimace and shows me his yellowed teeth. His gums have receded, as if retreating from the nicotine. I look at his hands and see he's letting go of whatever he'd been holding onto, and I hear him sigh as he closes his eyes, so I take one of those hands in both of mine and though he sleeps, I ask him, "Do you remember that day, when I was twelve...?"

And I tell him one of my favourite stories.

|6/6|

~

The short sequence of films known collectively as 6/6 stirred interest again recently by disappearing suddenly from YouTube where, in the past year, it had accumulated over 8,000,000 views[1]. It is unknown whether the footage was removed by the user NWhistler or by the host site, just as it is unclear as to whether it was done upon the urging of authorities whose interest in the film increased considerably after Mary Madison came forward claiming to recognise one of the participants[2].

Interestingly, shortly after the removal of the original 6/6 segments, other examples of the footage also vanished from the internet. The films first appeared on YouTube but were also easily accessible online via other venues, with several sites combining all six segments to create a short 36-minute piece. Many of these, however, have since been deactivated, and the few that remain only offer stills from the footage; any media samples either refuse to play or simply buffer without result.[3]

One theory holds that the footage is being removed in anticipation of the film receiving a cinema release. While no official statement has been made, award-winning director Denis Villeneuve did admit in a

---

1 This figure represents a round figure average taken from views spread over all 6 segments of film.

2 Although since exposed as an attention-seeking fraud in many respects, Mary Madison remains a valuable source of information regarding the 6/6 footage due to the proven accuracy of some of her claims and her successful polygraph test as televised on the *Fielding Investigates* Special, 5/5/2017. She continues to be a 'person of interest' in the ongoing investigation, and as such her statements regarding the recorded events remain worthy of consideration.

3 It is also worth noting that the awkwardly-titled documentary The House that Lack Built, which reproduces an extensive amount of the original footage, is no longer available from most outlets, listed as either 'out of stock' or 'recalled'. Private copies can still occasionally be found listed on auction sites like eBay but often for a considerable price.

recent interview with *SFX Magazine* that he had been approached to work on part of a feature length version of the footage that would also incorporate a 66-minute documentary (one assumes to bulk out the running time), but when pressed on the subject he declined to comment further[4]. Another theory maintains that the removed footage does not mark an effort to protect the film's cinema release but is rather an attempt to promote it.[5]

While the sequence of film is perhaps better known by the more colloquial titles *The Field House Film*, *The Birthday Film*, and *The Madison Footage*[6], it shall be referred to throughout this essay as 6/6, the official title by which it had originally appeared online on June 6th, 2016. Each segment of film will be detailed in consecutive order under subheadings 1/6, 2/6, 3/6, etc, thus following the chronological order in which they appeared online (and which also seems to indicate a linear narrative structure).

Comments posted online in direct response to each original segment will be reproduced within this essay wherever it is possible, useful, and ethical to do so, though such additional content will be limited due to a reliance on personal screenshots taken before examples of the footage were removed.

While the argument as to whether 6/6 is a creative endeavour or genuine footage of an actual event occurring naturally[7] is the most

---

4 Rumours circulate that Mary Madison may be narrating or playing a small part in the film, but she has been uncharacteristically quiet regarding the matter, neither confirming nor denying involvement.

5 In appearing first on YouTube, accessible for free by all internet users, 6/6 has so far been a venture without profit (save for anything made from advertising opportunities). It is possible that the participants responsible for the film were merely keen to gain exposure, and/or it may be that the film's release via YouTube was a way of striking out at the film industry as a whole, but until anyone claims the footage, we will never know. It will be interesting to see if the production or release of the film for cinema provokes a reaction from the original film maker, if only regarding issues of copyright.

6 Interestingly, having identified one of the participants of the film by name, it is Mary Madison who has come to provide an eponymous title for the film thanks to the media attention she both received and created, cementing her more firmly in its history or 'mythology' than those who contributed to the production of the film in a more direct way.

7 Or indeed *super*naturally.

persisting argument concerning the film, it is not the purpose of this essay to support either view. With copies of 6/6 quickly disappearing, it is the purpose of this essay merely to preserve the footage, albeit in written form.

1/6

The first segment, taken by itself, is a rather dull six minutes of film and no doubt generated many of its initial views only in the context of 6/6 as a whole, with viewers seeking it out or simply clicking on a suggested link after having seen later, more eventful, segments of the sequence. Shot in black and white (as are all the other segments, with two notable exceptions), it begins by focusing on the long grass of an open field, moving in a gentle wind. It seems, at first, to be an 'art' film or, as talespin28 expressed in the original comments, "hipster student shit". There is little sound beyond the whispering grass and, briefly, at 0:47, the single croak of some thick-throated bird[8], at which point the camera lifts and turns left to show a single-storey building[9]. A brief zoom brings it close enough to see it's made of concrete blocks, with a roof of rusted corrugated iron sheets. There are five dark square windows. The camera zooms out again to put it back in the grass field at a distance. As an establishing shot it is far too long, and early viewers would no doubt have lost interest after the second minute, if not the first. For 2:47 there is only the play of grass and the building 200 metres away, and a few scattered clouds passing overhead.[10]

---

8   Since identified as a raven, though whether it is the same raven seen in 5/6 is impossible to know (and perhaps pointless to wonder).

9   This is the so-called 'field house' of one of the film's alternative titles, also known by the misnomer 'fieldstone house', and though it is later revealed to be a basic kind of stable or cattle shed, very few people refer to it as such. For an interesting view regarding this reluctance, see the excellent essay 'Destabilising the found-footage genre: avoidance and omission in *The Field House Film*' by Stephen Volk.

10 Much has been said about the clouds, with several viewers noting anomalies such as how the direction in which the clouds move does not match the flow of the tall field grass, though this is easily countered by considering the different atmospheric and thermal conditions as well as the differing gradients of atmospheric pressure, not to mention the density of the grass, obstacles shaping the path of the wind, and other such geographical aspects. More startling is to observe that while the

Nearly 3 minutes into the film, the camera finally moves forwards. Handheld, it's a little shaky, offering occasional glimpses of the camera operator's legs[11] when lowered for shots of the grass folding down underfoot. Grasshoppers are disturbed into sudden movement, fleeing ahead for a few bounds before cutting sharply left or right and out of shot[12]. There are 41 seconds of this and then, 3:28 into the film, there is a voice. It is too faint to hear properly[13] but the camera turns and there's a sudden loud, "What?" from the camera operator directed at a woman walking behind[14]. She is bunching her hair into a loose ponytail when we first see her, wearing short shorts, a sports vest with the number 69, and a backpack[15]. When finished with

clouds cast accurate shadows over the fields, any darkness that falls on the field house is kept by the field house. That is to say, shadows do not pass over the building but rather strike it and then stop, the clouds continuing over the field and out of shot with no more shadow beneath them. Perhaps merely "a subtle and affective [sic] trick" as Kubrik_Khan commented, though it seems rather too subtle to be noticed by an audience not investigating the film's authenticity.

11 The legs are dark-haired, seemingly male legs, clad in ¾ length shorts, or cargo shorts. The shoes are Timberlands, possibly size 10 as suggested by a brief moment of comparative scale in section 2/6. There are no distinguishable marks such as scars or tattoos to help identify this mystery filmmaker, allowing for a great deal of speculation. One of the most popular theories holds that it is NWhistler (though there is nothing to suggest NWhistler is male), while others suppose the mystery man is Deborah Tanning's lover, though such a claim is impossible to either prove or discredit. He could, of course, be both.

12 Are the grasshoppers avoiding the people pursing them through the field, or are they avoiding the field house ahead? Or first one then the other? In fact, there is little strange about the movements of the insects, though some would like to suggest otherwise in support of a supernatural foreboding.

13 Investigations focussing on this voice have not yielded individual words, but the cadence suggests that the speaker does indeed say, 'Is this all there is?'

14 The woman was identified by Mary Madison as Deborah Tanning. Prior to this she was known as 'the backpack girl', 'the French girl', and 'the final girl'. There are logical reasons for each, though as Maura McHugh notes in 'A Girl Called Sid: The Masculinised Woman in Horror Film' "Whatever the modifier, she is still a 'girl', never a woman. The only early reference that does not call her 'girl' calls her instead 'Miss 69', reducing her to a number and sexual act, with a notable assumption regarding her marital status that presents her as 'available'."

15 Versions of 6/6 in which the colour has been restored reveal that the shorts are a tan colour like the camera operator's and the backpack blue, while the vest remains grey with black numerals. We never discover what the pack contains,

her hair, her hands go to the straps of the pack, pulling to ease the weight on her back, and she says, "I said, is this all there is? I thought there was, like…" The man prompts her with another, "What?" but she doesn't finish what she was going to say, only shrugs and says, "Doesn't matter." She has a slight 'estuary' accent to her English that suggests London[16], whereas his accent (heard more clearly later) is West Country, or perhaps Bristol.

She sweeps her arms forward, ushering him on.

The camera view turns with him as they resume walking, and the building is suddenly close, almost filling the shot[17]. It's a long building, perhaps 20 meters in length. Concrete breezeblocks have been cemented together with little care for the finished look. The windows are merely vacancies in the walls, with no evidence of there ever having been frames, sills, or shutters: each is simply a square opening regularly spaced amongst the blocks. There are no doors on this side. A ribbed sheet of iron leans against the wall where it has fallen from the roof which slopes ever so slightly towards the viewer. Rust has eaten away at the middle of this fallen sheet. In a move that seems perhaps *too* contrived to have been deliberate, the camera zooms in on the darkness of that hole and the segment of film ends at precisely 6:00.

2/6

The second segment of footage resumes directly from the rusted hole of 1/6, the camera turning without zooming out then bringing the building back into focus as the filming couple walk its perimeter, anti-clockwise[18]. On the other side of the building are five doors.

---

though there are many who suppose the contents include a blanket and candles; an unsurprising assumption, considering how the film develops.

16 Some critics believe this accent supports Madison's claim that Tanning attended RADA, though no record was ever found of Tanning attending the drama school. Madison, however, did attend, though she dropped out in her final year citing 'personal issues'.

17 It is much closer than it should be considering the short time they have been walking towards it, supporting the idea that the film has been edited.

18 Or 'widdershins'. According to superstition, 'widdershins' is considered unnatural due to opposing the normal course of the sun; it is therefore considered unlucky.

Three are made from the same corrugated iron as the roof. One of the other doors is made up of boards of various shapes and sizes cobbled together into a haphazard rectangle. The remaining door is half house door at the bottom and half chain link fence above. There are no handles or bolts or fixtures for keeping any of the doors closed and secured. To the right of each door is a small window, again simply a vacancy within the wall. The overall look of the building – the positions of the doors, combined with its long length and location in an open field – suggest something like a stable or some other animal shelter.

The slow perimeter walk is interrupted at 2:38 when the woman cries out from somewhere out of view behind, and the camera operator checks that she is okay; our view shifts suddenly with a quick twist, the camera coming down unintentionally as the operator asks, "You all right?". When the camera is raised again, the woman is crouching, filling the shot. She's feeling at one of her ankles. She's wearing Converse trainers. The hand at her ankle comes away bloody and she shows the camera directly. Beside her feet, lying flat on the ground, is another sheet of metal, partially concealed by the long grass around it. She appears to have walked into it.

"When did you last have a tetanus shot?"

She shakes her head. "Didn't come all this way to die of blood poisoning[19]."

"How is it?"

She hisses as an answer, wiping away blood with her fingertips. She has a tattoo around her ankle. A charm bracelet as an anklet, with several of the charms visible: a padlock; a feather; a horseshoe; a heart in two halves.[20]

---

19 Again, Volk's essay is of interest here regarding the ambiguities and interpretations of this utterance. "The lack of inflection makes it difficult to determine Deborah Tanning's meaning; could it be she did not come all this way to then simply die? Or is she claiming she did not come all this way to die of something as trivial as blood poisoning? Did she, in fact, have more grand plans for her own demise? Assuming, of course, that the film is not a hoax, and assuming, of course, that she does, indeed, die."

20 Madison claimed this tattoo was how she recognised Tanning, despite two earlier shots in the film clearly showing the woman's face. "She would add charms whenever she wanted another tattoo so she didn't have them all over

"Do you have any wipes or some, like, tissues, or something?"

"I might do. Let me—"

The camera lowers briefly, but a "Never mind," from the woman, "don't worry about it, I got one," brings it back into position.

"Sorted?"

"Yeah. It's just blood." She dabs at her ankle with a crumpled tissue. "If it scars, you can just get a new tattoo."[21]

She wipes her hands, discards the tissue, and stands, camera following her up then turning away from her. It turns back when she says, "Look. The tree[22]." She points, and the camera follows as directed.

It's a wide-limbed ash tree, denuded of all leaves. It's little more than a silhouette at this point of filming, certainly nothing notable about it that would warrant spontaneous attention, unless for how striking it looks, stark against the sky.[23] At 4:18 the camera turns back to the field building and the woman. She gestures forwards, much as she had earlier to encourage the camera operator onwards. "Let's go."[24]

---

her body." There has been much conjecture as to the significance of the charms which will not be repeated here, except to note that any symbolic significance to the narrative suggests a deliberately crafted film. How they might relate to the narrative cohesion of Tanning's own personal life up to this point remains unknown, of course.

21 It's worth noting that if the charms did carry deliberate significance to the film, a close up here would support the comment and guide the viewer's attention to the tattoo to reinforce the image. However, there is no such close up.

22 YouTube user Reggie Richards commented in response to segment 5/6 that this line could suggest a prior knowledge of the tree, noting the use of definite article "the" to suggest the tree is of some particular significance, that it has a reputation of its own. It may even be that Tanning's incomplete utterance in 1/6 alludes to the existence of this tree, that she is surprised to not see it. However, it is also feasible that, "Look. The tree." is merely an abbreviated version of 'Look at the tree', in which case "the" has no additional significance other than to indicate what should be looked at.

23 Though never referred to in the footage as anything other than "the tree", viewers who have seen later sections of the footage often refer to it as 'the hanging tree', for obvious reasons.

24 So ends the longest exchange of dialogue in the film. Joe Hill's short story, 'Let's Go', written in response to the 6/6 footage, not only takes its title from this line but also explores its potential use as a beginning and as an end, though the story

The camera zooms in and out of each of the windows beside the doors without moving forwards. Many have supposed that this is a last moment of procrastination, others that it is an attempt to create tension, though in the case of the latter there is little to affect the viewer, unless it is to create impatience. Certainly there is little of interest concerning the windows to a casual viewer. They are narrower than the squares vacancies we saw on the other side of the building but otherwise very much the same. However, as was first noticed by Simon_Carris2, enhancing the resolution reveals what might be a person stepping back from the third window into the deeper shadows of the room, wrapped in a blanket as if cowled against cold despite the summer weather.[25]

The film-makers do not act as if they have seen anyone and continue towards the building. They approach the first of the doors, which is little more than a leaning sheet of metal bending into the darkness behind it.

The film cuts here, at 4:45, to different footage entirely for 2 seconds. It is a jarring sudden cut in its shock of colour juxtaposed with the previous ten minutes of black and white, jarring as well in the incongruity of its content; it's a children's birthday party, the children sitting at a table set with bright napkins and a large cake. There is a snippet of song, the word "Happy" in a tone suggesting the penultimate line, the one that would normally end with the name of the person whose birthday is being celebrated.[26] There is nothing to indicate who this might be, however, as none of the children lean towards the cake with any sense of ownership or importance and the camera focuses on the cake itself, white-iced and alight with candles. There are six of them.[27]

---

will always be remembered for the chilling way in which the title later develops into the fuller 'let us go'.

25 If it is meant to be a shock moment in the film, it is far too subtle to be effective, impossible to even see without the viewer making some effort of their own. As part of a hoax, however, it makes for an effective detail.

26 At the time of writing, these children have not as yet been identified.

27 Of course much has been made of this number. Indeed, as there has been for every number appearing in, or suggested by, an aspect of the 6/6 footage. The most thorough analysis is perhaps 'Even Numbers are Odd' by Manisha Dutt, which appeared as an entry on her personal blog.

The film returns to the black and white footage and for 3 seconds we have the opening of the corrugated iron door and a step into the dark interior of a narrow room or stall.

Then the film cuts again to colour and we are in a bright garden where children are crying[28]. One is wailing particularly enthusiastically, pointing, and the camera turns its attention left to a swimming pool where a child floats facedown in the water. The camera is dropped but before it can land we're back inside the field building.

A panning shot takes in each of the walls, the corners, and then up into the rafters and the rusting roof. Light slants in through numerous holes, holding dust motes in slow movements. There is nothing in the room. None of the detritus you might expect of an abandoned building, no litter, broken glass, no graffiti. A concrete trough at the opposite end of the room, below the bigger window, holds only damp stains or shadows. The only sound is the occasional scuff of someone's shoe on the concrete floor.

We exit this first room back into the bright light of outside, glimpse the distant tree again, and turn back for the second room or stall. It is so much the same as the first that some have speculated it is in fact the same room, but it is easy to note some minor differences: there is a slight build up of cement around the window opening as if the excess was not scraped away properly by the builder's trowel; the camera dips into the trough at a similar angle as before, but there are no signs of the dark marks we saw inside previously; there are holes in the roof again but they are positioned differently. However, this time, when the camera is pointed upwards at the roof, sun slanting in, we hear the distinctive sound of metal flexing as if someone or something walks across the roof outside. Neither person present comments on the noise, though, not even when a fall of dirt sifts down from above as if disturbed by a moving weight.

---

28 Opinion is divided as to whether these are the same children from the birthday party. While they are not wearing party hats, there are some similarities in attire that are difficult to dismiss.

3/6

The third room or stall is where, with enhancement, the blanket-clad figure was seen. It is not here now. The far window is bare, just as in the previous rooms, but in the trough below is a line of candle stubs of various sizes, six of them, melted in place. Occasionally, as the camera moves over them, there is an instance of lens flare as if catching light from a flame, though none of the candles are lit. They are not mentioned by either party, though the camera lingers on them.

From the line of candles in the trough we pan up to the ceiling. Again, iron sheets sit on narrow wooden beams. However, the metal is in better condition here, the only light coming in from the windows at either end of the room. The woman is leaning out of the one near the door, bending over the sill on tiptoe so she is all taut legs and tight shorts and a line of naked waist where her vest has ridden up with the shifted weight of the backpack, but the camera does not spend more than a passing moment on that view and sweeps the perimeter of the room. Cement floor, concrete blocks. Back at the window we find it empty. The woman is now in the opposite corner of the room instead, standing in shadow. She steps forward suddenly, a blanket clutched in both hands which she thrusts at the camera when it finds her. It's clear she is angry even before she shouts, her brow furrowed in a scowl, lips twisted in a sneer. When she shouts, her words are French[29].

---

29 Madison claims that Tanning did not know French, nor any other language besides English. There are those who, believing the film to be a genuine recording of supernatural phenomenon, claim that at this moment in the film Tanning is 'possessed' or acting as a host body for something 'other'. There are some who agree that this isn't Tanning, but they agree in a more literal sense inasmuch as it is someone else entirely, the windows possible exit and entrance points for Tanning and a replacement. Indeed, in *Bon Anniversaire, Mon Ami*, a short featurette released a year after 6/6 was first uploaded, Agnès Domis puns on 'French exchange' in her close focus of this scene and reminds us that the woman's face here is either contorted by rage or obscured by her gestures with a blanket, allowing for a convincing double. Of course, as no Deborah Tanning has ever been officially identified, all of this is mere speculation initiated by Madison's own dubious testimony.

"Qu'est ce que tu as fait? Dis moi ce que tu as fait! Était-ce toi?"[30]

The camera operator retreats from her. She presses forward, *"Tu crois que je ne sais pas?"*[31] and he says, "No," though whether it is an answer to any of her questions or simply a denial of the situation occurring is unclear. The woman throws the blanket so that it drapes the camera entirely for a moment[32]. When the blanket is gone we are on a shaky run out of the building. There are noises from the roof again[33], faster this time as the camera operator flees.

He is followed by more French.

"Je le sais tres bien! Je sais!"[34]

As soon as we are outside in the light the camera is turned up to the roof, suggesting that this time, at least, the noises were noted, but there is no one there. The camera work is clumsier than previously as the operator runs backwards to keep the roof in shot, but even with some distance and a wider view there is no one. The camera lowers to the window of the room that was so hastily vacated and zooms in on the darkness there. The operator, loud and startling, yells, "Hey!" but there is no answer. The camera flits quickly from window to window, all five, then each of the doors, the camera operator muttering[35] before

---

30 "What did you do? Tell me what you did! Was it you?" It could be that she refers to some infidelity. It could be that she refers to some fatal negligence or deliberate action resulting in the death of an infant, if you consider the previous footage interspersed with 2/6. It could be anything.

31 "You think I do not know?"

32 This momentary obstruction of view allows for more theories regarding editing, the deliberate darkness allowing for a cutaway that would provide Tanning with a chance to leave the building ahead of the camera operator in preparation for later scenes, or to allow for the apparent time lapse in 4/6.

33 It is interesting to note that these noises are precisely the same as the ones heard in the previous room, only with less time between them as intervals so that each tremble and squeal of metal coincides with the footfalls of the fleeing camera operator. Again, this is cited as evidence of deliberate editing by some, either of this scene, the one prior, or both.

34 "I know it very well! I know!"

35 After some effort manipulating the audio, it has been proposed that one of the words muttered is either "Help", "Hell", or even "Hel", this last offered as a suggestion because Helen is reportedly Deborah Tanning's middle name – a tenuous link perhaps, but she wouldn't be the first person to go by a middle name instead of their first one.

yelling a final "Hey!" with the camera focussing at the third window[36].
Moving backwards, the camera operator stumbles and the building
drops out of frame and all we see is grass.

4/6

The grass is swept aside by the camera being picked up, aimed now
at a sheet of metal on the ground. It's the same sheet the woman
had stumbled on earlier, a discarded bloody tissue nearby. The camera
operator's right foot comes into frame and nudges at the metal, then
he's crouching and using one hand to part lift, part push the metal.
There's some difficulty due to the weight, the awkwardness of using
one hand, and the long grass that hinders it, but eventually he manages
to move the metal aside.

There's a hole, deep like a shaft or a well. The camera shows nothing
but dark inside until a mounted light is turned on and we see it is
indeed something like a well; the light reflects and flashes as if falling
on water. The camera holds on this for 9 seconds and then withdraws
suddenly with a cry from the operator – "Oh fuck!" – the picture
jerking as he scrambles back from the hole. After almost a full minute
(57 seconds) of heavy breathing and a focus on the edge of the hole,
the camera moves slowly forwards and again peers over and down into
the depths of the shaft. It holds there for another 12 seconds and then
– "Shit, fuck, shit!" – jerks back once more[37].

36 This is where some suppose they have seen a figure step back from the shadows
at the window. Some even claim to identify the figure as Tanning, wrapped in
a blanket she sweeps up over her head as she retreats into the dark. There is,
however, nothing in the footage to support such claims.

37 No amount of close scrutiny has ever revealed anything that might have provoked
such reactions; there is only darkness. Some viewers, however, claim to see a body
in the water, perhaps taking for their inspiration the earlier interruption footage;
indeed, some even claim the body is that of a child floating face down; there
were even those within the official police investigation who reported the same to
the press, although no visual evidence was ever produced. Examples of re-edited
footage circulate the internet, each borrowing from an existing horror film:
Samara from *The Ring* climbs up and out of the hole; Pennywise from *IT* offers
a balloon; one of the creatures from *The Descent* scampers up, hissing. In one
disorientating reversal of perspective, 'Buffalo Bill' from *The Silence of the Lambs*
looks simultaneously down a well and up, advising the viewer 'puts the lotion

There is no third look into the dark: the camera is upside down now and pointing behind as the operator runs through the grass. Glimpses of the pit and the building flash in and out of view, receding, more distant with each appearance until eventually, at 3:10, the camera is brought back around and the right way up. It is aimed low to show grass kicked flat and grasshoppers scattering. At 3:19 the grass gives way to hard-packed dirt, and protruding from the dirt are a number of what appears to be short sticks. The camera operator stops running abruptly to focus on these sticks and we see they are, in fact, tiny candles of a kind usually used on birthday cakes. The camera operator says, "What the fuck?" and "What the *fuck?*"

The view shifts dizzyingly fast back the way we have come to show the distant field building. The quality of the light has shifted so that it seems to be dusk, although it has been early afternoon throughout the footage up to this point. The more subdued light seems to be spreading outward from the building, as if the sun is going down on the other side. The sky is cloudless.

An abrupt *caw!* has the camera spin again, and it needs to refocus as we are standing too close to the tree seen earlier, looking up into the branches where the sudden flutter of a raven disturbs the uppermost limbs. For a brief moment the camera manages to track the bird's flight but in trying to hold the image centre frame misjudges the speed then overcorrects and the bird is lost.

5/6

The camera lowers back to the tree, slowly coming down from the higher branches to the lower boughs and panning down the trunk, moving across to where a hollow gapes like a slack mouth. It holds on this, zooming in steadily, when the lower half of a body drops into view and snaps up short of falling to the ground[38]. We have a glimpse

---

on the skin', before segueing for comedy into an advertisement for skin care cream. Another notable example includes a surreal cut to 1980s pop singer Rick Astley singing 'Never Gonna Give You Up'. Kim Newman has addressed each of these variations and more in his essay 'Meta-culpa: the intertextual dilutions and cultural pollutions of 6/6'.)

38 In horror film terms, it is a classic 'jump-scare' moment.

of bare legs suspended and twisting and kicking in spasm before one of the feet strikes the camera; there is a sudden close-up of an old Converse trainer[39] and the camera is knocked aside to land on the ground.

For nearly 4 minutes this is all: a patch of dirt, a scattering of candles, and the long grass. At 4:36 there is a singular scratching sound. Again at 4:45. Every few seconds, a scratch, sometimes twice in succession.

At 5:02 there is faint humming in the interval between scratches to the tune of 'happy birthday'.

At 5:10 a blanket draped figure crawls into the frame. They move from candle to candle, righting those that have been knocked askew and lighting each with a disposable lighter. When all we can see are lit, the figure crawls out of shot, though you can still hear the humming, and the regular scratch-scratch of the lighter wheel.

The fallen camera struggles to auto-focus, having too many options with the flickering candles sticking from the ground nearby.

6/6

The camera whirrs in and out of focus for 24 seconds before it is lifted from the ground. It pans around to show the tree surrounded by candles. For a moment the legs dangle in shot, feet limp and toes pointing to the ground. One foot, the left, is missing a shoe. The legs swing lightly. The camera doesn't linger on the sight, though when the hanging legs are no longer in view we can still hear the creaking of taut rope.

The camera angles up from the candled ground to take in the field. It is almost full dark now, despite the assumed timeframe of the shoot. The camera tilts further upward and there is the building, now aglow with candles. Tiny lights in the windows. Lines of light outlining the roof. The camera remains level with the building in focus then lifts higher so that there is no grass in the picture, only the building. It is lit up like a birthday cake. The image trembles a moment before moving higher still, though now the image moves

---

39 Although the same style and colour (as revealed in restored footage) as Tanning's shoes, and although stained with blood around the collar of the heel in the same place we saw earlier in the film, the ankle is neither injured or tattooed.

slightly from side to side, and tilts just the slightest bit with each movement[40]. We hear the branches of the tree shudder in a gust of wind that makes the nearby grass hiss and whisper and all as one the candles go out.[41]

The film ends. 6:00.

---

40 It is entirely possible that the operator is holding the camera up at full arm's length, though taking into account the momentary tremble and then the tilting side-to-side movement, there are those who suppose the camera was handed to, or taken by, the hanging person, an idea supported by the creaking sound of the rope that accompanies each side-to-side movement.

41 Considering some of the subtleties featured in the film prior to this point, it seems plausible that such an ending supports the film's authenticity, the conclusion so neatly contrived for a constructed narrative as to be disappointing. A better ending would have been to have the house remain illuminated, the final image one of tantalising frustrating revelation as well as birthday imagery, rather than the predictable, heavy-handed symbolism of lights extinguished. 'Out, Brief Candle' by Anon, criticises this in particular. In analysing 6/6 purely as a film and ignoring the possibilities of it being either genuine footage or a hoax, the anonymous critic paraphrases Shakespeare's *Macbeth* to deride not only 6/6 but all work that seeks to engage with it. "Out, out, brief candle. Life is nothing more than an illusion. It's like a poor actor who struts and worries for *her 36 minutes* [sic] on the stage and then is never heard from again. Life is a story told by an idiot, full of noise and emotional disturbance but devoid of meaning."

|Sideways|

Captain Sam Harding was a great pilot, a patriot, and a very close friend, so when I tell you I'm glad he died, know that I don't say it lightly. He augered in on November 4th, 1951, leaving behind a beautiful wife plus one. Sandra eventually remarried, and the child Sam never met grew up to be a good man, like his father. Tom was just a few months in Sandra's belly the day Sam came staggering out of that wreck like some flaming scarecrow in a field of fire. Sandy named the boy Tom because of how I was always there for her but says it was something she and Sam had already discussed. I don't know. I'm still not sure how Sam would feel about it now. When he made me promise to take care of his family if ever anything happened, I don't think he meant for me to marry his wife and raise his kid like my own.

Sam was a great husband, by all accounts. I believe it, and as his usual drinking partner I can testify to some of that assessment. He had an appreciation for the opposite sex, sure, but he never strayed. And he could have, very easily. He was a pilot, for Christ's sakes, and I haven't met a lady yet who doesn't go for a man in uniform. Never failed for me. And Sam was no ordinary pilot, either. Captain Harding was a test pilot for the United States Air Force, risking his life – and ultimately giving it – for the good of his country.

Sounds too good to be true, doesn't he. Well, that's how he was. Maybe God snatched him back when he realised. Maybe Sam flew too close to Heaven and caught the big man's attention. That's what I used to tell Junior when he asked about his real daddy.

Better that than the truth.

"It's like nothing you've ever *seen*."
"Unless you've seen an arrow."

"Okay, but as far as jets go—"

"Should you even be talking about this?"

I shrugged.

"So what's so special about it?" Sam asked, humouring me.

He and Sandy were having a barbeque. Throwing a bit of a party, really. They had the same sort of house as the rest of us, same dry yard, but for some reason theirs was where we usually ended up for barbeques. Everybody was there, the whole bunch, kids and all, adults standing around on the patchy lawn, sitting at the picnic table, milling around the kitchen, kids screaming and running and falling down and laughing. Nobody was listening to Sam and me discuss 'military secrets'. Hell, we all worked at the same base; everybody would know eventually.

"Well I was talking to Jonesy," I said, "and he reckons it's more like a rocket than a plane. You know, long. Tubular. And it has four wings, like this." I made a cross of my arms. "But set right back. *Too* far back, in my opinion. Like on the end of an arrow."

Sam leaned close and said quietly, "You know what I reckon it is?"

"What?"

"I bet... you say it looks like a rocket?"

I nodded.

"I bet, what it is..." He looked around, exaggerating caution. "It's a *rocket*."

I flapped my hands as if to brush him away and he laughed. There was no malice in it. I laughed with him.

"Hey," he said suddenly, as if the question had just occurred to him. "Why do they call it the Arrow?"

"Because it has four wings like – Oh. Funny."

As if in agreement, a burst of laughter erupted from where Bull was playing with the kids. He was holding one of them upside down by her ankles, shaking giggles from her as other laughing children clambered over him like a climbing frame. Kennedy was stood at the grill, apron on, beer in one hand and tongs the other. "You need a hand there?" he called to Bull. Ernst Kennedy would one day become 'Pres' as in president, but until then he was just Kennedy. "Nah," was Bull's answer, to which Kennedy replied, "I was talking to the kids." He put down his beer and tongs and began rolling his sleeves as if to join them.

"Honey, no," Claire protested, but she was laughing. The very idea of her husband going against Bull was hilarious. Bull didn't so much fly planes as wear them. Even Doc joined in, taking on that official voice we've all hated at some point – "For the sake of your health, I strongly advise against it" – and that got a laugh, too. Doc was our natural enemy, the only man on base who could stop any of us flying, but not today. Today was a good day, a happy day, and I remember it fondly as one of the last good times we were all together.

"Seriously," Sam said, drawing himself away from the kids at play and the sight of his wife in a crowd of his friends, "I have heard something about it that sits odd with me." I didn't ask where he'd heard it, or why. If there really was an Arrow, it would be Sam who flew it. Anybody could have told you that.

"What? It uses rocket fuel? Because it's a rocket?"

Sam didn't humour me this time. He just said, "It goes sideways."

I frowned at him but all he did was drink more beer. "Sideways?"

Sam shrugged, though I think he already knew a bit about it, even then.

"Maybe it rolls," I said, making a twisting motion with my beer bottle. It wouldn't be able to go sideways, but maybe it could alter its course in diagonal. Dangerous, though. Stability and control at supersonic speed were the two main concerns of most of our FTTs, each flight test technique measuring and evaluating these capabilities. Another problem at high speed was the damn thermal thicket, severe heating caused by aerodynamic friction causing all sorts of merry hell. But the Arrow wasn't focussing on any of these things. Not as a main priority, anyway. The Arrow was something very different.

"I've heard it's a spy plane," I told him. "Hard to detect."

Sam neither confirmed or denied the suggestion.

"You flying it?"

Sam smiled and said, "Can't tell you." His way of saying yes.

"Sandra know?"

Sam looked at where she stood with the wives and girlfriends by the kitchen door. The other women were laughing but Sandy only smiled, one hand on the swell of her stomach.

"She knows."

"She give you hell for it?"

She looked over as if sensing she was our topic of conversation instead of planes for a change. Sandy knew the job, and she knew the risks, but she liked to remind Sam from time to time that she didn't like it. Sam raised his beer to her and she turned her smile up for him, blew him a kiss.

"Just a little bit," Sam said and he smiled at her.

Sam flew the Arrow twice, the first time less than two weeks after that barbeque. You can believe Sandra gave him hell for it before the second time.

"I heard they brought some scientists in from New Mexico."

Sam's smile was suddenly gone and he said, "Not just scientists." Before I could ask what he meant, Fliss came out of the kitchen with a huge bowl of salad and a plate full of bread rolls and announced that Jenny was here, giving us a chance to tone down the humour before she stepped out into the yard.

Unofficially, this little shindig was her farewell party. It was the last time she'd be part of one of our get-togethers. We did it all the time, us pilots and wives. We barely associated with anyone else, actually. Drinks at someone's place, dinners, group nights out at Ratty's. But Jenny was taking the kids 'back home' to live with her mother for a while and we all knew she'd never be back. Kimble had augered in last month, a miscalculation in fuel consumption leaving him deadstick and spinning before plummeting in a fall he didn't or couldn't try to eject from. He'd crunched about fifty yards from the runway. That one was bad. They were all bad, but that one was ugly. I remember watching the duty officer on the phone trying to explain to someone what had happened and he couldn't do it. He just kept swallowing the words, choking on them, voice breaking with the effort to get them out. In the end I took the phone from him but I couldn't do it either. I'd put the phone down, then took it off the hook.

"I didn't know if she'd make it," Sam said.

For a moment, Jennifer stood framed by the doorway, her two girls looking around from behind her legs. A picture missing its husband and daddy. Then Sam called, "Hey Jenny!" and there was a chorus of "Hi!" and "Hello!" from everybody else, jokes called at the kids, and they were all welcomed back into the crowd.

We forgot all about the Arrow.

~

We all had to sign additional confidentiality contracts after the crash, documents swearing us to secrecy above and beyond standard military practice. There was no expiration date to those agreements, no disclosure after sixty years, exemption from the freedom of information, et cetera, et cetera. But there is an expiration date to this old sack of a body I'm trapped in, and I'm pretty close to it now. I'll go with a few regrets, like everybody else I reckon, but I don't want to go with any secrets because they eat you up worse than this cancer I got and I'm not sure they'll stop eating me even when I'm gone. I never used to be one for believing in anything after but I've seen things since then that changed my perspective. Knocked me sideways, you could say. Last thing I want is to go to wherever we go after this still being devoured by secrets. I've enough to worry about without adding that.

I saw the Arrow but I never flew it. Nobody flew it, as far as I'm aware, except Sam. I did get to see it up close though because I flew the modified B50 that carried it into the sky. Only for its first drop launch. The second time I saw it I stayed on the ground, and shortly after that I saw it again coming in fast, dipping down and flipping and hitting sideways, rolling and breaking apart into a fiery ball that opened up like a curtain to spit out the black charred pieces.

I loved the B50. She was a mighty bird. 99 feet long, 140 across the wings, decent cruise speed. Trustworthy. Reliable. Bessie, ours was called, with a long-legged redhead stretched out across her in vivid colours, head turned to smile at you as if she couldn't care less where she was flying as long as she was flying with you. First time I saw my precious B50 with the Arrow strapped to its belly, though, was the first time I didn't want to fly. There was something wrong about that thing. This isn't hindsight here. I felt a genuine sense of foreboding, looking at the Arrow, like the curdling you get in the stomach when you think you hear a rattlesnake. It was longer than I'd imagined. The B50 is nearly a hundred feet long and the Arrow was nearly half that, not including the length of what Sam called 'the lightning stick' pointing out from the nose. The wings stuck out like the flights of an arrow or dart and they looked flimsy, like thin sheets of aluminium. Must have been about as thick as a sandwich, at most. Far too short as well, I thought. Looking at it, I couldn't believe it even flew. It shouldn't have.

Sam was already inside. Normally he'd have climbed into it at 7000 feet but he needed to be fixed in this time. I knocked hello on the canopy, heard him knock back. The glass was reflective. In fact, the metal of the entire thing was so highly polished it shone like a sliver mirror. I didn't like the way it distorted our reflections either, bending our features around into strange shapes that seemed wrong, not just as representations of ourselves but because the Arrow didn't seem to reflect light right. I hated carrying it and felt the whole time like my precious Bessie was pregnant with some monstrous malignant parasite. It was a pleasure to drop the damn thing into the clouds.

"Twenty five thousand and climbing."

—*Roger that. How's she feel up there?*

"Feels fine," I reported. "Bessie's always a smooth fine ride."

—*Roger that.*

My co-pilot that trip was Kennedy. He looked at me and said, "Except she ain't." He had his hand over the mike, his words only for me. "She ain't right, is she Finn?"

Finn as in Huckleberry. I'm named after *Tom Sawyer*, which was the only book my father ever read, so of course everybody called me Huck, or Finn, or Huckleberry.

"Just a bubble in the pipes or something," I said. "She's fine."

She felt heavy, though. Whatever the Arrow weighed, Bessie was flying like she felt more than every pound of it, dragging her down. Her turns were sluggish and shaky even when there wasn't any chop.

"You okay back there Sam?"

"He can't hear you," Kennedy reminded me. Again.

I didn't like that, either. I didn't like Sam without a radio. No test pilot should be without a radio, and yet the Arrow didn't have one. Part of the stealth thing, maybe, but I got the impression Sam didn't think so. He said it didn't bother him. He'd always had a great memory and I'd seen the truth of that, seem him relay every change and movement after landing a test where the radio failed. He'd be doing that again now, this time on purpose, remembering everything his control panel told him as well as when. "But I don't think they're so interested in all that at this stage," he told me. "I think they just want to know if it works." And maybe that was a good thing. Too many pilots have crunched because they were paying too much attention to the controls, diligently relaying information when they should've been pulling up or pulling out of whatever envelope-pushing power drive they were in. When I think of how he came in on that second landing, though, I wonder if he forgot he didn't have one and I wonder what he would have said before the screams. I'm glad I'll never know.

"Hey Kennedy? What do you know about this thing?"

He checked the instruments more than he needed to when he answered, his eyes everywhere but on me.

"I don't like it," he said. "I know that."

I was both glad and worried that someone else felt it too.

"Nosing over at twenty-six thousand feet," I told control.

—*Roger that. Twenty-six thousand.*

"Let's dump it," I said to Kennedy. "About time Sam did some of the work around here."

He smiled. "Amen to that."

I could tell Kennedy was thinking the same thing I was, thinking 'better him than me'. Or, there but for the grace of God go I. Not that we'd have ever been assigned the Arrow. Something else it didn't have was the option to punch out, and there was really only one of us you could count on to never do that. I reckon about fifty percent of pilots have had to eject at some point in their career, but Sam wasn't one of them. I'd seen him land deadstick, *twice*, when his fuel ran out, rather than eject. He joked it was too dangerous, that punching out was just killing yourself before the ground could do it for you, but maybe he wasn't really joking. When you eject, you're fired from the jet by a blast of nitroglycerine like a human bullet, and a lot of men got hurt hitting the edge of the cockpit on the way out. Some even died. One guy I heard of, caught in a spin, ejected sideways and was torn apart. The air you're fired into is like a wall at the speeds we flew. Which was why so many tried to bring the plane down no matter what problems they were having. And, of course, for many it was an issue of pride. Not me. I've ejected three times. First and second time bust up my knee, and the third time broke both ankles but luckily there was never any permanent mobility damage. I was hurt badly each time but I survived. Maybe I could've wrestled the plane down and escaped injury altogether, but maybe not. Maybe I'd have died.

For the Arrow, Sam had no choice. He was bolted in. The only parachutes the Arrow had were drogues, chutes to slow it down for landing. Not that a parachute would necessarily help you much anyway. We'd seen plenty of chutes fail to open, too, pilots – friends – hitting the ground and becoming puddles or long smears on the sand. No, when Sam landed, a ground crew had to get him out. He had the means to do it himself if he had to, but it was pretty cramped in there and not an easy thing to do, Sam said.

He managed it that second time, though. Even after all that rolling, with fire filling the tube, he managed to pop that top off and clamber out, but by then it was far too late.

One of the first things Sandra asked me was if there was any pain, and so of course I lied. I told her Sam died on impact. That it was all very quick. I don't know if she asked anybody else. I don't think so. You wouldn't, would you, once you had the answer you wanted, even if you suspected it was a lie. Especially then, I think. I told her that her husband died a hero and a patriot and she slapped me. She told me, *reminded* me, that he died a husband and a father, and then she beat at my chest and then she clung to me, handfuls of my uniform bunched in her fists as she sobbed. I could feel her bump between us, and I'm sure something thumped there, too. A kick or throb as Sandy cried. It broke my heart. She kept blaming the machine. A lot of wives did when it happened. It's understandable. Speak to any surviving pilot, though, and he'll tell you they'd have done it differently, somehow. Whatever was wrong with the damn plane, however good a friend the dead pilot might have been, the rest of us would be convinced we could have landed it safely, and in kidding ourselves we placed blame on the dead. It wasn't fair, and it wasn't right, but we did it so we could keep flying. But Sam was the best pilot I'd ever known, and I'd seen the Arrow, and so when Sandy cried, "It was the plane, it was the damn plane," I was inclined to agree. None of us thought we could have handled it better. After a moment I held her, and a while after that I stroked her hair and said the things people say when it's the tone of voice that matters more than the words. Awful things, like everything was going to be okay. You'll be okay. They'll look after you.

I held her like that a few times. She said seeing the uniform reminded her, so whenever I visited after work she had to go through it all again. I stopped visiting after that but one day she phoned and told me to wear my civvies. She reminded me of my promise to Sam, my obligation to her and their unborn child, and though she had her girlfriends she worried that her grief was beginning to bore them, or wear them down, remind them that their own husbands faced the same risk every day. Back then, in the 50s, test pilots died with alarming frequency. Jets were new, experimental, and fighter pilots were keen to test themselves as well as the planes. Some reports put the deaths at one each week across the country and I can easily believe that. We knew it, and we faced it, even enjoyed it most of the time, like it was an enemy to be beaten. Flying at those speeds, being in control of that kind of thrust, you felt the power of the machine all the way through you and you were free, so long as you could control it. Nothing held you down, nothing held you back, when you were up there, and as well as free you felt kind of… separate. From everything. Special, I suppose. The world was below you and you just… were. You existed, and you pushed that existence to its limits.

The money was good, too. $5000 a year, in those days? I know it motivated Sam. He wanted his kid to go to the best college they could afford. It was never just about the money though, not even for Sam, and however attractive it seemed financially, it was always hard on the families. I didn't have one myself, but I saw it. Saw it all the time. Deborah Pattern, she had a full nervous breakdown after Tailor crunched. Inflight explosion, no chance of survival. When Kimble ploughed a new ditch into the airfield, Jennifer took the kids back home. Same with Lenny, Hamilton, Lee, all of them friends. All of them leaving wives behind, leaving children. I used to say this was why I stayed single. Then, all of a sudden it seemed, though really it had been a long time coming, I had a ready-made family of my own to worry about.

I can't tell you the first time I kissed Sandra, but I remember it was as she broke away from one of those comforting embraces and I know she kissed me back at first. After that, I went back to not visiting for a while until she asked. I don't think she ever really loved me, not in the way a woman should love her husband, and certainly not the way she loved Sam, but we made it work for a while. I do think she saw me as a good man. Someone who would take care of her. And she knew how much I loved her, knows how much I love her still, which is an awful lot even if she can't give it back the same way. But sometimes I wonder if she wasn't the only one who saw our relationship as a way of staying close to Sam. It was a complicated and sometimes painful marriage but I took care of her and Tom as best I could.

I tell this to Sam sometimes but I don't know if he hears me.

I couldn't fly the B50 the second time Sam went up. I was still drunk from the night before and I made sure Hobday knew it so he wouldn't let me fly, when usually I'd have just flushed my system with an oxygen mask. He gave me an earful but nothing I wasn't expecting and it was a far better option than carrying my friend into a dark he dreaded but wouldn't resist. By then Sam had told me all about the first flight. He shouldn't have, but we'd been drinking then as well. Seems the Arrow brings that out in people. The night before that second flight I'd gone round to talk to him but he and Sandy were having a bad one. He phoned later but only said a few words. He was drunk, and by then I'd emptied most of a good bottle I had at home as well. Neither of us made much sense.

So, Pres and Cramshaw took Bessie up and I was ordered to drink coffee because they'd use me on the ground instead.

Last I saw of Sam, the Sam I knew and hoped to see again, he was pulling on the strange flight suit he had to wear. He was doing it in the coffee room.

"Tom—" he said.

"Don't."

"I have to."

"You don't."

"Not for them. For me. I have to see. I need to know if any of what I saw up there was real. You understand that?"

I held a cup to him, offering coffee, but he shook his head and pointed to the crotch of his suit. "You see a bag to piss in?"

It was the standard suit in much of its design, but it crinkled and shone like silver paper and there was piping coiled up and down his limbs. Narrow tributary wires sprouted from this to wrap his arms and legs. It was like his veins were visible on the outside. Over his chest he wore a mesh of golden filaments.

"Hurts my eyes to look at you," I said, shielding my face in an awkward salute against each flash and dazzle of his suit as he moved. I'd meant it as a joke because of how shiny he was, but as soon as the words were out of my mouth I realised it was the same as something he'd said the week before. He realised it, too.

"You get a good breakfast in you?" I asked him, just to change the subject.

Sam smiled and nodded.

"Because you need to keep those blood-sugars up."

"Yes, Mom."

I tried to smile back at him but I couldn't do it. "Don't," I said again.

He kind of growled at that and left me holding coffee while he went to do a man's duty for his country.

He'd left the helmet on the counter. We didn't fly with helmets back then, not crash helmets anyway. Just the leather ones like those used in the war. Not that this looked much like what you'd call a crash helmet either. In fact, it looked dangerously fragile. It was a sphere but flat on one end, like an upside down fishbowl if you could make such a thing out of mirrors. I'd seen it before but Sam had been wearing it then. This time I could touch it. I picked it up and peered through it without putting it on but saw only the kitchen. Outside, through the window, I saw the rest of the base and some of the runway. Everything looked normal. Of course it did, what did I expect? I set the helmet back down, carefully, when I should have smashed it to pieces.

I could've waited for Sam to come back for it but there was no need to speak to him again. I had nothing to say he hadn't heard or would listen to. I stirred milk and sugar into my coffee and left.

I had a bad feeling, a very bad feeling, and I should have tried harder. I should have said something better than *don't*. Something like goodbye. Who knows, maybe that would have done it. I did wave, but by then he was underneath a canopy I couldn't see through, the men around it twisting bolts tight and slapping the fuselage for luck when they were done. I raised my hand without knowing if he saw me, and then the Arrow was getting towed to where Bessie waited for her unwanted passenger.

Cramshaw was leaning against the landing gear. He looked around him, didn't see Hobday, and said, "Hey Berry, you wanna take her up?" Cramshaw was a good kid. Youngest we had, with a mop of red hair and freckles that made him look more like a farm boy than a pilot. Standing next to Bessie he looked like her kid brother. He died in '53 testing the X2 but right then, standing in the sun beside the B50 and the Arrow, he probably thought he was going to fly forever. "I know you two go way back," he said. He meant the B50 but I thought of Sam.

"No, that's all right. I don't much want to fly today."

He gave a broad smile as if I'd made a joke, shrugged, and asked if I'd be going to Ratty's later. It was a pointless question, we always went to Ratty's later, especially after a test, but I answered yes anyway and tried to massage the hangover from my head. Tried not to think of my last conversation with Sam.

Ratty's was the best beer joint off base. It's gone now, sort of, turned into a restaurant called The Grill, but back then it was just a bar with good music and plenty of girls to look at. Sam used to tell me to find one worth sticking with and whenever I saw him and Sandra together I thought he had a good point, but in the meantime... Well, Maisie and her friends were in, distracting everyone with the way their skirts moved around their legs as they danced. Sam didn't even glance at them. He had other things on his mind.

"It was dark," he said. "I mean, pitch. And that messes with your mind, let me tell you, soaring through blue sky one minute and the next minute black. And not like night time, either. Black like your eyes are closed. No stars. Nothing."

That was what Sam told me about going sideways. I wish he'd left it at that. He'd talked about the Arrow once already – the speed, the way it handled, all of that – but now the boys were embarrassing themselves over by the jukebox and the empty glasses had mounted up so Sam started talking about it all over again, only differently.

"You remember I said it went sideways? At the barbeque?"

Kennedy seemed to be having some luck with a pretty brunette. Meanwhile, her pretty friends were listening to everything Bull had to say. One of them touched his arm a lot. There was a pretty blonde who kept glancing over at me and Sam. They were all so pretty.

"Tom?"

"Yeah, I remember." I let the girl go. "Was I right? Does it roll?"

"It spins, but it never changes direction while it's doing that. In fact, it's slow making any kind of turn. But that's not what it means, the sideways stuff."

"Well, what does it mean then?"

He leant in close. "It's got this fixture on its nose, right? Remember that? The metal rod?"

"I remember."

"It makes lightning."

I smiled, brought my glass up only to see it was empty, and set it down again. "Lightning."

"Yeah. It fires these pulses of light," – he opened and closed a fist at me – "kind of like a flashlight only a hundred times more powerful. Perfectly straight bursts of light." He performed a fast sequence of those hand-flashes and then sort of danced his fingers back at himself. "And then the Arrow is washed with lightning. Bright white lines crackling all over, and then they shoot forward from the nose, from the… the *lightning stick*, let's call it that, because the other name won't make any sense—"

"Because so far all of this is just—"

"—and this electrical discharge, it creates a tunnel of low-density air for the Arrow to fly through. To reduce drag. It tears the electrons out of the air molecules to make an ionised channel for the Arrow."

I didn't know if it was the beer, but this bit was beginning to make a sort of sense to me.

"Mach 3, Finn. *3*."

I stared at him a moment, then repeated, "3."

"Yeah."

You have to remember, this was 1951. The Bell X2 wouldn't break Mach 3 for another five years. It wasn't so long ago people thought the sound barrier was exactly that, a barrier, and that even Mach 1 couldn't be done.

"But you told the boys—"

"3, Finn. *At least.*"

"At least?"

"Hard to tell for sure because after that the readings went a bit... strange."

"Well that's it, then. Dodgy data."

He batted that away with his hand. "It doesn't matter anyway because after that it went sideways and speed wasn't important anymore."

Saying speed wasn't important, a *test pilot* saying speed wasn't important, was like the navy saying they didn't care if their ships floated or not.

"Mach 3, and then those bursts of light became one long beam of it and then..."

"And then?"

He was quiet for a moment. Bar noise filled the gap; music, conversation, laughter. I wondered if this was all building up to some sort of joke but Sam wasn't the joking kind. So I waited until he finally spoke.

"And then sideways," he said.

I don't think he meant it to be dramatic. 'Sideways' didn't follow some metaphorical drum roll, we'd been talking about it the whole time. It's just that he had been remembering, gone from Ratty's to sit in the Arrow once more, and then part of him remembered he was meant to be talking so he said, 'and then sideways,' before returning to his moments in the dark. I waited for him to come back again until somewhere a glass smashed and a woman shrieked and that noise, or its combination, brought Sam back with a shudder.

"Except it's not really sideways," he said. "It's still forwards. Sideways was just how they explained it to me, like overtaking when the traffic ahead is slow."

"You changed lanes."

"I don't know that I did anything," he said. "And I don't know where I went."

He had vanished from radar for a while – the big boys were very happy with their new toy – but he returned when he was near the base, bringing the Arrow down without incident.

"The way they explained it, the simple way, they took two pieces of paper and put one across the other like an x. On the bottom piece, at one end, they wrote 'base' and at the other end, on the same piece, 'base' and then they drew a line connecting them. My route, right? The line went right across the top piece of paper, which they took away to show me that a long line had become two short ones with a big gap in the middle. A start and an end, with nothing in between. That piece of paper, the removed piece, that was the sideways. It was like I ducked out of the sky for a while, then came back."

"Okay, where did you go? You stray off course?"

"I don't know where, I told you. But it was dark. Instantly dark."

"Have you told them this? You passed out, buddy. Hypoxia. Pulling more gees than—"

"I didn't pass out, Tom. There was light, and then lightning, and then I was somewhere else. It was so still. She moved so easy. Not that I moved much – couldn't deviate from the flight path – but I tried it some and there was no struggle. I had full control. No thermal barrier to worry about, no aerodynamic friction, best I could tell. No pitching, no buffeting. She was gliding."

At high speed the centre of pressure shifts, you've got aeroelasticity factors with the fins, you're not stable, and you struggle with control. Sam was telling me something that shouldn't be true, not at Mach 3. If that's what it was.

He looked at me and I swear his eyes had that wet look of tears in them.

"What is it?"

He held my hand. It felt strange, that kind of contact, but there was no getting away from it, especially when he put his other hand on top of both of ours. He kept his eyes on me. I'd never noticed until then how blue those eyes could be. Sandra must have loved them. I'd seen intensity in them before, but not like this. Not shining. "You have to take care of them for me if anything ever—"

Here I pulled my hand away. Snatched it back, in fact.

"No," I said. "I'm not saying it."

"Finn—"

"Don't you say it, neither. You're just drunk."

"Tom—"

"Of course I will, okay, you don't even need to ask so don't, and you don't need to ask because it'll never happen that way anyway. You're the luckiest son-of-a-bitch I know."

He nodded. Just once, quick, accepting what I said. My agreement, I think. Probably not the lucky SOB bit, considering what came next.

"I have to tell you more."

I rubbed my face as if I could wipe away the cloud of alcohol I was stuck in. "All right."

"It was dark," he said. "I mean pitch. And that messes with your mind..."

Shortly after that, he messed with mine by telling me what he saw there.

Sandy used to have terrible anxiety dreams. Nightmares. Long before anything ever happened to Sam she'd dream of looking out the window to see one of us, usually me, in full dress uniform coming up the path to deliver bad news, only in the dream they, me, whoever it was, never made it to the end of the path. They just seemed to keep walking and never reaching her, so she never knew what had happened, only that something had. First she felt fear and then frustration, all tinged with a sadness so deep she seemed to fill up with it, ready to burst, "like I'm waiting to become that expression, 'burst into tears'," she explained to me once. "I'm entirely water waiting to be released, and as the dream goes on the pressure builds and I never know what's happened to him, what's happened to my Sam."

In another dream she's hanging the washing out and hears a thunderclap, "like the zoom and boom, only I feel it under my feet". When she looks up in this dream she sees a plume of black smoke rising from the horizon, angled with the wind. In the dream she always thinks, 'Sam's back,' and then gathers in his washing again, leaving the rest on the line. She's always so calm. She says that one scares her the most.

She still has them occasionally, these dreams. Still tells me about them from time to time. If it's a really bad one, she'll call me in the middle of the night. Sometimes it's not Sam in the dream but me. Sometimes it's both of us, or we blur together so that sometimes we're one and sometimes the other yet somehow both at the same time. She told me once, during one of these phone calls, about how Sam looked at her differently after the first time he flew the Arrow. How he used to look at her, and her pregnant belly, and seem suddenly frightened. He never talked about it, not to her, but she knew there'd been something wrong with that flight. Something that scared him.

I used to have a few bad dreams when I still flew. Mostly they were about being in a cockpit I couldn't eject from and the plane would spin and spin and all the time fall towards the ground and I'd wake just as I crunched. Since giving up my wings, I've had worse. Sometimes Sam's in them. Sometimes, those things he told me about are with him. Or on him. Part of him. I don't tell Sandy about those ones.

Just lately I've been having the cockpit dream again. It's not about flying anymore, though. It's about this cancer. Not that it was ever about flying anyway, I suppose. Occasionally Sam will be a co-pilot, even when there's no room for one. Dreams are like that, aren't they. He'll be there, by my side, telling me what to do, only I can't hear him. There's no voice. His mouth just opens and closes, blinking at me.

"He's still coming in too fast."

Hobday looked at me as if I could do something about it. "Sir," I said.

A line of us watched, me the only one using binoculars, waiting for one of the drogues to deploy, but it never happened. And then the angle changed. There was a sudden and severe drop as the Arrow nosed over.

"He's coming in too steep."

I was reminded of last year, Hendry passing out at high altitude. A connection problem with a hose in his oxygen system and hypoxia took care of the rest: Hendry crunched nose-first and left only pieces to bury.

Hobday turned to issue orders but the fire truck was already starting up. He yelled anyway to hurry them along. Medics followed, speeding down the runway behind it, but if Sam continued on the trajectory he was on he was going to hit the runway early and wrong and so fast he'd only need the fire truck.

"Pull up, Sam," I said. "Come on. Get it back."

Had there been radio contact, this would have been where Sam declared emergency. No pilot liked to do it, and some would rather crash – some *did* – but with Sam it would have been different. If he couldn't handle it then it couldn't be handled. A lot of pilots thought that way, but with Sam it was true and he knew it in a modest way we all admired. But there was no radio contact, and a cynical part of me now wonders if they anticipated problems they'd rather not hear about, whereas any problem reported after the plane had come down wasn't really a serious problem at all.

This was. Anybody could see that. And with the binoculars, I knew it better than anyone. It made me glad Sam didn't have a radio.

"Oh no. Oh Christ, no."

"Captain," Hobday warned.

I brought the binoculars down. I didn't want to see. I even started to back away from the crowd gathered around the welcome wagons, as if I might turn and flee into the desert. Everybody was looking up but they did it with the naked eye. I wanted to tell them what I could see but although my mouth was open I couldn't get it to do anything else.

"Come on," said Hobday. He grabbed me by the arm and pulled me towards his jeep. Shoved me at the passenger side. I managed, "No," but by then I was already sitting down and buckling in, a couple of the others jumping in behind me. "No," I said again anyway, watching as the Arrow came in at the ground. Then it lifted, more suddenly than I'd have thought possible. An overcompensation that set it spinning, a tossed silver stick flashing sunlight back at us in a Morse code of distress anyone could read. Inertia coupling, I thought – the X3 Stiletto had shown us how bad that could be, and later it would nearly kill Yeager – but really, I knew different. It seemed to disappear and reappear, showing us long side then rear, so narrow it was barely there except for the cross of its four wings. The kind of tumble that only got worse as you tried to correct it, all aerodynamics gone. When it struck the ground it did it sideways. The flimsy wings broke away as it rolled but first they steered the Arrow like it was a rolled skittle pin, digging chunks out of the runway before it was thrown back up into the air, cartwheeling across the ground in clouds of dirt and dust before finally breaking apart into fiery pieces that screamed flames.

We sped towards a blazing ruin, feeling its heat in the air that washed over us and smelling the smoke that rose like a blooming dark flower before the wind took it away.

'Burnt beyond recognition' was the euphemism we used. He looked like meat forgotten on a barbeque, blackened and blistered and parts of him greasy. Smelled like it, too, beneath the putrid chemical stench of fuel and plastic and cloth and metal. Everything burns in a jet fuel fire. Everything. He was only a small lump with smaller lumps protruding, legs stiff and feetless, arms angled out like wings of his own but not much left below the elbows. His head was half its usual size, a shrunken seed, shrivelled and crisp and without any facial features. He was checked carefully, not by Doc but by some guy they brought in 'specially who prodded and cut and finally burnt Sam all over again. Cremated him, whatever his wishes might have been. Nobody ever told Sandy why. We scattered him on the airfield. Sandy said he would have wanted that, though it was clear she felt some final resentment, like she was being put second one final time.

Sam dying put my life on a different course. Or Sandra did, but Sam had to die for that to happen. With Sandy I became a different man, a better man. For a while, anyway, and a long while at that. Had Sam's shoes to fill, didn't I. His memory to live up to. I never managed it, of course, though Sandra helped me cut down on the drinking when other women had failed, and I stopped chasing other girls, now that I understood why Sam barely even noticed them. There'd only ever been one for me, and I think she knew it long before Sam was gone. I took a sidestep at work, still flying but only the transports and after a while not even those. I suffered conversion symptoms more and more frequently and even knowing that's what it was didn't help. Blurred vision. Tremors. All in my mind, but real as well.

The sidestep at work was a sidestep out of the fraternity as well. I still flew, but I wasn't one of the jocks anymore, and though we remained friends, there was always something missing. Maybe it was Sam. I was safer, though, which was what Sandy wanted. She managed to stay in the loop because she was still one of the wives, though she was always 'Sam's wife' first and it got so that I began to feel it. I became a father to Tom Junior and though I never had any of my own I don't regret that often. Tom was enough. He asked about his real dad a lot as a child, but as he grew older he asked less and less. He could have resented me, I suppose, as the new man stepping in to take his father's place, but he never did, even as a teenager. Maybe he would have, if he'd had the chance to love and admire Sam as we did.

He visits me occasionally, even now. I think he's sorry for how things turned out. I think we both are. Of course, neither of us has ever actually said it, just as we never talk about Sam anymore. There are things men say, and things they don't, and sometimes we get it wrong.

"If I don't fly it again, someone else will," Sam had said. "You want to?"

It was a pretty mean way to make his point, especially for Sam, and I sensed in his question a judgement of my courage. Like finally he was admitting what he felt of me as a pilot. That I would never quite have the right stuff, or at least not as much of it as he did. But he was drunk. I was drunk.

He'd told me, again, about the lightning. He'd told me, again, about the sudden dark and how it felt like it wasn't quite sky but a tunnel through it. Or a tunnel *of* it, like the sky was bent around him, a tube to pass through where no stars shone. And yet...

"I could see things. Out on the wings. On the nose. The canopy."

"Things?"

He was seeing them again now, I thought. We were in Ratty's of course, and his eyes were on the table in front of him, but he was looking out of the Arrow. The jukebox was playing, people were yelling and laughing and dancing, but he was probably only hearing jet thrust and maybe the bubbling of fuel. Later he'd tell me he heard none of that, that the whole time in the dark was silent, like he wasn't moving at all. Trapped in a long blink, he said, just himself and the Arrow. And yet, in that dark blink, there were things he could see. I don't know what he put it in his report. Part of me suspects he told them everything and they let him fly anyway.

"They were all over me. At first I thought the plane was falling apart, that I was seeing pieces of the Arrow lift up to tear free. But they were only flat *at first*. As they peeled from wherever they were on the fuselage they took on other shapes. Filled out. And it didn't seem to matter none how fast we were going, they held right on and made shapes of themselves that shouldn't've have stayed at that speed. Fleshy clumps that spread whenever the lightning flashed, in sudden bursts just like the lightning that zig-zagged over me. You seen creeper vines, Huckleberry? They were like that, like the fastest growing creeper vines you ever saw, only with these… these… *masses*, like… you know when you've got a bad cold, and you blow your nose or hawk something up and the stuff, it's really thick? Like that. But they had other shapes, too. In the lightning. In the dark. They had arms and legs, I'm sure, and maybe even wings too, and they had too many of everything, and they could bend them into… into these *angles* like nothing I ever saw. Stuck all over the Arrow, like those things on a ship. Like limpets or barnacles. Only without the shells."

"Sam—"

"And they were filled with holes."

He took a drink then, but I'm not sure he knew he was doing it because he kept the glass tipped and still worked his mouth even when there was no more beer coming. Finally he put it down again and said, "I don't know if they were holes. They might have been mouths. They might have been eyes."

"Sam?"

"They might have been both. I think maybe they were both."

I could only look at Sam as he stared at the tabletop. "Holes in holes in holes," he said. "Holes filled with mouths. Filled with eyes. Eyes with holes in them."

He glanced up then, pulled back into Ratty's through what looked like his own force of will, and he said to me, "It hurt to look at them, Tom." He massaged his head, fingers at his temples.

I took him home. It wasn't far to drive but I took it slow, partly because I'd been drinking (though not much, not once Sam had started talking) and partly because Sam might have had more left to say. I though it better he said it to me than to Sandy. She'd already called me once to talk about the things Sam said. In his sleep, mostly, but sometimes at odd moments. "He's not here, Tom," she said, "not all the time. He is, but he's somewhere else, too, and when he's there it's not me he's talking to. And what he says scares me."

He didn't say much on the drive home. He mostly sat swaying beside me, happy to be a passenger for a change, leaning forward in his seat with his arms on his thighs like he was back in the Arrow, nodding a little forwards, lurching back to overcompensate, and keeping his eyes on the dark road ahead of us.

"Hey, you remember the truck?"

I smiled and said, "I remember," knowing he'd bring it up. He always did on this stretch of road. All pilots think they're great drivers and we used to race each other out here. Sam won, more often than not, and when he didn't I strongly suspect it was his choice not to. But one time we were so busy looking at each other, parallel, that we didn't see the military truck coming right at us, bedded down with parts. Death, heading right our way. I saw it first and dropped back so Sam could nip in front. He almost nudged me, and the truck nearly crunched us both, but we survived, suffering only a scare neither of us admitted to, only laughed about.

Sam was looking sideways out of the window and I thought he was remembering. Which he was, only not what I thought.

"I think there were more of them I couldn't see," he said. "In the black. I think there was something bigger and I think the black might have been it, too big or too close or just everywhere all at once."

"You're kind of all over the place yourself," I said.

It made him suddenly rigid, suddenly straight. Sitting to attention. "I'm a damn good pilot," he said. A statement of fact that was as close as he came to bragging, and only when he'd been drinking.

"You are."

"Straight as an arrow," he said. He made a zooming motion with one hand, a thrust forward like a jab to an unseen opponent, and laughed. The spluttering laugh of a drunk being childish. "Arrow," he said.

"Yeah, you're straight as they come."

But soon he was rocking again with however the car moved, back and forth and side to side. He'd made a pillow of his jacket and kept trying to rest his head against the window.

"I think they were just babies," he said.

"Right."

"Or pieces of something bigger. Full of holes."

"Full of holes, Sam. Okay."

"They could see *everything* Huckleberry. I think those eyes... I think..."

As he fell asleep or passed out he said, "I think they wanted to eat me."

When they told me I had liver cancer the first thing I thought of was what Sam said back then. It wants to eat me, I thought. Hepatocellular carcinoma. At first I thought it was just stomach ache, but eventually I listened to Sandy who told me to get it checked out. We'd been separated a while by that point, but we were still friends. Well, we were friendly. Phone calls, Christmas cards. Anyway, I went through the surgery and treatment but it had spread to my gastrointestinal tract, or had originated there and spread to my liver. It doesn't really matter which way around. I'm okay with it now because it feels like I've lived too much of my life from the outside. I remember the early days pretty well, and I can see the end coming, but everything in between is on a separate piece of paper somebody took away. There's a big gap where I lived for a while, where my life went sideways. We always think there's something else going on around us we're not quite part of, friends having babies, friends dying, and before you know it your own beginning has an end and that's it, it all happened when you weren't paying attention. Twice now I've been told I have six months left, and there was a kind of relief the first time, seeing the truck coming at you instead of being surprised by it, and I lived those months well, fully aware for what felt like the first time. But it's like my body doesn't know when to quit. Maybe I've bailed out on too many things already and this time I'm not allowed. The crunch is coming, though.

Until then I've got plenty to think about.

When they rolled out the X-15 in '58 I thought of the Arrow and its lightning stick and its sideways roll into black. The X-15 looked nothing like the Arrow but it could reach 280,000 feet, taking a pilot out of the atmosphere right to the edge of space. Not sideways, but up. Still, I wondered what they might see there. And for every 'Spam in a can' rocket project after that, Sputnik, the Apollo missions, I thought of those holes in the dark Sam said he saw looking at him. I remember speeding towards that fiery ruin of his crash and feeling its heat wash over us, smelling the smoke. A thick black plume of it leaned in the angle of his descent, a trail of fumes like a dark tunnel from the sky. And maybe that's what it was because those things, the ones Sam talked about? They flew in it. They followed its path up and away and fell, spiralling down to earth as if struck. Some were spread across every available surface of the Arrow, coils of flesh wrapped around it, bodies flattened into thick fluids that held them in place, clutching underneath the fuselage at whatever they could find of the landing gear until it flipped, rolled, exploded and they were cast aside with the fiery wreckage. Limp rags of meat, hanging limbs, wings torn or flapping in flames.

This was what we sped towards in the jeep. There was a heavy thump, the smash of a headlamp, then something folded up onto the hood and rolled at the windshield. A loud crack from that and whatever had hit us was finally tossed away. Not before we'd seen the things that dangled from its segmented body, though. The loose sheets of skin. The ropey lengths of flesh.

Sam was right, there was something about what you saw that made your mind hurt, like you were looking at pain that could travel through your eyes to your brain. Looking at them, you felt yourself... going. I don't know where. There was less of you, somehow. I saw them first when the Arrow began its spin, long angled limbs like fleshy lightning running across the aircraft seeking grip or suction. I had the binoculars, remember. But close up they were even worse.

Hobday brought the jeep around in a sudden squealing stop but none of us got out. Even when we saw Sam, a staggering man of fire, miraculously emerge from the smoke, we remained seated. We could only stare. Sam slapped at his body, but not at the flames, twisting and turning. Part of his helmet was gone, the front smashed away, and he was screaming and yelling in pain and panic. A lot of his words were lost to the chaos around him but I pieced a few together, then and later, often in dreams and drunken half-dozes where I remember better. "They're coming after me!" is what I thought he screamed, but I don't think so now.

When Sam came out, they were attached to him as they had been the jet. I've come to believe they were the reason he survived as long as he did. That they shielded him from the impact and the flames somehow. He slapped and pulled to get them off, and one of them, the one settled over his face, spread a single membrane wing. A raised flag that Sam tore away before falling to his knees. One of the medics got close to him but came to such an abrupt stop when he saw the things on Sam that he fell on his ass, kicking his feet to scramble backwards from where Sam struggled with something at his head. I like to think it was what remained of the helmet, I *try* to think that, but I don't suppose that's really how it was. Then he collapsed forwards, arms and legs spread. A fallen star.

For long moments he still moved – parts of him writhed and fluttered, pulled and stretched – and then blasts of foam obscured everything as the fire crew tackled the blaze, washing away what they could from where Sam lay. He was already dead by then. I could tell. Not because of the limp way his body moved beneath their hoses, or because the things leeched onto him began to withdraw, but because I felt it. Like a change in pressure. And I was glad. Seeing him ricochet on his feet, pulling at his body, hearing him scream, hearing what he said… I'm glad he died.

The things that spread away from him began to pop and pool. Some of them seemed to inflate, bubbling with air like isolated lung-sacs. Others spewed these long ropes that lay like the wet lengths of a mop head. A few of them burst. I saw one of the medics stamping on them, jumping on the bodies, crazy-dancing on the things, twisting, grinding the empty skins into the ground. He slipped at one point, landing hard, but he got right back up again to mash what was left under his boots.

I've wondered many times since that day if Sam didn't put the Arrow in a spin himself. That he nosed down deliberately to kill the things coming out from the blackspace with him. If so, it worked.

Sam? It worked.

None of us there that day ever spoke about what we saw, and it wasn't because of anything we signed. A bad psych evaluation got you kicked off the programme quicker than failing eyesight, but it wasn't that either. In time, I think a lot of the others came to doubt what they'd seen anyway, and you can't blame them for that. The brain has a wonderful coping mechanism like that. A sort of mental ejector seat. But me, I think of Sam's last days all the time now that I'm living mine.

Sam tells me the dark is coming, and everyday it seems I see some truth of it. I see him, too, sometimes. In my peripheral vision. He'll be right there beside me until I turn to look, a fluke moment that lets me see him out of the corner of my eye, and then he's just the smell of chemicals and cooked meat.

Corner of my eye. I'd never thought how odd that was until just now. An eye with angles to look from.

Anyway, sometimes Sam's here for me to see, and it hurts to look at him. His face is full of holes, all of them watching. Porous judgement waiting to be filled with what's left of me. Sometimes he's wearing the helmet but that's no better. It reflects my face back, distorted, and I hear what he said that day in the fire. Not, "they're coming after me," I don't think he said that anymore. "They're coming *out* of me." That's what I think he said.

They're coming out of me.

What if looking at them put them inside? I don't want to go like that.

When Tommy Junior used to ask about his daddy, I told him he flew too close to heaven and God saw him. Maybe it *was* something like that, only I don't think it was God who saw. I think it was something else. Something made of holes.

So now I'll go back. I'll return to base. Somewhere in the desert, anyway. Some wide open place where there can be nothing either side of me. Where I can take care of things under a vast blue sky which I'll make black, but only briefly. A plume of smoke headstone for the wind to take as I burn the holes that might be mouths, might be eyes. Holes within holes.

Eating me up, and seeing me from the inside.

|Child of Thorns|

~

The cabin's single room was small, but three people in it made it smaller still, and Jessie's screaming made it worse, filling the room – what was left of it to fill – with a jagged howling that just about tore the world apart.

"You gotta push harder, Jessie-Belle, come on girl."

"It hurts—"

"I know."

"It hurts like worse than—"

"Seems that way, but lots of women gone done this before."

Danny kept thinking there should've been something erotic about the way Nessa crouched at his wife's crotch, her face between his woman's thighs. She had her hands on his woman's knees to keep them spread. "Should I boil some water?" he asked her.

"What for, Daniel, you making tea?"

Jessie wailed, clutching at the edges of the table beneath her, head back, and that should've been erotic too, or could have been, but it weren't.

"Okay, here it comes."

Danny went in close to see – didn't need to take no more than a step or two – but moved away again with his wife's next scream. He put his hands to his ears and looked at Nessa but she was suddenly too busy to spare him a glance. She grabbed at the nearby cloths, but not before Danny had seen the gush of blood spreading from between Jessie's thighs. He was glad she was up on the table – their bed was too low, just a mattress on boards on the dirt floor, and it was a mattress they couldn't afford to ruin. The blood ran to the table edges and kept running. It weren't so much dripping as pouring. The sound was like their porch in the rain, the broken guttering dropping vertical streams to pound the ground into muddy holes by the front door. Here, in the kitchen, bloody puddles soaked into a soil floor pressed firm by a thousand thousand footsteps. Jessie was still screaming but she was trying to cry, too. She looked wretched, like a dog Danny had once that he had to shoot when it got sick.

"She gonna die, Nessa?"

Nessa looked at him and he almost smiled at her. His face didn't want to quite hold it there, but she saw it. He had stripped down to his jeans. His chest heaved with nervous breath but she couldn't tell what kind. She looked at the woman spread before her, knees up and legs open, belly round as a pumpkin, and said, "No she ain't gonna die."

"I just thought—"

"You shut your mouth on those thoughts, Daniel Erlson."

Jessie wailed again, but strained, and pushed, and pushed, and Danny came in again to see. He put a hand on Nessa's shoulder. She didn't shrug it off.

He couldn't make sense of what he was seeing. He'd never seen birth before except with animals but this didn't look right. Maybe because he'd never looked so long at Jessie's nethers, never seen them open and unfold, but he could tell it didn't look right to Nessa either because she'd stopped doing anything but watch, blood soaking the rags in her hands as something brown and gnarly emerged from an opening too small for it, too... *tight* for it. It weren't so much expelled from there as torn free, a knotted ball of briars shredding Jessie in its exit.

"What?" said Danny. "*What?*"

Nessa crossed herself, though Danny never knew her to be a religious woman, then she put her hands to either side of whatever the hell it was that twisted its way out of—

"Jessie, that's it, come on girl, nearly, it's nearly ou – *oww!*" Nessa snatched her hands back. She almost put the thumb of one to her mouth but it was wet with blood that weren't hers so she didn't.

Another heave from Jessie and more skin split, tore, *unseamed*, as something with barbed shoulders emerged from her. Its chest was spiked with thorns, body a wrapped tangle of brambles. Nessa tried to find a place to hold it, tried another, but Jessie pushed again before Nessa found anywhere clear. Withdrawing her hands, it was like she drew the baby out with magics, summoning it without touching. It slid in the blood it had made, this baby of briars, and was suddenly free.

Nearly. A spiked vine like a limp rose stem curled from its navel into Jessie's ruined crotch. Nessa cut it like she had so many other cords.

"What is it?" Jessie asked. Her voice weren't no more than a whimper.

"I don't know," Nessa said.

It lay trembling, a tough brown lump with points that scratched at the table as it tried to move. Nessa dropped bloody cloths over it. Danny thought it was dead or dying and that she meant to hide it but she only padded the thorns of its torso so she could hold it safely. She picked it up and offered it to the new mother but Jessie had collapsed, her eyes fluttering too much to see anything even right in front of her. Nessa held it to Daniel but he backed up a step. Would've taken more if there'd been room.

"Take your child, Daniel, I gotta see to your woman." She pressed the ragged thing to his chest.

Danny felt it prickle through the wrapping. He felt the bumps and hard ridges of its padded thorns.

"It don't weigh no more than kindling," he said.

Nessa said nothing. She was too busy doing something with Jessie as Daniel looked at the wood-whorled face of his... whatever he had.

"Is it a boy or a girl?" Daniel asked, too dumb to realise the answer was no. He unwrapped it, tugging at rags that pulled on hooks and sharp-tipped triangles. One wicked curve of thorn tore the swaddling into frayed threads and Danny picked these away, dropping them to the floor as the little thing turned its head left and right. It waved its bramble-bound arms with a sound like foliage passed through, and it kicked its legs with the sound of dried twigs stepped on. Between them Danny saw wood grain, a knot curl, the nub of something that might sprout, and knew nothing of what it meant. "It don't matter," he said.

"What did you say?"

Nessa had the look of someone who'd asked a question Daniel'd answered wrong.

"Nothin'."

"Good. Because she's gonna need to rest now." Nessa wiped her own brow with the cleanest part of her forearm. It still left a streak of blood across her forehead. "She's torn up pretty good, but it ain't nothin' Doc can't fix."

"Do we need Doc?"

Nessa looked like she had an answer right away but she kept it in.

"Only, he'll cost us some. And, you know. He's from the town."

Nessa stepped closer to Danny and the bundle of briars she'd delivered. Looked at how it rasped in his arms. "No," she said. "I don't suppose we gotta tell no one."

She looked at Danny like she had a question for him but he looked away before she could ask it. She said, "Congratulations."

Danny swore and looked at new lines scratched in his arm. They turned pink and welled with dots of blood.

"I'd wrap that one in sack cloth, I were you," Nessa said, then set about fixing up Jessie-Belle as best she could, cooing and swabbing and sewing where she had to. Danny tried to talk but she ignored all that and when she left she left without cleaning herself or gathering her things.

Danny saw as she went that it was nearly morning. The door opened on the sort of grey light you could smell as well as look at, but he couldn't remember what day it was. Not that it mattered any. It was today, and there'd be others after, all of them different to the ones he'd known before.

The baby voiced its first cry. The sound was a series of broken sticks, like a small tree falling.

The wood split right down the middle and fell away in two parts, toppling into twins either side of the stump Danny used for cutting. He wrenched the axe free, bent for another block, and set it upright. Swung the axe back-around-up and down, splitting another piece with a sharp crack and the double thud of fallen pieces.

That would do.

He'd gathered an armful when Nessa appeared out of the trees. She was wearing her good cotton dress but with a shawl wrapped tight around her shoulders and over her hair. She didn't smile, only nodded.

"Cold to be out," she said.

"Had to," Danny said. He tipped his arms to show her why.

"Got a name for it yet?"

He was surprised by the abrupt question, "Not yet," and then by the way Nessa looked right after. She'd made a mistake, he realised. "Firewood," he said, tipping his arms to her again so she could properly see what he cradled there. What he didn't. "Little one's inside," he said.

Nessa strode past him, letting the hand he put on her shoulder fall away again, not shrugging it off or nothing but not waiting or letting him hold her there neither. She knocked on the cabin door, "Jessie?" and went inside.

Danny'd hung a sheet up at the door because it didn't reach right down to the ground and the untreated wood was split. Nessa gathered the cloth aside with her arm and stepped into a snug room warm in the way that stifled breath and made a person drowsy.

Sure enough, mother and child dozed by the fire. Jessie-Belle was breathing deep, the bundle in her arms still and quiet. She sat with her breasts exposed, fat and heavy and wetting the bib of her dress with a seep of milk that made Nessa think of tree sap. She had pale breasts and dusky nipples and even in the room's soft light Nessa could see they were pricked and scratched with welts, crusty with the raised ridges of tiny scabs. Around her nipples especially, bleeding dimples like pock marks, punctures of flesh given no time to heal.

Jessie stirred and covered herself as she woke, refastening her dress as if she'd felt Nessa's looking. She blinked, saw her nurse, and blinked a few times more. "Got coffee if you want," she said.

"I'll do it."

Nessa checked the pot on the stove. A bitter smell had been burnt into the metal. She added water to the dark silt at the bottom and stirred before setting it back on the stove. "How's the little one?"

"Sleepin'."

From outside came the irregular crack and thump of split wood. Nessa'd thought Danny had finished that particular chore but apparently he needed something to keep him busy awhile. Keep him outside.

"And how are you? Are you sleeping all right?"

Jessie smiled. "Like a baby."

Like a log, Nessa thought. She eyed the bramble-bundle bunched in the crook of its mamma's arm. Jessie pulled it to her scratched chest. "You've not told Doc, have you Ness?"

"I've not said nothin' to no one."

Jessie rocked slowly, quietly, and glanced down at the gathered thorns in her arms. "What about Stray Dog?"

"Not told Merrin nothin' for years." Nessa smiled, a forced one, but Jessie was still looking down at her bracken-born and cooing quietly. "How are you feeling, Jessie-Belle?"

There was nothing forced about Jessie's smile. She raised her face to share it. "I'm fine. Better than."

Nessa pointed vaguely to the woman's lap. "I mean…"

"Oh, I'm torn up plenty. Hurts to move much, and it burns when I pee." To the child of thorns she said, "Worth it, though."

"You've gotta keep yourself clean and—"

"I know."

"To avoid infection."

"I know. It's fine."

Nessa had seen this plenty. The transformation from scared little girl to all-wise woman, the mother of a child. It rankled, sometimes, like they was gloating or something, preening a sense of having surpassed Nessa in some crucial way. Maybe because she had none herself and couldn't ever, even if she wanted to. Merrin didn't mind any, though. Stray Dog that he was, or used to be, he might have plenty anyways, and most of the time Nessa didn't mind that neither.

The child reached for its mother with clumps of fist that spread open like vicious flowers but closed again before Nessa could see anything more than the terrible curves of hook. The same thorns pointed this way and that from its body. For the most part it was a thatch of bramble and briar but occasionally it took the shape of something limbed. Nessa saw pips for eyes. They opened and closed, split seeds blinking.

"Hungry *again*? Hmm? You hungry?"

Jessie unfastened the top of her smock dress. Nessa turned to make the coffee. She heard the woman hiss, sucking up her pain as the little one fastened on to suckle.

"I'll take a cup to Daniel," Nessa said. At the blanketed door she glanced back and saw the thorn child fixed to its mother with spread limbs, spider-like against her body. The sharp face had pierced its place at a large swollen breast. "Does it hurt?" Nessa asked. "Much, I mean."

"It hurts," Jessie said. "Hurts plenty. But love does, don't it?"

Nessa had no thoughts on that topic anyone could consider new. She took the coffee into the yard, blinking at how bright it seemed in comparison and relishing the sudden bitter chill.

Daniel chopped another log into twin pieces of firewood.

"Expectin' a storm?" Nessa asked him.

He looked at the sky. "Should I? You got one coming your way?"

"You've got the shutters on." Nessa gestured at the cabin. "It's real gloomy inside."

Danny left the axe buried in the stump and wiped his brow. "Don't want no neighbours pryin'."

All the property Danny and Jessie-Belle owned was the outside kind, save for their tiny cabin, with miles between them and any neighbours. Even then, those neighbours were Nessa and Merrin.

Danny said, "Got something for me?"

Nessa thought yes, and no, and don't know, and maybe, and in that time Danny pointed to the coffee warming her hands. She nodded and Danny wiped his sweaty palms on his overalls before reaching for the hot cup. It reminded her of the grasping baby.

"There's no milk," she said.

"Don't need none." He sipped and winced. Could've been the heat, could've been the taste.

"How's family life suit?"

Danny winced again. "I don't know what to do."

"Daddies everywhere say the same thing."

"I ain't sure I *am* the daddy," he said. "I mean, how could I be?"

"You take that back, Daniel Erlson. Jessie don't give her honey to no one else. No one. Clint named her wrong in more ways than one regarding that. She's been yours since she first bled."

Danny looked into his coffee. He stared like the cup was great-lake deep and he was waiting for something to surface there and swallow him.

"Maybe some devil came in from the woods," he said.

"Danny..."

"It came in from the woods and—"

"*Daniel.*"

He scowled at her but that was all right. Let him scowl.

"You're all cock and swagger and not much else besides, Daniel Erlson, and I should have known. Of course you're going to give it to Jessie. Who wouldn't?"

"Ness—"

"And sometimes those miles must've seemed like long ones. Too far, even for neighbours."

A silence stretched between them as wide as the barren yard until Danny said, "There *is* devils in the woods, though."

"There's devils everywhere. Never bothered you none before."

"I can still come see you, Ness. I still want to."

"No. You can't."

"We can still leave."

"Can't do that, neither."

Danny set the cup down on the tree stump beside his axe and when he turned back he was smiling that crooked-tooth smile of his. "Don't you want me no more?" He went to her, all cock and swagger, just like she said. "Nessa? Don't you want to?"

Nessa glanced at the shut-up cabin. Danny took her hand and she let him. His were warm, but only from the coffee. She let him take her into the woods with only one more glance back at the cabin and chose to say nothing else.

Nessa walked a track back that had been pressed into shape only by the tramping of feet. Mostly those feet had been hers and Danny's. Long grasses grew close around, yellowed in places and dry and swishing against her long skirts in a constant rasp as she brushed it down in passing. A rapid dry breath that matched her steps, rasp-gasp, rasp-gasp. Occasionally a stand of nettles tangled across her route and she would clutch her skirts at the groin, bunching the material in her fist, to step over. Danny used to say he'd cut them down but he never did.

She regretted visiting, and she looked forward to next time, and she hated herself for one of those thoughts.

"You said you never went to her no more," Nessa'd said when they were done. "You said she don't let you no more."

"Sometimes she let me."

He was looking at her pale thighs and between them. "You're pretty."

She'd let herself smile because she knew he wouldn't see then fussed her skirts back into place, shuffling back from where Danny had spilled on the ground. She didn't let him finish, not inside. Not this time. A small pool glistened on crushed leaves and hard scraped soil. She thought again of sap and adjusted the rest of her clothing, brushed twigs and dirt from her hair as Danny tucked himself away. He wiped his hands on his knees.

Jessie's voice, "*Danny!*" had startled both of them.

Daniel had looked back towards the cabin yard. "I gotta go."

"I ain't stopping you."

And she hadn't. Danny'd nodded and hurried away. Maybe he'd grab more firewood on his way, or maybe he'd tell Jessie it was the call of nature, which had a bit of truth to it, but Nessa didn't care what he said. She knew he could be charming if a woman wanted him to be. So she waited, still breathing a little quick and staring at where the leaves glistened with Danny's seed. She'd scrunched up a handful of dirt and grasses to cover the spot and made for home.

Now the woods were thickening with cool shadows. The soft path held a smell like old well water. The woods did not scare Nessa, though she knew they earned being scared of. Mr Splitfoot lived in the woods. Devils burrowed up from the sour soil to take them that paid no mind to what they did. There were things with teeth and things with claws. There were poisons and there were magics in the naked woods, and there were men.

It was getting dark. Merrin would be home. His Stray Dog days were over now, or so rare nobody cared, not Nessa anyways, and he'd be filling the cabin with his musky bulk or draping the yard trestles with fresh skins for scraping. Used to be he made her feel that way, stretched taut and roughed into something smooth and pliable, and it weren't a bad way to feel a lot of the time. Now'days, thoughts he never shared darkened his mind and only the fire he stared at put a light in his eyes. It was a depth she used to crave in a man but there weren't much use for it when it only ever stayed his.

She was nearly home. The trees leaned, drunk or weary. Weak light slanted through the branches and crossed her path. Swollen blackberries drooped on withered bushes that looked to Nessa, now, like a tangled crowd of children. She expected the dark fruit to blink at her, to pucker open with a spill of juice. She saw the twisted shapes of thorn-hearted things.

"Damn you, Danny."

She wouldn't cry for him, though. Stray Dog was a far better man and there'd been few tears for him so she'd not spare water for Danny. Jessie-Belle had earned a few maybe, but then she was the type who'd shed plenty on her own. Clint had been a tough father and cause enough for crying, and marrying Danny wouldn't help her none down the track, but what was a little sorrow when you were young and beautiful? Jessie would be fine.

"Damn you."

She said it several times on the path that took her back, letting the curse follow her or find its way elsewhere without caring much what it chose to do. She thought of lies and wishes and promises and how they tangled together and soon, too soon or soon enough, she was home.

There'd been an old swing frame outside Merrin's place since before Ness ever lived there. Never a swing seat for as long as she'd known, but Merrin used the rusting metal to hang corpses for butchering. There was one there now, a hulk of red flesh stripped of skin, sweetening. Meat and muscle, veined with thin white strings left behind, dangled over a bucket. The head was propped in place by its own antlers. The throat was open and dry. Nessa took up the bucket as she passed so nothing would come sniffing for the blood.

A truck rusted at the side of the house, sitting on bricks, hood open. It had been there almost as long as the swing frame. Nessa glanced inside as she always did and saw it empty, just as she always did. Saw all the way through to black, oil-stained ground. It made her sad, that absence. Like it'd had a heart once. There'd been nights that engine's heat had warmed her back. Nights when Stray Dog still had some straying in him, picking up town girls until eventually the girl was only ever Nessa.

He was asleep at the table, head resting on his forearms. There was some money crumpled by his elbow. Nessa counted without touching. Weren't much. She set the bucket down on the table.

He stirred when she lit the stove.

"What time is it?"

"Late enough."

He grunted something and wiped his face more awake. He saw the bucket. "I'll cut it down after supper," he said.

Nessa nodded. She lifted the lid from yesterday's pan and saw plenty left for warming.

"Where you been?"

"Jessie-Belle's. Check on her and…"

"Danny?"

"The baby."

He stood from the hard chair and leaned to crack his back. "The baby," he said. "Ain't much more than babies themselves." He came to the stove to look at what she stirred around. "How'd we get so old, Ness?"

"Day by day."

She flinched when he put his arm around her waist. Surprised was all, but he pulled away after.

"Merrin—"

"I'll go finish up outside."

He closed the door quietly behind him as if they had a newborn themselves he might wake.

"Motherin' suits you," Nessa said.

Jessie was in the yard, standing but leaning over to hold the outstretched hands of her russet child. It had bulked out some with nest-like weaves of thicket and thatch stiff as a broom head. "Yeah," Jessie said, but not to Nessa. "That's it. Come on." The child was stumbling forward with a fireplace crackle and snap. It had grown a lot and done it fast and already it staggered like a toddler. Jessie, standing close over it, shuffled tiny awkward steps behind.

"Healing all right?"

Jessie glanced at Nessa. "Still a mess down there," she said. "But I'm doing most things all right again." To the child she said, "Yeah, that's it."

Nessa listened for Daniel, looked about for him, but was brought back to Jessie when she asked, "How long before I can…"

"Before you can…?"

Jessie laughed. It was forced, or sounded that way to Nessa. The false friendly only girls ever bothered with. "Danny's behavin' like he wants another one already."

"Really?"

That laugh again, shrill as a strangled bird. "Keeps me up at night more than this one."

Jessie looked at Nessa and held it so long that she missed her kindling-child wobble and fall. "Whoops!" She pulled it up by its barky arms and set it back on leafy feet. "Whoops-a-daisy!"

"Where is he, anyway?" Nessa asked. "Left you on your own, has he?"

"He does his share. I know folk called me foolish for pickin' him, prob'ly said all sorts about getting away from daddy, but they was wrong to say so and now everything's good again."

"Didn't know it was bad before."

"Come on, Ness. You know it was."

Only men called her Ness. Men, and women older than this one.

Jessie raised her child with another "whoops-a-daisy" and gathered the bundle of branches into her arms. "Not now, though, eh? They're good now. Yes they *are*." She brushed at tufts of sprouting green and the thing made a keening wind-blown sound, the sigh of treetops in a breeze. Laughing, seemed like. Jessie was tickling a baby born of bark and it laughed.

"Danny's people's not got much learning," Jessie said. "Some, but not much. And mine've got no better, maybe less." She looked at Nessa, smoothing the foliage hair on her young's knot-head. "We got country-magics, though. We know who to ask and how when we want something."

"Jessie-Belle, what did you do?"

"I ain't losing Danny," she said. "Not to no one. Even if I like her. He ain't much but he's mine and I need him even more now."

The gnarly bole bundle of leaf and branch broke away from its mother for a short staggering run. Jessie clapped, delighted, "That's it!" and then again when she saw, "It's daddy!" He had a beaten box of store goods and he looked tired but he grinned and called hello to his sprig of a child. He set the box down and stayed crouched after, opening his arms to the stumbling bark-skinned thing. Daniel winced with the hug but he drew it close and held it. Did it with affection Nessa knew he had but hadn't seen.

"Hello, Ness."

"Daniel."

He glanced at his wife and made a wary but obvious assessment – a man like Danny had a face you could read better than books – but Jessie was too busy smiling her love to notice.

"Ness just came to see how we're doing," Jessie said. "We're doing fine, aren't we Danny-baby?" She squatted near them and Nessa felt some horrible joy at the pain she saw, the girl's grimace of cunt-stitches, then felt pain of her own at what she saw after. The bracken-sapling thing of thorns and acorns pulled them both together with ivy-vine arms. It was a sturdy tree trunk with buds that flowered as Nessa watched, roots that thickened and thorns that spiked to hold Danny and Jessie together, pinning them, draping them with fruiting tendrils and unfurled leaves. It brambled them in a fierce sharp hug of bark and bough until that was all Nessa could see.

Nessa lay in bed staring at cobwebbed rafters, listening to Merrin's heavy breathing and the quiet of the night outside. When she was a girl, her mother told her the best way to catch a man was to not want him but her problem growing up had been deciding which ones she wanted and which ones she didn't. She often got it wrong. When Merrin was Stray Dog, he told her they were similar that way. He'd taken her out to one of the great-lakes, fucked her on the truck the way she liked back then, then wrapped them both in a blanket to watch stars fall from the sky. "Make a wish," he'd said, and "I never know what to wish for," she'd said back, and that was how the conversation started. He'd told her love was something you couldn't hunt, but when you found it you had to trap it quick. She'd moved into his cabin shortly after that, as natural as seasons changing.

Nessa rolled over to look at him. His back was bunched with muscle and thick with hair she used to run her fingers through. She used to say of all the pelts he could ever sell his would be the best of them. The hair had silvered now and there were bald lines, wounds he'd earned and scars he didn't deserve. The back of his head was balding too but the hair there held its colour.

"Merrin?"

He didn't stir any, but then she'd only whispered his name in a hush he'd barely hear awake, so it wasn't any wonder.

Outside, something moved quietly on the porch. The wood was weather-warped and it creaked beneath the slightest weight. Nessa wondered what animal it might be and what it was looking for. Food and warmth if it was wild. If it were a stray, well then it would want those things too but someone to love it as well, most like.

Nessa shifted onto her back to hear it better. The noise was scratchy. Used to be there were trees growing right up to the cabin and when there was a wind the branches would move against the walls and roof, scratching at the wood with naked spindles of twig in winter, brushing leaf-sweeps of hush in the summer months. What she heard now reminded her of that. An uprooted bush, tumbling back and forth across the boards.

Danny's child, she thought. Jessie's knot of brambles.

Nessa leaned away from Merrin and slowly left the bed. She put on the fur slippers he'd made for her and gathered a tattered blanket around her shoulders and went to the window.

The yard was silver with moonlight. It frosted the metal of the empty swing set and the rusting hulk of truck. Nothing moved out there but for clouds, darkening the stars away and back again.

Merrin slept.

Nessa left the bedroom, easing the door open, closing it slowly, treading her way across rugs of fur and spread pelts, stepping where the boards wouldn't creak. She peered again at the vacant yard from a near window but that didn't ease her mind any so she opened the front door and stepped out onto the porch.

The night air was cool but not overly cold. It carried inside it the scent of sap and dew-damp soil.

The rustle came again, nearer some, right beside her, and Nessa was startled into turning and stepping back from what she saw. A thing of broken sticks and autumn leaves and hand-pulled grass. A sulphurous yellow crop, damp and rank. This was not the child of thorns she had delivered on Jessie's kitchen table. This was some coarse child of her own. It reached for her with hands of mulch. When its tiny fists unfurled, flowers opened in the palms.

"No," Nessa said. "Back to the woods with you." She pulled the blanket tighter around her shoulders. "Go on."

Fronds of fern and spiky foliage, the bundle tumbled at her and clutched her naked legs with limbs that prickled. Nessa couldn't shake it free. When she bent to lift the thing away it clutched her arms and peppered her skin with tiny punctures, scratched lines that swelled pink and beaded blood, and held her firm. Its bark-skin chest was weak with rot and nettles grew in a stinging thatch between its legs. It bulged all over with the nubs of clipped branches, swirled with open knots, and looked at her with eyes like chestnut husks, soft-spiked and sickly green. It smiled with a mouth of seedling teeth and when the mouth opened, a cavernous oak-hollow too large for its broken bough face, it spoke. Its voice had the plump softness of windfall fruit. It dropped over-ripe syllables like tiny pine cones onto compost.

"*Ma*ma."

Nessa scooped it up and ran. It scratched beneath the blanket, tried to suckle as she fled with it into the woods. She didn't want this, this was Danny's work. He could have it back, a sibling thing for his other shrub.

The child scratched at her, rubbing against her skin, scraping her raw, and she tried to pull it free. She snapped what she could find of it, tore clumps and chunks from it and tossed them to the track as she ran. The nubs on its bark skin sprouted and fattened into berries. Clusters of blue and purple and black plumped and burst in her fingers, sour tumours sticky with poisoned juice. She ran. She tore. Leaves browned, blackened, and fell away like paper ash; brambles that tried to wrap her legs and snare her feet turned brittle and tugged apart with her strides. Soon all she carried was a wild but weed-strewn brake that broke, crumbled, scattered, and she only held fragments of forest floor. She cast these to the wind, panting, and dusted pieces from her naked skin, allowing herself a single sob and telling herself it was relief, though she only ever believed lies men told her.

She returned home.

The figure that waited for her on the porch this time was Merrin. His bulk was a bear's shadow blocking the door. He wore blankets and pelts and his breath was frosty, a puffed cloud around his nose and mouth.

"Can't you leave him be awhile?"

Nessa said nothing. She fidgeted her blanket tight.

"Fire's going," Merrin said. "Warm yourself up, if you're still needin'." He turned away from her but stopped short before going inside. Stepped back. When he turned around again his face was darker than Nessa'd ever seen a night sky.

"What's this?" he said.

She'd never be rid of it, looked like. There'd always be something of the woodland life to bind her to the mistakes she'd made, tie her like a creeper vine to a man who sowed his seed in another furrow, a fertile furrow. But when the child moved, Nessa saw a face freckled with mould and a moist crop of fungus. It sagged, limp and autumn-coloured, withered eyes weeping long lines of lichen down its split shape to a soft-bark chest scooped almost hollow. *Almost.* The moss-furred stump of a tree felled long ago but still ripe with life.

"Merrin," Nessa said, "I think it's ours."

The clod of vegetation smiled or grimaced, and the flower of its mouth blossomed, drooped, and wilted. Petals fell in a slow sequence of loves-me, loves-me not.

Nessa chanted each one down and wondered who the words were for.

|The Wrong Shark|

~

When Darnell Jackson was a boy, a film crew came to the island where he lived and made a movie. The island was Martha's Vineyard, and the movie they made was *Jaws*.

40 years later, feeling like a tourist, Darnell came back to the Vineyard. He came back on the Wood's Hole ferry like he was summer-people, only it wasn't yet summer, it was early May, and there was a bite in the air that had him holding his coat closed at the throat as he stood on deck for the approach. They passed the West Chop lighthouse. It wasn't on, but he felt its warning.

Stay away. Stay away.

It was cold, but as he remembered it the weather was much the same back when filming started all those years ago, actors and extras doing their best to pretend it was summer-hot. The aim had been to get most of the shoot done before the real tourists arrived and turned 6,000 people into 60,000. For Darnell, though, this time? He had come straight from his father's funeral, renting a car with little thought to where he was going until he was already most of the way there. Still wearing his black suit, his black shirt, his good shoes. Appropriate, in its own way, as something of Darnell had died here long ago. He'd mourned it his whole life.

He headed for his rental as the ferry began the docking process. He tried to ignore the appetite that had been building throughout his long journey. He didn't want to spend much time in Oak Bluffs. There'd be no lobster roll from the Lookout, no Big Dipper ice-cream. No nostalgic visit to Inkwell Beach, either, as much as he'd loved the place as a child. His mother used to take him, before *Jaws*, because of how much he'd liked to swim, but his father had hated the place and the racist roots of its name. He thought going there was volunteering for segregation.

There *were* more people of colour on the island these days, Darnell noticed that right away. Better off than he'd ever been – shit, they were downright *affluent* – but that was okay. That was probably good. The Black Hamptons, some people called it. His father would have found a way to be angry about that, and he would have found a way to blame white people, but that was okay, too. That was his right. The island had been home to the same families for centuries, and progress was always ever slow. You had to keep swimming against the current until the current changed, that was all, and as his therapist was fond of saying, it was swimming against a current that made you stronger.

He was swimming against the current in coming back. That's how it felt, anyway, after years of moving deeper and deeper inland. As if things would get better depending on how far they removed themselves from the ocean. But jobs were scarce everywhere – or his father was bad at keeping one for long – and Darnell quickly discovered that the fears he'd started harbouring on the island were carried with him, regardless of where they went. They were like memories that way, which are the wake you make in moving forwards.

And all that moving didn't mean shit because the sharks would always follow.

Sharks have a kind of sixth sense, thanks to a remarkable electroreceptive system. The black spots on a shark's skin around the eyes and mouth and snout are the ampullae of Lorenzini, which allow the shark to sense the electromagnetic fields and movements of other animals. It means they are especially good at locating and homing in on prey.

On his way to Edgartown, Darnell stopped to walk the State Beach and look at the American Legion Memorial Bridge. Or '*Jaws* Bridge', as it was better known. State Beach was where the Kintner kid was killed, where the camera so famously zoomed in on Brody while everything else seemed to zoom out behind. On State Beach you could run upon the same rocks as Brody on his way past the bridge to the pond – Sengekontacket Pond – where his own kid was playing, sent to the estuary because Brody had thought it safer than the open sea. It had been so cold for that scene. People on the beach and in the water were freezing their asses off in shorts and tees, swimsuits, bikinis, all of them dressed like it was already the 4th of July, all of them with jackets hidden in their beach gear for the time waiting between takes. The sun had rarely been out, and the water held its chill because the Gulf Stream didn't shift until late May, early June, and unless you were in the Polar Bear Club you wouldn't want to swim State Beach until then *at least*, but people went in the water anyway. You had to, if you wanted to be in the movie, and *everyone* wanted to be in the movie. Like everybody else, Darnell would loiter wherever there was filming, hoping for an opportunity to get involved. For many people that tactic paid off.

It never worked for him, though.

Darnell walked beside the rocks he could have run upon and watched the sea. He watched waves sweep up the beach, each one the result of some distant force, pushed and pulled to their inevitable destination. Building to violent force in some cases, smashing against whatever tried to stop them, often to their own mutual destruction. Not these ones, though. Not today. They merely hushed their way up the beach to dissolve and disappear back the way they'd come. Darnell wondered if it was a sign that he should do the same.

The sea withdrew, and the sea came again. Did it remember what it once lifted, carried, deposited on distant shores? Did it remember what it consumed or regret any of them it drowned? He didn't think so. The tides were as cold and careless as time.

At the bridge, he remembered how he used to watch older kids jump from it, splashing into the water below. Judging by the warning sign on the rail it seemed they still did, probably even more so now it was Jaws Bridge. He imagined children joking about sharks before they jumped.

Jump the shark. Wasn't that something people said these days? About taking things too far? Darnell wasn't sure. And how far was too far, anyway? Hit back harder, that's what his father used to say. Pay it back with interest. Darnell had rarely agreed with him but now that he was gone, he felt adrift. Not that his father had ever been any kind of anchor. More often than not he was that current Darnell swam against. He didn't feel stronger for it, though.

He waited for a gap in the traffic and crossed the street to look at the pond where Brody's kid and his friends had been knocked from their dinghy. One of them – the Rebello boy – was nearly eaten. What was his name? Darnell had sort of known him once. He used his phone to Google. *Chris.* That was it. There'd been a time Darnell was envious of him, only to learn in later years that he'd been so scared of that fin coming at him over and over that filming needed to be cut short. Even knowing it was all fake, he'd been terrified. Darnell wondered if the experience still came to him at night the same way his own experience haunted him, or if he'd managed to reduce it to an amusing anecdote, something to dine out on. He Googled again, curious to see what the kid – what the *man* – was doing now.

He was dead.

Darnell looked again at the pond, remembering the kid's face as the camera came at him in the water and wondering, shit, did the shark get you after all, man? Because your thirties are far too young for a heart attack, aren't they? He scrolled down a few more links on his phone but found something disturbing about the younger Brody brother and put the phone away without reading more.

People were like oceans, he thought. Pushed and pulled by similar tidal forces. Prey to all the vicious things that swam within them.

He looked at the ocean and thought of all that lived there, sleek and secret beneath the waves. He thought, predictably, of sharks. Of bulls and blacktips, makos and hammerheads. Of tigers and threshers. He'd become something of a shark expert over the years, 'a black Richard Dreyfuss' as he'd explained it to a partner once, when he still trusted enough to confide such things. Learning all he could about sharks was the therapy he'd prescribed himself long before he ever had a professional session.

Hammerheads have 360-degree vision. Great whites can grow 10 inches each year. A shark's heart is an S with two chambers. These were some of the things he still remembered. He found comfort in the natural facts of them, albeit a cold one. Better to remember details like that than how a shark's skin felt against your own, or how sharp their teeth could be.

How hard laughter could bite.

There was a churning in his stomach he'd hoped was a lingering effect of his ferry-crossing, but now his breathing came quicker and shallower and he knew that what was happening had little to do with the ferry and more to do with where it had brought him.

"Okay," he said. "Okay." He knew what he had to do.

He looked and saw the sea. It was the same grey as the sky. He saw a boat. He saw gulls. He saw a distant buoy.

Okay.

The breeze. It carried the ocean with it as a thin mist that settled on his skin. He clutched the satiny lining of his pockets tight in his fists and held the coat open like twin sails to feel the cold.

Okay.

He turned an ear to the breeze and listened. Heard the gulls calling back and forth. Heard the clanking halyards of nearby boats. Heard his own slowing inhalations which brought to him a fishy odour and the ocean's brine. The latter was so strong, he could taste salt on his lips.

"Okay."

All those hours of therapy – all those dollars – and the best thing he'd learned was the 5-4-3-2-1 technique. The rest of it was all trite, soundbite wisdom. Like 'face your fears', that was a classic. Face your fears so as to better overcome them. But then that was what Quint did and look what happened to him. Days scared in the water waiting for sharks to eat him and the rest of his life hunting them in an effort to defeat that fear, only to have it come back monstrous and chomp him down whole. The shark was an instrument of karma, that was how Darnell saw it, because as far as he was concerned, *Jaws* was Quint's movie. He'd watched it over and over – facing his fear – and the more he saw it the more he was convinced. Quint was the lead. Quint was the one with history and past trauma to overcome. That he fails just makes the film honest.

Fear never went away. Quint knew that, and so did Darnell. It accreted like coral. It built like a wave. Shit, there were people who *still* wouldn't go in the water thanks to *Jaws*, that's how strong fear could be.

Darnell turned away from the pond and headed back to the car. The breeze, as if to encourage him, strengthened into wind to push him on his way.

The colour of a shark's skin helps it hunt. The blues and greys of the ocean, combined with a pale underbelly like the sky, help render it near invisible when seen from above or below. Many are named for their colours, such as great whites, brown sharks, and blacks.

Spielberg had a thing about colour, but not the way Darnell's father said. As far as Darnell could tell – and he'd followed the director's career over the years – the man was not a racist. He *was* particular about colour, though. Like how he didn't want the colour red in *Jaws* so that when the blood came it would really pop. If Darnell had realised, he wouldn't have worn his lucky tee – the *red* one – every time he showed up for a part. He wouldn't have worn his favourite – red – baseball cap. He supposed they could have given him a different shirt if they'd really wanted him. He could have taken off his hat.

Down-island, walking through Edgartown, he remembered that cars had been moved out of shot if they were red. He remembered the red had been replaced with orange in the bunting they'd put up all along Main Street for the 4th of July celebrations. He remembered the atmosphere, the excitement and expectation that came with the novelty of a movie crew on Main. Now, that same street was quiet. Much of it had changed, too, and yet at the same time it had not. Not really. The differences were mostly surface details. As if another film set had been erected in the time he was away, the buildings given new identities with false façades. He had a sense of floating between worlds, between past and present and something else. He recognised many of the clapboard and redwood buildings, the old whaling captains' houses, but some of the businesses were new. He remembered the hardware store that had briefly become a music store so Quint could buy piano wire for fishing line. The scene had been cut. The store was a restaurant now.

At the junction of Water Street and Main he saw where Brody had picked up his supplies for the 'beach closed' signs. Afterwards he had driven the wrong way down a one-way street because it was only

Martha's Vineyard that had the one-way system, not Amity, and back then, when Darnell was a boy, the topsy-turvy use of his hometown had amused him. Amazed him, even. It had shown him how rules he thought were fixed in place could be broken. Showed him how the world he thought he knew could change, or at least seem to.

"If he's not racist, how come you ain't got no part in his damn movie?"

His father's voice, able to cross time to find Darnell wherever – whenever – he might be.

"Everybody else is in it, why ain't you?"

Almost all of the other kids got parts, that was true. Some of them even got two; the Edgartown kids in the marching band were the same as the Boy Scout group swimming in the sea (even though the parade and the swim were meant to be happening at exactly the same time) because who was going to notice the same kid twice? Darnell was patient, though. He'd hang around the cast and crew, collecting autographs, making sure he was seen and hoping he'd be remembered. But…

"Shit, there ain't no one black in that movie. No one."

That wasn't true. Darnell had checked. There were people of colour in the Wood's Hole ferry scene, *and* on State Beach, right before that pasty-pale mayor started hogging the camera.

Not Darnell, though. Every time his father asked he had to shake his head no, not today, hating to see his father disappointed yet again, not just by him but by the world they lived in, and he'd move quickly to show him the new signatures in his autograph book, though his father never cared for it.

"Looks blank to me," he'd once said. "Look at all them pages. They're so damn *white*."

The largest of the predatory sharks is the great white, or Carcharodon carcharias. *It relies on its heavy-hitting power, sometimes leaping out of the water to attack.*

The tiger shark, or Galeocerdo cuvier, *is a stealthier animal. It hunts mostly at night, drifting slowly before suddenly striking.*

~

It was a tiger shark they'd used for the scene on the docks. Thirteen feet long, or thereabouts, tied up by its tail and hooked through the mouth so it hung with its jaws gaping open. It wasn't local. Best they'd managed to catch off the Vineyard were a load of threshers and blues that lacked the striking visual impact required for a summer blockbuster. With time running out, they'd sourced the tiger shark from Florida and FedExed it in a crate of ice. Darnell hadn't known that at the time, though. He'd assumed Spielberg had said, 'I need a shark,' and someone had hooked the tiger right out of Vineyard waters. The idea had terrified him. Knowing there were sharks like that near Inkwell Beach? Shit, no wonder his father never went swimming.

While the hunt wore on in real life to find the right kind of shark, everyone else was filming the other hunt, the first of the chaotic dock scenes. All those different crews hurrying and jostling each other and getting in each other's way. All of that, plus the film crew, too; it made for a lot to watch. The film crew were easy to spot because by then most of them were wearing those screen-print t-shirts Darnell had liked so much, an open-mouthed shark coming at you over JAWS, and the boat crews were easy to spot because they were locals, all of them stepping around each other and bumping left and right and swamping each other's boats in their eagerness to get out there and catch a monster. Anyone and everyone who had a boat was in that scene, and getting paid twice for it, too: once as an extra, and once for the hire of their boat. Darnell's father wasn't into boats, so he missed out on that, but he could bullshit with the best of them and managed to land himself a background part. He still complained, though. "Doubt you'll even see me," he'd said, but Darnell had gone along to watch anyway, sitting in the cab of his father's truck with the engine running for the heater.

It was May and it was cold, raining enough that there were long pauses between takes and a lot of hanging around. "Hurry up and wait," was a joke Darnell had heard plenty of times without really understanding it, and with so many people to organise for this scene, and rain as well, there was even more waiting than usual. But then suddenly the docks would come alive with a cry of 'action!' and sure enough there'd be lots of it as men overloaded their boats and bumped each other and even fell into the sea in their haste. Then they'd cut and there'd be shouting through a bullhorn, "Rick! Rick! Get over here!" and there'd be pointing and taking new positions and nodding and a lot of standing around to wait all over again. Some of the men drank from flasks they'd brought along to keep the cold at bay – and Darnell had no doubt his father was one of those – but with the rain and the cold and no coats or waterproofs, because it was meant to be July, all that waiting and waiting and waiting became too much for some of them.

Darnell's father had been one of those, as well.

"Look at this shit!"

Darnell had been staring at a truck opposite, one of the rentals the film people used. He'd been trying to figure out what they'd done to the AVIS logo to make it read JAWS, eventually seeing how lines of tape had been used to make a J, while another line from the V to the I made a W. It was clever, Darnell thought. Like the clapperboard he'd seen with its white stripes altered to a double row of teeth: snap! He smiled, thinking of that. Then the door beside him was wrenched open, startling him, and his father was shaking a flimsy fishing rod in his face.

"Look at this shit! Like this'd catch a shark. Shit, this wouldn't catch *nothin'*."

He threw it aside to reach in for his jacket.

"Catch a *cold*, though, you bet I can do *that*."

He pulled his way out of the wet sweater he'd been allowed, put his jacket on, and yanked the sweater back down over it best he could before slamming the door closed again to stomp his way back to where everyone else was hurrying up to wait.

Safe in the truck, Darnell had laughed at how suddenly fat his father looked with the jacket under his sweater, stopping only when the new cold in the truck had him looking around for his own.

Standing on the dock years later, he let his coat flap open in the wind, welcoming the cold –

an awareness of discomfort is proof of a desire to live

– and looking around at the boats and buildings. He was surprised at how little had been done to mark the *Jaws* legacy on the island, especially here. He'd half-expected a fibreglass replica of the shark to be dangling on the docks, a background prop for tourists' selfies. In the absence of such a thing, he was able to better remember the real one.

"Looks like a lynching," Darnell's father had said when they first saw it, hanging there. "It's the wrong way up, but that's what it looks like. And look at them. Bunch of happy white folk."

That had been some time after the first dock scene and by that point Darnell's father had no desire to be in the film no more. He'd agreed to let Darnell keep trying, though. Maybe as a kindness, maybe to prove a point. Either way, that was how they found themselves at the docks again, approaching the dead shark hanging in the crowd. A hook through its mouth kept it open, its rows of teeth on gruesome display. It had been stabbed and cut, and something like a crossbow bolt or harpoon protruded from its side.

They could smell it long before they were close.

The meat of a shark is different to that of other fish. It decays quickly because it's all just simple proteins and no bones, only cartilaginous tissue. For the 800lb tiger they'd strung up, that decaying process had begun in Florida, was slowed a little by ice, then hurried along again quick just as soon as it was out of its crate. When they hung it upside down, gravity went to work on its insides until the guts kept piling up in the fish's throat. Darnell had been both delighted and repulsed to see them bulging out of the animal's mouth, ready to drop and slop on the docks. As he watched, someone stepped close to push them back in, push them back up.

"Yuck," said Darnell.

"It's just a fish. You wanna be in the film, you gotta get closer."

Darnell had felt his father's hand on his back, guiding him forwards with a final, not gentle, push. He'd felt a similar thing at his grave, once the service was over. Something steering him away from where his father lay buried and pushing him towards Amity. Back towards the Vineyard.

Close up, the shark had *reeked*. It was dead, and doing what dead things do, which was rot. There could be no bringing it down between takes to store on ice because the more they handled it, the more it would fall apart, and so it stayed there, hanging in the sun. Unless you had to get close for a shot, you made sure you stayed downwind of it.

Many of the locals had complained about the hanging shark and its stench – for all those keen on the film and all it provided, there were plenty who resented the disruption of their normal lives – but whoever was running the docks back then was getting more money from the *Jaws* people than all of those complaining put together, so the shark hung there, rotting, stinking, spilling its guts and blood, while everyone waited and filmed and waited again.

Darnell had waited with them, making himself part of the crowd around the shark. He'd even had to step out of the way once so Richard Dreyfuss could measure the span of the open mouth, *and* he'd been there in the background as Dreyfuss explained to Brody it was the wrong shark, but he'd never yet spotted himself watching the scene back. They'd run that scene quite a few times, though, and much of the time he'd found himself distracted by the shark. He'd looked into that mouth, his hands over his own and over his nose, and he had been revolted. He had looked into those eyes, those dead, dark eyes –

lifeless eyes, black eyes

– and he had not liked what he saw there. Had not liked, either, what he couldn't help imagining: the whole shark descending from its unravelling rope to swallow him whole.

More than once his nightmares had put him in that shark's place. He'd be packed in ice and FedExed straight to the docks where he'd grasp and pull the sudden noose at his neck, gasping his last breaths while people in screen-print tees and hoods like teeth gathered round to watch. Someone would yank his legs and he'd wake with a clapperboard snap, freezing cold and sucking for air.

That was one of the better dreams.

Darnell heard some children laugh and the sound pulled the present into sharper focus while the past dropped away, like in that famous dolly zoom. Only there were no children on the docks, there was only him, leaning into the wind coming in off the sea and staring at where a shark used to be. The ghost of young laughter lingered, clinging to him like the smell from something dead and rotten.

As well as extraordinary electroreceptors and excellent eyesight, sharks have a great sense of smell. A great white can detect a drop of blood in an area the size of an Olympic pool.

~

Far from Martha's Vineyard, two years after they'd moved away, Darnell's mother convinced him to try swimming in the local pool. Not to face his fears, as any of his therapists might have put it, but because her little boy had once loved to swim, and she was keen to bring that joy back to him.

He'd been anxious, but they took some time for him to control his breathing and to quietly note his surroundings, and eventually she was able to lead him to the pool edge and into the shallows and never mind who might be watching, you're doing real good, and with her help it had worked out all right at first. The water was cool and then comfortable, and the chlorine smell was nothing like ice or the briny scent of sharkskin, and the room was so big it echoed, throwing back the cries of other children and the occasional whistle-blow of a lifeguard keeping them safe. And the light! It was so bright, and the water was clear, and there were no sharks, not a single one.

Still, he stayed close, facing his mother, holding her hands until she eased him away to tread water on his own and told him that's it, that's *good*, see? You're doing it, you're doing it. And he was. He turned and saw adults swimming lengths of the pool and he saw children splashing each other, the youngest of them wearing inflatable bands around their arms to keep them afloat, and as he watched he saw...

He saw a shark.

He saw a dark shape in water that suddenly breached, lifting one of the children shrieking into the air, shrieking with laughter, and he panic-splashed himself around again to face his mother but he couldn't turn quick enough, remained frustratingly in the same place, his left hand slapping the water one way and his right hand the other, both too fast, too choppy, splashing like he was swatting at flies and that splashing would draw more sharks, he knew that, but he couldn't stop. He saw the shadow of one coming for him along the bottom of the pool and another bumped him from behind and now he couldn't breathe, he was drowning in the air while his legs kicked and his arms slapped and splashed and the water was so suddenly cold, *freezing* cold, gripping him around the chest, and the reason he couldn't breathe was because all the breath he'd had was coming out in a scream. A shark fastened its teeth on his arm and pulled and his scream became so shrill that something of the sound broke and he could only expel air and suck in sobs as his mother's fierce grip pulled him close and she waded to the edge of the pool with her son in her arms.

It was the first time his fears had taken hallucinatory shape in the waking world, surfacing from his nightmares to frighten him into a state that had him shaking so violently that his mother, holding him tight, trembled with him.

Darnell woke from that remembered terror, shivering. He was on the floor of his hotel room. He'd consumed the contents of his minibar and fallen asleep foetal by the open door of the refrigerator. He remembered listening to it hum until the sound dragged him into sleep, the cold seeping deliberately into his bones.

An awareness of discomfort is proof of a desire to live.

He groaned with the ache of straightening, sitting up and putting a hand to his head. It throbbed like a boat's motor. A taste for alcohol was one of the things Darnell had inherited from his father and he'd liberated the tiny bottles from the minibar in an effort to drown the laughter that had followed him back from the docks, hoping to sleep so deep the dreams wouldn't find him.

Only the powerless are at the mercy of their trauma.

He snatched up the bottles and threw them into the wastebin under the dresser, wincing with each knock of the metal and clink of glass. Was there anyone more powerless than a child? How can a man overcome trauma born at such an early, powerless age?

You can't. That's what Darnell had learned. Instead, you drag it behind like a trawler drags its net or a shark its barrels.

It was late but still light outside, so he splashed his face, ran his wet hands over the buzz of his hair, and left the hotel.

As a child, Darnell had lived in Oak Bluffs, but coming back he'd decided to stay down-island in Edgartown. Edgartown was where most of the film crew had stayed all those years ago because it was only 15 minutes away from Cow Bay, the area so perfect for *Jaws*, and just as Edgartown had been conveniently located for their needs, so it was for Darnell's, too. He didn't want to be driving all around the island any more than could be helped, even as small as it was. He'd do what he had to do and be gone.

He drove slowly, though. The cocktail of different drinks from the minibar was still foul in his mouth and swimming in his bloodstream. He leaned over the steering wheel to look left and right at the large, handsome houses as he passed.

A child was playing in the front yard of one of them, throwing a baseball straight-up high and watching, watching, ready to catch it with that flat, rifle-shot smack in his mitt when it came down. He was white, wearing the full baseball kit to go with his mitt. The Red Sox colours, not the purple of the Vineyard Sharks. The cap reminded Darnell of his old favourite, forever lost now.

"I know where they keep the *real* shark."

A boy exactly like the one across the street had said that once. Darnell had thought he was talking to him but when he'd turned to ask, "Where?" he saw the boy was addressing his own group of friends, all of them talking about the shark hanging on the docks as they waited between takes. Darnell recognised a couple of them from school. The kid in the baseball shirt was Brad. Bradley Ladson. He was the one claiming to know where they kept the real shark. One of the others had at that moment reached forward to pull at the arrow sticking out the shark's side and then the lot of them were ushered away by an angry adult, Darnell included, even though he hadn't done nothing.

"My brother says he carved his name into it but he's full of shit," said one of the boys Darnell didn't know and the others laughed and agreed, just so they could say "full of shit" themselves.

"It's way bigger than that one," said Brad, and pointed back at the hanging tiger. Someone was measuring its mouth again, but no one was filming. They measured the distance between the mouth and one of the actors.

Can't be no shark bigger than that one, Darnell thought.

"What did you say?"

It had taken him a moment to realise that this time someone *was* talking to him, and only then because someone pulled him around by the shoulder. Not aggressively, but not exactly gently, either.

"You said something," Brad said. "What did you say?"

"He said it wasn't bigger than that one."

Had he spoken out loud?

"I bet you haven't even seen it," Brad said. "I think only people in the movie get to see it."

Darnell could feel something stirring in the air between them, something that even as a child he recognised as the vibrating thrum of violence waiting. Darnell wondered if he was going to have to fight and hoped the choice wouldn't need making. His mother had always told him to walk away from fights, especially with someone white. His father's advice, had he ever given any, would have been the opposite – he was a man of action – and of the two parents there was one he was more afraid of disappointing.

He looked for his father in the crowd around him.

"*Nobody* gets to see the shark," he said absently. "It's locked away and secret."

Someone took his hat.

Darnell turned quickly and saw Brad wearing it. He snatched it back, too quick for Brad to dodge.

"Hey, I was just trying it on."

Then he called Darnell a bad word.

The others tried to laugh as if it had been 'jerk' or 'butt-wipe' but it was much worse than that and all of them knew it. They didn't fully understand *how*, but they knew it was a bad word, awful, maybe a dangerous word, and their laughter reflected some of that confusion in trying to be something it wasn't. Darnell even saw a flush of shame pass over Brad's face, but it was only brief.

Without thinking – which frightened him a little then, and a lot in later years – Darnell took up a boxing stance, fists as tight as the sudden silence they made. One of the actors, the police chief, Roy, had shown him how. He used to be a boxer, and sometimes he liked to play with the kids between takes, throwing slow jabs or sweeping his whole arm for them to duck under while encouraging quicker, hard punches back from them, BAM!, into one of his open palms, WHAM! He called it the old one-two, WHAM-BAM! Once, he'd called Darnell 'Tiny Tate' while shaking out his palms and pretending Darnell had hit him too hard.

So Darnell put his fists up and though he didn't know if he had it right he must've had it close because he saw Brad back down. Not physically – Brad still had one arm up himself, a fist cocked back – but something went out of his eyes. Darnell relaxed his own stance and straightened up a bit, the moment fading, and Brad threw a pretend slap at him with such exaggerated slowness and with such a comic-book sound effect that there could be no mistaking it was just a joke. "Ka-POW!" Darnell stepped back from it though, and one of the other boys pretended to be struck instead, spinning in slow motion with his hands at his jaw, eyes mock wide and mouth growling in feigned pain as he ricocheted from a bystander like a sluggish pinball. It led the others back into a more comfortable laughter.

Brad said, "Hey, remember when that lady hit him?" and he mimed a slap again – and again, and again – making a whip-crack noise with each one. There was no need to ask what lady, or hit who, because they'd all watched it. Take after take after take, a grieving mother had slapped the police chief, over and over. For real.

"His face was all pink!"

"She slapped him so hard his glasses came off!"

"I bet they use that in the film."

Darnell said, "If you get attacked by a shark you should punch it on the nose and it will leave you alone."

Everybody looked at him.

"What?"

"They're very sensitive."

Everybody laughed again, but it was okay. They weren't laughing at him. They were laughing at the idea of punching a shark. And just like that, the rest of the violent tension they'd been wading through receded.

"Come on," said Brad. "I wanna show you something." He pushed his way through the crowd who were still hurrying to wait for the next 'action!' and his friends followed him down the dock. Darnell watched them go, feeling their fleeting acceptance slip away like a slow wave when you're standing barefoot in the surf, sand sinking beneath your feet.

Brad turned, running backwards for a moment to throw a question back at Darnell.

"You coming?"

He didn't wait for an answer. Just turned back to continue running.

Stunned for a moment by the invite, then giddy with inclusion, Darnell ran to catch up, grinning.

~

The thresher shark has a very long tail fin that measures half the length of its whole body. It uses this to lure prey, tricking it close only to swat it away and attacking once it's stunned or otherwise disabled.

~

They gathered in one of the boathouses of Norton & Easterbrook dock, standing a short distance away from a large freezer. The docks had a walk-in refrigeration unit but whether for purposes of secrecy or perhaps permission, the film crew were using a large freezer like you'd find in a regular store – only bigger – to keep some of their potential props fresh. That's what Brad said. A generator chugging nearby kept it running. A flap of cardboard torn from a box was stuck on the freezer with a piece of raggedy tape and the outline of an open-mouthed shark had been markered on the card as if to devour the sign's instruction: KEEP CLOSED.

"What's in it?" someone asked.

"What do you think?"

"The real shark?"

"The *real* shark is fake," said Brad. "It's all mechanical and fake and nowhere near here. But they caught lots of real ones like that massive son-of-a-bitch out there."

This time there was no laughter at the swearing, no joking elbows to the ribs. They were too curious, too much in awe of what might be in the freezer. They were too afraid.

They shuffled each other forward as a group, leaning to look rather than get too close. The freezer lid wasn't see-through, though, wasn't frosted glass or nothing like that. It was flat, and metal. There was a clasp with a bolt to keep it closed.

"Get it open," Brad said. "You'll see. My dad told me."

Someone pulled the bolt and flipped the clasp open and started to lift the lid and then other hands were helping. The freezer released a cold cloud that enveloped them as they bowed slightly to look inside.

Their gasped sounds of amazement and disgust drew Darnell closer, and he pushed his way amongst them like they'd been friends forever.

"Look at them all!"

A pungent smell came at him out of the frosty mist, but it was nowhere near as bad as the stink from what was hanging outside. Nor were the sharks he could see anywhere near as big. But there were so many!

"There's more underneath!" someone said.

"Look at that one!"

"There are *loads* of them!"

The freezer was *full* of sharks, all of them twice the size of Darnell, easy. Head to tail and tail to head, rows of them stacked on more rows of the same, none of them suitable for some reason or another but kept anyway, all blue and grey with pale bellies. They had fins like half kites, and tails too on the blue ones; the others had tails so long to be nearly ridiculous, coiled or folded like something wilted. Their torpedo bodies glistened, frozen forever wet, and slit with gills like tallies counting recent kills. Darnell reached in to touch one. He ran his palm over the skin. It was smoother than he expected. He rubbed the other way and found it rough, like sandpaper. Eyes black as night stared docile through cataracts of ice. Their mouths were open sickles of teeth.

"Even the chief couldn't punch this many on the nose."

Brad said it quietly, like it was only meant for Darnell, and the new intimacy of it was startling but welcome. Darnell glanced at him, smiling wide, then turned his attention back to the sharks. Imagine swimming into this many! He shuddered, imagining them alive and writhing around him, thrashing to bite, and for a moment he thought his imagination had flexed, like it was a muscle that could tense or spasm, because he felt something clamp around his legs and he cried out, thinking 'Shark!' as he was lifted like a caught kill, breaching. He soared high as Brad stood from a crouch behind him, his arms wrapped around Darnell's calves, his shins. Darnell flailed his arms as the others laughed and he was carried, panicking for balance he'd never achieve as he twisted in Brad's grip. His hat was knocked flying and then he was coming down, dropping, deposited backwards into the ice chest. Those gathered around it backed away fast, their laughing faces disappearing quick as his head struck the side of the freezer and the lid came down to plunge him into darkness.

The dark was so absolute that he thought he'd passed out, but he could feel the cold and he could hear the laughter that felt the same and he could smell the–

fish, it's fish, just fish, lots of fish

–but he couldn't move. He lay in a dark so deep it filled his mind like seawater rushing into a capsized boat and he felt himself sinking. He couldn't move and he couldn't speak but he could *feel*, and what he could feel was all the sharks beneath him and beside him, the sharks all around him in the cold pitch dark. Their hard bodies, tight with frozen muscle. The press of fins in his ribs, the scythe-blade sweep of a long tail against his neck. Prickling his skin were teeth, everywhere teeth, all of them seeming to bite as he tried to fight the fear that held him frozen amongst the sharks, so many sharks he was drowning in them, breathing the stink of them – he could breathe, he was still breathing, oh God, oh God – but he couldn't do it properly, was doing it too quick, in/out, in/out, giving him nothing, like he might not be breathing at all, and waves of shock carried him so that his chest rose and fell like a fast tide and all the sharks swum out from him, out from within, and with each attempted breath they wanted back in, *they wanted back in*, and he couldn't… he couldn't…

The paralysis was dragged out of him, pulled like sand and stones by a receding sea, and taking its place before the sharks could fill him was a titanic burst of panic that made him mighty; he thrashed and turned and kicked, beating at a lid that wouldn't open, and as he shoved and shook in his fit of fear the teeth around him opened his skin and cut a low noise out of him, stuttered grunts connecting for a keening growl rising in volume until he was *screaming*, screaming like the sound itself might free him as he tried to beat his way out of a cold darkness filled with sharks that wanted to drown him and eat the flesh that shivered from his bones.

A group of sharks is called a shiver.

Darnell thought of that now as he watched the boy across the road throwing his baseball, catching his baseball. He had the air conditioner running, keeping the temperature in the confines of the car purposefully low.

A shiver of sharks.

A shark's skin was smooth in one direction, but if you rubbed it the wrong way you got that sandpaper roughness he'd felt as a child because a shark's skin is made up of placoid scales that point back to the tail, tiny teeth-like formations called dermal denticles that help reduce friction as the shark swims.

Even its skin was all teeth.

The chill in the car had raised the hairs on Darnell's arms. He rubbed them, one way and then the other. What was skin, anyway? The cells on the surface were dead already, shedding to replace themselves until no one was the same person they once were, not on the outside.

Some sharks shed and replace so many teeth that they get through 50,000 in a lifetime.

Darnell watched the boy play. He wondered if he had many friends and thought, of course he does. A white boy in Edgartown would have lots of friends. This whole place was once Amity, friendship by definition. A place where you could give a beach a racist name and watch it stick throughout the years. Where people like Darnell were only welcomed as friends if they had money to spend, and even then not for long, thank you. Hurry up, we're waiting for you to leave.

The sky was sharkskin grey with held rain, and though he had the windows closed, the smell of the sea came to Darnell thick and tangy. It tasted like something spoiled. Like childhood.

He looked at the boy and then the house behind him. White clapboard façade, large windows, a white fence that might as well have been fucking picket, all of it ghostly in the fading light. He'd only known the upper floor of a shared house, growing up, and when they moved across to the mainland they downsized again while his father looked for work. It didn't help that Darnell's sessions with doctors had cost them, as had his medication, and they could never afford either for long. His father would rage about the film people and white people and everyone else he blamed for Darnell's terrors, including Darnell himself once he'd blamed all the rest. "You gotta be strong, boy. You gotta hit back and hit back harder. Show them they're messing with the wrong—"

With the wrong N-word.

Darnell's father had been so angry, all of the time, right up until he was too old to hold it anymore and it killed him, that's what Darnell thought. It ate him up from the inside.

If you cut a shark open and throw it back to sea, it will rip itself to pieces and devour itself.

A lot of the time, therapy had felt just like that. A self-feeding frenzy of anxieties and emotions once you've opened the box you locked them in.

Darnell had come out of the dark of that freezer like he was surfacing from deep water, cold and gasping for breath. He didn't remember the lid opening, or the sudden light, just that eventually he realised he was being carried. He didn't remember being lifted out from that icy shiver of sharks, but he remembered being carried, knees to his chest. Like he'd fallen asleep in his father's truck.

When a reporter managed to sneak a peek at the mechanical monstrosity to be used in the film's finale, a security guard was fired. There was no such punishment for anyone after what had happened to Darnell. A prank gone too far, an accident, that was all, and where was Darnell's father anyway when it happened? Of course, Darnell's father had raged, threatening violence, and his mother had threatened legal recourse they couldn't afford, and eventually they did receive a little keep-quiet money as compensation, but it didn't last long. It certainly didn't cover all of the help Darnell would need.

He was given a screen-print tee.

By the end of September, almost all signs that the film had ever been made were gone. Quint's boat was still around, and the barge they'd used to film from, out on the water, but apart from that and a few newer cars on the roads, a few newer boats, the island went back to how it had always been, and life carried on as it always had.

Except for Darnell. Thanks to Brad.

"Hey, Dad."

The kid across the street threw his ball to the man stepping out from the house who caught it effortlessly, as if he was always going to pluck a ball from the air right there.

"Hey, Roger Clemens. Better get your butt inside. Getting dark."

The resemblance between father and son was striking. Not that Darnell had needed to see Brad again to confirm he had the right place; looking at his son was like looking back through time. Like looking at the same kid twice. They were ghosts of each other, in different ways.

Brad put his hands on his hips to watch his younger self pitch a ball to the sky and the gesture spread his jacket open. Darnell saw the uniform beneath and was not surprised because –

bull sharks were the most dangerous of sharks, the most aggressive

– because of course Brad was a cop. *Of course* he was.

But shit, it didn't change nothing.

"How about we catch a few together tomorrow, you and me?"

The ball came back down; a star falling to the kid's mitt.

"K."

He threw the ball back up to the dark.

"Maybe we could go down to the cages?"

The boy kept his eyes to the sky, mitt snug to his chest until he knew where to put it, and said, "K."

Darnell found he had as much hate for their easy relationship as he did for what was done to him all those years ago. The relationship he'd had with his father had never been the warmest, but after the sharks it was never anything, though the man forever directed the course of Darnell's life. And though he understood how the world worked, how it belonged to the great white man – he'd endured countless discriminations his whole life, just as his father had – it was to this particular one that his hatred held fast. And there he stood, with no idea of what Darnell had lost because of him. He just waded through life, kicking up sand from the seabed and paying no attention to the mess he left behind.

As he passed his son, Brad swiped the Red Sox cap from his head –

"Hey!"

– and tossed it back, saying, "Inside, kiddo, before your mom gets home."

I should have punched you, Darnell thought. Right on the nose.

A police cruiser pulled up at the sidewalk and someone inside called a greeting to the kid in the yard as Brad opened the door and dropped into the car. The kid waved and there was a blerp of siren in reply. A quick flash of the lights as they went, like bioluminescence in the wet air.

Darnell had managed to put a lot of what happened behind him, but it was always there. Coming back had not helped. You had to keep moving forwards to live. All he'd done was chum the waters and now something worse than his terrors had surfaced, dorsal-sleek and sharp with teeth. It fought to come out, bulging its way from his mouth until he grew tired of pushing it back in, pushing it back down.

He wasn't here for revenge. He was an instrument of karma, that was all. A wave some 40 years building, ready to smash up against the shore.

The boy continued to play, even as a light rain began to fall. Darnell turned on the wipers so he could keep watching the boy throw and catch his ball. Up it went, and down it came. Inevitable.

The male great white matures at around nine, ten years of age. They have teeth as early as embryos and eat their siblings in the womb. From the outset, before they are even born, they are as dangerous as their parents.

Darnell looked into the rearview and saw, behind him, sitting upright in the backseat, his father. A chill, colder than the air con, settled over him and he closed his eyes. He felt the sharks pressing their icy bodies close, fighting to bite, to strip skin from flesh and flesh from cold, white bones.

When he opened his eyes and looked again his father was gone.

Grief was how you drowned. Better to be a shark.

He knew what he had to do.

Most shark attacks occurred in shallow water. Exactly where you thought yourself safe. Like in your front yard.

This time when he looked in the mirror all he saw was himself. His eyes were full. Lifeless eyes, black eyes. The descending dark filled his car and the cold shadows enveloped him, slipping over him like sharkskin he could wear as armour.

He who makes a beast of himself loses the pain of being a man.

The windshield wipers slowed –

thump-thump…

thump-thump…

– as a cloudy rime of ice crackled across the glass, and a quiet voice from somewhere behind him said, "Action."

Darnell stepped out into the wet, the frosty drop in temperature following him from the car. The door shut behind him with the finality of a freezer's lid.

Alerted by the noise, the boy paused in his play and looked at Darnell.

"I like your hat," Darnell said as he approached.

He smiled.

He showed the boy his teeth.

|Painted Wolves|

~

I've seen things few other people in the world have ever seen. And it's a pretty big world, you know. The expression 'small world' is a bullshit expression used to explain coincidence, if you believe in that sort of thing. I know *you* don't, Jenny. "Everything happens for a reason," you said once. As if it's part of some plan. But whose? I don't know. I believe in Darwin. If there's a God, and if He has a plan, then He not only works in mysterious ways but cruel ones, too. I've travelled a lot of the world in this business, and it's a bloody *big* world, and it's beautiful, absolutely beautiful, but it's fucking brutal. We're all part of that.

When the sun came up today I was thinking about how lucky I was to see the things I see. We were looking down at those zebras. You were drinking from a bottle of water. Tony and Eddie were prepping their cameras. The sky was lightening into shades of red and you said, "red sky at night", which didn't make much sense at the time because it was morning. Later you told me the rest of it: red sky at night, shepherd's delight, red sky in the morning, shepherd's warning. You didn't know what it meant, though. Anyway, I was watching the sun rise and I was glad to see it, and I was watching you, and I was glad for that as well, and all around us Africa woke up. The rising sun brought the volume up with it, wildlife waking in a rich medley of calls and caterwauls. You didn't have to be a sound technician to appreciate it.

"Beautiful," you said.

Eddie clapped – "Okay, let's go," – and we took our positions. You put one foot on a rock, hands on your knee, and watched the sun fatten into a fuller shape, all for the camera. I remember wondering how many of our future viewers would watch the sunrise and how many would focus on the way your shorts clung to the curves you made in that pose. You knew I was looking. You knew we all were.

"Africa," you said, turning to face the camera. "Still very much a wild continent, even in Kruger National Park. Perhaps *especially* in the park. Here, over a thousand different species exist together in a purposeful circle of—"

"Perpetual."

"Perpetual. Fuck."

Tony swore, too. I let the furry shape of the microphone dip into shot while I rested my arms (you take every opportunity) and you apologised to Eddie.

"Go again."

Your face was red in the glow of the rising sun. "Africa. Still very much a wild continent…"

This time you messed up the name of the park.

"Fuck, fuck, *fuck!*"

"Gee, do we need to have the sun coming up as she says it?" Tony asked.

"There's always tomorrow," I offered.

"No," said Eddie. "There isn't. We lost too much time with the lions. Come on, go again."

The sun was almost up, drifting away from the horizon to add a bloody colour to the soil of—

"Africa…"

∽

"Fucking *cunt!*"

Tony peered into one of his cameras. Some dirt had gotten in despite his precautions. I remember you covering your ears, claiming, "Ladies present," though we'd all seen your *Big Brother* footage and knew better.

"Fucking *Africa!*" Tony yelled. Fucking Africa got its own back, though, and Tony jerked his head down with a squint and another, "*Fuck*," rubbing wind-blown dirt from his eyes.

You laughed, I remember that too. Tony glared. You covered your mouth with both hands.

The others didn't like you much. You have to remember, the three of us had worked together for a while, sharing tents and toilet paper in some right God-awful places. Then you came along. We get our biggest gig with guaranteed TV time but there's a condition attached and the condition is you. "Time to put a pretty face in front of the camera," they told us. "No more voiceover." Admittedly, your celebrity status, such as it was, gave us something of an Anti-Attenborough advantage. Tony and Eddie both admitted that much, at least, even if they did call you 'the tits with the script'. One of the magazines said of *Park Life*, "I'm sure there will be lots of interesting animals, but most eyes will be on the beautiful creature that is Jenny Friars." You pretended to hate it, said it was sexist and patronising, but you didn't mean it. It would get you more work and us more viewers, and you understood that. All we had to do was film the damn thing.

"Calm down, mate," Eddie said. He was squatting at the stove with a sandwich on a stick, making jaffles. Real food, apparently. Just Eddie being the typical Australian, I suppose, only happy when burning food over an open flame. He was a canyoneer with legs like a rugby player and muscled everywhere else from years of carrying heavy gear. He was spooning something from a can to his mouth even as he cooked.

"I hate this country," Tony told him.

"You hate every country we film in."

"Yeah, well, every country makes it difficult for me." He puffed breath at the lens and tilted it to catch the light.

Tony and I had worked together on a series called *Rainforest* and after that we'd done *Outback*. With *Rainforest* we picked up a dose of dengue fever and botfly. With *Outback* we picked up Eddie.

"You okay, Tom?"

You asked me that a lot. When you looked up, you smiled. I'd been staring at your midriff as you tied a knot into the front of your shirt. I suppose you must have noticed. I tried to smile back but you had a way of making it feel crooked, like I'd forgotten how.

"Hot enough?" you asked.

A more confident man would have turned that into some sort of flattering joke, directing the 'hot enough' back at you somehow, but me, I just laughed and wiped the sweat from my brow. My shirt would be soaked before breakfast. You, though, you wore yours with a sort of serenity. Even khaki looked good on you.

"Hey, Tom," Eddie called, "chuck me my bag, mate."

Do you remember asking me why I let him push me around? It was the 'mate'. Every time Eddie said 'mate', it didn't feel so bad. "He's okay," I'd told you, "once you get to know him."

"You just mean he's a dick but I'll get used to it."

I'd laughed. You knew a bit about people and how to put up with them, I suppose. Seemed that way, on *Big Brother* I mean, but that might just have been the way it was presented. That's the thing with TV stuff. It's all about the editing.

Tennyson once wrote that nature was "red in tooth and claw", and it's true. I've seen it. In Africa alone I've seen a baby giraffe pulled to pieces by a pack of hyenas, a wildebeest split apart in a crocodile tug of war, and an elephant brought down by a pack of hungry lions. I know it's supposed to be a *pride* of lions but when you're sitting in the middle of it, 'pack' feels far more appropriate. Pride suggests a nobility that just isn't there. It's hard to see a lion as the king of beasts when his mane is matted with blood where he can't lick it clean. If he's a king, he's a savage one.

Following that herd of zebra, we were actually hoping for some of that tooth and claw. We'd filmed them interacting, of course, their feeding habits, social activity, but really we were waiting for something else. They're beautiful creatures, zebra. Serene. Born to be on the screen, it seems, but doomed to be prey. *That's* what we were waiting for.

And that was what we got.

You were the first to notice it happening. "They've seen something," you said. "Or maybe they've heard something."

You were right.

Eddie pointed. "Look."

"Beautiful," said Tony.

In the grass, rising from the dusty ground, was a motley mix of colour. Orange, red, brown, and black, all of it blending together in dirty patches. Spots of colour like rusty stains.

"And there. Look."

"How many's that? Ten? Twelve?"

African hunting dogs. Wild dogs. *Lycaon pictus*, or 'painted wolf'. A formidable group of them, too. They're small, but what they lack in strength they more than make up for in numbers.

By the time we had the cameras on them they were trotting towards the herd of zebras at a steady six, maybe seven, miles per hour.

"They're picking up the pace," I said.

The herd saw them and fled.

"Look, look, there they go!" You checked to see which of the cameras was on you and turned back to face the action. I had the boom pole overhead, ready for whatever you might say.

"They've singled one out."

The African hunting dog is a pack hunter. With agile prey like gazelles or impala, they have to be, flankers cutting off escape routes and narrowing the choices of their prey. With the zebra, though, it's a straight chase.

"Look at them go!"

The pack focussed their attention on one of the young females. When the first of the dogs leapt you startled me with a sharp gasp. The dog tore into the zebra as it landed, dragging its claws across the animal's hide as it slid back down over the rump. It was kicked away by a rear hoof as the zebra fled but rejoined the chase as a new lead dog attacked, leaping to grab hold of the zebra's muzzle. It sank its teeth into the soft sensitive flesh of the zebra's mouth and clawed at the face. With its head forced down, the zebra slowed enough that the other dogs could attack its hind legs, clawing at the muscle, piling onto its back. They tumbled together in a cloud of dust and a high cry of pain from the zebra. There was a mad scrabbling as the zebra tried to stand, dogs tearing at its flesh, but it was too late. It had been too late from the moment it hit the ground. One of the dogs got hold of an ear, more by accident than design, and tore it free. Worse than this, though, the soft flesh of the zebra's underbelly was exposed. We watched as the animal was disembowelled alive, the pack clawing out its insides as the poor beast kicked for all it had left. One of the dogs actually burrowed its way into the stomach. Two others yanked at the legs, making a wide V of them until eventually one was torn free from the body. And still the zebra struggled, writhing and rolling as best it could beneath a mass of dirt-furred bodies. I was relieved when one of them finally clutched the zebra's throat closed in its mouth and yanked the animal dead.

We actually celebrated, do you remember? Eddie, Tony, you, me; we all gave muted congratulations, hissed a quiet "yes!" of success and high-fived like we'd played a part in the spectacle ourselves. I guess we had, in a way: we'd watched and done nothing. Nothing but film it, anyway. But the African hunting dog, the wild dog, is one of the world's most efficient and *elusive* predators and we had caught the entire thing on film. It was amazing, something to put us with the heavy hitters. Shit, even *Planet Earth* hadn't caught a wild dog kill on camera. It was just luck, really. Ours, not the zebra's. We'd been in the right place at the right time, that was all. It would've happened whether we'd been there to see it or not.

Although we'd been quiet with our congratulations, something aroused the attention of the dogs. Maybe the wind changed. They looked over at us, a dozen or so animals all at once. It was eerie, that shared reaction. They didn't run, not with a fresh kill, but they watched us as we watched them. One of them held the zebra's severed tail limp in its mouth. It was a great shot.

Nature, red in tooth and claw. Caught on film.

"But the African hunting dog is also a very social animal…"

My words, your voice, right to the camera as we filmed follow up footage. With some animals the violence didn't necessarily end after the main event – there could be fighting over the carcass – but the dogs, they shared their spoils equally. Even a latecomer who had missed the hunt was provided for.

The remaining zebras stood grazing, not very far away at all. They could probably see what the dogs were doing if they looked but they kept their heads down, safe for the time being as the dogs ate and played and napped.

"Let's do that again without the but," Eddie said, covering other editing choices; the kill may have been the first thing we filmed but it wouldn't necessarily be the first thing you saw by the time it hit the screen.

"Why, what's wrong with my butt?"

You turned your back to the camera and bumped your behind left and right, shimmying it down in a provocative wiggle. This was the Jenny we knew from *Big Brother*. A little bit of z-list celebrity, shining through, wanting to be a star.

"Fuck's sake, Jenny."

Tony had only been filming for a few minutes but he was already getting irritable. A few minutes feels a lot longer when you're lugging camera equipment around under an African sun. I was feeling the same strain. I had the sound mixer in my shoulder satchel, cans clamped over my ears, and the boom pole raised so that the armpits of my shirt were exposed for all to see just how much I was feeling the heat.

You did that thing where you wipe a hand down over your face, straightening your expression into something more serious. 'Emotional re-set' you called it. Or Davina did. Someone.

"The African hunting dog is a very social animal…"

Occasionally, as you spoke, one of the dogs would raise its head from where it dozed with the pack or look back from where it stood panting in the dry air. Did you feel them watching? I did. I can still feel them, even now. All the way down here. Their breath is hot on my skin.

It happens to everyone at some point, I'm told. This connection between man and animal. A friend of mine once saw an elephant brought down by lions in the dead of night. He watched the whole thing unfold in green-tinged light on a night monitor and it stayed with him forever after. Elephants bleat, did you know that? My friend used to hear that sound in the dark whenever he tried to sleep, an elephant's bleating struggle as a tawny carpet of lions writhed on its body. Someone else I'd known a few years ago saw a komodo dragon bite a buffalo then stalk it for days until the poison claimed it. You're not supposed to interfere in this job. You just let it happen and record it, impartial, as nature runs its course. But it gets to you sometimes. I mean, how natural is it to watch something suffer and do nothing?

Not that there's anything I could have done. Not about the dogs. Not about any of it.

"…prowling for prey in highly organised units, or simply relaxing together, howling in play."

I liked the rhyme of that. It chimed well. Prowling and howling. Prey and play.

"Good," said Eddie. "Now the other way around."

You turned your back to the camera again – "Like this?" – and began reciting the same lines. I don't know if you were joking or not but Tony made no attempt to hide his frustration either way. "Christ, Jenny, stop pissing about."

The narration felt clunky second time.

"Okay, cut there," said Eddie.

I brought my arms down with relief and you stepped away from the descending microphone, exaggerating your dodge and ducking dramatically with a cry of, "Watch it!"

The dogs skittered. They didn't move far, but they were suddenly alert and looking our way.

Nobody said anything. Your smile disappeared without needing an emotional re-set.

We waited.

Slowly, one by one, the dogs began to leave. They took as much of the carcass as they could carry.

"Shit."

"Film me," you said, motioning to us all with beckoning hands, "film me, film me."

"Jenny—"

But Eddie had his camera up and so Tony followed suit. Eddie said, "The dogs," and Tony turned to film them walking away.

"The pack moves in single file, the alpha male leading, but for much of the day they will sleep the heat away in the shade…"

And so on, as you improvised a way for us to edit the footage together. Eddie encouraged you with quick hand-rolling gestures and I tried to think some script your way. You even shifted your position, squatting down in the dirt so the shot could look like a separate occasion, gesturing behind as if the dogs were still sitting somewhere nearby. It was good.

"In Kruger National Park, there is a predator easily identified by the blotchy colours of its coat. Shades of orange, brown, and black, with a long tail tipped in white, this is the 'painted wolf', better known as the African hunting dog…"

I kept glancing at them. The heat rising from the ground turned them into wavery shapes, phantoms, and before long they were gone altogether.

~

"You okay, Tom? Want some water?"

You tried to pass me your own bottle but I had little chance to take it, grabbing wildly at the side of the truck instead as we bounced high and came down hard. We always sat in the back with the equipment, you and me, because we were the smallest. Even as cramped as it was we spent a lot of our travel time up in the air and then slamming our behinds. We got banged around a lot making sure the equipment didn't.

"Woah! That was a good one. Here."

I took the water, more because you'd offered than because I was thirsty.

"Do you think we got enough back there?"

You were worried you'd screwed up.

"We got enough," I said. "We'll probably only use three minutes or so."

"Really?"

"Yeah. Probably just the kill, and a little bit of what came after. Lucky we were running behind schedule or we might have missed it."

You smiled, and said, "Everything happens for a reason."

"Yeah. I suppose it does."

Eddie slowed the truck. I looked around in case he'd spotted something and I thought maybe—

"What's going on?" You had to shout to Eddie over the sound of the engine.

"Dogs," I said.

But after a quick look you shook your head.

I couldn't see them either. The sky was taking on a darker hue. The sun was going down, a trick of its light and heat making one end seem squashed as it slipped below the horizon. Shadows were growing long and dark around us.

"Looking for a camp spot," Eddie yelled back.

"But the caves are so close. We might as well keep going."

"Not in the dark."

"You've driven at night before."

"Yeah, but it's rockier now, and I don't really want to be fixing a tyre again, not out here. Not at night."

We were already on our last very-patched spare, and the early hours of evening increased the risk of puncture, maybe worse, thanks to the poor visibility.

"But it's okay to *camp* here at night?"

You had a good point. "I'm sleeping in the truck," I said.

"I'm done with sleeping in the fucking truck," Eddie said.

And of course, Tony supported that. "Nothing to be scared of here," he said, "There's nothing but us."

"Well, I think I'll join Tom in the truck." You smiled. "If that's okay with you?"

As if it wouldn't be.

In the early days of the shoot, sleeping had been difficult. Do you remember? We'd been following those lions, sleeping whenever they did, which often meant during the day, which always meant we were hot and sweating and attracting flies and not actually sleeping much at all. In the open bed of the truck there wasn't much protection against the incessant buzzing of flies *or* their frequent landings. Not much protection against lions, either, for that matter, though they turned out to be rather dull. Placid. Did you ever play that game, sleeping lions? We used to play it at school. You had to lay down and pretend to sleep while someone else played hunter, moving among the sleeping lions and trying to get them to move. You weren't supposed to touch them but you could get close and whisper, say things to make them stir. Of course, we couldn't do that, not with real lions. We took turns napping at night, but following lions over the rise and fall of Africa made that nearly impossible, and even when we were able to stop driving for a while the lions growled constantly. A low, throaty sound. Engines in muscled flesh. All of it made everybody tired and irritable. A bit tense, as well.

It was like that the night after the dogs, too. Unpacking the truck, setting up camp, I could feel a building growl, and little irritations flitted around like flies.

"If only we had a heli-gimble," Tony said, looking back the way we'd come. Thinking of the dogs, probably.

"If only you'd stop saying that."

That got you the middle finger without him so much as glancing around. From me, a smile, but I doubt you noticed.

"If only we had a helicopter to mount the heli-gimble on, eh?"

That was the best I could do.

Tony was right, though; it would have been a great bit of kit to have. Three-sixty-degree filming, good long shots, good *close-ups* from even a kilometre away... But bloody expensive, and we were still low budget. None of this 'three years in the making' with us. No slow-motion predator action or time-lapse prey decay.

I was setting up a light in the back of the truck, along with a monitor and one of the cameras we did have. I wanted to check the infrared for when we were in the caves. I wanted to distract myself.

"You all right, Tom?"

"Hm? Yeah, I'm fine. Just, you know..." I held up a memory card, titled and dated, adding the details to the index in my notebook. If I didn't do it, nobody would.

Eddie glanced at us. "He's not fine," he said. "That kill got to him. What's wrong, mate? Tooth and claw and all that shit, remember?"

That annoyed me. Partly because he was right, it *had* bothered me, but also because until that moment the distraction had been working just fine.

"You're either spots or stripes in this world. Dog or a zebra. Sad, but true."

"I'm fine," I said again. "Looking forward to the caves."

That was a lie, but I thought it would change the subject because Eddie was looking forward to them. A seasoned canyoneer, much of his campfire talk had been of his hikes and climbs in the Australian Blue Mountains. Sorry, the 'Blueys'. Not really mountains but a plateau eroded into mountainous shape. Anyway, it worked, although he quickly turned the conversation around to one of his 'Nam stories, climbing around the caves of the Annamite Mountains. He'd also explored some of the Hang Son Doong in Phong Nhake Bang which was supposed to be our next stop after Africa. The Hang Son Doong, or 'mountain river cave', is the biggest cave passage ever measured. The Echo Caves, though, are some of the *oldest* caves in the world. They haven't been fully measured yet and we had special permission to explore further than any of the offered tours.

"You really staying in the truck?" Tony asked. I was spreading my sleeping bag out on the floor near the monitors. I shrugged.

You tossed your bag to me as well.

"Let us warn you about Tom, love," Eddie said, but that was all I heard. I looked up to see him making a tiny hook with his little finger. Tony laughed.

"Never had any complaints," I said.

You gave me your most dazzling smile yet, said, "Tom, you sly dog," and I remember thinking *this* is what I need to be like? This is how I get you to notice me?

"Friend of mine did this cave a few years back," Eddie told us. "For *Planet Earth*, I think. Gomantong. You guys see it?"

I knew the episode and nodded with Tony.

"Yeah," Eddie said. "Gomantong." He smiled at me. "That was full of shit, too."

Tony roared with laughter.

"No offence, mate," Eddie said.

I ignored Eddie to look at you. You gave us all a sort of half-smile. "I don't get it."

"Gomantong cave," Eddie explained. "It's—"

"A shithole."

Stealing his pun was the best I could do for retaliation. He scowled at me but recovered quickly.

"Yeah. It's a shit hole. A cave literally full of shit. Guano. Friend of mine, Scud, good fella, he said that pile of bat crap was a hundred metres high and swarming with all sorts of things. Cockroaches, centipedes, crabs. All sorts of creatures. They never even had to leave the cave. That steaming pile had its own fucking – what do you call it? – ecosystem."

"You ever get crabs from a dirty hole, Eddie?"

I don't think you were sticking up for me. You were trying to get involved in the conversation. The new girl still trying to fit in. We'd talked about it before and you'd compared it to that *Big Brother* house, how it took the group a while to accept anyone new. It's the same with animals, although with animals it can be even more brutal.

Tony and Eddie barely acknowledged your joke before discussing between them the technical difficulties we'd face filming in Echo Caves. I was concerned about the sound quality but of course they were preoccupied with the visuals. One of them said a rope pulley and counterweights would do it, and the other wanted a crane shot, but either way it was going to be a hassle lugging all the equipment around. You sided with Eddie, and Tony said you didn't know what the fuck you were talking about, you were just the tits with the script and you even managed to fuck *that* up. "The script part, anyway."

I said something pathetic like, "Hey, guys, come on," but it worked. Enough to create an awkward silence for a while, at least.

Tony, surprisingly, was the one to finally break it.

"Anybody got a beer?"

It was a joke wearing thin – he'd asked every night so far – but this time it was funny again and I think it was sort of an apology. Maybe that's why you gave me up.

"Tom's got a bottle of something."

Were you still just trying to fit in? Or were you doing your bit to accept his apology? Maybe you were simply deflecting the attention away from yourself for a moment.

"Is that true, Tom? You been holding out on us?"

I'd bought a large bottle of mampoer but I was saving it for celebrating the end of the shoot. I busied myself checking the connection between camera and monitor, pretending not to hear the question. Infrared is invisible to most animals, including humans, but the camera picks it up. I was able to see everybody in the camp even with the lamps off. It was sound that would be a problem in the cave.

"What are you doing, mate?" Eddie asked.

"Giving the gear a test run before the caves."

So much for pretending to not hear him.

"He's filming us for the DVD extras," you joked, and everybody laughed. I went along with it, glad some more of the tension was lifting.

"Is Jenny right? About the beer, mate?"

How could I not give it to them?

"Mampoer," I said. At Eddie's puzzled frown I added, "Brandy. Sort of. To celebrate our last day in Africa." I added that as a final attempt to put them off.

"*Brandy?*"

I smiled, and nodded, thinking Eddie's mockery might mean he wouldn't ask for it. And he didn't, because Eddie never asks.

"Let's have it, then," he said. "This is pretty much the last day anyway."

Everything is green and black when you film at night. Your skin was green on the screen. Eddie and Tony, too, though their eyes, looking at you, were dark pools of shadow. Shark eyes. You were crouching, doing an impression of Attenborough as if he was stalking around the campsite; good enough so we knew who you were doing but bad enough that it was funny. I'm half convinced it's how you got this gig in the first place, because you did the exact same thing in the *Big Brother* house for one of their challenges or something. Everybody was laughing.

"And *capturing* what has *never* been seen be*fore*, not even by *us* at the BBC, with all our budget and big names like *me*... an *Af*rican *wild* dog hunt."

"Fuck yeah," said Tony, raising his cup.

And you, still Jenny-Attenborough, "*Please*, Tony. Watch your *fuck*ing language."

The camera loved you. I zoomed it in.

You seemed to sense what I was doing and struck a provocative pose. "Make sure you get my good side."

"Which side is that?" asked Tony.

"They're all good," said Eddie.

"Aww, thanks, Eddie mate," you said, exaggerating your vowels, switching to Australian, "Not bad for a sheila, eh?" You turned and posed and turned again. Catalogue poses. Magazine parodies. Eddie smiled with his mouth but not with his eyes, not on the black and green screen.

And then behind Eddie, stepping quietly out of the night, was an African hunting dog. I could see it, panting, just over his shoulder. Behind Tony there was another.

"Yeah, that's good. *That's* your good side," said Tony. You were on all fours and looking behind with wide-eyed feigned surprise.

One of the dogs, with its head down, made a single bark at the ground. It was how they called to the pack, drawing them to the echo.

"Don't," I said.

"What was that, mate?"

You were all looking at me now.

"The dogs are back," I said. "They followed us."

Eddie and Tony looked at each other. Eddie took another mouthful of mampoer. "They're miles away."

"No," I said. "They're here."

You couldn't see because of the dark, and because of how the lamps had ruined your night vision. Didn't stop you looking around, though. "Where?"

They were gone.

I checked back and forth between the monitor and the darkness around us. "They were here. They looked… I don't know. They looked hungry."

Tony exaggerated a sigh. "You're not going to start quoting Tennyson again, are you?"

"You're still shook up from the kill," Eddie said, "that's all. There's nothing out there."

He was right. Or half right. I couldn't tell. I panned the camera around but found nothing.

"They must be hiding. Waiting. For the right moment."

"People love to anthropomorphise animals," you said. "You know; project human characteristics onto them. Maybe that's what you're doing?"

'Anthropo-what?" Eddie said. "That's a big word, sweetheart."

You grinned. "Oh, I like them big. The bigger the better."

"Seriously," I said. "The dogs…"

But you waved that away, "Don't worry about them," and teased me with, "I'll take care of you."

"You can take care of all of us," said Tony.

For him, you turned an imaginary crank at your fist to raise your middle finger. "Fuck you, Tony."

He raised his cup. "That's the spirit."

You raised your cup as well, but aimed the smile at me. Were you trying to include me? Or were you just posing for the camera? "To nature," you said. "Red in tooth and claw."

"And a bitch to get on film," said Eddie, tipping his cup to you.

Your eyes were vast dark circles, like the empty cavities of a skull. Caves in your face. I looked away from them and searched again for the dogs. I couldn't see them, not even with the night monitor, but I felt them out there in the dark.

Waiting.

I've seen things few other people in the world have ever seen. I've seen birds of paradise performing their complicated mating dances, flashing their feathers like capes in a fashion show of arousal. I've seen colourful lizards leaping like acrobats to feed on swarms of black fly, a bright rainbow devouring a buzzing cloud. I've seen the peaks of the Himalayas, Ayers Rock, Victoria Falls. I've seen lots of beautiful things.

I've seen you.

But I've also seen a crocodile roll its prey. Heard the thundering chaos of splashing and devouring. Seen Komodo dragons wait patiently for the inevitable, heard them hiss at a buffalo already dying. I've seen a zebra, serene, brought down by dogs that tore at her flesh and burrowed into her body. Seen them shove their way inside and—

"You okay Tom? Where are you?"

You...

    ... you...

        ...you.

Now I can't see anything. The dark here is absolute. But I must be quiet. Sound travels far down in the Mpumalanga escarpment. Down in the Echo Caves.

They exist because of erosion, these caves. Limestone. It covers approximately ten percent of the Earth's surface. Rain shapes it. Rivers sculpt it. The water, slightly acidic and loaded with carbon dioxide from the soil, slowly eats away at the rock. But over time it builds, as well, depositing calcite to make stalactites and stalagmites. It breaks and it builds, it wears down and it hardens, and all of it is very natural.

"Tom?"

I'll not say a word.

In Deer Cave, Borneo, there are three million bats. Three million *at least*, all flapping around in the dark. They use echo-location to navigate, hearing to see. Some animals do away with eyes completely in the caves, that's how dark it is. The Texas cave salamander, for example, devolving so it has no eyes at all. It doesn't have to see a thing. I envy it. Sometimes it's better not to see. There's a cave in New Zealand that has a ceiling of stars, cave constellations held in an underground night sky. These beautiful glowing lights attract insects, drawn in by what they see, but the stars are not stars. The bright lights come from the bodies of glow worms that drop delicate strands of silk to trap their prey, hauling it up like a fisherman's catch.

Safer, sometimes, not to see.

"Tom? It's okay."

But just because you can't see something doesn't mean it isn't there. When oil in the Earth's crust releases hydrogen sulphide, a cave can be filled with dangerous toxic fumes. Poison you can't see. And when it mixes with the oxygen in water you get sulphuric acid, eating away at the world around it. That's how I used to imagine Hell. But Hell is a black and green screen that I'll carry with me forever. It's whimpering sounds, grunting sounds, growling away at my insides. Hell is the things I heard with my eyes closed. It's the sound of wild dogs with prey.

"Thomas!"

My name resounds in the dark and I hear an echo of it fade like the hiss of Komodo dragons.

"You can come out now."

The 'now' echoes in the cave like a series of howls. They surround me. They keep me cowed, hunkered down in the dark.

I won't say a word.

"What do you like most out here?"

I wonder what would have happened if you hadn't asked that question. I wonder if, without that to think about, it would have been a normal night.

"The brandy," said Tony, upending the bottle.

"The wilderness," that's what Eddie said. "All this space and nobody around to watch everything you do. The *freedom* to do whatever you want."

"How about you, Tom?"

I shrugged. "You?"

You didn't hear it as an answer, but then you weren't meant to. You heard the question passed back.

"Same as Eddie, really," you said. "On *Big Brother* people watched everything I did, and most of it was stupid or embarrassing and *really* badly edited. They made me look like a bimbo. I like being a part of something serious now. None of that messing around in front of the camera."

"You've done that," Tony said.

"Exactly."

"I mean you've done that *out here. To*day."

"Hey, come on."

Eddie and Tony laughed.

"Seriously, they made me look like an idiot."

"I thought you looked pretty good," Eddie said.

Tony nodded. "The Jacuzzi," he muttered, but you heard him. You were meant to.

"That was part of a stupid game thing, and we were all drunk."

"*We're* all drunk," Eddie pointed out, though I don't think he was. Not at all.

"Yeah," said Tony, "So let's play a 'stupid game thing'." He spun the empty mampoer bottle. A teenage game. A *Big Brother* game for no one to see but me.

I looked out into the darkness for the dogs. There was nothing at first. A turn of the camera, though, and I had them on the monitor. Two of them, maybe three, standing with their mouths open, panting despite the cool night air. Their eyes flashed from empty black to bright green when I moved the camera over them.

"We can't play that," you said, reaching to stop the bottle. "I'm the only girl."

"I know." Tony moved the bottle away and spun it again. "This is just for deciding who's first."

You laughed. It sounded false to me, but to the others I don't think it made any difference.

You stood. "Right, that's it. Time for bed."

"See," said Eddie, "she gets it."

"Sorry, I've been fucked enough by a film crew already. Good night, boys."

On the screen the dogs were pacing. Agitated. There were lots of them now. Some of them growled. You looked around and I wondered if you'd heard them too but then, "Whoops," said Eddie as if you'd stumbled when really he'd pulled you down to the ground, into his lap. Maybe it was meant to be playful at first, I don't know, but then he gave you that crude grope – "Like that?" – and you clearly didn't; shoving him away should have been answer enough, never mind the way you spat his name. But like I said, Eddie never asked. Maybe he was telling you to like it. Maybe he just meant *he* did.

"Of course," Tony said, "It's only natural."

"Come on, Jenny, nobody'll know."

"No."

I heard you from over by the truck so they must have heard you, too. Even when the dogs started yipping and barking I heard you say no, and no, and I heard you say stop.

But Eddie didn't stop.

And afterwards, neither did Tony.

"Tom? We know you're in here."

I just want you all to leave me alone. So I push my way deeper, groping in the dark, forcing myself into narrow fissures of rock. It's wet, or cold, or both. I can't tell.

"We can wait, Tom. You'll have to come out eventually."

Troglodytes can go months without food. If I go deep enough, maybe I'll find something hungry enough to end this.

There are plenty of things in here with me. There's a baby giraffe. There's a wildebeest. There's an elephant, a buffalo, a zebra. You brought them with you, you must have done. Or maybe I did. They glow like stars that aren't stars, and they thrash and they mewl and they kick, fighting tooth and claw against something unseen. Maybe the darkness. I've seen these throes too many times. Heard them, too. Nature sounds wonderful when the sun's coming up, but it sounds very different in the dark.

"*Tom.*"

Crouching in the darkness, hiding in caves we will never film, I hear the echoes of my name. It bounces my location back to you.

I imagine you surrounded by those others I've seen destroyed. I imagine you leading them, a procession into the dark to find me. A slow and ghostly stampede. I'll be mauled, gouged, rendered to chunks by tooth and nail and claw, crushed and broken by hooves and jaws. You're coming for me, and you're bringing all of them with you.

Teamwork. It's the key to successful mammal behaviour.

What I fear most, though, is that you'll find me and do nothing. That you'll just look at me. Record it in your memory and remain unsatisfied.

Something down here growls. It may have been me.

I can still hear the smacking sounds of flesh against flesh. I can hear the dogs, howling and barking and rutting in the dark.

It would have happened whether I'd been there or not.

There's nothing I could have done.

The things I've seen, the things I've heard. They wear me down, like water on limestone. And they harden me beyond calcite.

These caves are well named: I have become your echo: "No. No. Please. Don't."

Don't...

    ... don't...

        ...don't.

"Don't worry, Tom. Nobody will know."

No...

    ...no...

        ...no.

Rocks scatter under scrambling feet. Yours, mine, theirs. The animals.

"She's coming for me."

Laughter in the darkness. "I dunno about that."

Those sons of bitches.

"Did you film it, Tom?"

You know. You must know. I feel for the memory card in my pocket. Is that what you're after?

"Something for the DVD extras?"

Your words, but I'm no longer sure the voices down here have been yours. Maybe you're pretending to be someone you're not as well.

You're either spots or stripes in this world. Someone said that once. Was it you? Dogs or zebra. Predator or prey. But they get mixed up don't they? Plus tigers are striped, so that fucks up the analogy. It helps them hide. Helps them blend in.

But I'm no tiger. I'm a sleeping lion. You're just trying to get me to move and make a sound. You stir things up, that's what you do. Something you did, something you said, it stirred something up. In Eddie, in Tony. In all of us. Woke something. A sleeping dog best left lying.

I am Gomantong Cave. I'm full of shit.

"It's just nature, Tom."

"Come on, mate."

Come on. Mate.

I hear the dogs in here with me. They howl. And eventually, just as before…

I'll join in.

|In the Shadow of the Lightning Tree|

The ground had been baked hard and the long grass dried brown. The field rose only gently, the very slightest of inclines, but under the sun on such a clear day it was enough to make Will sweat. He could feel the damp in his armpit. He was carrying the cooler. Demi had insisted on carrying the hamper, even though it was heavier, the amount of food they'd packed. She carried it with both hands. She was wearing the summer dress he liked because of how the skirts flowed around her thighs in a breeze, though there was no breeze today. A large hat kept her shaded. Sunglasses protected her eyes. Hid them from Will.

"Not so fast, Lucy! Wait!"

A shrill quality had crept into Demi's voice whenever she spoke to Lucy. And always when she spoke there was a warning or reprimand or both, even if it wasn't in the words themselves.

The girl was only a little way in front, but she slowed her walk. She was kicking at the ground, occasionally jumping on the spot, mannerisms Will recognised from when she played in the rain. She was watching the dust rise up around her feet, enjoying the novelty of the summer's heatwave.

"Lucy," Will said. Not because she needed reining in but because Demi needed to hear his support.

Demi shifted the hamper to one hand so she could squeeze Will's briefly with the other. She was pretending not to struggle with what she carried.

Lucy turned to wave at them. I heard you, the wave said. I'm okay. She had dressed as much like her mother as possible, with flowers on her dress and a large hat, though her sunglasses were a sharp bright yellow, the lenses shaped like cats. Nine lives, thought Will. Imagine that.

"She asked about a kitten again yesterday, on the way to school," he said.

Demi said nothing in reply. Eventually, she gave him a huff of breath and said, "It's hot."

"You okay with that?"

Demi hefted the hamper. "I'm fine."

It wasn't just food. Lucy's things were in there, too, because she didn't want to wear her backpack today and she was discovering she could get away with things like that at the moment.

"Lucy!" Will yelled. "That way, honey." He pointed to the only tree in the field, and she diverted her course seemingly without looking.

"We'll have some shade up there," Will said.

The tree was old and leafless, bleached to a tan colour so pale it was almost grey.

"Looks haunted," Demi said.

Will laughed and looked at her, surprised by a joke, but her face remained sombre because of course it wasn't a joke. Everywhere was haunted to Demi now, even places they'd never been.

"It's a good spot," Demi said.

An apology. Will wanted it again. "Yeah?"

"Yeah," she said. "No roads."

No roads. No anything. They had the whole field to themselves.

At the tree, much of the ground was bare, hard-packed and cracked. Demi set the hamper down and wiped her hands on her skirts.

Lucy was peering into where some of the bark had split. A jagged scar had divided the tree.

"Miss Dyson says that trees get hit by lightning so you shouldn't stand under them when it rains unless it's been hit by lightning before because if it has then it won't happen again."

"Come and eat, sweetheart."

Lucy leapt over to them, a sequence of jumps, trying for as few as possible. "Three!" she announced.

"Are you sure?" Will asked. He was playing for time while Demi set out Tupperware and cling-filmed plates.

Lucy jumped back to the tree, counting aloud this time.

"I packed the blanket underneath," Demi said as they set food aside, colouring books, a cuddly cat toy. The frisbee.

She lingered with the frisbee. Lucy must have packed it.

"Can we play?" Lucy asked.

Demi stood, but not with the frisbee. "Maybe later." She shook out the blanket and dragged it back down to the ground. Will thought of a matador.

"Come and eat," Demi said.

Lucy went straight over the blanket for the cakes. She'd spied their bright frosting through the plastic container.

"Sandwiches first," Demi said.

To her credit, Lucy didn't pout, protest, or persist; she took a paper plate and began eying up the sandwich options. Tiny triangles, but with the crusts still on because, as Lucy liked to point out, she was a big girl now. She lifted the bread to inspect the contents. Satisfied, she loaded her plate and sat on the blanket to eat.

Before Demi could tell her to move, to make way for the food, Will began setting out the plates around her, making a joke of it. In moments, Lucy was surrounded. She would be the centre they moved around, now. He took a juice box from the cooler and pressed it to Lucy's bare leg. She squealed and giggled and fidgeted at how cold it was. Will only moved it to her other leg, and she collapsed back as if tickled.

"Lucy!"

She'd crushed a plateful of crisps and squashed the quiche.

"My fault," Will said.

Lucy tried to look at the back of her dress. Demi tried to save the quiche.

"Honey, it was me."

But Lucy was sullen now, and Demi was snatching up plates of food and moving them more quickly than she needed to.

"It was my fault," Will said again, but no one was listening.

Will set the juice box down near Lucy's lap. He glanced at his watch. They would share at least an hour here together. Lucy needed more than the tiny garden to play in. Demi needed more than the quiet house.

"Can I have a cake now?"

"What's the magic word?"

"Will, she's barely touched what she has already."

"Can I have a cake now, *please?*"

"Eat one more sandwich and then you can have a cake."

Lucy pushed a whole triangle into her mouth. It was so sudden, so eager, that it surprised a laugh from both adults. Lucy didn't understand why but she laughed as well, keen to be a grown-up too. Her mouth was still full of sandwich.

Demi peeled back the lid from the cakes and offered the tub. Lucy took a cake and when her mother put the container down she took another.

"Hey, young lady," said Demi, "one at a time."

"The blue one's for Danny because blue's his favourite."

It was as sudden and surprising as the stuffed sandwich, only it worked the opposite way. Will released all the breath he had in one exhalation then covered his mouth as if there was more he might lose. Demi slumped where she sat, turning her body away from them.

"*What?* Blue's his *favourite.*"

"I know, honey. Eat the yellow one, okay?"

"What's wrong with mummy?"

"Nothing, sweetheart."

"What did I do?"

"Nothing."

"Mummy?"

"Your mother's okay. She'll be okay. Now eat your cake, Loopy Loo."

Lucy took a mouthful of yellow icing. She looked at her mother's back and watched how her shoulders shook.

Will wrapped the squashed quiche so that he had something to do. He put it back in the hamper. The frisbee sat at the bottom. He looked at Demi who was trying not to cry and he left it there.

"Do you want to do some colouring in, now?" Will asked Lucy.

"Yes."

"Yes, what?"

"Yes please."

Will handed her one of the colouring books and a packet of felt tips. "Go sit in the sun for a bit," he said. "The light will be better."

"Okay."

"Wait."

He handed her a juice box and a new paper plate with some apple pieces and grapes. She held it like she'd seen waiters do on TV and carried it out of the shade, colouring book and pens tucked under her other arm.

"I can't, Will," Demi said when he sat beside her.

"Yes, you can."

"Sometimes I think I can, but I can't."

"You're doing fine."

She leaned against him and let him hold her.

Lucy lay on the dry grass, the colouring book spread open before her and the pen in her hand rubbing backwards and forwards too quickly to be doing anything neat. Will watched her swapping colours. Watched her flick the pages whenever a picture bored her.

"How do you not fall apart?"

She said it quietly. More to herself, Will thought, than to him. But he heard it. He heard the tone. Maybe an accusation.

"Daddy!"

Both parents were quick to look up, but the urgency was only a desperate need to play. Lucy was standing in the sun, a paper plate tucked in the crook of her elbow, ready to throw.

"Lucy, don't."

"It's okay, Demi." Will stood, ready to catch it.

"If you throw that, you'll be littering."

"Go on, sweetheart, I'm ready."

Lucy threw the plate. She hadn't mastered the flick of the wrist yet and threw with her whole arm. Sometimes it meant the throw went wide. Sometimes it meant the frisbee turned vertical, rolling through the air like a thin wheel. Rolling on the ground, across the pavement, into the…

But Will caught it this time. Nobody had to run for it, grab for it, chase it away.

"Lucy!"

"Demi, it's fine."

"I said not to throw it."

"But I *caught* it."

She stared at him but whatever pain she had to show was lost behind her sunglasses and he didn't know how to respond.

Demi began packing up the picnic. "She always gets what she wants."

Lucy was standing where the tree's shadow met the grass. She held herself in a hug and turned left and right. She'd started doing this if her parents fought, or cried, or did anything they didn't usually do like shout or stare at her.

"Show me your colouring in, sweetheart, yeah?" Will said. "Let's see."

He stepped out from the cool of the tree's reach and into the sun and was suddenly so much warmer at his daughter's side. He sat at her feet and picked up the colouring book. "Which one's your favourite?"

She sat beside him and leant into his lap where he flicked slowly through the pages.

"That one."

"The cat? But you've not even coloured that one in."

"I don't know what colour it should be yet."

"How about… yellow?"

"No."

"What about… blue?"

"*Daddy.*"

"With pink spots."

Lucy laughed, then lay on the grass again to sort through her pens.

Will turned the page. He saw a sailing boat on a sea of blue scribbles. On the next page, jagged colours zigzagged through a smiling sun.

"I like this one."

Lucy glanced at it. "Danny did that."

"Did he?"

But Lucy was too busy to answer, or she knew she didn't need to. Will traced the lines with his fingertips, up and down the peaks and troughs that spread further and further apart before turning into a horizontal flat line.

"Did he do any other ones?"

Lucy shrugged and he didn't ask again. He turned the pages, keeping a finger in the book to mark where his son had once coloured a smile, looking for more.

"I'm sorry," said Demi.

She was standing beside him. She held the hamper in one hand. In the other she held a cupcake thick with blue icing.

"I'm sorry," Will said. "It was my fault."

She put the hamper down and squatted next to him. She looked at Lucy.

"Honey, what are you doing?"

Lucy was colouring in. She'd cupped a handful of dry grass into her palm and with the slow strokes of a felt tip pen, she coloured them.

"Sweetheart?"

"The grass is all dead because it's brown so I'm making it green again."

Demi squeezed Will's thigh.

"It's okay," he said.

"Will, she's getting ink all over her hand."

"I'm making the dead grass better again."

"Lucy, here," Will tried. "Use your colouring book."

"I don't want my colouring book."

"Lucy, stop it. You can't make it better; you're only making it worse."

"Demi—"

"Will, help me."

"I'm trying."

"Lucy, stop. Stop it, Lucy." Then, "You can have a kitten."

Lucy let go of the grass and twisted around to check if her mother was telling the truth. She tested her with, "What colour?"

Demi had no answer. Looking at her, Will said, "Whatever you want."

Lucy said, "Yay!" and dropped her pen and clapped and bounced on the spot.

Demi looked down at the cake she still held. Will looked at the tree that lightning might've struck once. "We'll be okay," he said.

In a world of her own beside them, Lucy was pulling up all the grass she'd coloured green and letting it fall. There was no breeze at all to catch it.

|The Tigers of Myanmar|

~

The General motioned with an impatient jab of his hand for the mirror to be moved, then again when the new position failed to satisfy him. The two soldiers holding it between them awaited further instruction, but this time their *gyoke* merely admired his reflection. He gave no nod of approval, but he made no other gesture to move the mirror, so with only eye contact for communication between them, the soldiers agreed to lean the mirror back against the wall before making a respectful retreat.

The General did not admire his reflection. He examined it. He searched it for signs of weakness. Trying, as he always did when this moment came, to see where death would come for him. To identify where on his body it would strike. The woman never told him. She *could* not, or else she surely would. She only told him that it would come, and that if he did not do as she advised then it would be violent and it would be soon. "There will always be blood," she'd said. "Blood, and fear. You cannot help that now. But do as I advise and the blood will not be yours."

Blood, he thought. *Fear*. But he looked at himself and was not afraid. His uniform was crisp, green as the jungle of his country, and he wore it as a shield against fear. He wore his honours as shields against fear. The laurel bands on the peak of his hat were wards against it. He was an imposing figure. He did not feel fear; he inspired it.

On a silver tray, a fresh slab of meat sat red and wet in its puddle of juices. He picked up the tray and flipped it. Meat slapped the floor – a heavy, singular sound – and glistened beside his polished boots. He stamped his heel upon it, stamped blood from the meat in a sudden splatter. He raised his foot and brought it down hard a second time, a third. He trampled the meat beneath his booted feet, hammered it, twisted the tread of his boots to tear it, grind it, pulp it flat. All part of his *yadaya*. His ritual. Exactly as he had been advised, with only one final action to perform.

He looked again into the full length mirror, drew his sidearm, and fired at the self he saw reflected in the glass.

The blood would never be his.

The morning was thick with held heat, the sun a bright white hole in a hazy sky. A radiant sun. The General stared at it through the tinted window of his car, comfortable in the air conditioning while the people in the streets sweated beneath the burdens they carried to and from the nearby market, their backs wet with exertion and the close proximity of other suffering bodies. Wide cane hats cast dark faces into shade that did little to cool them. Men were bare-chested or wore their linen jackets open, *longyis* hitched up to the waist. The women wore floral patterns but each *htamain* was far from fresh. The General saw saffron robes and he saw military uniforms. He saw far too many foreigners, but was pleased to see fewer Chinese. 100,000 had left so far. It was a good start. There were still too many people, though, crowds of them filling the streets, and the traffic moved slowly, adding engine heat and exhaust fumes to the stifling humidity of the city. Hard to believe this was once the Golden Land. Hard to imagine forests of teak and ebony where elephants roamed and tigers stalked, where sapphires and rubies winked and glittered like stars in your cupped hands. And yet…

There. Moving among the people. There were still tigers to be seen if you were the right person to see them. This one passed among the people unseen by all but the General. Graceful, weaving left, weaving right, pressing between the people of the crowd. Serene despite the heat, as if its fur was as cool as amber, its stripes dark vents to cool its growling engine as it padded through stilled traffic, turning its body between vehicles. Tigers had a quick and brutal strength and they influenced all other life here. They were a good omen. A powerful sign. The General watched the tiger as it paused, watched it yawn, and saw its mouth wideful with teeth and tongue. Saw eyes that blazed with sun-shone gold. Radiant suns.

The General watched until the tiger was swallowed by the sluggish river of people. As if it had never really been there at all.

The meetings were secret. Everybody knew about them.

The building was no different to any other in this part of the city, no more special than the building next to it, or the building next to that. The concrete walls were dull with grime. Occasionally a curtain shifted in the vacant darkness of an open window. The General's car pulled alongside and one of the soldiers hurried to open his door. A few people in the street stared but they were quick to avert their eyes from the General. Someone saluted. The General removed his hat and entered the building holding it in his hands. His men remained behind, at the building's door and beside the car which idled with a low rumbling purr.

The General stepped from bright sunlight into the cooler gloom of a windowless foyer. The walls were dirty. Faded rectangles marked where pictures had once been, the shapes almost as dark as the walls that defined them, mere ghosts of old views. There were rows of metal boxes for post, each thick with labels of tape, one over the other, names and symbols in heavy black pen. The General walked past them and up the stairs, counting each step as he went because numbers were powerful and the total, when he reached her floor, was divisible by nine. Nine was very powerful.

The corridor was almost as busy as the street outside, though everybody here was keen to look elsewhere when the General passed. The rooms were meant for housing but many were also businesses. While the government slid further towards bankruptcy, many of the country's people thrived through smuggling, black market trade, and other questionable services, many of which took place around the city in buildings just like this one. Ahead, someone extended the grate that served as a door across the front of his apartment, the rattle of metalwork loud in the narrow space of the corridor. He padlocked it then retreated from the General without glancing back. The General paid him no heed. He had reached the room he needed. The smell of jasmine floated out to him. He saw the glowing tips of incense inside like amber stars in the dark. Tiny suns. Tigers hiding in shadows.

"I knew you would come today," said the woman inside. She always said she expected him when he visited. Perhaps she thought it added credence to her profession. She motioned to his feet and he unfastened the laces of his boots in her doorway. He stepped from them, positioned them side by side, and pulled the metal frame across behind him to seal them inside the room. It did nothing to shield them from prying eyes or eavesdroppers, and he would have his back to the diamond gaps, but there was a symbolism to the action he felt important. The gate only secured the room against the theft of its contents, but it marked a closing off from the outside world he thought the spirits and his ancestors would appreciate.

She beckoned him in and down – "Sit, sit" – the only woman who gave him orders. The General sat cross-legged before her, the tiny table between them aglow with burning cones of scented ash. Carved chips of ivory were scattered in a pattern he didn't understand. They seemed to glisten in the subdued light.

The woman was old. Her dark skin creased around eyes that squinted at him, and her forehead was forever furrowed, deep gorges in flesh filled with wisdom. Her skin hung in loose folds on her long neck, mottled and sagging. Her head rolled as if the neck was too long, too weak, to support it. The General wondered if that neck had ever known the brass rings of the Kayans. She seemed to experience, permanently, the stupor of someone fighting sleep or the effects of narcotics.

"More dreams of orchids?" She tilted her head back to look at him down the length of her face. Her cheeks were burnished with some powdered colour. Her eyes were narrow, almost closed.

The General nodded.

"But this is not why you come today."

"No."

"You'll soon hold counsel. You want to know what will follow, and to hear the wisdom of your own words."

She dealt cards to the table between them, a face-down row, and she tossed pieces of ivory upon the line.

"The orchid will be a problem for you," she said. She had not yet turned a card or examined any of the ivory tokens. "You will come to me about her eventually."

"Her," the General said. He had trained his voice never to give sound to questions, but the woman nodded as if he had asked.

She gestured over the table and said, "But the cards…"

And so it began.

The General listened. This woman kept him safe from assassination. Kept him stocked with mirrors and fresh bloody meat. She had told him of tigers, and one day she would tell him of orchids, but now she read his cards and listened to the *nats*, spirits that whispered and warned and spoke to her of his future and the future of the country.

"The children of fire will come again," she said. "And the men who blossom blood."

The General nodded. He expected them. The woman always predicted ghosts and she always predicted history's repetition and the General knew they were the same thing.

"You will continue to fight sword with sword," she told him, "spear with spear. It will serve you as it always has."

The General nodded.

The woman made no such motion. She was staring into places the General could not see.

"It is not power," she said. "It is not power that corrupts." And then she said, "Fear."

The General leaned forward.

"Fear… of losing power… corrupts…"

The General turned an ear towards her.

"Fear," she said again, "corrupts those who wield it."

The General waited but nothing else came. He put his hand on her arm and shook her from the trance, or shook the trance from her. She looked at him with eyes that saw through his and spoke with a quiet, dream-thick voice.

"Beware the tiger with flowers in its mouth."

The message hung between them like spoken incense, dispersing then gone. Eventually, the General nodded. "It means me harm," he said.

The woman's head rolled on her neck in a blurring of yes and no and she was awake. She passed her hand over the cards, brushing the spread line into a single pile before adding another card from the remaining stack nearby. She turned it and smiled.

The card showed a lady with a dress of petals. The General did not ask the woman questions, not verbally, but he looked one at her with hard expectant eyes. The woman only smiled, and bid him take care.

The General always took care. Of himself, and of his country. In 1941 he had trained in secret to fight for independence from the British, taking the radiant sun as his new name. In 1945 he had fought against Japanese occupation. And he fought now. He would always fight. When he had been Prime Minister he had brought order back to this country and how was his government known? The caretaker government. As if he had merely kept somebody's seat warm and restored nothing. It was with a glad heart that he seized power again two years later. The armed forces he had been trusted to rebuild were his to use, and he used them well. The military was a professional institution and the people trusted it. They trusted it more than they trusted their inept government. Their weak, corrupt, government. The country needed someone who cared for it to take control and lead the way and the military provided the necessary stability. The country was not ready for democracy. A tiger did not let its cubs fend for themselves until they were ready.

Beware the tiger with flowers in its mouth.

Flowers did not feed a nation.

When the country's poverty demanded it, the General and his ministers had eaten *mohingka*, a poor man's meal of fish and noodles. He would eat flowers if he had to.

Beware the tiger with flowers in its mouth.

The General did not mind the enigmatic nature of the soothsayer's predictions and warnings. The process of considering their meaning provided a path to clarity and enabled him to recognise the wisdom of his own conduct. His interpretations led to decisions, and his decisions led to action. Sometimes these actions were actions of violence but his violence always came with the approval of the numbers.

When the woman had invested him with the power of the numbers the General had rescued the country's economy with notes of 45 and 90 *kyat*, notes that were divisible by nine, and in the process he crippled those hoarding 100s. Those who made their money on the black market, those who funded insurgents; a legacy left to him by prior government. Leaving the soothsayer's building, the General nodded at one of the soldiers who had waited for him and gave him some of this money. The soldier gave a nod in return that was more of a bow and went inside to pay the woman, while another soldier opened the door to the General's air-conditioned car.

Two corpses sat inside.

The General knew better than to grab for his pistol – he had learnt to expect them, and he had been forewarned only moments ago – but still he glanced at the soldier beside him. If the soldier saw the dead girls as well, he remained calm about it. Despite their charred skin, their roasted flesh. If he could smell them, as the General could, then he gave no indication.

The General's dark passengers looked at him, smoke rising from the red-black meat of their bodies. They looked at him with empty sockets, tiny craters gaping in ruined faces. Their skin was crisp where fat and flesh had cooked in a heat the general did not feel. He only knew they were girls from what remained of their dresses. They were students, perhaps from the burnt school, perhaps from the demolished university, it was difficult to tell. One of them turned from him to look out of the window. Her hair was gone, her head a cracked and smoking dome. The other girl bared her teeth in a lipless smile she couldn't help making. A rictus grin as she shifted in the seat to make room for the General.

The General sat beside them. They were all his *otta-saunk*, these visitors, forever bound to him. He accepted them now. With the door again closed, they sat in a silence broken only by the occasional pop and sizzle of smouldering skin as the car moved into the crowd, easing among the people and joining traffic on its way out of the city.

"What do you want?" the General asked. He always asked, though they never answered. Perhaps they couldn't. Not with words. Perhaps they thought they'd told him enough when they were alive.

Outside, in the street, everyone they passed was suddenly burning. Fires licked them from the feet up. Clothes caught and shrivelled, hair flared as bright and as brief as muzzle-flashes. There was little sound – the car was a sanctuary of dulled quiet and cool air – but the General knew that even if he were to open the window he'd hear only the normal street noise, feel only the normal heat of the day.

The student beside him turned her head to look outside with her companion. The General heard skin crackle. He saw crisp flakes of it fall from her neck to the car's upholstery. He brushed them to the floor but they vanished into powder at his touch, dusting his skin with ash. The girl put her hand to the window as if seeking to touch the burning people. Her thin fingers were red and black. The back of her hand was a raised blister, waiting to burst. She opened her mouth. Her jaw creaked with the effort then fell away fast in a puff of dust, the fallen bone crumbling as it tumbled to the floor. Her shrivelled tongue hung like a dark rope, descending to a chest that went in instead of out beneath her shirt, a sunken cavity where her breasts used to be. When she breathed, the General could hear the soot-muffled rattle of debris held inside her body.

They were passing through what used to be the university district. Two decades ago the General's men had fired upon protesters and destroyed the union building. He had denied involvement, of course, conveniently abroad on the advice of his soothsayer, and publicly he had blamed his deputy. Privately he thanked the man. The General had not fared well at university. He was never meant to be a doctor. Different things were expected of him.

As they drove, the General saw the ruined shells of buildings gutted hollow by fire and knocked empty by controlled explosions. It had diverted public attention from inflation, from the rising price of rice, but there was meant to be a lesson in the destruction as well, albeit one they refused to learn. There were more protests. There were more riots. There was more violence. Students and factory workers were burned and shot. They were imprisoned, exiled, kept out of sight. He saw them now, though. Saw them move among the district's ruins and rubble as a burning, bleeding, crowd.

The General tapped on the glass partition separating him from the driver and told the man to circle the area before continuing. Nine times, he instructed, making his own *yadaya*. He had once walked a bridge backwards, dressed as a king, because his soothsayer had advised it. In the ninth minute of a new day, he had crossed the river and taken the city backward to a more prosperous time so it could know its own wealth again. He had changed the city's driving regulations on the advice of a wizard, vehicles moving in left lanes instead of right. He had done many things in the name of *yadaya*, rituals that kept his country strong, rituals that kept him safe. He would not be weakened by the past, or shamed by it. He would use it to control his future, and the future of his country's people.

On the ninth pass, his *otta-saunk* companions collapsed into each other. Their bodies merged, a shared cloud of smoky ash as their bones fell to the floor where the movements of the car and its engine-rumble growl vibrated the pile to dust.

That night, the General dreamt of orchids. A field of them bloomed in a wave from the west as the sun descended. Steel orchids, shining under bright Burmese stars.

The woman brought him tea as he took off his boots and she said, "You are surrounded by those who oppose you."

The General nodded and took his tea.

"Expect the best, but prepare for the worst," the soothsayer said.

The General had heard those words before, but not from her. He was haunted, even here.

She took him deeper into the shadows of her small room.

"None of the spirits here are enemies, but there is one who troubles you. He is a ghost. He is the past made present by an ancestor."

The General was reluctant to give her a response but she stared at him until he nodded. He only nodded for her to continue, though in truth he also agreed.

"His face is on the currency, and her face is his face." She smiled. "But... with more feminine tranquillity. A resolute grace."

The General put his cup to the table with some force. Tea spilled onto the cards but he made no apology. "Tell me what you see," he said, pointing to his facedown future. "I hear enough of this talk elsewhere."

"You hear it, but you don't listen."

The General scowled, opened his mouth to speak, but the woman's words came before his. "You will have a daughter yourself one day," she said. She tilted her head left, then right. "Two. Five."

"Which is it?"

"You will care for nine children," she said. "One of the daughters you will prize above others."

Nine children. Nine was good.

"Be careful who she marries."

"Of course."

The woman shrugged. She emptied a cup of her own, gulping tea as if in a hurry, and turned card after card before her.

"Your trouble comes from far away," she said. "From the past, from..." She gestured beyond the room they sat in, made a rolling motion with her hand and said, "away."

"I shall eliminate her."

He had removed 100,000 Chinese from his country; he could rid himself of one woman.

"You will not."

The mystic glanced up from the cards when she felt the General move away from them. He was angry. "You would turn her spirit into something far stronger," she said. "Another martyr. Like her father."

The General had his hand on his gun and the soothsayer saw a future there, but it blurred as if beneath water and was gone as quickly as a river passing.

She turned the remaining cards quickly.

"Make the promises people want," she told the General. "Bring peace. If there is peace she will have no cause to trouble you."

The General looked away and around the room. He looked at the smoking incense and the statuettes on shelves and the fabrics hanging from the walls. He looked at a folding screen draped with colourful clothes and saw himself in a tall mirror leaning nearby. He released his grip from the gun.

"Do this, and you will have a quiet death," the soothsayer told him.

"Do this," she said, "and you will have a quiet death, many years from now."

The General grunted. The woman took it as a question, or a signal to go on.

"When the century is new," she said. "You will join the river. The Hlaing will carry you in peace. Is this not a good death?"

He watched a thin line of jasmine scent, the smoke blue-grey in the fading light. He passed his finger through it, dispersing the line, and watched it reform before breaking it again, taking more truth from that action than anything the woman had ever told him. He nodded.

"I saw a tiger," the General said.

"Tigers are good. Tigers are strong. They have the blue dragon as a grandfather."

"That is a Chinese belief."

She shrugged. It didn't matter to her. "The tiger's head came from the heavens. Its body came from the earth. It breathes the moon in its lungs. The tiger's bones are made of stone and its heart from iron. You will see the strength of burning stars in its eyes." She smiled. "Radiant suns."

He thought of its stripes. Of its prowess and longevity. What if this tiger was not his? What if it was hers? What if it was here for the woman who had returned?

The soothsayer, for the first time, looked comfortable. She was never intimidated by him – he'd noticed that before – but this time she was perhaps even amused.

"Beware her claws," the woman said.

The General stared. The tiger's claws came from the vulture. The woman clutched at one of her necklaces, some symbol at her throat. She touched the cards, moved them. She did not meet his eyes.

"I must go," the General said, and saw relief in her curt nod.

He stopped beside his boots. He put them on and laced them tight. "Prepare for the worst," he said, and with those words he went. He left her to wonder if it was advice he'd taken with him or a threat he'd left behind.

From the roof, the General saw the full extent of the crowd gathered below. In his time as Prime Minister he had prohibited gatherings of five or more, yet here he looked upon thousands. Tens of thousands, pressed close as a field of crops. A rally, men and women, young and old. The monks had gathered too, obvious in their orange robes and striking in their numbers. Unseen by all except the General, though, moving among them, were lines of the burnt and blackened dead. As he watched, this mosaic mass of people, the orange-robed and the charred-black-skinned, they became the vast outline of a tiger's head, striped with lines of corpses; a multitude of *otta-saunk*. And there, the dark green of his soldiers, and there, on the other flank. Emerald eyes that looked back at him and narrowed as the men spread within the crowd. They would take the outspoken ones, the most eager supporters of this woman's cause, but they could not take them all.

And there, where the crowd parted and came together again, the mouth of the tiger's head opened wide around the woman who passed among them. Their beloved 'aunt'. Their *Daw*, and Star of Burma. Famous daughter of a slaughtered hero whose face smiled from boards held high, a silent voice from the past that encouraged her to speak his echo. The General knew that women embodied karmic punishment, that they had transgressed in past lives as men and in their new lives were punished with a female form, but he saw in this adversary some residual male strength. He saw her father, and more.

The woman, slender as a reed, had a voice that was calm and quiet and considered, but here she had a stage, an audience of thousands, and the General had no choice but to hear her roar, in every line of rhetoric, *"I urge you all to embrace democracy."*

The tiger-stripes in the crowd were spreading as people listened and said the words back to her, back to each other.

The General turned away from it. Those who heard her words would turn into tigers and he needed to be ready. They wanted an election: he would give them an election. You didn't calm a tiger by beating it. You gave it meat. You gave it something it hungered for, and while it was distracted…

You could kill it. Or cage it, and hide it away.

Her house on the shore of Inya Lake became her cage. Number 54, a multiple of 9. The General did not like this. 5 plus 4 is 9. The General did not like this, either. He did not like placing his adversary under house arrest when her house had such numerical power. And it was her family home: she would have the strength of her ancestors.

He ordered the numbers removed, along with the banners and political papers, all the people who convened there to plot and conspire. Her family. All of it, all of them, everything, gone. All except for this single flower from the west. This woman who cared so little for her country that she married a foreigner, yet now claimed to love the land she once abandoned. She was like the *ouktazaung*, roaming free for years before returning to her treasure, luring men to her with a siren's voice.

Well, she could not cause much trouble from behind her walls. With no family, no phone, no access to the outside world, she would soon give up and the people would forget her.

The General was pleased.

~

The General was wrong.

~

The people in the street did not disperse when the General stepped out from his car. Some even dared to look him in the eye, and maintained that look until he pointed at them and soldiers pulled them away. He looked up at the building and saw the dark marks on its concrete walls were spreading like underarm stains. Yes, he thought. The sweat of fear. You *should* sweat. All of you.

The General marched from the heat of the street into the coolness of the building's interior. He barely noticed the exertion of the stairs up, nor the humidity and stifling warmth of the corridor. There were people here, and as usual they hurried away from him to other stairs or their own rooms, closing doors, pulling at metal shutters. Some of them, though, shouted before they left, turning their heads to yell so he wouldn't see. He ignored them. Those who remained were smouldering, black with soot and their own smoking skin, reminders of a necessary past. Perhaps here, in this building, they were also a forecast of the future. They grinned at him with faces burnt down to teeth, and they slumped in corners, sagged against walls, because the cooked muscles in their limbs could not hold them. Fat melted and dripped slick like sweat, forming dark puddles on the floor. Torsos and torn limbs no longer bled but cooked and rotted, ripe with a human incense only the General could smell.

The woman was throwing her belongings into a case, stuffing garments into a blanket she had folded and tied, but she stopped when the General entered. She stood calm, a lesson learned from orchids, and she faced him more directly than she ever had when telling him the things she thought he needed to hear. She was *nat-kadaw*, a spirit's wife, but the General saw her now as a desperate woman who tried to control the world around her when all she should have done was know her place in it.

"Did you know I would come today?" he asked her.

He stepped closer, moving beyond the small welcoming area of the room where he once removed his boots. Sticks of incense formed lines of smoke, a row of ethereal columns. He waved a hand through them to send the smoke curling. The cards lay stacked on the same shelf. He swept them to the floor and they spread and turned as they fell in a fluttering of fortunes. The woman glanced at them but said nothing of what she saw. The General trod on them, grinding numbers and symbols beneath his heels as he had so many chunks of bloody meat. Numbers were indeed powerful. He had never had so many united against him. When had words become more powerful than guns? When did personality and character suddenly hold power over rank and authority?

"If you saw any of this, you kept it from me," said the General. "And if you didn't see it, then you are flawed, or a fraud, and I have no use for you."

The woman nodded. Her head lolled on her long neck and she smiled. "You are no tiger. You are *Belu*. You are *Pan-kike Belu*. You are *Yama Yazar*."

She spat the words at him. Shape-shifting man-eater. Flower biter. Lord of Death.

"This will not be Burma anymore."

He stood opposite, close enough to feel the heat of her old body and something sour like fear. He drew his pistol, pushed it to her chest, and fired.

The woman shattered. He had expected her to wilt, a flower to step away from as it fell, but there was a blast and a smash and a thousand pieces cascaded in a shattering splash and tinkle of glass. Her image collapsed before him and the General faced only himself in the mirror behind. Cracks lightninged from where the mirror held his bullet, the General's chest a mass of zigzags, but he looked away from that. Looked, instead, to the woman who lay in pieces at his feet. He moved his foot over her, pushing pieces aside with his boot. In one he saw an eye. In another, a mouth that still moved, tried to speak. He squatted beside the fragments and turned his ear to hear but there was only the noise of the city outside. The voices of its people.

He holstered his gun and scooped the glass pieces of his soothsayer together with both hands, made them bloody yet again. Where he should have seen a hundred warriors he saw only her. Fragments, but each broken piece could still bite, each new shape a sharp one he'd made himself, more dangerous now than they'd ever been before. So many of them. And numbers could be powerful.

He looked into the pieces and saw the woman within them disappear until what he held in his bleeding hands, what lay scattered around him at his feet, were the pieces of a broken man.

He made fists around them and watched his blood fall upon the floor like tiny blossoming flowers and at last he was afraid.

Outside, tigers waited.

|Things I Learnt on the Afan Trail|

∼

Things I learnt on the Afan Trail:
1.	Pay attention to signs at all times.
2.	Jason's idea of a bike ride and my idea of a bike ride are two very different things.
3.	Mountain-biking is not the same as cycling.

We arrived at the Afan Forest Park later than intended and that was my fault. We'd taken a wrong turn coming out of some valley town or another because I'd ignored or missed a sign somewhere, and while Jason tried to get us back on track I faffed with his sat-nav, which was a silly thing to do because I'm at that age now where all technology hates me, so I only succeeded in making things worse.

Speaking of getting older, you know you're middle-aged when the first thing your mate says upon arriving at such a beautiful spot of Welsh countryside is, "Only a pound to park all day? That's excellent value."

"Bargain," was the best I could offer in reply.

Jason and I had been friends for most of our lives. We didn't see each other as much as we used to thanks to work and partners and, you know, *life*, but it was one of those friendships you could pick up again whenever and carry on from wherever you left off as if nothing had ever changed. Except this time something pretty significant *had* changed, namely that Jason had just become engaged, and our bike-riding trip around Afan Park was a sort of celebration of that. I'd never pictured him settling down, to be honest, and I kind of judged him for doing it, to be *really* honest. I mean, he was already saying things like 'gosh, what excellent value' about a carpark.

"Good to see it's not too busy," I said.

Despite the bargainous parking price, there were only three other vehicles at the park. We'd taken the day off work midweek for exactly that reason, and I was especially glad of it. Jason's okay, he's been climbing ladders for years as part of his job (maintaining mobile phone towers and the like) and although he insisted he hadn't cycled for a while, he was still in very good shape, whereas me? Well, I'd been sitting on my arse for the last five years in a safe but dull office job, and even before that I wasn't exactly active. Now I'm what you might call 'portly', if you were kind and made rather quaint use of the English language. A bit chubby, to be frank. The fewer people watching me struggle for breath, sweating a lake into my t-shirt, the better.

"We'll get the bikes and then get changed," Jason said.

"I'm good to go."

I had my three-quarter-lengths on already and an oversized t-shirt that had been part of some company promotion or another. It was oversized when I got it, anyway. Now it fit me pretty well. Bastard thing.

"Right," said Jason. "I'll get my gear on in a minute, then."

"Don't tell me you've got all the Lycra stuff?"

"Okay," he said, smiling, "I won't tell you."

I laughed, but it turned out he wasn't joking. He had the clingy shirt, the *super* clingy shorts (obscene, really), padded gloves, the whole lot. Everything was mostly black, but with glaring yellow sections in thin bright stripes. He looked like a giant wasp, especially with the wraparound glasses. In that get-up I'd have looked like a bumblebee. One of those so loaded with pollen that it can't fly.

The guy at the bike rental place was young and efficient and someone who obviously embraced the outdoorsy way of life. I've never really rated dreadlocks on white people, and I don't know if that makes me racist or them – because, you know, appropriation – but whatever, they suited him. He was pierced, too – eyebrows, nose, ears – and his arms were a tangle of those Celtic-tribal-style tattoos, you know the ones. Vines with thorns that hooked back on themselves like snakes with sharp turns. They'd faded from black to bluey-green but they still emphasised his arm muscles the way they were supposed to.

"So this is your suspension here," he told us, "just flip it down to the six o'clock position for downhill. And this one gives you some bounce at the front." He shoved down on the handlebars to demonstrate how they pistoned. "Saddle," he said, pointing at a lever for adjusting it, "and all the gear for punctures underneath, including a new inner tube. It's covered in the hire price, just let me know if you use it so I can replace it."

Jason nodded throughout the spiel. He asked something about the brakes and seemed suitably impressed by the answer, so I nodded as well and made some sort of pleased noise. They used technical terms and named various manufacturers while I thought about the old spokey-dokeys I used to have and a Tony the Tiger clip-on reflector that came free with my Frosties years ago. It was *grrr*eat.

Dreadman looked from Jason to me and said, rather tactfully, "Just ride around the car park first to get used to them."

"Will do."

He handed us our helmets. "Play safe."

And so it was we circled the parking area, click-clack-clunking through the gears and squeaking the brakes. That old saying, 'it's like riding a bike', is bollocks, by the way. This was almost as alien to me as the first time, only now I didn't have stabilisers or a parent holding the back of the saddle to help me. I got the hang of the balancing part pretty quickly, but the brakes would take some getting used to. They were so good, so abrupt, that you stopped in an instant. The first time I tried the brake I immediately wobbled and fell off balance. Only off balance, though. Not off the bike.

"I'll be honest," I said, "I thought we'd be cycling to a pub or something. I didn't expect an actual mountain."

I was exhausted just looking at it from the carpark.

"Technically, these are just hills, mate."

"Potato, po-*tarto*."

Jason laughed.

There were notice-boards set up near the bike hire place with maps showing various routes around the park, each colour-coded. Turned out the colours also referred to the difficulty level, but I didn't notice that until later. I wanted to do the Blue Scar because there was a photo of children doing it and I figured it would be easy, but Jason wanted to tackle the Penhydd route because it would be more interesting and give us a better view. All I saw for Penhydd was that the markers we had to follow were red and decorated with a stag head, which seemed appropriate considering this was something of a mini stag-do. The route itself was a spaghetti mess of lines in tangled curves and I took a picture on my phone in case it was the sort of route you could get lost on.

"You ready?"

"Not really."

Jason laughed. "All right," he said. "Let's go."

~

Things I learnt on the Afan trail:

4.   Uphill, downhill, it's best to keep your mouth shut.

5.   The levels of hand-eye coordination achieved through mastering the complexities of Guitar Hero doesn't mean shit on a bike travelling at high speed down a mountain.

6.   Falling off a bike travelling at high speed down a mountain hurts.

We were shaded by trees initially while the gentle (at first) slope switch-backed on itself again and again, winding its way up, and I found myself thinking maybe this wasn't so bad. I was standing on the pedals for those first few turns of the path, actually close to enjoying myself.

"Man, I haven't been on a bike in *years.*"

Last time I'd been on a bike, I had a paper round.

"We should bring the girls out here next time," Jason suggested.

"Chrissie wanted to come today, but I said it was lads only."

Lads. Like we were still twenty-something.

"Yeah, she'd like it, I reckon," Jason said.

Chrissie was in far better shape than me. She had a weekly dance class she went to, *and* a 'Bums n Tums' thing, and she was even a bit outdoorsy, sort of. She liked sunbathing and festivals and drinking prosecco in beer gardens, anyway. In fact, we'd met in a beer garden. Jason had dragged me away from our usual pints at the Hare & Tortoise to some new place in town and there she was. Chrissie. Like it was fate, or something.

"Man, I can't believe you're getting *married,*" I said for the hundredth time. "Did *not* see that coming."

Jason smiled. Olivia may have been the latest in a long line of girlfriends, but something about that smile told me she'd be the last. I was happy for him. I was. So I told him, "I give it less than a year."

"Fuck off."

"I'm just saying, statistically, most marriages—"

"Fuck off."

I laughed, he smiled, and for a while we cycled in comfortable quiet (only the quiet was comfortable, not the bike) until I asked him, "How do you know? That she's the one?"

I genuinely wanted to know, but I was also hoping he'd talk about her for a bit because I was already short of breath and needed what little I had for pedalling; my enthusiasm for the uphill climb had already diminished and I no longer stood as I pedalled. In fact, I now stayed firmly seated, pedalling round and round in first gear. Jason called it 'circling the drain'.

"Some things you just know. You know?"

"No."

He laughed. "It'll be you next."

"No rush."

"Seriously? You know Chrissie's way too good for you, right? You should secure that, asap."

"Cheers, mate."

"And, you know, her body clock's gonna be ticking."

"She'd love to hear you say that."

"I'm just saying, she'll be thinking about the future, even if you're not."

"Has she said something?"

"What? No."

But I wondered. Had I missed some obvious sign? I didn't want to lose her, but marriage? That wasn't just a relationship that had gone up a level, that was a different relationship altogether, with a whole different set of ups and downs, and I wasn't ready for any of that. I just didn't have the guts. Jason did, obviously, but not me. As for kids, hell no. I was still a kid myself, really. And what if we split up? I didn't want to be that guy dragging his sprogs to McDonalds every other Saturday. Nothing against McDonalds – I love a Big Mac, and the nuggets are so good they should be currency – but there's more to parenting than a Happy Meal, I imagine.

"I just don't want things to change," I said.

"Things change anyway, mate, whether you want them to or not."

I shook my head and gave a mock tut. "*You've* changed."

Jason grinned at me and said, "Yeah, I grew up. You should try it."

There was a building coming up. A ruin, really; roofless, with walls crumbling into long grass growing wild around it. I suggested stopping so I could take a picture but really I wanted to catch my breath and lower my heart rate. I offered Jason, "Water?" and pointed the bottle his way.

"Nah, not yet thanks."

So I pretended I didn't need any, either.

"What do you think it used to be?" I said, pointing to the ruin. A carpet of red flowers bloomed where the floor had once been and spilled from the gaps between old stones. I took another picture.

Jason shrugged. "No idea. This area used to be all mines and stuff before it was turned into mountain bike trails. You know, because *things change?*"

I gave him the finger.

"Some of these bike routes are old slag heaps, actually."

"Speaking of old slags, how's your mum?"

Normally, that would've got me a laugh, or a retaliating insult about *my* mother – usually both – but instead, Jason pointed into the ruin. "Hey, you been here before, mate?"

I'd just noticed the same thing myself: my name was on one of the walls in a spray of graffiti. The large bubble letters had been crossed through with a thick black line, but you could still read them easily enough. A sad face emoji painted next to it had crosses for eyes.

"Well that's not creepy at all."

"Come on, it's a *perfect* place for a selfie."

I could think of better places (such as in a pub, with a nice cold beer and maybe a juicy burger) but we squatted next to the name and Jason pointed at it while I played sad and scrunched my eyes closed.

"Classic," Jason said, and sent the picture to my phone.

Shortly after the ruins the trail zig-zagged up at a steady, steeper gradient and then we were rewarded – if that's the right word – with some downhill riding that took us into a cleft of valley side. Here the bike became something of a boneshaker because I'd forgotten to set the suspension and lower the saddle as recommended. I was a bit rattled metaphorically speaking, too, by the sudden speed. Ahead of me, Jason leaned back on his bike at full arm's length, arse hanging low over the rear wheel, and he sped away down the mountain, leaning into the turns. I couldn't watch him for long because I had to keep my eyes on the ground to see where it bumped and dropped and twisted, applying the brakes most of the way down until I realised that going slow was worse, shaking me more and fucking up my balance. The suspension soaked up some of the lumps and bumps, but the bike still came down hard on the rockier areas. As I picked up speed, the more it felt like I was flying, leaping from stones the size of paving slabs and landing on loose ground that kicked up beneath my wheels. I'm not at all what you might call an adrenaline junkie, not even close – the only thrill I would get from this was not the joy of cheating death but the relief of having survived, which is rather different – but it *was* exhilarating. I even cheered at one point, a quick "Whoo!" as I came down after a particularly dramatic drop and, "Yeah!"

I swallowed a bug.

Jason was waiting at the bottom of the slope, legs down either side of his bike as he chewed on a cereal bar. He grinned at me. He had an oat or raisin or something stuck in his teeth. Maybe he'd swallowed a bug, too.

"Ready for the next bit?" He gestured with what was left of his muesli stick to where the route climbed again, steep and relentless.

"Just a sec."

I took the opportunity to scoff a king-sized Snickers. You know. For the energy.

The climb was hard going, and despite the crappy weather I was really sweating as I struggled, circling the drain the whole way. The trail was rough stone and gravel and sometimes my tyres slipped, trying to find grip, or the front wheel lifted in accidental wheelie when I pulled too hard on the handlebars. It was hard work. And my arse was killing me.

Jason talked about his plans with Olivia most of the way up, like he was showing off how much breath he had to spare. Listening to that was hard work, too.

"Bloody hell, mate… When did you get so… live, laugh, love?"

"You wait. You'll want the same soon enough."

"I dunno… Isn't it… meant to be… all downhill… after marriage?"

Although I had to admit, downhill sounded great right about now.

Jason looked at me but didn't say anything and I realised maybe I'd offended him or something. The thing is, I'd always wanted to be more like Jason, but here he was becoming someone else entirely and soon it would all be DIY projects and teething problems and whatever else married people with kids talked about.

"But hey," I said. "Who knows… what the future… might hold?" I tried to sound all ominous and mystical but sounded fat and out of breath instead because that's what I was.

"You're nearly forty, mate," Jason said. "You better get a move on." Then he did exactly that, pedalling ahead with a cry of, "Meet you at the top," thrown back over his shoulder as he left me behind.

I followed with an ugly mantra of heavy breaths and swearing.

By the time I reached the summit I was doing all of my breathing open-mouthed. Panting, really. *Gasping*, if I'm honest.

"You all right?"

Jason was standing with his hands on his Lycra-hips, surveying the landscape, barely out of breath at all. His bike leant against a very welcome bench.

I dismounted with no grace whatsoever, dropping the bike in my eagerness to swap the sharp triangle of saddle for the flat boards of the bench and collapsing onto it. I sat with my elbows on my knees, head down to exhale at the ground, all the while feeling grateful that I wasn't clutching at my chest mid-heart attack. I decided that 'Afan' or 'Penhydd' must be Welsh for 'you're going to die out here, chubby'.

Jason paced a bit, sipped some water, and lunged to stretch his legs while I recuperated. I took the opportunity to swipe through my phone, accessing the picture of the route to see how much we'd covered. Or, more accurately, to see how much we had left.

"*Bloody hell*, Jason."

"What?"

"It says this is for people wanting a challenge."

"It's not that bad."

"I'm dying here."

"Nah."

I gathered some of my t-shirt to mop my face but it didn't help much because the material was already soaked with sweat.

"Pour some water on the back of your neck," Jason suggested.

It was a good idea.

"Better?"

"Yeah."

"We're nipping in and out of trees next," he said. "It'll be much cooler."

Before that, though, the route was enjoyably flat, offering a pleasant view of the forested hills. The motorway was down in the valley, a faint noise of normal life, and for a moment I was genuinely glad to be up on the trail instead, but then we were directed through a narrow gate to a gloomy, wooded trail down and—

"Here we go!"

He was gone, speeding ahead into the dark.

Here's the thing about cycling in a forest – you can't see shit. Not at first, anyway, moving from an open hilltop into the shadows of close trees. So there I was, unable to see, trying to weave when the path weaved and dodging branches on a route that was a rutted line not much wider than the tyres that had probably made it in the first place. The ground was still loose with rocks but now there was tree-litter as well, fallen leaves that rain had softened into treacherous mulch.

"Oh-shit-oh-fuck-oh-*fuck*."

Sticks and stones were thrown into my spokes and shallow puddles hissed into halves as I split them with my tyres and through it all I reacted and panicked and basically just tried not to die. A couple of times the path opened up to the sky and it was briefly lit by angles of daylight, but that only made the dark much worse when it came back. It was like riding through a silent lightning storm.

At one point I thought I saw someone in the flashes and then – yes, *there* – a sudden blur I swerved to avoid. The bike jarred against something, probably a low line of rock. The handlebars were twisted hard from my hands. I got my foot down quick to stop from falling, but the bike spun out from under me. I turned against it with a wild over-correction and turned sharply back the other way. One of the pedals scraped skin from my ankle. The other bashed my shin. I didn't fall, but I careened from rock to tree and back to the trail, ricocheting, still somehow racing forwards until the trees were suddenly gone and I was out in the clear again.

On a suddenly steep, zigzag down.

"*Shit!*"

The first of those sharp bends cut a high-cambered turn and I took the outside of it with a scattering of gravel. I must've been going too fast because the bike wanted to keep going, up and over, which would have put me down the mountainside *really* fast if I hadn't pumped the brakes and yanked the handlebars to a near ninety degrees. I slewed in a short skid, spraying a fantail over the edge and down a drop I really did not want to think about, but I stayed on the trail.

Jason had stopped to wait and I only noticed him at the last moment, pulling the brakes hard and turning the bike sideways to stop. I heard stones tink against his bike and he put a hand up to shield his face just as I hit the ground.

I cracked my head pretty hard and was suddenly very glad for the silly helmet. I slid a few feet on my side, stones and gravel scraping me raw before hitching my t-shirt up to cut across my back and stomach as I rolled. The bike was somehow still between my legs for some of it but then it got away from me and I felt a tyre run up my back and something metal carved a fresh line from my skin and then the bike was over me and gone and in the dirt upside down, both wheels spinning.

Jason managed to sidestep with his bike still under him, a casual bunny-hop to avoid mine, and said, "Shit, man, are you okay?"

I'd been groaning for a moment, I think, but with his question I laughed. I was bruised and bloodied, red raw and scraped and sore, but I was all right and I couldn't stop laughing. I struggled to get up, feeling very much like a turned turtle trying to right itself; I had to roll to my front and kneel before standing, one hand down to help me. I wiped myself clean of mud. I'd been scoured down to new skin in long, wide patches, and blood ran from numerous thin lacerations. My skin was singing with fresh cuts and stings. My t-shirt was torn.

"Mate."

"It's okay," I said, laughter subsiding. "I never liked this shirt anyway."

"You all right?"

"I'll live."

The words felt like a lie and killed the rest of my laughter. I dabbed at my blood and winced.

"There was someone back there," I said.

"What?"

"Yeah. Or I thought there was, anyway. In the trees, or just stepping out from them or something. Scared the crap out of me."

We both turned to look back, expecting someone to come out of the woods to check on us – on *me* – to make sure I was okay, but nobody did.

"Do you think I might have hit him?"

"Mate, I don't know, *did* you?"

I thought about it and said, "I might have."

"Shit."

We couldn't see anything beyond the first few trees. Jason sighed.

"We better go back."

Things I learnt on the Afan trail:

7.   We never should have come to the Afan Trail.

We walked the bikes in deference to my injuries, though Jason made it subtly clear that it was just a breather and we'd be cycling again just as soon as we'd checked on whoever it was I'd seen, or thought I'd seen, and maybe even *hit*, back in the wooded area of the trail.

"You know, the more I think about it, the more I think I couldn't have hit anyone. I definitely hit something – a few things, actually – but a person would have cried out or yelled at me or something, wouldn't they?"

"I expect so."

"If there was even anybody there."

"Only one way to find out."

But I really didn't want to. I just wanted to get back on our bikes and go. I didn't know why; it was just a feeling. I didn't think we should be heading back into the trees. So I hesitated, just for a moment, but because I couldn't explain my reluctance I ended up wheeling my bike across the threshold anyway and we were back amongst the trees and their shadows.

And that was it. That was the whole extent of me trying to change the course of events. A sudden gut feeling which I pushed aside.

This time the wooded area seemed even darker, though the shadows seemed slower in encroaching. Like they were trying to sneak up on us. The sounds of the distant motorway, already faint, disappeared completely. The sudden hush was like something tangible, settling on us like a chill. The only sound was a quiet *thwop, thwop, thwop* noise from my bike as I pushed it along beside me.

"Ah, shit," said Jason, and nodded at something behind me.

I flinched, looking back as I hurried forward, but there was nobody there.

"Your tyre," Jason said.

"Oh."

It was a pancake.

"Shit."

"Yeah, that's what I said."

I looked again to the route out and down. "Think it'll be all right getting back to the–"

"You *have* to change it, mate. Can't keep going with it like that, you'll damage the wheel." He was unzipping the tiny wedge-shaped pack nestled beneath his saddle. I looked for a puddle. I had vague memories of my father submerging an inner tube in a bowl of water, finding the puncture by watching for bubbles as he fed the tube around in his fists.

"We'll just put the new tube in," Jason said. "It's paid for anyway." He handed me the kit.

I stared at the offering and took it eventually but when Jason asked, "Want me to do it?" I handed it back, grateful.

"Cheers. I've not fixed a puncture in… well, ever."

"Takes two minutes. Come on." He put the stand down on his bike and took mine. He flipped it over as I inspected my wounds again.

"Sore?"

"A bit, but my arse hurts more."

"Friend of mine said if you ride often enough it toughens the perineum," Jason said, "but who the hell wants that?" He laughed.

I didn't quite know what the perineum was, but I knew I didn't want a toughened one, so I laughed with him. Or I tried to. It came out wrong. Like I'd never done it before, or changed my mind part way through.

"Seriously, you all right?" He was levering the flat tyre away from the wheel rim.

I wasn't all right. I had a feeling inside like weather on the brink of turning, but I didn't know how to explain it.

"Bit shaken up I suppose."

"Not surprised, mate."

I looked around. Up the track and down. "We should go back."

"Soon be done. Then we can tackle the Blue Scar route if you're still up for it? Or get a drink and a bite to eat if you're not. Either way, plenty of time."

I didn't think there was, but I said, "Okay," when no was what I wanted to say. No, thank you. *Fuck* no. Let's just go.

But I said okay.

Jason had the inner tube flopping in his hands. He looked for the puncture even though we were replacing it. "Yep," he said, "definitely fucked," and he dropped it into his lap before feeding a new one around the wheel. "Won't be long now."

A long gust of wind channelled through the trees, picking up leaves from the trail and casting them around. A noise came with it, more of a low vibration than anything particularly loud, and as it passed over me I felt something of myself seem to slip away with it.

"Did you feel that?"

Jason was squatting beside the wheel, pumping at the tyre in a way he thought comically obscene until whatever he saw in my expression caused him to stop and his grin faded. He started to say my name but suddenly stood and backed away instead. He tried to speak again but gave up and pointed.

There was someone standing in the middle of the path. He had a beard that was mostly white like his hair. His eyes were wide and deep in a face that seemed to sag around them. I couldn't make out what he was wearing. It looked like a white bedsheet which he wore like a poncho, tied at his waist with rough knotted rope, but I gave that no more thought once I'd seen the knife. It was long and pale, curving like a hook from his fist. Like a small scythe or sickle or whatever. It felt like I stared at it for a long time.

When the man spoke, his voice croaked from his throat like he hadn't used it in a while. "Are you lost?"

"No," Jason began, but then the man on the path said my name, my *fucking name*, and—

"Do you know what's going to happen?"

He walked towards me with surprising speed.

"No," I said. And, "Not me." I backed away from him, putting my bike between us. "*Jason.*" I pulled at one of the wheels and bent my fingers painfully in the spokes dragging it closer for protection. It fell. I crouched and reached for the handlebars while trying to avoid the reach of the man.

Behind me, I heard the fast, ticking sound a bike wheel makes when rotating without resistance and I knew Jason was turning his bike around to cycle away. I glanced back thinking he'd already be halfway up the mountain, leaving me behind, but he was right there beside me, bike held up before him like a ridiculous shield. He was holding the frame and brandishing the entire thing like, I don't know. Like a lion tamer with a chair.

"Go!" he said. "Get out of here!"

I don't know if he meant me or the other guy, but I yanked at the handlebars of my fallen bike and picked it up as I stood. The man was still pointing his knife or whatever the fuck it was but with his free hand he grabbed my bike's rear wheel. He pulled, and for a brief moment it was a tug of war between us, but then Jason was there with his bike up, pushing the strange man back. It gave me enough time to get on the saddle.

My feet slipped off of the pedals first time I stood on them, *and* the second, but third time I was lucky and stayed on. The bike was still in a high gear though and I barely moved, so I stupidly thumbed the lever to lower it and fell from the pedals yet again with the clunk-click of the changed gear, wondering suddenly why the fuck I was bothering with the bike anyway.

I pushed the bike aside and ran.

I made it about two steps before a tangle of rubber looped my ankle and I fell. I got my hands up in time but still ate dirt. I barely felt it.

Certain I'd be stabbed or slashed across the back, I rolled over. I tried to scramble up but only scuffed at the trail with my heels, my feet tangled and kicking at the discarded innertube.

Jason shoved his bike again, but the man knocked it aside with one hand before bringing his other forward in a quick swipe. Jason dropped the bike. I thought for a moment he'd been winded by the man's punch, judging by how the air came out of him and how he staggered. But he hadn't been punched. Or not just punched.

The man's knife was red-wet and dripping. When it slashed again, just below Jason's stomach, it split Lycra and skin and meat and, *fuck*, this wasn't happening, how was this *happening*?

Jason was unseamed. Split open. Right in front of me. He put his hands to the man's shoulders to try and keep him back while the man had both of his wrist-deep in Jason's wound as they moved past. The man was twisting his hands, turning them, rummaging inside my friend, and I saw Jason just... I saw him fucking *emptying*. He sort of... *unspooled*, right in front of me. Red ropes hanging beneath his stomach, dropping in loops. He made an attempt to catch them, keep them close, even press them back inside, and I experienced an awful feeling of déjà vu thinking *innertubes* and *inner tubes* as Jason unravelled to the path right before my eyes.

"Tell me what's next," the man said.

Jason glanced at him, then back at the wound he was cradling. When he fell it was a slow collapse to the ground, like he merely needed to sit down for a moment.

He looked at me and his eyes were...

He had this look...

It was something like wonder. He opened his mouth like he had a secret to tell but then the other man was beside him, squatting to hear it, bloody hands scooping more from Jason to spill steaming across the ground.

I have no recollection of getting up. Whatever shock had held me, I somehow shook it loose enough to do that. I must've backed up a few steps, too, because I was standing next to Jason's bike instead of my own.

Jason was sitting with his head bowed, looking down at his lap where warm, wet parts of him glistened.

The man beside him followed the loops of intestine with the point of his knife, making quick movements above the entrails as if writing something over them, or like a new learner finger-traces words as they read. He was muttering something I didn't want to hear.

I retrieved Jason's bike from the ground and ran downhill with it so that when I leapt into the saddle it was already moving.

I imagined the old man behind me, giving chase, but I didn't look back.

I would never look back, not for a long time.

Things I learnt on the Afan trail:
8. ~~Control is an illusion.~~
9. ~~Everything happens for a reason.~~
10. It should have been me.

I went back to Afan because I thought it might be good for me. My therapist wouldn't comment either way as to whether it was a good idea or not, but he did admit that some people found closure in revisiting sites of past trauma. He was useless, really. He was the one who suggested writing 'a survivor's list' of the things I'd learnt from my ordeal in order to take something positive from it, but that hasn't helped. The only one who really helped was Chrissie.

"Are you sure this is what you want?" she asked as we sat in the car, because of course she had come with me. Months had passed, but it didn't feel like it. In that time, I'd healed a broken wrist, three broken fingers, a fractured ankle, and a pretty serious skull fracture, but all of that was physical stuff and it healed pretty quickly. It was the rest I had trouble with.

Even today, I barely remember what happened right after Jason. The ride back down to the bike centre is mostly a blur. Some of that's because of how fast I went. I barely touched the brakes, leaning into every turn like Jason had shown me. Sometimes the pedals hit the ground or the rocky sides of the trail hard enough to scrape sparks and it would set the bike shuddering for a moment, but somehow I managed to readjust and keep going.

I have a vague recollection of leaving the trail. A sharp twist of the handlebars and I was careening down a steeper route, a dangerous short-cut that wasn't a track at all, just ridges and scree. I took a few jarring hits that the suspension didn't like as I sped down the technically-not-a-mountain, juddering over loose rocks that tumbled under me, riding on flat stones that were themselves sliding on pebble bearings, slipping beneath my wheels on a coarse lubricant of gravel. I dipped and bounced and bumped my way down, bike shuddering, and my feet were shaken from pedals that still turned and hacked at my shins and ankles as I see-sawed down the near-vertical slope. At one point I thought Jason was riding beside me, laughing, asking, "Are you fucking crazy?" and really, I think I was for a little while.

The man with the dreads who worked in or owned the bike hire place was still working there when I went back with Chrissie. He saw us crossing the car park and nodded hello through the frame of a bicycle he was repairing, just being friendly. He didn't recognise me or anything. I was much slimmer than the man he'd seen before, and I had a wife with me this time. My beautiful, pregnant wife. We were having a boy. We were calling him Jason.

Chrissie noticed the bike man and asked, "Is that the man who helped you?"

I nodded, and so Chrissie waved. Just polite, no big deal.

When Jason's car was the only one left in the parking area, this guy with the maybe-racist hair and the tribal tattoos grabbed a bike to come and find us. He found me first, sprawled in a state of shock, and believed enough of my babbling to call the police instead of looking for Jason by himself.

Chrissie and I walked to the noticeboard. It was a weekend this time, and a much brighter day than before, so the trail was busy. It was strange, being here again but with people around and the sun shining. Children were laughing. There was a ring-a-ling of bicycle bells in the air. There was a family standing at the board, tracing out a path on the map, the father following red loops with his finger. I recognised the stag's head symbol. Part of the track was labelled 'widow-maker' and I thought of Olivia, Jason's wife-never-to-be.

"Hey," said Chrissie. "Hey, I'm here. I'll always be here. You're okay now." Eventually she asked, "Do you want to go back?" but

I wiped my eyes without giving an answer and she took my hand again.

We walked together like that, holding hands, making our way slowly up those first few curves of the trail with a long quiet between us until Chrissie said, "They still don't know who he is."

I didn't follow the case anymore, but Chrissie occasionally Googled it, hoping to find something that might somehow help me.

I tried not to ask, but the question came anyway; "Has he said anything?"

Chrissie squeezed my hand. "No."

They'd caught the guy easily enough because he'd made no attempt to flee. They found him right by Jason's body, in fact, exactly where I said he'd be, still covered in my best friend's blood. One of the officers, far too forthcoming with information, said they'd found him wearing parts of Jason looped around his neck. I don't know why he told me that. But they could never get the guy to talk about who he was or where he'd come from, and he never said why he'd done what he'd done, except, "To show the way." He did ask to speak to me, apparently, but I said no. I don't want to hear anything he might have to say.

"It's beautiful here," Chrissie said, then immediately apologised for it, but it was okay. She was right. It *was* beautiful. The Afan Park was just a place. It held no memory of what had occurred.

But then I saw the ruins and realised, yes it did. Of course it did.

"What's wrong?"

I pointed to where red flowers grew, and around them four partial walls. This was where my name had been painted and crossed out. I still had the selfie Jason had taken and sent to my phone. His last message, me being an idiot in front of the graffiti.

But my name was not there now. The sad face with its crosses for eyes, that was still there, but my name was gone and there was another in its place, a dark line striking it through.

Jason.

Chrissie looked at the name and then to me.

"Baby?"

She took her hand from mine so she could hold the bump of her belly with both of hers and as she cradled the life she carried inside I thought of the writing on the wall and the sacrifices required of me.

|Steel Bodies|

With a subtle turn of the outboard, Abesh steered them towards a narrow gap between the two nearest vessels. Before they slipped into the dark channel, Samir cast another glance along the coast, taking in all of the tankers and container ships beached there. Some of the vessels were still very much intact, and if they did not look as good as new they at least looked functional. Others were merely skeletal outlines of steel, stripped down to holds empty of all but shadows. Or so they seemed.

The ship Abesh was taking him to was in a state of only partial decay. Several attempts had been made to take it apart, but work was now far behind schedule. It usually took 3 to 6 months to break a ship, but the *Karen May* had been sitting in the mud for nearly a year.

They passed massive propeller blades that sat only half submerged, huge fans of rusty red-brown metal hanging mud-crusted over seawater they had once twisted into currents, churned into froth. And then man and boy were past them and between ships, moving through the shadows of giants.

A sudden chill enveloped Samir as they left the sun behind, its warmth and light eclipsed by the ships either side. The metal walls channelled a cool breeze between them as Abesh steered them in and through with the tide, bump-bumping over the small waves that swelled in the reduced straight space of the sea. The shadows here were deep, deep as the cavities exposed in the steel, the metal skins of the ships pock-marked and stripped of material. Enormous superstructures, rising out of the water, they threw a vast darkness that seemed to leak from their hulls, casting them into premature dusk until there, suddenly, from high above, a shower of shooting stars that were gone before they could reach the water. Sparks from an acetylene torch somewhere nearby. Someone was working late.

Abesh muttered something, his Chittagonian fast and clipped with urgency. He put a finger to his lips to hush Samir, though he wasn't the one to have spoken.

"They will tell us it is dangerous," Abesh said, his voice low.

"It is," said Samir.

Abesh cut the engine and they drifted, carried by their momentum. It was the same way Samir had travelled for years, now. Momentum. All that had ever happened drove him towards all that was yet to occur.

"Listen," said Abesh.

Samir could hear the waves slapping against the sides of their own small boat and the enormous ships to their left and right. From somewhere hidden within one of them came some deep gurgling, the throaty rumble of an ocean contained, longing to escape. He heard the resounding clank of something heavy, its echo swallowed by other settling noises.

"Can you hear them?"

Abesh was joking, or trying to, but Samir said, "Not yet."

The boy shrugged. "This is it." He pulled their drifting boat closer to the structure beside them. The sea lapped into an exposed corridor or hold, Samir couldn't tell, and a set of steps led deeper into the vessel. "This is a good place," Abesh said, as he roped them to the framework.

"That's not what I was told."

Abesh laughed. "Are you scared?"

Samir shook his head. "No," he said, but he was lying.

Samir had come to Chittagong three days ago. More specifically, he had come to a single stretch of coastline where ships came to die. Not so many years ago, it was a part of Bangladesh that would have been dense with mangroves. Now it held more than 100 ship-breaking yards, the mangroves cleared to make way for the ever-expanding and always-profitable business of destruction.

For Samir's first visit to one of those yards, he'd arrived at low tide and watched as a line of men and boys – too many boys – dragged heavy lengths of cable through the mud towards a row of beached liners. The mud that sucked at their legs and caked their skin was loaded with all sorts of toxins – poisoned blood from the beached vessels dying on the mud flats – but all they wore for protection were shorts and t-shirts. It was exhausting even to watch. The cable would be used to heave pieces of ship inland, vast sections of steel excised from vessels that had once known the glory of the open water but now stood mired in mud. They had been tourist attractions, once, even in their ruin; there was little else this region had to offer. Now each yard was fenced off. Some were even patrolled, or so Samir had been told, though he had seen no guards. Only signs that promised danger. Signs warning against trespass. Signs forbidding photos. Samir had looked at one of those signs and had taken a picture of it because it would have amused Kamala. She would have admonished him, laughing or shaking her head.

Samir shook his head now, watching the men at work. Danger, said the signs, and yet beyond the fences people worked. The rest of the world had strict health and safety regulations, Samir had no doubt. In Bangladesh, safety precautions ranged from optional to non-existent, and there would always be plenty of men in the local shanty towns desperate enough for the dangerous work that paid so little. If it meant they could feed themselves and their families then they'd face the physical hazards of injury and fatality, risk poisoning from a range of toxic materials Samir could only guess at. Ship-breaking was big business, and almost all of the local men worked in one yard or another. Children, too, like Abesh. They were cheaper. All of the ones Samir spoke to said they were fourteen years old, but most of them were lying; it was the minimum age for ship-breaking work. Children or not, they were no less aware of the dangers and difficulties. They wore the same slack expressions of exhaustion as the men. It was what they had for a uniform, along with their filthy t-shirts and grubby shorts and the mud they wore up their legs and arms. Some already had their own 'Chittagong tattoos'. That's what they called work-related scars. The shantytowns were filled with men carrying such marks. Many of them were missing fingers. Some were missing entire limbs, or were disfigured in other ways, bent and crippled. More than a few carried the clean, smooth scars of burnt skin. But still they worked the yards, and the children followed their example. They had little choice.

"Our bodies are made of steel," one of boys had said, flexing his scrawny biceps. "Strong."

One of the other boys had pointed to Samir's face and said, "Tattoo," for the scar that cut a line through his beard. When Samir tried to smile it twisted like a broken snake.

"Tattoo," he agreed. It was work-related, so he supposed it counted.

A foreman of some kind, or someone who wanted to be, came over and yelled at the boys, his Bengali quick to emphasise the hurry. He clapped his hands once, and children who thought they were men rose to their feet to get back to work. They trudged through the mud towards a line of waiting vessels. Boys against giants, Samir thought. Every ship a Goliath waiting to fall.

"They're very young," Samir said.

The man looked at Samir. "You here to work?" He clearly didn't think so, not the way Samir was dressed.

Samir nodded. "Yes."

The man shook his head. Said, "There is nothing here for you."

The ground reverberated beneath their feet at that moment and thunder boomed, shaking the beach. The enormous noise of fallen metal as a huge section of ship collapsed down the shore. Many days of cutting through deck after deck after deck had cleaved a massive section from the main body and it crashed to the ground in a shower of sparks and sharp metal, slapping hard enough into the mud to reshape it. None of the boys walking away were startled by the noise, but Samir had ducked and the foreman had laughed at him. The thunder lingered in Samir's feet, and charged his legs with a quickening tingle.

"I'm here to work," he said.

The man sighed his laughter to an end and shook his head again. "Follow me."

A crowd of workers gathered down the beach to the section of fallen hull. The metal plate would be dragged across the mud to a waiting truck, dragged using chains and rollers and the flagging strength of malnourished men and boys. Thousands of pounds of metal moved by skinny people in tattered shorts and sandals. *Sandals.* Some of them even barefoot, risking tetanus at the very least. And there, clinging to the framework of what remained like fiery barnacles, were the cuttermen who sliced the ship into pieces. Samir saw how they leaned for hard-to-reach places, an assistant paired with each to hold not only the trailing hose of the acetylene torch but also the cutterman's free hand as he suspended himself over a fatal drop.

Samir said a prayer for them, and as he concluded he saw the ship he had come for. It loomed over the other vessels from further down the beach, as if creeping slowly back out to sea. A hulk of steel, rusted red like some scabbed wound. The *Karen May*.

Brine and diesel. The smell of it seemed to cling to Samir's skin even just sitting close to the ship. Abesh stood and leaned to clutch at one of the exposed struts of the *Karen May* and pulled them closer.

Samir tipped away what was left of his water and refilled his bottle from the sea. He fastened the lid tight and tucked it away in his bag as Abesh tied the boat secure.

Samir looked inside the exposed section of ship and saw only shadows and absences where once there was steel and substance. It was disorientating, so many missing walls and floors in this section of the ship, and each missing floor a missing ceiling. Samir leaned to look further in and up. There was a rectangle of sky above where a stairwell used to be. The sky was tinged orange, with hues of pink turning red, a fire suspended above him that shed little of its light into the ship.

"Tell me about your brother again," Samir said as he eased himself into a standing position in the small boat. He'd made a list of those killed in various accidents over the last year in the ship-breaking yard, and of those he'd made a second list that he'd brought with him of those killed or otherwise lost on the *Karen May*. Abesh's brother was on that list.

"Ibrahim?" Abesh asked. He was little more than a dusky shape in the shadows of the ship, a grubby baseball cap and thin limbs and, incongruous with Samir's question, a bright smile. He made the sound of a blast, miming an explosion with his hands. Bravado, Samir thought. *As I walk through the valley of the shadow of death, I shall fear no evil*, performed with a simple gesture and sound effect.

Abesh's brother had been a cutterman, slicing up sections of the ship when his torch ignited a gas pocket. He was killed in the explosion.

His assistant, too. Abesh had seen it happen from the beach, he'd said. Saw them both thrown hard against metal and engulfed in sudden flames. He'd told the story like it was a film he'd seen. Like a story he'd heard from someone else and hadn't been a part of himself. "It's okay," he'd said. "I have lots of brothers."

He was looking into the ship now as if his brother might still be in there.

Perhaps he was.

"How old are you, Abesh?"

"Fourteen," the boy said, and grinned.

Samir climbed from the boat into the remains of the far larger vessel they'd anchored themselves to. "I never had any brothers," he said. "Just a sister. Kamala."

Abesh made a sympathetic noise.

"I lost her when I was just a little older than you claim to be."

Abesh had no additional sympathy for that. Perhaps he thought it was worse to have a sister than to have lost one. The only sound was the boat knocking against the ship, and the water lapping.

"We were living in Munshiganj when Aila hit. Do you remember Aila?"

"One of the storms?"

Aila had not been a simple storm. Aila had been a cyclone, killing hundreds, leaving thousands homeless. But Samir agreed.

"Yes, one of the storms."

Abesh shrugged. "I remember lots of storms. They are all the same storm."

All the same storm.

Samir remembered how the water had rushed into their home. How it had filled the rooms and toppled the mud walls. Remembered how his sister had reached for him before the water took her away. He told Abesh some of this, staring into the *Karen May*. What remained of his family had fled to Dhaka, already crowded with those running from other floods. Other storms.

All the same storm.

Samir had often looked for Kamala in those crowds.

"Why are you telling me this?" Abesh asked. He had stopped looking into the ship's shadows and instead looked set to follow Samir.

"Wait here," Samir told him.

Abesh looked disappointed, but he sat down.

"I'm the only one left," Samir told him. "I told you about Kamala so that you can remember her."

He shrugged his bag into a more comfortable position on his shoulder and pulled his way deeper into the *Karen May*.

The foreman had taken Samir to an office made from an old cargo container. It sat on short stilts of recovered scrap but still it sank into the mud at one end. The lean was even more obvious inside thanks to the papers, maps, and notices pinned to the walls.

"Wait here," the man said.

Samir waited.

The paperwork on the walls all concerned the ship-breaking, of course. Each vessel had its own hanging clipboard of papers, and a large map of the beach illustrated where they were located with barely legible script, circled numbers, and shorthand symbols, like some mystical chart. The trappings of a spell that summoned wealth. Samir read some of the details, though he'd already done his research. Ships were bought by an international broker, and a suitable captain – a *good* captain – was hired to beach it properly on the narrow strip of mud-beach like someone else might park a car. Then more people were paid to take the thing apart. A ship had a lifespan of only thirty years or so and then they became too expensive to maintain, too costly to insure. With profits dwindling, each ship became more valuable as scrap, with more than 90% of each vessel recyclable. A lot of the material was resold right away: the liquids, machinery, the easily-removed fixtures; it all got sold on to salvage dealers. Engines, wiring. Everything. Samir saw a list detailing all the copper pulled from one of the vessels, and the sum beside it amazed him. The steel would be converted into building materials like rebar, tension devices to reinforce larger constructs. Samir thought of the workers standing in bent shapes or taut with the strain of some heavy task, sticking from the mud; they were like exposed rebar themselves, holding the yards together. Profits in excess of 83 million taka, depending on the price of steel, were built upon their strength, and at great cost. He had a list of dead men who knew the truth of that.

He turned from the records when the door behind him opened. A large man stepped into the office. Samir knew already that this would be Mabud Kibria. He barely glanced at Samir, making his way to a heavily loaded desk and rifling through the papers piled there. The foreman who had escorted Samir earlier followed.

"This is the man looking for work."

Judging by the number of clipboards and the red underlines on the map, there would be plenty of work for those who wanted it. India may have dismantled more ships each year, but here in Bangladesh they recycled more deadweight tonnage than anywhere else in the world.

"I'm not *looking* for work," Samir reminded the foreman.

Mabud gave Samir more than a glance this time, clearly annoyed that whatever little time he was going to spare had already been wasted.

"I am here *to* work," Samir told him. "Rokeya Begum sent me."

Samir fumbled for a handrail he'd forgotten was no longer there as he climbed. He would start from the top and work his way down. He had to be careful; the handrail was missing, but so were some of the steps themselves. The portholes had been taken from the walls, and in many places the walls were gone as well. Inside the ship was an absence that expanded. Samir walked within a steady decomposing of steel. There were no railings on the deck, either. Samir passed mounts for missing cranes. Saw signs for lifeboats that weren't there.

Out to sea, in the fading light of the setting sun, children were playing in the dieselled waters. They swam around a raft of wreckage, clambering up only to throw their young careless bodies at toxic water and whatever scrap metal might lurk submerged there. Despite what they might have thought, their bodies were not made of steel. Each was susceptible to breakage, all too easily opened up and spilt empty, or filled with fluid instead of breath. Samir had to look away from their play, unable to stop imagining the worst.

Port and starboard, the Bangladeshi beach was an open graveyard. The ships here did not sink, they slumped; rotting, rusting corpses alive only by day with the men who took them apart reducing them to rivetless pieces. But in the dark they looked almost whole again. It was easy to imagine each as it might have once been. Their slow progress across the world's oceans; the sudden climb and plunging fall over waves the size of mountains. Leviathan, each of them, forging paths that disappeared almost immediately behind them as they fell and rose again. These were cruise liners and tankers and container ships from all over the world. Who had sailed them? What had brought them to the ships, and where had each ship taken them? And what else had each ship carried? Here they were now, these amazing constructions, at their journey's end. Waiting to be torn apart, they spilled silent stories into the mud, into the sea, like slicks of oil, each sinking or getting dragged away with every outgoing tide.

In the bridge, every monitor and machine, every button, every wire, had all been taken. Samir stood at the where the windows used to be, imagining himself the captain looking out at a vast ocean and a sky full of stars. Now, windows empty of glass framed a landscape that was all mud and lights coming on in the city inland, or from the fires on the beach where workers kept the evening chill away burning unsalvageable materials in old oil drums. Burning asbestos and worse, probably.

Samir retrieved a small bound bundle of sage from his bag and wedged it into a tight corner of metal. He lit it, and wafted the aromatic smoke with his hands as he recited a prayer. He was combining his faith with 'smudging', a Native American ritual which cleansed a space of negative energy, and with science; sage cleared the air of bacteria.

He would descend now, and wind his way through the corridors until he found the 'dark heart' of the ship. It was a suitable metaphor. Much of what Samir did was couched in metaphor. That was how faith worked, and it made the supernatural easier to understand. He had grown up Christian in a Muslim country but he knew all the faiths now. He liked the stories. Stories were useful. Powerful, sometimes.

Inside the ship again, it was difficult to remember the noble majesty he'd imagined from the bridge. What he saw here, in the beam of his torch, was decrepit. There was no engine thrumming life through the body of this giant, and no rhythmic movement of tide around it that he could feel. Yet there was something. Some vibration of life inside, something more than silence. Sounds that rose from its own depths. The sudden clank-spank echo from some unseen place as something fell. The metallic groan of steel grinding on steel, like the drawn out inhalation of a final breath. From somewhere deep came a steady ticking, like a swinging chain striking a wall in a hidden chamber. And always, everywhere, dripping. Wherever Samir touched, his hand came away wet, red-brown with rust.

Throughout the ship, Samir inhaled the thick smell of the saltwater mud sump it sat in, breathing in the sharp odours of steel and copper and whatever else remained to oxidise. He could smell oil, and some pungent chemical that wasn't altogether unpleasant. He fancied he could feel the odours on his skin, and the dark he moved through, too. He rolled his sleeves down against it.

Samir explored. He found a galley stripped of its sinks, seeing only rectangles in the metal where they used to be. He cast the beam of his torch over holes where once there were pipes. He found a sockets and vents in a long line – a laundry room, maybe, or somewhere for computers or some other kinds of machines, all of it gone now. Yet for all the absences, the atmosphere was still oppressive. The passages were tight, and stepping through doorways stripped of their hatches seemed to take Samir into closer confines instead of opening up into empty vacant spaces. He was walking a labyrinth of steel that seemed to narrow around him.

He needed some air. What he was breathing was thin, like others had exhaled it countless times before, leaving little for him. It was metallic and sharp like blood. And though what he breathed in seemed thin, the air around him seemed dense. A thickening of atmosphere that pressed against him. He had experienced such contrasts before, such oppressiveness and shortness of breath, but even in Dhaka it had never been as severe as this. He took a small canister from his bag, fixed a plastic piece that would cover his mouth, and pumped a deep fresh breath from it. Another.

Stepping aboard the *Karen May* had been like stepping into the inhalation before a scream. Some had told him the ship was brooding, waiting for someone to come aboard, and he'd felt that. Now he felt like he walked poised on a pendulum at the highest point of its swing, waiting to plummet.

He descended walkways that hadn't felt footsteps for months, maybe a year. The sound each step made was strangely muted, stifled before it could echo fully. Surprised to find a handrail at one section, he had taken it, only for it to come away from the cancerous sheet metal. He dropped it in surprise and it made only the briefest noise in falling. Even with the torch beam cutting a way ahead of him, Samir felt like he barely had any presence of his own. Like his passage through the dark was a temporary unseaming of the shadows he walked through, shadows that sealed up again behind him, and for a moment he couldn't shake the impression of having been swallowed whole. Like Jonah, in the body of Leviathan.

The thought brought him comfort. The whale had swallowed Jonah to protect him from a storm.

All the same storm.

As if to mock Samir's train of thought, the ship released a sudden low groan and, on the tail of it, came a soft stuttered sound. Like someone sobbing in the dark.

"Peace be with you," Samir called. It came back to him only in part, a repetition of peaces –

pieces?

– and then a sudden scream. Shrill, and brief, like wrenched metal.

"Samir?"

The voice came quietly.

"I'm here," Samir said. He set his bag down and swept his torch behind, and up, and down. It showed him only narrow passageways like ventricles and walls red with rust and he thought again of being held inside the body of a beast, only now he thought of the other Jonah, the one sailors thought bad luck. He took another puff of air from the canister and flinched at the hiss of it. Thought he heard it come back to him, closer than it should have been, and sharper. A gasp of sound. He swept the torch behind again and was startled when a shape pulled away from the wall. A body peeled from the gloom, dark but for the wide eyes and the teeth suddenly grinning.

"You frightened me!" said the boy.

"Abesh!"

The boy spoke again before Samir could admonish him fully.

"I want to see my brother."

Samir sighed. "He's not here."

"Then where is he?"

"He's with you."

"But what if he's here as well? Like the others?"

Previously, Abesh had feigned to not believe the stories. He had scoffed at the idea of a haunted wreck and, according to Mabud, was not only unafraid but actually keen to work the ship, though nobody would work it with him. Now, though, it seemed the stories had convinced him, at least partially. Only partially, because still the boy was still unafraid.

"Will you help him?"

Samir nodded. "I will help him. Now go. Back to the boat. It's dangerous here."

Abesh did as he was told. Samir only stopped him when he heard a quick rasp and saw the sudden flare of flame that came with a lit match. The boy held it aloft to light his way but dropped it, startled, when Samir yelled at him.

"Dangerous!" he repeated, and handed the boy his torch. He had another.

"You'll help him?" Abesh said again, shining the beam close enough to Samir to see his face. "You promise?"

"I'll do all I can," Samir said.

He watched the child carry the light away until it was gone.

Rokeya Begum had served Samir *choddo shaak* almost as soon as he'd arrived at her house. It was a vast dish, made up of fourteen different vegetables, but he was hungry and thankful for the meal and did not care that this was not the right time to eat it, that this was not *Bhoot Chaturdashi*. She had prepared it thinking of how it might help him, but he ate only to satisfy his hunger. He would welcome the protection, but he had other wards, other charms. Symbols of his faiths, which were all the stronger for being plural.

He had, in his bag, a selection of photographs he'd taken of the ship after speaking with Mabud Kibria at the breaking yard. He'd zoomed in on the vessel after downloading the pictures to his laptop, and had printed several copies of what he'd found. He retrieved them now, as he ate.

"Please, look at these. I took these this morning. What do you see?"

Even enlarged, the pictures showed little more than the ship. Presented in a state of partial deterioration, it held shadows like blemishes, and looked in places as if the picture had not developed fully. There were many dark spaces. But if you looked long enough…

"Faces," Rokeya said. "I see faces." She pointed. "There. And there. And – there are so many of them."

Samir noted how she would not touch the photograph. Didn't poke them when she pointed, hadn't picked up a single one, just looked at where they lay on the table amongst the dishes of food. "Are they all…" But she didn't finish her question. She looked at Samir and said again, instead, "So many."

"Your son?"

She nodded.

"Where?" He tried to hand her one of the pictures but she recoiled, albeit subtly; she half-stood and leaned across the table to fetch him more water.

"Will you help them?" she said, refilling his glass.

Samir gathered up the photos.

"I'll do all I can."

"Muhammed Goswami said you helped him. In Dhaka?"

Samir touched the scar on his face but turned the gesture into a rub of his beard, remembering. "Yes."

It had been difficult, but yes, he had helped.

"You are Christian?"

"I am."

Less than one percent were in this country, but Samir had been taken in by missionaries after Aila and though they hadn't forced any of their teachings on him, he'd learned from them anyway.

"Christian," she said. "Not Muslim."

"Muslim too."

What did it matter, he felt like asking. God is the ocean, and religions are the ships that carry us.

But of course, it did matter.

He drank some of his water. It tasted salty. "I can help."

Rokeya sighed. She had little choice but to let him try, at least. They always had little choice by the time they were requesting his help.

"I want you to free my son's spirit," Rokeya told him. Samir knew this already; she was only saying it to hear it herself. "Release him from that terrible place."

It was likely that the only ones he would be setting free were those left behind. Those who grieved, and held on so hard that it hurt. Like squeezing a handful of keys. He would ease them of that, at least.

He looked around the room as he closed his bag on the photographs. There were many pictures of her son. He was well remembered. This was good. It would help him more than the *choddo shaak* he was eating.

"Tell me about him."

She nodded again, but said nothing for a long time. "There was an accident..." she managed eventually.

"I know. Tell me about him before then."

She found that much easier.

The Bengali word for ghost is *bhoot*, or *bhut*. It is also the word for past. So Samir listened to all of her stories, and he ate all of the vegetable she gave him, and he hoped it would be enough.

Samir had been told, once, by a man in Jamalpur, that ghosts could only exist for as long as it took their body to decompose. Samir could understand how such a belief might be born, how it could stand as a metaphor for the grieving process. He could see, too, how it might appeal to those who'd had little time to prepare for a great loss. A transition period in which loved ones could linger but not be trapped, able, still, to pass on to whatever it was that came next. For the brief time he had known Dr Shahid, a missionary he'd met in Dhaka, he had come to recognise a different belief. That the dead remained, in some form or another, for as long as there was someone else to remember them. This was how Christ could still be with us, she'd explained, and Samir had nodded like he was supposed to, and stored the story away with all the others that made up the different faiths he carried with him.

When it came to the *Karen May*, he was more inclined to believe Dr Shahid's version than what he'd heard in Jamalpur. He thought of Abesh's brother, incinerated in a blast; what had remained to decompose in a case like that? He thought of Nasir, Rokeya's son. He'd fallen through a hatch, plummeting deep into the vessel's hold. Enough water had flooded the wreck that the fall didn't kill him, but he broke so many bones on the way down hitting struts and part-walls that he couldn't keep afloat or swim and the man had drowned before anyone could help him. His body had been recovered. It had been cleaned, shrouded, and buried, as according to Islam. No doubt something of him still remained in his grave, though for many he was already forgotten. Rokeya remembered him for who he had been, Rokeya and Abdul, but Mabud Kibria in the ship-breaking office hadn't even remembered the name, was reminded only when Samir explained how the man had died. That's all he was now. A death. Like all the others. Every dead worker had become the method of their ending: the one who fell, the one who burned, the one who suffocated. The one crushed flat beneath tonnes of freed steel. The one thrown and broken by an unexpected blast. Each of them united in that their work had killed them.

And that this ship had taken them.

The ship wanted him, too; Samir could feel it. Not Samir specifically, just someone; it had been so long. Nobody would work the vessel anymore. It was the only reason he had been allowed to even take a look. Often Samir would need to convince people to allow him to complete his work, persuade them with a mix of cajoling or something spiritual if they seemed that way inclined – he knew various faiths well enough to talk about them with authority. This time, though, he had been granted permission with little hesitation or reservation. The men in charge were more interested in profits than prophets and didn't care what had to be done, so long as people would work the ship again. Whether Samir could cleanse the ship or not didn't matter, so long as they had been seen to try. The workers would be less afraid.

Samir found a suitable spot for his purpose and stopped. He estimated he was near the middle of the ship, both regarding its length and his position between decks. Where he stood, the passage branched off in two directions. Taken with a missing wall opposite, he was positioned at an improvised crossroads. Not exactly the points of the compass, but it would do.

"This is it, Kamala," he said. He took a final puff from the canistered oxygen and readied other items from his bag. "You ready?"

Of all his faiths, his sister was the one Samir believed in most of all. Reciting her name was as much a part of any of his rituals as any sacred text or practised gesture. She looked after him still, just as he cared for her in carrying her with him. She—

From the dark ahead, the opened room, came the tiny scrape of furtive movement. As if a sandal had trodden rust underfoot.

"Abesh?"

But Abesh would be behind him, would be back at the boat by now, and the boy had been barefoot.

From the dark again, another sound. Someone panting, like the breaths between hard sobs. Or the noise someone might make as they suffocated.

Whimpering.

And from over there, a muttering he couldn't make out. A trailing of words he couldn't quite hear, quick but quiet, like a desperate prayer or the hasty promises someone made when in trouble.

Samir set his torch down on the floor, leant it within the loop of his bag's strap, opened both arms to all he heard, and spoke so they might hear him.

He told them about his sister. He told them she liked ice cream and the way birds flew in patterns and how she hated to be called Kami. He told them about how she died, too, and how she was forever with him.

This was how he always started.

A standing shape came into the corridor, rolling in from behind a door frame as if detaching itself from the wall there. It was a man. He had a shredded face. His skin was hanging in thin wet ribbons from his brow, cheeks, and from his jowls where the front of his throat was open. Lower, and Samir saw the chest was open, too.

"My name is Samir Zakir Hamid," he told him, and his voice wavered. He could see the broken bones of an exposed ribcage protruding from the man. He nudged his torch so the grisly sight was illuminated clearly and saw amongst those bloody bones rows of metal struts curving from the flesh. Rusted bars, like railings or corroded pipes.

From deep below, beneath his feet, a wallowing groan swallowed its own echo in rising through the decks. It engulfed Samir, heavy but brief, and faded like some distant whale song.

The sudden stench of charred meat announced a second presence. Emerging from further away, clambering up from the floor as if it had knelt there all this time, a red-black man scorched featureless of all but wet glistening limbs and a blacked nub where a face used to be. It took faltering steps towards Samir, guiding itself by bumping into one wall and then the other as it stumbled forward.

"You don't have to—"

And now there, from between the legs of the first, came another. Drawing itself across the floor with torn arms. A man whose torso marked the end of his body, save for what trailed out of it. He reached for Samir with the hand that wasn't pulling him forward, the left, then the right, in some tortured dry-swimming crawl.

Samir looked back the way he had come and saw more shadows than had been there before. He nudged the torch with his foot and saw others of those who'd perished here. Brought them into life by seeing them. They had changed, forced into new shapes by what had killed them and wearing scars that disfigured them beyond any Chittagong tattoo, each carrying some aspect of the ship. This one rusted where it should have rotted. This one with struts like splints, another with rivets where eyes should be, or a gaping porthole for a face.

Their stories were mingling. All who died here found their identities bound together, and bound to the ship.

Samir talked about each of the men who had died on this ship, knowing those who approached were some of those same men. And as corrupted as they had been, as disfigured and reduced, they recognised something of themselves in what Samir said. He had a notebook filled with what their families had told him, and he had photographs too, but he relied on his memory, speaking in a rush not because he was afraid – though he was – but as a sort of litany, a tribute given not to appease but to convince. I can keep you alive, his stories said. I will remember you, and you can live on in me. Not here, in this rusting hulk of cold metal. In the flesh and blood of me, where my own spirit is anchored. Where my sister lives. And Christ. And Allah. Ninety nine gods, and more. Replace this vessel with me. Let me carry you.

"Nasir?"

The nearest dark passenger of the *Karen May* made a guttural sound, a thick growl that bubbled from a throat choked with water. It reached for Samir with hands black and slick with oil.

"Your name is Nasir. You fell and you drowned."

He saw it happen in more detail than he had been told, saw it more vividly than was contained in any written report. He saw how quickly and quietly the man plummeted, and how he landed across a beam as yet untaken. Saw him fold over it, heard the crack of spine and the way his feet kicked against metal as he flipped around it, and fell. Saw him facedown in the filthy water, drowning in the ship's black dregs.

The man pulled a fistful of Samir's shirt, yanking buttons from their threads and tearing one half of the garment almost entirely free. It exposed the crucifix he wore. The blue peacock eye of a nazar boncuğu amulet. The scriptures he'd tattooed across his chest. Whether from one or the sum total of all, Nasir recoiled vampire-like, though perhaps it was simply the momentum of his violence as he staggered back with a wet handful of Samir's clothing.

"Your name is Nasir, and you lived with your mother Rokeya and your father Abdul who is too old for physical work but loved to hear about yours. Your mother told me. She remembers your life well."

What had once been a man came again at Samir, pushed him hard to the wall and went in quick to meet him and…

Was gone.

"And which one are you?" Samir said to the next. "Did you fall, did you explode, did you burn or bleed? Because I remember all of you, now. I wasn't there when you died, but I've heard how you lived and I'm here now; I can take you away with me when I go."

There was a sharp, high-grinding whine of metal from somewhere within the ship. Sheet metal torn and folded. A deep wailing came up from the bowels of the vessel as a foul-smelling wind. A fetid stench, channelled to Samir through empty chambers and corridors stripped down to metal bones. It passed over him like breath, sour and dank. With the buffeting of his clothes, the tousling of his hair, some of those Samir had come to see collapsed back into the steel that had taken them. One fell, and burst into red flakes of rust that were dispersed by that same air. Another staggered into a wall, then a second wall, ricocheting in frantic spinning turmoil before falling against a space where a wall only used to be and tumbling into a dark that swallowed him whole. The ship would regurgitate him when it needed, unless…

"There's more to remember you by than how you died," Samir told those who gathered to him, moths to his flame of hope. "There are others who remember you better than this."

The crowd was dispersing and growing and dispersing, all in flux. Some were taken by shadows, others birthed by them, but there were those who flared, consumed suddenly not by fire but some bright burning light.

"Yes," said Samir. Memories and ghosts. Each so easily became the other.

Still, many remained. Those whose families Samir could not find or would not speak to him. Those who had no one but those they worked with, who knew them now only as ghost stories.

"Tell me who you were," Samir said. "Before this place."

One by one, they came to him. They held him tight in desperation, pulling him hard to support their listing forms as they breathed their stories into his ear. They smelled of rust and oil and mud, burnt flesh, blood, and the bilge of old flooded compartments. Their words fluttered like scraps of wind-blown tarpaulin, and with the last whispered one, so did they.

Samir, exhausted, lowered himself to sit when they were done. His breath came in thin bursts, like he'd run some long race, so he took another full blast from the mask and canister he'd brought with him. Then he began unpacking other items from his bag.

He wasn't finished.

Some had called the *Karen May* haunted, and others had called it cursed, when in fact it was merely dying and trying not to. The *Karen May* had slowed her own demise by creating a new identity. Rather than suffer an undignified death, at foreign hands on a dirty shore, she would make others suffer, and she would live.

"You've sailed every ocean," Samir said, fumbling at the claps in his bag, "sailed all of them so often to know there is only really one. We give it different names. The Atlantic. The Pacific. The Bay of Bengal. We recognise the strength that comes with a name. The containment."

Samir grabbed handfuls of paper and cast them about the floor in front of him. Maps and charts and travel records.

"You are the *Karen May*, and you have known the power of the sea."

He spread rolls of paper and weighted them at the corners with piles of salt, lined the edges with it to hold them. It was used in many rituals, but this was the first time he'd used it to represent the sea. He cast photographs of the *Karen May* upon them, none of the ones he'd taken, nor those from the ship-breaking office, but pictures of her in harbour, at sea, loaded with crew, with passengers, containers. He splashed water over them, anointed them as if with something holy but using the sea he'd brought in with him in his water bottle. There was an article from a newspaper he read aloud before adding it to the pile, an itinerary, a manifest of documents and statistics and records that he shared, though he mentioned nothing of money or of costs, said nothing of profits. He did not reduce her to that.

Her. Like all ships, she had been given a name and personified. Given life. Why would she not be bitter about seeing it end?

These ocean-going giants were never meant to be broken. They had withstood the world's most ferocious conditions, crossing oceans that rose like mountains and dropped like valleys, burdened with cargo or passengers and taking them safely to wherever they needed to go. And now they sank only in mud, with the sea behind them. Sliced into sections and repurposed, more savaged than salvaged, and all they'd ever done before was forgotten.

The *Karen May* was not a graveyard, haunted by those who had died within her. She was a corpse, haunting the shore and doing all she could to be remembered. That was the problem. She was a ghost, existing only for as long as it took to decompose, but with no one willing to take her apart anymore. Or existing only for as long as she was remembered, but being remembered wrong. Every life she took became a new story and built her anew, created a cursed or haunted ship none would dare venture aboard, prolonging her own destruction by building her into something terrifying.

"We are each of us vessels, in the same turbulent sea."

Samir thought of everything people did to stave off their gradual collapse into irrelevance and insignificance. Whenever Samir's faith faltered, he found another to cling to. And another. That was their beauty, that was their strength. Surely it didn't matter to God?

The salt piles shifted in a gentle trembling. The papers moved askew and some were picked up in a new breeze. The torch fell from where it nestled in the bag strap and began to roll, turning half-circles this way and that and jittering with the new vibrations that were passing through the ship.

Samir stood. He clutched at the nearest support.

The lost engine, and all the ghost machinery of the vessel, was making itself heard for a final time. From somewhere distant came the sound of water churning. For a brief moment Samir wondered if it was his turn to be taken and was glad there were few to remember him. Then the ship listed and Samir staggered with it. He clutched at a frame where a hatch used to be and his legs kicked out into open air as the vessel suddenly slumped violently to one side. Pieces of it fell. Lots of them. A thunderous succession of crashes, metal clattering on metal. Samir felt a wash of heat, and for a moment shadows were cast into dancing shapes by some blooming flare of orange somewhere distant in the ship's belly.

The echo of whatever blast that had been faded like a sigh.

Samir found his feet again, though the floor he stood on now was angled and it groaned as if the weight of him was too much to bear.

Samir scooped up his torch and ran.

He'd done it. What he hadn't expected, though, was the quick disintegration of the ship once it had let go. Now metal buckled beneath his feet and he stomped booted-prints into each panel as he fled. Each step of the stairs bowed in the middle as he climbed, the last few giving way entirely under him just as he set foot on the next. He stumbled onto the deck and rolled, got back to his feet. The entire ship was leaning, as if pitched in some slow violent sea, and Samir was disorientated. His torch still worked but he might as well have been in darkness; he did not recognise where he was. Until there, on the ground, a spent match. This was the way Abesh had come. And there – another. He followed them quickly, found more stairs, and hauled himself up as parts of it crashed away beneath him.

He burst out of the ship's confines into the free fresh air of its uppermost deck and saw they were being swept out in a rush to sea.

Pulled from the shore that no longer held them, water washing in and around them as the land receded, receded...

Samir threw himself overboard. For a moment he held a graceful dive, like he'd seen the boys doing at dusk, and he panicked, recognising how he had been tricked. He had been expelled, jettisoned like spray from a cresting whale, and he had a moment to worry that he had flung himself from a great height towards mud flats that would smack him dead. But there was tide enough to catch him after all, and though it was so shallow that he felt the seabed in his kick to resurface, it held him safe.

Beside him, looming huge where it had always been, was the mud-mired steel-picked wreck of the *Karen May*, hollow and unhallowed. Sullen and spiteful, and silent now, but for the quiet hush of the shallows around it, and the bumping of the boat in which Abesh had brought them, still tethered to its hull and empty of all but shadows.

|The Swans|

~

"Be careful, little man, I don't want you falling in."

The canal was shallow at the bank where they stood but still deep enough to worry about, Helen thought. And four or five feet deep in the middle; plenty reason enough to insist Charlie wore his lifejacket at all times on deck. Standing here on solid ground she had let him go without it and she regretted it already.

"Charlie?"

"I'll be careful."

The wild way in which he flung his bread said otherwise, his arm coming all the way back then arcing out with sudden speed that was efficient but clumsy.

"Break the bread up a bit, honey. They can't eat pieces that size."

The sodden slice of white was sinking uneaten, the swans slow and lazy in their pursuit. There were two, one significantly larger than the other, both of them sleek yet slow. Perhaps they were tired of the haphazard delivery system; Charlie's throws sent bread left and right but never directly to them.

Helen was glad of the swans. Was glad of some time away from the all-too-narrow boat. Now that Charlie was tearing the stale bread into pieces, she was pleased for the little extra time it would take to feed them as well. She didn't like the boat much. It was beautiful on the outside, bright and colourful, but the inside, as neat and efficient as it was, felt too enclosed. Her first night had not been a good one. Too many bad dreams, some of them true.

"Can I feed one?" Charlie asked. One of the swans was approaching him at the bank. The big one.

"You *are* feeding them."

"I mean can I feed one?" He held out a piece of bread then looked at her for permission.

"Just put it in the water, sweetheart." The swan was gliding to her boy's hand, so she said again, "In the water, go on."

Charlie dropped the bread and the swan snatched it up. It would have had his fingers for sure, Helen thought, wondering if it was true that they could break your arm. Were their wings really strong enough? Perhaps a child's arm, yes. But had it ever happened? Why did people say it?

"Throw it out," she said, "Far out, across the water. See if you can hit the other side."

Charlie turned his body with the action, throwing the bread like a discus. The ragged shape of it spun up the canal rather than across it, but the swan followed anyway and that was the main thing.

"Good boy."

Helen and Charlie were the only two on the waterway this morning, but it was still early. A thin mist clung to the water and seeped into grassy banks rich with the smell of fresh dew. The boat was moored nearby. It was far too big for their needs, but it had been the only one available. She'd been able to rent it for the same price as one of the smaller vessels, though, so that was good. The steering took some getting used to, that was all.

"Charlie, honey, be careful."

He wasn't paying attention, looking at her instead of the swan that was returning for the next piece of bread in his hand.

Helen pointed – "I think he's hungry, sweetheart" – and Charlie turned to see the swan stretching its long neck forward. His cry of surprise sounded exaggerated, but she laughed as he threw the bread high into the air. Another full slice. It slapped down on the water and the bird darted for it, beak snapping it into pieces quickly gobbled down.

"Do *all* swans belong to the Queen?" Charlie asked.

"I think so."

"Even these ones?"

"I think so."

"Does *she* ever feed them?"

Helen smiled. "I don't know. Maybe."

"What about the King?"

"Is that bag empty now?"

Charlie looked inside. "All gone."

"Then shake out the crumbs and put the bag in your pocket so they know."

"All gone," he said again, letting the crumbs fall into the water. Before he could pocket the bag, though, a breeze took it from him. It floated past Helen before she could catch it.

"Quick, Mum!"

There was no urgency. The bag had caught in some of the long grasses or reeds – she wasn't sure of the difference – that nestled close together in a tall thatch rising out of the canal. Helen plucked the bag free and scrunched it into her pocket, glancing down at a spot where the reeds beside the towpath had been flattened down. It took a moment for her mind to register what she was seeing.

"Stay there," she said to Charlie.

He would have done exactly that, had she not told him. "Why?" he asked, making his way over.

"I mean it," she said, and Charlie could tell. He stopped.

"What? What is it, mum?"

"A swan," she said.

"What's wrong with it?"

She hadn't said anything was wrong with it, but children just knew, didn't they? They heard your thoughts even when you were saying something else, sometimes.

"It's all right," she said. "It's just sleeping."

The reeds had been flattened down in a circle and the swan was displayed in the centre. It wasn't all right, and it wasn't sleeping. The swan was dead. Not just dead but killed; its head had been cut off all the way down at the base of the neck where it normally joined the body and, oh, how she wished she hadn't seen that neat red circle. A bloody full stop on feathered paper. The wings were folded into the body, a neat white parcel except for its open wet wound.

Helen looked at the other two swans, wondering if one of them could have possibly caused such damage. She wondered how they were able to tolerate the loss. They were gliding back down the canal, carried by a current too slow to see or perhaps paddling their hidden webbed feet furiously. Secret effort for a seeming grace. One of them briefly examined the gap between the boat and the bank but detoured around the vessel instead.

"Come on," Helen said. "Let's go. Hold Mummy's hand."

Charlie was too old for Mummy now, she didn't know why she'd said it, but he did as he was told. She led him away from the grisly nest, back towards the boat.

"Can I drive?"

Helen remembered the silent stare of the shirtless man, saw again the way he clenched his jaw, but she said, "Yes, all right." She understood there was some kind of trade off here, even if Charlie didn't quite realise he was doing it.

"Just let me get us started."

Charlie hurried ahead, pulling her after him, eager to get back onboard.

The early chill of the morning quickly faded and the low mist on the water burnt away under the warmth of the sun so that Helen and Charlie puttered onward in a lazy haze of sunshine, wending their way at a wonderfully slow pace. The hum of their engine was the drone of honeybees, drugging Helen into drowsiness, a pleasant state of in-between. The low fields on either side of the canal were spotted with the fluttering forms of butterflies, and wisps of dandelion seed hung in a gentle breeze. Meandering with the waterway, they eventually passed into countryside that was farmland, thick with colourful crops and home to lethargic cows. Helen had seen the canal in the city suburbs, had smelled its dark waters and grimaced at the sludge that clung to its litter, but here the water was dappled with sparkles of sunlight and the air carried the subtle scent of distant manure and rapeseed. Helen felt almost calm, this far from the city. The noise and the people, the relentless energy and startling vitality, the traffic, the pollution; it all tired her. Here she could enjoy a temporary respite from all but the most simple decisions. Though it was supposed to be a time for making choices, Helen found she was really enjoying the lack of them: their world, for a few days at least, was a stretch of canal forever straight and narrow. There was no urgency to be somewhere, somewhen, and it left her with the feeling that they'd stepped aside for a moment while the rest of the world carried on without them.

Despite the fine weather, they'd not seen many people on the canal. Occasionally they'd glimpse the stern of a boat ahead of them, which they never seemed to catch, and once a boat had passed them the other way, but that was all. She had expected more, especially on a long weekend. And she had expected more people on the towpaths, too. At one point they'd seen a chair and a rod set out for fishing, a small picnic of lunch laid out beside it, but no sign of the owner.

"Mum?"

"You're doing fine, sweetheart."

He was. They were well under the four miles-per-hour limit, and when he steered he did it gently and with plenty of time, his small hands comfortable now on the long-stretched S of the tiller. It took a bit of getting used to, that was all. He'd learned his lesson.

On the first day, within the first half an hour, Helen had allowed Charlie to take control of the boat. She had steered them out of the boatyard, negotiating the channels between the jetties – and that had not been easy, not with such a large vessel – but immediately after that they were on the straight course of the canal and Charlie had begged and so she'd let him. There were still many other boats around but they were moored at the banks, semi-permanently from the looks of most of them, so Helen had thought it would be all right. Even when Charlie steered them too severely she'd thought they were fine, talking him through how to correct the turn, speaking calmly, explaining that he had to turn the tiller in the opposite direction to where he wanted to go and then pointing to where he needed to take them. But he was anxious about how slowly the boat moved, the length of it taking an age to straighten out, and he overcorrected while increasing their speed, sending them across to the other bank. Helen had needed to take the controls, desperately trying to alter a course she could tell was already fixed as they headed at one of the boats tied up at the side.

They'd bumped it hard. Both of them lurched with the impact, Helen grabbing for the lifejacket Charlie wore, steadying him, while she tried to straighten the boat. A man had come out from the other vessel almost immediately. He was wearing jeans, but barefoot and bare-chested. He was lightly muscled and handsome. Helen had apologised several times before he could say anything himself, embarrassingly close to him as they were carried past. She could see the grey shadow of stubble on his jaw and the way he clenched it as she apologised again with the second bump as the rear of their boat struck his. The man had grabbed the doorframe and cabin roof for support but only stared, red-faced and breathing hard but saying nothing. Helen would have preferred shouting, or a good swear word thrown her way. She didn't belong here. He could have told her to go home.

"*Mum?*"

"Mm?"

Charlie pointed this time.

There was a family on the canal, each encased to the waist in the blue shell of a kayak. They were travelling single file, led by the father, a pack secured to the front of his craft with a criss-cross of elasticised rope. He stopped paddling and indicated for his wife and daughter to do the same while they waited for Helen and Charlie to pass. He smiled.

"Okay, let me," Helen said, stepping to the tiller.

"I can do it, Mum," Charlie said, but he was already turning them the wrong way.

"Charlie."

Charlie hesitated, then stepped away for her. "Careful," he said.

There was plenty of room, but Helen steered close to the bank anyway and cut the engine completely to drift. Charlie went over to the side and leaned to look at the family.

"Morning," said the woman, and, "Morning," said her husband. The girl smiled and nodded hello.

"There are swans down there," Charlie said, pointing.

"Well, we might have something for them," said the man, patting the pack in front of him.

"We fed them already."

"*Charlie.*" Helen smiled at the family but said to him, "They might be hungry again."

The man raised a hand to block the light from his eyes, watching as they cruised by. Helen wondered if she should say anything about the swan she'd discovered in the reeds. She didn't know how to bring it up, though, not with Charlie around.

The kayaks rocked as Helen and Charlie passed; only a gentle side to side wobble in their wake, an easy up and down, but Helen apologised anyway. It was dismissed with a wave that became a proper wave goodbye as the family started paddling again, father in front. Strong slow strokes, she noticed, watching him go.

Charlie watched too.

"That man kept looking at you."

"Did he?"

"The man in the canoe."

Helen glanced behind but they were already too distant, too low to the water, to see clearly. She hadn't noticed the man looking. Barely noticed him at all. Maybe that was a good sign.

"Kayak, honey."

"What?"

"The boats they were in. They're kayaks."

"Why was he looking at you?"

"I don't know, honey. I don't know that he was."

"He was."

Charlie was looking up at her, squinting into the light, one hand curled at his brow in an awkward sun-shielding salute.

"Maybe he was looking at the boat," she said. "It's a beautiful boat."

"But he's got a canoe."

"Kayak. It's a kayak, honey."

On either side of them, bushes of bright white flowers crowded the banks and dipped into the canal. She recognised the image as one from the tourist guide. There was a lock coming up soon, and a pub shortly after. She'd factored it into their route; their last stop before turning.

The bright summer light made a mirror of the canal's surface. It reflected the white-flowered bushes so that clouds seemed to float in a long straight line of fallen sky.

"It's a palindrome," Helen said, and explained. She told him it was a word that made sense however you looked at it. Palindromes were strong words, solid words. Good words. She spelled dad. She spelled kayak.

Charlie said, "Mum."

Helen shook her head and said quietly, "Mummy's not a palindrome." She didn't know what she was. She pointed at the large double gates blocking the canal in the distance ahead. "A lock," she said.

The first set of gates were angled open to them, the water level for their approach. The second set were closed, of course, barring their way. She thought of all the water held behind.

"Look, sweetheart, another swan."

It was gliding out from the lock, drifting across their path.

"Out of the way," Charlie said. "It's my turn."

Was he talking to the swan?

"Ready to take charge, Captain?"

Charlie grinned, nodded, and saluted, all at once.

As the swan neared, it dipped its head into the water. Helen watched its body pass, following the course the man and his family had taken. Heading away, heading away, until gone.

The locks seemed easy to operate. They'd had a brief tutorial before leaving the boatyard. It was alarming, Helen thought, how you could control the course of water simply by opening and closing a gate. One simple action.

Charlie was unimpressed. He was of an age where everything operated to his demands anyway, Helen supposed, so going uphill in a boat was nothing to him. It was just as well, because she needed him to wait onboard while she took care of the lock mechanism.

At the front, up on the walled bank of the canal, Helen couldn't see Charlie, but she kept her eyes on the rear of the boat as she turned the windlass. Water began to gush from one side of the lock into the other and the boat began to rise with the water level. It began to drift forward.

"Take us back a bit, honey," she called over the rushing water. More because she wanted to give him something to do than out of any concern. When the boat continued drifting forward, unpowered, she glanced back for Charlie but her view of the stern was blocked by the angle and the raised roof.

There was a semi-circle of tyres gathered at the bow of the boat and they bumped the lock gates but Helen barely noticed. She called again for Charlie, hurrying back along the wall, looking down into the rear of the narrowboat.

Charlie was not there.

"Charlie!"

There were no ripples in the water that she could see, or rather there were too many because of how the surface churned and she couldn't tell if he'd fallen in or where he'd fallen in or—

He appeared from the cabin in a hurry, glancing back inside as if he'd left something behind, and Helen felt that blend of anger and relief reserved for concerned mothers. Charlie must have seen some of it in her face. "There was a swan," he explained.

"Stay there."

She ran back to the front of the boat.

One of the tyres at the bow had caught beneath a horizontal beam in the gate structure. As the water level rose, so did the boat, and as the boat rose, so did the gate.

"Go back!" Helen called. "Quickly!"

He'd be too late now, but she called it anyway, grabbing the gate paddle and trying to shift it, move it away from the boat, opening the lock chamber early. In part she was successful, pushing hard and somehow managing, but the boat continued forward with it, still caught and still rising.

"Reverse!"

She heard the engine, but still the boat moved forwards. The paddle she pushed to lever the gate open suddenly ceased resisting and, as the last of the water filled it to the appropriate level, the lock opened up. One gate was about a foot or so higher than its partner now, though.

"Charlie, rever—"

The boat began easing backwards, angling so that the front worked itself loose from the gate and the gate dropped down in the water. Now it was *lower* than the other one. Helen had a horrible idea as to why; they had lifted it from whatever pin mechanism held it or hinged it, had separated one section from its mount, or something like that. In short, they had broken it. She would know for sure when she tried to close it, but—

"There was a swan," Charlie said again, emerging with the boat from the confines of the lock chamber. Helen ignored him, stepping aboard, and moving him aside from the controls.

She guided them away from the lock, leaving the gates open behind them. She didn't want to check if one of them was broken because she knew it would be. She could tell it sat on the bottom of the canal just by looking. It wouldn't budge.

"Can I—"

"No. You've caused enough damage."

She sent him back inside so he wouldn't see her cry.

They arrived at the pub later than Helen had planned. The guidebook had advised adding the number of miles you intended to travel to the number of locks on the route and then dividing by three for the number of hours it would take. With only one lock it had been an easy sum, and yet it was still nearly evening by the time they arrived at the Still Waters. There were many boats already moored, and quite a crowd outside enjoying dinners and drinks. It was one of the few places with space enough to manoeuvre a boat around, the canal deliberately widened into a lake-like expanse. It was green with weed but picturesque in its own way. Helen supposed couples and families would pose for photos beside it.

The pub was so close to the canal that from the picnic benches you could see the tops of the moored boats over the hedges. Helen thought the only reason the hedges were there at all, interrupting the view, was to prevent the playing children from running right into the water. She sat with her back to the canal, though. She needed to face the play area to keep an eye on Charlie.

It was a simple set up. A pair of mock trees were connected by a rope bridge, the ground thick with those soft wood pieces that miraculously prevented most injuries. A line of swings was suspended from the branches of one of the trees, each of them a child-bearing pendulum swinging back and forth, forth and back, while a huge tractor tyre twisted in circles from another branch as the children on it leaned their bodies one way and then the other. A slide dropped down from one of the treetops too, half its length an enclosed tunnel painted faux bark. It was from this that Charlie repeatedly emerged, screaming his joy into the world only to return to the ladder and climb back in. Helen grew tired watching him. She picked at what remained of her ploughman's, trying to enjoy what was left of the evening sunshine. She shined an apple on her sleeve. And there was

Charlie again, coming out of the tube head-first. As soon as he was on the ground he ran around for another go.

Helen pressed her apple gently to check for bruises. It felt all right, but you could never really tell.

"Are you done?"

One of the pub's waitresses was beside the table reaching to take Helen's plate. She was a pretty thing, in the middle of girl and woman and enjoying the change, it seemed, judging by her makeup and how tight she wore her clothing.

"Yes," Helen said, "I'm done."

There was a man talking at Charlie in the play area. There was another boy with him. The boy was crying.

"Great."

Helen grabbed her handbag. The man was pointing at Charlie but being careful to not actually touch the boy.

"Charlie, come on, time to go." Whatever he'd done, it would be punishment enough, and she wanted to avoid a scene. She was careful not to make eye contact with anyone else.

"He pushed in," said the man. "He wouldn't wait for his turn."

Charlie pushed him. He used both hands and he did it hard enough that the adult staggered back.

"Charlie!"

Charlie had both hands out, ready to charge and push again, but Helen grabbed one of his wrists. She spun him away with her, dragging him behind as she marched them back to the boat.

"I want another go."

"I know you do, sweetheart, but you can't."

"Why not?"

Helen, her mind suddenly taxed with all she thought she'd left behind for the weekend, wanted to tell him you couldn't always have another go once you'd done something bad, but she replied with every parent's favourite fallback answer instead.

"Because I said so."

"It's not fair."

Helen was old enough to know that rarely mattered.

~

Her second night's sleep on the boat was as poor as the first. She'd dreamt of the kayak family. Charlie's father was supposed to be with them but his kayak was empty, a vacant stretched O in the middle marking his absence, and she woke from the dream before much could happen. She woke suddenly, fully, denied even the brief pleasure of wondering where she was. She held her breath and listened for any noise that may have woken her. She heard only the quiet slap of water against the boat. Her dream faded into fragments, ebbing away in the dark.

Helen checked the bed beside her. It was empty, but warmer than it should have been, and she remembered Charlie sleeping there, scared of something he didn't want to talk about.

Perhaps his rising had brought her awake.

"Charlie, baby?"

Her dressing gown was hanging on the door. She shrugged into the sleeves and rubbed a crust of sleep from her eye. "Charlie?" She swept the gown closed and stepped out into the galley.

He was in the small lounge area at the front of the boat, kneeling on the curve of sofa and looking out the window. He was wearing his father's sweatshirt, the hood up. Helen had brought it. She wasn't sure why.

"Hey, little man, what's wrong? Why are you dressed?"

And why are you wearing that?

Charlie tensed at her voice, his body suddenly rigid. Then he slid down from the sofa, retrieved something from the cushions, and faced her. The sweatshirt was too big for him, the hood so low that it was a mask over his face, all shadows and gloom. She heard a strange clacking sound as he approached, arms swinging at his sides. She saw what he held in each hand.

"Charlie?"

In each fist he gripped the long, severed neck of a swan. The heads dangled down by his knees. Helen's surprise gave him a few moments to get nearer and then he swung one of them at her. She managed to get her arm up in time to block it and the white length of neck folded around her wrist. She heard the unhinged beak snap against itself on empty air. Then the other one was coming down at her. It struck her across the chest. "*Charlie?*" She held her hand out to protect herself, fingers spread, and was struck across the palm. The hard beak gouged a line in her skin. Then the next came up from beneath, underarm. She pushed it away before it could strike between her legs. "Charlie!"

The heads swung at her again and again, beaks clacking. At one point a neck wrapped around her arm and she managed to yank it from his grip. It fell somewhere behind her. He was beating her into retreat, though. When she passed the door to the bathroom, she flung it open to block the narrow corridor but any advantage it gave her was lost when she stood on the fallen swan neck; the severed length was soft beneath her bare foot, a white-feathered snake that rolled with her step and sent her toppling backwards. Charlie fell with her. She fought to keep him off, pulling at his hood with one hand, groping inside with the other for his face. Her hand sank in too far, her arm swallowed up to the elbow, and then she had the hood down and there was nothing there. Nothing. The hoodie collapsed upon itself, empty, and fell into her lap where she lay on the floor, sprawled and panting for breath.

"Mum?"

Charlie was crouching over her, gripping her shoulder, the bathroom door open behind him. Helen looked down at herself and hitched her nightie back down, pulled her dressing gown closed again. She clamped her legs together and felt something awful between them.

"It was a bad dream."

She wasn't sure which of them had said it.

"Can I sleep with you still?"

"Of course, honey. Get to bed, I'll be there in a minute."

But she lay there for another five, slowing her breathing, waiting for him to fall asleep in the other room.

It was still dark when Helen went out on deck, but it was cloudless and silvery with moonlight, the air sharp with the fresh smell that belongs only to such secret hours. It was cold, too, and Helen felt it in the shallow cuts that criss-crossed her wrists and arms. She was still wearing her dressing gown, only taking the time to pull on some jeans and shoes. It didn't matter, there was no one around to see. Not yet.

A light had come on in one of the nearby boats when she'd started the engine, but nobody came out to say anything and she was able to take the boat into a slow and awkward five-point turn, using all of the widened lake area. The canal curved away from it and she used as much of that as she could as well to help her manoeuvre. She didn't bump anyone.

Once they were clear of the moored vessels, Helen eased the throttle forward and rushed them away faster than was strictly allowed on the canal, sending a breaking wash against both banks. It was hardly high speed, but enough that their wake was probably eroding the sides of the canal as they went, adding silt to the shallows. Helen couldn't care less. She only hoped the noise and movement wouldn't wake Charlie. Perhaps the vibrations, the dull throb of their progress, would actually soothe him and keep him under.

The sky was greying with early light when Helen saw an early morning dog walker. He was walking slowly along the towpath, his head down. She saw no dog, just the empty lead in the man's hand swishing back and forth. When he looked up at her she looked away. Neither of them spoke. After him she slowed the boat to a legal speed. She looked for the fisherman's chair with the abandoned rod, but she didn't see it. She couldn't remember if it was before or after the lock. Perhaps some boy had come along and pushed the chair into the canal, stolen the rod.

When Charlie woke, Helen stopped so she could change her dressing gown for a blouse while he ate at the tiny table.

"Aren't you having breakfast, Mum?"

"Not hungry," she said.

She ate her apple at the tiller. The sky began to fill with white cushions of cloud, but the sun remained bright and by the time they reached the lock the day had warmed considerably. At first she thought that was why so many boats had gathered in lines, bow to stern, at the banks. She thought they were moored because it was such a beautiful day, perfect for an outdoor lunch, but a woman waved to them from one of the closer boats as Helen neared.

"Lock's broken," she said.

Helen eased the engine down and then into reverse, drawing level with the woman. "Sorry."

The woman heard a question. "Lock's broken," she said again. "One of the gates has come off its mount. They've called for a crane but we're still waiting. You best moor up somewhere, could be a while before things are fixed."

The woman was about Helen's age but in much better shape. Whereas Helen was wearing a sensible blouse, this woman wore a turquoise bikini top and probably matching briefs, though a sarong was draped around her waist. She probably didn't have children. She probably had her choice of men.

"We have to keep going," Helen said, hating how pathetic it sounded. "I've got to get him back."

The woman shrugged. She sidestepped the length of her boat to where a towel had been laid out on the bow. There was a book there, too, but Helen couldn't make out the title.

"Look at all the boats!" said Charlie. "There's a thousand of them!"

"Yes, lots and lots of boats."

"Are we parking as well?"

"We have to, honey. The lock's broken."

She took them backwards. They would have to wait with everybody else.

"Can't we go back?"

"Not yet."

Maybe never.

She looked at Charlie, thinking she should say something more reassuring about what they were going to do next, tell him everything would be back to normal soon, but he was bouncing on the spot and pointing.

"Look! Look at all the swans!"

There were suddenly dozens of them. Some were gliding by, quiet on the canal, dipping their bills to the water or into the narrow gaps between boats and bank. Others were on the boats themselves, waddling on cabin roofs, nestling into comfortable positions on the decks. She saw a mother and two children sitting with one, a blanket spread between them piled with snacks for a picnic. The swan snaked its neck forward to take bites from the sandwiches, nodding its head back after each mouthful as if throwing the food down its long throat.

An abrupt shriek drew Helen's attention back to the sunbathing woman. One of the swans had settled nearby, opening its wings to her, wide, wide – such a wingspan! – as it puffed up its chest. The woman swatted playfully at the swan with her book, laughing, as if the feathers of its enormous wings tickled her. The bird waddled closer, settling on her towel, engulfing its dark webbed feet with its own body as it draped itself over hers.

"Do we have anything to give them?"

"No, honey. Everything we had is gone."

She took her hair out of the band she'd worn for days and ran her fingers through it, shaking it into shape. She unbuttoned her blouse.

"What are you doing?"

"Sunbathing."

She stripped off her blouse and dropped it to the deck but the air it caught falling took it to the water where it floated a moment before sinking. It didn't matter.

"You don't have your costume on," Charlie said.

Her brassiere was a good one but still very clearly a bra, and its colour had been washed out long ago. Her arms were scratched, darkened in places by ugly bruises. She looked around to see if anyone had noticed but everyone was busy, each with their own swan.

"I need to change," she said.

She went inside.

The bed was still unmade, quilt tossed aside. It looked vaguely human in its gathered shape. Helen stepped out of her shoes and jeans but instead of finding something suitable for sunbathing she sat on the bed in her underwear. She pulled the pillows to her lap and made a nest of them around her.

"I can't," she said.

She looked at the bed, one she would usually share, and saw the vague shape in the sheets of someone not there. She struck at it, punched it flat, threw it this way and that, straddled the quilt and brought both fists down upon it again and again. She tried to keep the noise down, grunting and growling instead of crying out, but Charlie heard anyway and came to see what was happening. When he saw what his mother was doing on the bed, he joined in. He dragged the duvet away from her and she snatched up a pillow and beat at that until the fabric split.

A flurry of feathers rose up around them both, too many feathers for such a pillow, and she beat at them as well, swatting them from the air. She scooped them up and swiped handfuls of them back again as they fell, crushing them in her fists, slapping at the blizzard that swept around them. Charlie climbed onto the bed with her and bounced on the mattress, up and down and grabbing. Helen's noises had become a series of desperate exhalations, hitched and laboured, almost sobbing, but Charlie's yelling was victorious joy.

The room was thick with feathers, and sometimes there was a shape in them Helen almost recognised.

|Trapper's Valley|

~

Laquita Baptiste had seen plenty of dead bodies, but not like this.

"Bear," John said.

Laquita looked into the trees as if it might still be around, but there was too much snow and not enough light to see more than shadows. The trees were taller here in the valley. They offered more hiding places.

"Aren't the bears hibernating?"

John shrugged. "Some wait until the very last moment, filling up."

Laquita saw nothing in the trees around them, but she withdrew her gloved hands from under her armpits just in case, though getting to her gun would be awkward. She'd tucked it inside her parka to stop it freezing.

John continued to stare at the body in the snow. "Cold first, *then* bear."

"Right."

"Baptiste? It's gone. Don't worry."

Ba-*teest*, she thought. Ba-*teest*. No p, except on paper. She looked at John, a giant of a man beside her, and thought about telling him again. But she'd told him twice already. He was doing it on purpose. Testing her.

"How do you know?" she asked.

"Because if it wasn't gone we'd know by now."

"I mean how do you know cold and then bear?"

She knew, she just wanted to hear his view of it. A little test of her own.

"Not enough blood. Bear's been chewing a popsicle."

Laquita glanced down at the body again. A man, judging by the build, but laying face down and frozen to the ground it was difficult to tell for sure. One arm outstretched, the other folded under him. One leg ending at the knee, the other gone almost entirely. The gnarly twist of an empty hiking boot. Ragged torn fabric in the middle of the jacket and some exposed meatless spine.

"Blood back there," she said, pointing behind them, "sheltered by the deadfall we just passed. And a boot print that was probably his." She nodded at the body. "Back when he had feet."

John trudged back to the fallen tree to confirm what she already knew.

"He stopped briefly, bleeding, but pushed on," she explained as John looked. "Either because of the cold or because he was being pursued." She slapped her gloved hands together a few times and stamped her feet. "Fuck, it's cold."

Over at the deadfall, John grunted.

Laquita knelt at the mauled body and tried to turn it, but it was part of the terrain now until the spring. Breakup, they called it here.

"Some blood on top, too," John said, coming back. "He went over instead of around."

"Quicker."

He'd been chased. Or followed, at least. The hand under his body would be holding a wound, a gut shot, and the one outstretched was an attempt to break his fall. Once down, he'd probably thought it a good idea to stay there. He'd have been tired, and cold, and losing blood, and the body didn't always know the difference at this point between what it wanted and what it needed.

"This your teacher?" Laquita asked.

John nodded. "Reckon it is."

They'd already found a discarded pack with frozen textbooks inside. John thought it could only belong to a man called Prait, a local teacher who delivered books to the homesteads for home schooling.

"Got more spine than I gave him credit for," John said, but he didn't laugh, looking down at the corpse and its exposed vertebrae. "Looks like he's the one learnt a lesson here." Dark North Country humour, as harsh and mirthless as the landscape you found it in. It reminded Laquita of the jokes you heard at a crime scene. And she was sure this was a crime scene.

John swept the snow with his boot. "He would have had a rifle."

"Maybe he dropped it. Maybe someone took it."

"Who?"

She wondered how long this man at her feet had lived out here, in the wild, among countless things that could kill him, only for his death to come from a city thousands of miles away.

Laquita looked at John but he was still searching the snow. "Trooper Bruak is all you've got out here?"

John nodded. "We'll tell him, but there won't be much doing until breakup and Prait will be gone by then. Bear'll come back. Wolves." He smiled to add, "Maybe the bushman."

Laquita said nothing.

John shrugged. "Won't be the first body to have been disappeared in this valley."

He'd told her this already. Made a point of talking about frontier law on the drive up, before telling her they took care of their own undesirables. She understood from his tone that undesirables included her. A 'government busybody', that was how he'd put it. She hadn't flashed a badge or any ID but she still carried its authority. You learnt to wear it like a gun until flipping the credentials was only ever a formality. And once you got to that stage, you couldn't stop. Couldn't turn it off.

"So we leave him for the animals?"

John knelt in the snow, drew the knife he wore at his belt, and cut away at the man's ass. The pocket, Laquita realised.

"They'll eat everything, even the bones," he said, working his knife. He prised a wallet free and breathed on it a few times, cracked it open in the cloud of his exhalations. He nodded and handed it to her. "Roger Prait," he said.

There was a picture (two men) and a driver's licence.

"Other fella's *his* fella."

John smirked as if this was juicy gossip. Laquita only nodded.

"His lover," John clarified.

"I'm from New Orleans," Laquita said, handing the wallet back. John said nothing. Maybe he didn't know anything about New Orleans, or even that it existed. Maybe he didn't know it was the '80s. Maybe he didn't care.

Laquita hugged herself again, stuck her hands back into her pits. "Fuck it's cold," she said.

John grunted. "*Chechakos*," he muttered.

Tenderfeet. He'd said it a lot these past few days.

"*Ta gueule,*" Laquita said. Then, "Pardon my French."

John continued north. Laquita, took another look around, peering through drifting snow and into the trees, then shook some warmth into her limbs and followed.

Alaska was one of the last places in the world where wildlife outnumbered people, but to hear John talk it seemed all of that wildlife was in Trapper's Valley. As well as game like moose, caribou, beaver, you had timber wolves and black bears and grizzlies. Not to mention the bushman (and once you were out here that didn't seem such a far-fetched idea). They were nearly a hundred and fifty miles north of Fairbanks, heading north towards the Arctic Circle, though they wouldn't go that far. Still, the temperature could get as low as 70 below. For now, though, travel was relatively easy. Not jump on a tram easy, but the snow smoothed the ground flat, and the rivers had frozen into highways. That would have been more than just a metaphor if they'd had a snowmobile, but Laquita didn't want to break the quiet with the sound of its engine, not while they were still able to travel on foot. It wouldn't be out of place, that sound, but she still preferred the quiet snow-crunch of their footsteps. Even if it did mean she might freeze to death.

"A thousand ways to kill you," she muttered.

John looked at her.

"It's what Jack London said about this place."

John grunted. Laquita thought perhaps a man like John didn't get many visits from a man like Prait, but what he didn't know from books he more than made up for with his knowledge of the valley.

John pointed to a tree. It had been savaged with claws some ten feet from the ground. "You're walking a little lower down the food chain around here," he said.

"Grizzly?"

He nodded. He was looking on the ground but any tracks that might have been there were buried under fresh snow.

"A black bear will eat you if it's hungry," John said. "A grizzly just doesn't like you. It needs no other reason." He looked at her as if he shared the same sentiment. Probably did. Not because she was a woman, or even a black woman, but because she was from the Lower 48. And a 'government busybody'.

"They were here first," she admitted. "We're the ones trespassing."

John nodded. He was very much a bear himself. When someone had described him as a mountain man she'd thought it meant outdoorsman, which was exactly what she needed, but when she met him she realised it applied to his size as well. The man barely fit in the cab of his truck. Some of his bulk was layers of clothing, of course, most of it fur. That, plus his full beard and shaggy hair, made him look like one of the grizzlies he hunted. When he'd offered his hand she'd expected a padded paw with claws. Even with gloves on, hers looked dainty by comparison. She'd been mildly embarrassed to realise he hadn't meant to shake, nor had he been offering to take her bag, which he tossed into the truck. He'd wanted the money, and he counted it right in front of her.

"Not bad for a walk in the woods," she'd said.

"Better than oil work." He'd tucked the cash into a pocket and looked her over, apparently liking, or at least accepting, what he saw. She was well bulked out herself, with decent boots she'd broken in already.

"What you here for? Hunting?"

She'd been tempted to say yes. Instead, she'd said, "Heard there's some trouble with a T and M claim."

She'd overheard a conversation in town regarding a certain Mark Hooper who owned 80 acres intended for trade and manufacturing. In his case, the tourist trade, which was hunting and trapping. She'd also heard, buying gear in the store, that there was some sort of dispute regarding Hooper's claim. He'd come in on the last years of homesteading and still had to significantly improve the land in order to claim the full 80 acres. Problem was he'd turned to gold prospecting midway through his five years and it ate up a lot of his time.

John had accepted the story. Or at least pretended to. She doubted he cared why she was out here, except that she was prying where she didn't belong.

"Black bears stick to the deep woods," he told her now as she examined the clawed tree, "but grizzlies wander wherever the hell they like, because they can. They're the biggest land predator in the world. Fast. Mean. Strong enough to pull you to pieces." He looked at her. "Nothing like facing a bear out here to remind you how much you don't matter."

Laquita would matter. She'd come all the way out here to matter.

"How far to the Hooper place now?"

"We're already walking it. First cabin's just up there." He pointed.

The snow crunched under their feet. They left deep prints, the snow sometimes as high as Laquita's knees. John moved with ease and surprising grace but Laquita was slow. Clouds of breath puffed from her with each step. She was the wrong kind of fit out here. City fit, not country.

"*Chechako*," she muttered, and increased her pace.

John looked back at her. She held her breath to stop it puffing until he looked away again.

"How many cabins are out here?" she asked, just to prove she could talk and walk. "Four?"

"Three and a half. He's not finished." He glanced at her again. "But you already know that."

He stopped at where a strip of trees had been cleared away and stomped on the ground. Laquita realised the strip of cleared ground was actually a creek, frozen and snowed over. John made his way across. He dragged his feet to make the going easier for her, which she both resented and appreciated.

The bitter wind really made itself felt here, channelled through the lack of cover to freeze the areas of her face not quite protected by hood and scarf, driving snowfall enough to make her squint. It seemed to whisper, an ongoing *shush* that muffled other sounds. She wouldn't hear if the ice under her feet began to crack.

"There it is," John said when they were back among the trees.

Laquita could barely see it. The cabin wasn't hidden, it just blended well with its surroundings. The logs were spruce, and they were vertical, which surprised her. Snow had banked up part of one narrow side.

"Roof's caved in," John said. "I told him it would."

Laquita was already hurrying to it, as much as the snow allowed. She shrugged out of the pack that was slowing her down, let it fall behind her.

"He doesn't winter here," John said.

She was reaching into her jacket.

"He's not in there."

No, but somebody else might be.

She burst into a cabin choked with snow and swept her gun to each corner. It took only a second to establish it was empty.

John stepped inside as she was putting the gun back under her jacket. "You're not here for a T and M claim," he said. He put her pack on the floor and shrugged out of his. He inspected what was left of the roof.

"We'll rest here tonight."

The stove worked fine, its chimney set in part of the roof that was still intact, but they cooked outdoors to avoid melting the snow that had filled half the cabin. They were well sheltered from any wind that might carry the aroma of their meal but John still advised eating quickly so they could retreat indoors.

"Bears can't see all that well," he said, "But they have a great sense of smell."

Dinner was rice and beans with chopped tinned sausage. It wasn't the tastiest thing Laquita had ever eaten (Gammy's dressed po-boys, extra hot sauce) but she ate it with enthusiasm. It was almost gumbo if she pretended hard enough.

"Aren't you supposed to tell a story around a campfire?" she said. "Isn't that what the tourists want?"

"You're not a tourist." But he shovelled a final spoonful of food into his mouth and said, "You know this area leads into Great Bear Pass?"

She nodded.

"Well, some call it *Grey* Bear Pass, or just Grey Bear. They also call the grey bear 'ghost bear'."

Laquita set her bowl down. "This is more like it."

He frowned at her, checking for sarcasm. Waited for some when none was found. Then continued.

"Supposed to be he's an old bear, so old he's grey, but some say he was killed a while back. By a *chechako*, like you." He smiled. "He was a lazy forager by then, sniffing around carcasses and garbage. But the grey was so angry, being killed by a tourist, that he stuck around as a ghost bear. That's what people say. And now, every time a bear is killed by a true pioneer, a frontiersman or homesteader, its spirit is said to go to the grey bear, keeping it in the world for as long as the shot bear would have been, had it lived."

Laquita nodded.

John gathered up the bowls and the camp stove.

"That's it?"

"That's it."

Laquita stood and brushed snow from her legs. "Can't wait for the movie."

They returned to the cabin.

"Has anybody ever actually seen it?" Laquita asked. "The ghost bear."

John nodded. A little reluctantly, she thought. She wondered if he was more accommodating with the tourists. "Might just be an old bear, though," he said. "And an old bear's still a dangerous bear."

Laquita thought of Muir and agreed. He'd be seventy now. She heard the usual addition of "if he's still alive" but it wasn't her voice, it was everybody else's. She knew he was still alive. And she knew he was out here.

"Eskimo Bill's seen him," John said, rescuing a chair from the snow and brushing it clean with his hands.

"The grey?"

He nodded. "But then Eskimo Bill claims to have seen the bushman, too."

"The bushman," Laquita said. "Right. You mean Bigfoot."

John grinned at her. "Big everything."

Laquita shook her head.

"Indians up and down the Yukon used to talk about how he'd steal children from their homes. Sometimes, right from their beds."

Laquita thought of Muir again. If only they'd had such cautionary tales in the city.

John nodded at a bed that sagged in the middle but otherwise seemed in good shape and said, "It's all yours."

"We safe in here?"

"From the bushman?"

"From the rest of the roof falling in and crushing us while we sleep."

"Would have fallen in with the rest if it was going to happen."

Laquita unpacked her bag onto the mattress. "Then I'll take it. You can call me *chechako* all you want."

"You're no tenderfoot," John allowed. "Not sure what you are. But you ain't here for no land dispute."

"Never said I was."

"No. Don't suppose you did."

Laquita unrolled her sleeping bag and took off her jacket. The room was warming up with their body heat but not by much, not with half the roof in the room, and she shivered. She'd need the jacket's warmth in the morning, though, and sleeping in it wouldn't give her that. She tucked the gun into her sleeping bag.

Finally John came right out and asked. "Why you out here, Baptiste?"

She considered the question. It was more complicated than John realised. Eventually she said, "Hunting the bushman."

John nodded. "Thought it was something like that."

He picked up his rifle and sat with it across his lap. He'll probably sleep that way, Laquita thought.

"G'night, John."

He nodded. "Don't use that pillow. Man like Hooper out here on his own gets lonely, I imagine."

Laquita was already tossing it aside because it was frozen solid. She puffed her jacket into shape and lay on that as John laughed.

"Sweet dreams," he said.

There was nothing sweet about them. In one she chased a man through a snow-filled New Orleans only to 'wake' and find she was being eaten in bed from the feet up by something as large as a bear that wasn't a bear. Its long hair was grey and wet and *all* of it was hair except the face. The face was Muir's face, red-lined teeth smiling at her from a beard of her blood. She woke from that one properly with a sudden shudder.

Still, it was better than the ones with the bus.

John was sitting nearby, facing the door. His rifle leant against the wall beside him as he worked. He barely glanced at her.

Laquita rubbed her eyes. "Are you sewing?"

He didn't look up from what he was doing. "You get three times as much for mittens or a hat than you do for just the fur." He showed her what he was working on. "It's not woman's work," he said. "It's just sensible."

"I can't sew to save my life, and last I checked I was a woman." Her watch had stopped. "How long have I been asleep?"

"Twenty minutes."

Her watch hadn't stopped. She slumped back down.

"Good night," John said again.

Laquita spent the rest of the night running through New Orleans chasing a grey-haired beast that kept disappearing into snow that shouldn't have been there.

The snow had stopped in the night and the next day was crisp and bright, the air sharp in Laquita's nose and lungs. Her legs ached but somewhere along the line it had become a warm ache, almost comfortable. Trapper's Valley didn't get much sun at this time of year because of the mountains, but they'd been walking for a couple of hours and some light had managed to rise above the surrounding snow-capped range to reflect off the freshly fallen snow. The brightness was pleasantly dazzling. Here was fir, spruce, aspen, larch, birch, willow, cottonwood, all protected from the worst of the wind by those same mountains that reduced light to six or seven hours, and they were able to grow beyond the stunted size of those she'd seen coming into the valley. Even in the early stages of winter it was beautiful, a stark setting striking in its simplicity and somehow spiritual, more hallowed than any church she'd ever known. She imagined the fall would be spectacular, a range of reds, oranges, yellows, and golds setting the valley afire.

She followed John out of the trees into a cleared area far too straight to be natural. It wasn't a frozen creek this time. Trees had been deliberately felled, some cut down to stumps, the lumber stacked, others pulled up roots and all. John told her it was an airstrip, or the beginnings of one. Small parties of tourists would be brought in by Cessna, but it seemed Hooper was in no rush for them.

"The Shaws are a couple of miles that way," John said, pointing. "They're wintering over, part of a deal with Hooper. Or there's Eskimo Bill, lives about another mile that way." He pointed in an almost opposite direction.

Eskimo Bill had nothing to do with Hooper. It meant John had abandoned any pretence regarding Laquita's T and M investigation. He was giving her options that might help with whatever it was she *was* doing.

"Bill gets around a bit, even in winter. The Shaws, though, they'll be hunkered down tight."

"They a family? Kids?"

"Dog breeders. No kids of their own yet, but they're trying." He grinned at her. "I've seen Luke's wife, though. He might not be trying all that hard or all that often."

Laquita pointed.

"I don't suppose that's one of theirs?"

She was already undoing her jacket because she knew what John's answer was going to be.

"No," he said, slowly unslinging his rifle. "That's a wolf."

It was standing beside one of the felled trees, its long head peering from the cloud of its breath. It must have been six feet long from nose to tail. As they watched, another seemed to come up out of the ground beside it, rising from the snow. The fallen tree would have left a hollow where its roots had pulled from the ground, and the exposed roots themselves provided perfect shelter for a den. This one sunk down to its forepaws. Its muzzle curled back from a wicked grimace of teeth. It growled. The sound was low but loud. An engine warming.

"This is where you tell me they're more scared of us than we are of them," Laquita said.

John raised his rifle. "No. It's not."

Laquita held her own weapon ready in a two-handed grip, pointing the gun down at the ground until John made the decision. She was reluctant to fire because of the noise but she would if she had to.

Another wolf trotted out from the trees to join the first two.

Laquita's fear wasn't the sharp kind. It wasn't icy. Her hairs didn't stand and her skin didn't prickle with goose pimples. That was a fear she liked because it kept her alert. This fear, out here, was more like grease in her veins. A slow oozing fear that clogged her heart and made her heavy.

"Baptiste."

"Yeah?"

"Check the trees."

John was statue-still, rifle ready, staring at the wolves ahead of them.

"The—"

"Trees. Check the trees, both sides."

She checked the left first and saw nothing. She turned right and saw—

"*Merde!*"

She brought her gun up quick and fired at the animal racing towards them. The shot puffed snow from the ground but it gave her a point to adjust from. The wolf had already turned, though, running back to the trees. She turned to face the others just as John's rifle cracked. They were scattering, retreating from the open space. Laquita pointed her gun at each but didn't fire and then she was hit hard in the back and fell face down into the snow.

The wolf that had leapt on her from behind had made no noise until now. Now she was on the ground it growled and snapped. It tore into her jacket. She felt it claw or bite her scalp, a fiery line of pain, and she rolled, *tried* to roll, but it must have weighed 150 pounds. She couldn't roll it with her, but she did manage to turn beneath it. She brought her gun up and under its jaw but before she could fire it turned its head sideways and snapped its teeth into her hand. Its breath was hot and moist on her face. It stank. Saliva dropped into her eyes. Her own blood warmed her throat but it hadn't got its teeth there yet: blood from her hand was running into her mouth.

Another bulk loomed over her suddenly and she thought, that's it, I'm fucked, but it was John. He grabbed the thick pelt of the animal, trying to wrestle it off.

"Move!" she yelled. "Move!"

He moved as she swapped gun hands and she fired. The wolf's muzzle showered up in a spray of blood and fur. It fell sideways and she rolled clear the other way. On her knees she shot it a second time then cradled her bitten hand and looked around the clearing. It was empty.

The snow at her knees pattered with drops of blood from her clutched hand. She tugged her glove off carefully but quickly to inspect the damage.

"You all right?"

She had bloody punctures through her palm and furrows scraped across her knuckles. A gash spiralled around her wrist.

"Broke a nail," she said.

One nail had in fact split down the middle to the cuticle. Half of it hung away.

"Head's bleeding," John said from behind her. "Hood got the most of it, but your head's torn up too."

"Just a hickey," she said. "How's my hair?" Her laugh came out like panting and she shook with adrenaline.

"I got a hat you can borrow," John said, and she laughed some more.

"Tourists must love it here."

Laquita glanced at the wolf beside her and felt sorry for having killed it. Except for its ruined muzzle it looked like a sleeping dog. That was an illusion granted by death, though. A moment ago it had been far from harmless.

"I'll clean those wounds for you."

Her scalp sang a stinging line and her savaged hand throbbed. She pulled the hanging half of her fingernail away, growling through clenched teeth.

"It's okay," she said. "I've got it."

John went to the tree.

"They've got a kill," he said. He squatted and poked his rifle into the hollow its roots had left behind.

"Who is it this time? The mailman?" Her hand was clean. She wrapped a bandage around it and taped the tip of her finger. It was her trigger finger and she worried about that. The glove already made shooting more awkward than she was used to.

"Caribou," John said. But he looked around as if for something else. She thought maybe he even sniffed the air. Maybe it was a show he put on for tourists.

"What is it?"

"I don't know." He palmed snow from his beard. "They'll attack that way sometimes. Distract the prey while another one strikes in surprise. But attacking people ain't all that common, 'specially not two. 'Specially not when they've already got a kill."

"Protecting what was theirs."

"Maybe. Or maybe something already had them spooked."

He trudged back towards her, rummaging in his open pack. He gave her one of his hats.

"Soft," Laquita said, stroking the fur.

"Caribou."

It surprised a brief laugh from her. "Got anything in wolf?"

John led them away from the abandoned airstrip, eager to put some distance between them and the wolves' den. He didn't like that they'd attacked. Laquita hadn't liked it much herself. Her injuries throbbed but she tried to ignore them, focussing instead on her walking. She walked in John's steps, but the going was still difficult. She didn't bother hiding her exertion anymore.

She glanced up when she no longer heard the snow-crunch of John's walking. He had stopped.

"What?"

He pointed. "Tracks."

She found energy from somewhere to hurry then, clumsy in the snow because she had to lift her legs high and turn her hips more. Sure enough, crossing their intended path, was the kicked-up trail of someone walking the snow ahead of them.

"How old?" Laquita asked.

John shrugged.

"Come on, John. This is what I'm paying you for."

He looked again at the trail. A light snow had been falling all morning. "Not long."

"Then we're close."

He nodded, leading them parallel to the tracks rather than taking advantage of the cleared snow. He said to her, over his shoulder, "Close to what?"

She let a silence hang between them for a while.

"His name's Muir," she said eventually.

"He's a bad man I take it?"

"He's a monster."

Martell Muir was wanted for the kidnap and murder of at least seven children. That they knew of. Three of those had come from New Orleans. It became an FBI case when they realised he was the likely suspect for two kidnaps and at least one murder in Mississippi as well, and even if he hadn't been the right man for those, little Leroy Moore had been taken across the state line into Texas. Leroy had been caught on camera at a gas station, peering out the back of a stolen car. The car was never found.

Leroy Moore was.

"His usual MO was to incapacitate one or both parents so they could see him do it. So they could see him take their child."

Laquita was breathing heavy, but only some of that was due to their trudge through the snow.

"GSW to the stomach," she said, clarifying, "Gun shot wound."

John said nothing.

"Mary Bellerose, mother of Josie Bellerose, she died, but all the others lived to know the horror of a missing child. And later, the horror of a child found."

She looked up at John to see how he was taking the story but all she saw was his broad back and pack. He dragged his legs through the snow same as before. He worked his arms economically and efficiently.

"You got kids, John?"

"You found them? The kids?"

"In a warehouse."

She didn't need to tell him they were dead, and she didn't want to tell him they found the children naked as the day they were born, each in a varying stage of decomposition. Muir had sat them all in a school bus. Some had slumped in their seats. Rats had eaten through the string Muir had used to pose them. She still dreamt of that bus and its passengers of dead children.

"He kept their clothes," she said. "You know, as trophies. Sent us photos of pyjamas and nightgowns in neat, folded piles."

John made a noise and stopped. He rummaged inside his clothes and handed Laquita a photograph.

"Sometimes I get sent things like this," he said. "This was the first one, and it's the only one I've ever kept. Reminds me who I am."

A man with a drink in his hand smiled in a handsomely furnished study. He pointed at a bearskin rug he had mounted on the wall between two well-stocked bookshelves. He looked proud. He did not remind her of John at all.

"A hunter kills to satisfy a need," John said. "Might be hunger. Might be he needs the fur for warmth or maybe trade. But trophies? Trophies are for men eager to force themselves on the world. Trophies are for tourists."

Laquita handed the photograph back and John pocketed it again without looking. She thought of Muir's needs. His ugly hunger. But she thought as well of his cries for attention. The photos.

"I think Muir is both," she said.

"And you think he's here."

"Well he sure as shit ain't in Mexico."

Mexico was the official thinking. But Laquita knew better. Laquita knew he was in Alaska.

"How do you know?"

"I just do."

She couldn't explain it. She wouldn't try. Sometimes she just knew things. Like who'd shoot and who'd run, or when to zig and when to zag in a pursuit moments before she needed to. One time she radioed for back up two minutes before an armed robbery went down in a bank a block away. Most times it helped her, sometimes it didn't. They used to call her Hunch. She didn't like it much.

"New Orleans to here," John said, "that's—"

"Four thousand, three hundred miles or so. Yeah. About as far away as you can get."

But she knew.

They beat their path in silence for a few minutes. Eventually John said, "I thought you people worked with partners."

"I'm off the clock."

They'd done as much as they could through official channels, and they'd gotten close too, she knew that as well. Then the photos stopped, and the case died. She'd investigated in her own time as much as she was able. Right up until ordered otherwise. Then she'd taken a leave of absence. Or she'd quit. Was fired. She wasn't really sure anymore.

"So this is a hobby," John said.

"Something like that."

He stopped and turned around. He was grinning. "Then you *are* a tourist."

Laquita began to smile in return but movement over John's shoulder drew her attention to a shape among the trees. It was burly and furred and heading right their way. She grabbed at the zipper of her jacket. Pain seared through her hand with the sudden action but she managed to yank the zip down and get it open.

"It's all right," John said.

Laquita was aiming past him, sidestepping as best she could in the deep snow.

"Baptiste. It's Eskimo Bill."

The figure ahead of them, thick with furs, ploughed a steady path through the snow but stopped at the sight of Laquita, or rather Laquita's gun, and raised a wary hand in greeting or surrender. The other held the strap of a pack over one shoulder.

Laquita lowered her weapon. "We've been following Eskimo Bill's tracks?"

John nodded.

Laquita holstered her gun. "I thought they were Muir's."

"I never said that."

John turned away as Laquita struggled her jacket closed. "Hey, Bill," he said.

"Hey yourself, mountain man. Got anything good to drink?"

Eskimo Bill was a trapper and fisherman. That was how John introduced her, neverminding to fix fisherman to fisherwoman. She was a gruff voiced woman and much older than Laquita had supposed from her movements. Or maybe she was young but didn't age well. Maybe nobody did out here. She'd widened the opening in her furred hood to drink the hot coffee John offered and Laquita saw a tan-coloured face like a screwed-up grocery sack someone had made an effort to flatten out again. She had small eyes.

"Got yourself a girlfriend," Bill said. She said it into the steaming cup she held with both hands before tipping it to her mouth again. It must have been scalding but she swallowed it down easily enough. "Heading to the Hooper place?"

"That's right," Laquita said.

The woman nodded. "Was heading that way. Heard your shots. What did you get?"

"Scared off some wolves," John said.

"Why were you heading to the Hooper place, ma'am?"

Eskimo Bill looked at John and her face cracked open in a wide smile. A couple of her teeth were missing. "Ma'am," she said to him.

To Laquita she said, "I got the parts but I'm not ma'am nor lady. Ain't Eskimo either but for a little bit."

"Which bit?"

This time Bill's smile was all for Laquita and it became a thick laugh, as if the woman had wet fur in her throat she couldn't dislodge. "She's quick as a trap," she said to John.

"What's at the Hooper place?" Laquita asked.

Bill addressed her answer to John. "Went out there with my dogs," she said. "Thought I'd see if he'd left any food in the place that wouldn't be no good to no one frozen over. Dogs went crazy mad before I could see. Going back there now without them for another look."

"What spooked your dogs?" Laquita asked.

Bill swirled whatever was left in her cup and watched it. "Nothing much, usually," she said. She took another mouthful and tossed the remaining silt into the snow. "Look at us, standing around in the cold yapping like *we* the dogs." She handed John his cup with a nod of thanks. She shrugged her pack further up her shoulder and drew the strings of her hood tight again, closing her face up into a snug ball of fur. She turned to go.

"We're coming with you," Laquita said.

Without looking back, Bill said, "Free country."

~

The cabin was another made from vertical spruce logs. Laquita knew from what John had said in the previous one that a build like this instead of horizontal meant Hooper had worked alone. Cutting, de-limbing, and skinning the trees was doable by yourself if you didn't mind hard work, but when it came to hefting them into position you had to do it vertical if you were on your own. The vertical logs also meant it blended well with the surroundings. It would serve well as a hideout.

"Look." Bill pointed from where they waited in the tree line, watching. Someone had cleared the snow from the generator's housing.

"Don't look like anyone's here now, though," John said.

"Yeah, well, can't hurt to wait a minute," Laquita said. "Just to see."

"It can hurt if you get your nuts frost bit, standing around."

John headed for the cabin.

He was better in the snow than Laquita. She couldn't overtake him. She walked wide behind him instead, gun pointing down at the snow. "John," she said. "Rifle."

His only response was to shrug it into a more comfortable position on his shoulder.

Laquita glanced back at Bill. The woman was following in John's trail but looking to either side of it, her head sweeping left and right.

The snow around the generator was discoloured where oil had been spilled. There were tracks, too, though they were little more than soft indentations, the prints filled with wind-swept snow.

John called out, "Anybody home?" Laquita dropped into a squat at the sudden noise and quickly turned to face him. She had her gun half up.

Bill was still a good few yards away. She was looking into the trees.

John opened the door before Laquita had a chance to say otherwise.

Again, the cabin was a single room. It was sparsely furnished – four beds, table, stove – but it was clean, except for a small heap of snow near one of the walls. The roof looked sound. Laquita approached the heap of snow and saw a torn sack lay beside it. Closer still she saw the snow wasn't snow but spilled flour. Under a table, lying on its side, was a tin of beans. Like it had rolled there. Like someone had gathered up their provisions in a hurry, dropped it, and let it roll there.

"Don't see your man," John said.

Laquita retrieved the tin of beans and held it up. "He was here, though."

John toed the flour.

Bill's voice came from outside. "You want to see this or not?" She was at one of the cabin's narrow ends, the side closest to the tree line. She was looking down at the ground. When she saw Laquita she pointed.

As Laquita closed in on the woman the air around her thickened with a stench that had her covering her nose and mouth. "*Fils de pute!*" She breathed in the leathery scent of her glove but still there was a pungent odour behind it, a cloying smell like a butcher's stall in summer. She expected to see a body at Bill's feet. All she saw was a large depression in the snow.

"What am I looking at?"

Speaking got her another lungful of that meat-sweat odour. There was a wet fur smell to it, too. A musky dampness. It hung in the air like an invisible fog.

"This is why I didn't bring the dogs," Bill said. "There are more prints heading that way, but this is the best one. He sheltered here a moment, out of sight, out of the wind. See? The print is clean, and the snow has frozen around its shape. Those ones," she pointed, "they've filled up some, but you can still see them."

"This is a footprint?" Laquita supposed it had some of that shape to it, but it was easily 40 centimetres long. And if it was a footprint then there was no indication of a shoe. "Wait a minute…"

John had joined them. He looked at the ground, laughed, and patted Laquita's back as if she was now part of a joke with him.

"Bigfoot?" she asked.

"The bushman," Bill said. "That's what we call him around here when we call him anything." She looked at John.

"Baptiste's man put something down for a moment," he said, "that's all. And those –" he pointed to the same indentations Bill had noted "– are *his* prints."

"Those strides?"

"He was in a hurry," Laquita said, thinking of the forgotten can. The split sack of flour. But why was he hurrying?

Bill had a different question, though.

"What man?"

Laquita looked around, into the trees and shadows. "A very unpleasant one," she said.

Bill looked at John just as he disappeared back into the cabin. "Well shit, you already found one of those."

Laquita couldn't tell if Bill was joking. The woman wore her furred hood tight and the opening for her face was filled with shadow. The sky had darkened considerably in the last hour. "How far's the next cabin?"

"You got the Shaw place that way a few miles. And I think Hooper started one down by Gullet Creek. Not been there for a while, don't know if he finished it yet. Some fancy boat lodge."

"How far's that one?"

"Too far for today."

"Two miles? Three?"

"Something like that. Dark before then, though." She squatted down by the frozen print near the corner of the cabin. "You don't want to be wandering around here at night."

Laquita looked up at the sky.

Bill stood. "Expect John's getting the stove going." She tramped her way through the trodden snow. "Get some hot food in your belly. You're skinny as a spruce."

Laquita lingered, looking into the trees the way Bill had pointed for Hooper's boat lodge.

At the door, Bill said, "Might be I saw that man o' yours." Then she went inside.

Laquita sighed. She holstered her weapon and followed.

"I first saw him back in '34," Bill said, "when I was a little girl. I'd gone with my father to check the traps. He made them himself back then, branches tied together, and we found a few of them all bust up, tracks as big as that one out there all around. And that smell. That beast-odour, all warm and wet, that lingers after."

Laquita wanted to cover her nose again just remembering. The memory of the stench was still in her nostrils.

"Four traps. No blood. No sign of what it took. Just tracks."

"But you saw it?"

Bill took a gulp of coffee and nodded. "Saw it hunched over by the river. Full daylight, sun shining off the snow, off the water, off the ice building at the banks. I saw it clear as the day was bright. He was just sitting there. Looked big even crouched down. Broad across the back. Muscular. Three hundred, three hundred and fifty pounds, I reckon, all covered in thick hair. Dark in places, but mostly grey."

"Should've shot it," John said. "You'd get a lot for the bushman's hide."

"Maybe should've."

"Did your father see it?" Laquita asked. It was clear she would have to sit through this bushman stuff before the woman told her what she wanted to know. She probably didn't talk to people often. Or only to people like John.

"No. And I couldn't say nothing right then. I was stuck watching. Eventually he stood up and waded across the river. Yellow Brook," she said to John, and he nodded.

"He moved easy, holding his long arms out of the water. Halfway across he stopped and turned." Bill grinned her gap-toothed grin at Laquita. "And he was definitely a he."

Laquita raised her eyebrows and hoped that was enough. Bill chuckled. "He's in proportion," she said, and her chuckle turned into a cough. She hacked her way through it.

"Anyway, he stopped, and he turned, and he looked right at me. I was just a tiny thing in the tree line, in the shadows, but he saw me. Looked right at me."

Laquita glanced at John. He had his boots off and was warming his feet near the stove they sat around. His socks had been mended several times, Laquita noticed.

"Teddy Wade said he saw it once," John said. "Back when he was a boy, camping out. Said it got a hold of his sleeping bag and yanked him halfway to Anchorage."

Bill nodded but said, "He ain't exactly known for honesty."

"He'll show you scars around his ankles. Said it had nails like chisels."

"How many times you seen it?" Laquita asked Bill.

The woman was rolling a cigarette on her knee. "Saw him a few times since. One time we went fishing together."

Laquita looked at John. He was smiling.

"Right," she said. "I get it. Stories for the *chechakos*."

But John shook his head and Bill said, "No, no, I don't do that. That kind of fooling is a man's sport."

John said nothing.

"I was gathering up one of my nets, but it kept slipping away from me. It was getting dark, so I hadn't seen him at first, but there was a kind of grunt and a snuffle for air. On the opposite bank. And there he was, tugging at my net whenever I wasn't. I don't know if it was the same one as before, all those years back, but he had the same thick hair. The same pale face. Squashed up nose." She put her palm to her face. "Squashed flat. I could even see teeth because its mouth was open. Mouth was like a man's, but the teeth weren't, from what I could tell."

Bill put her cigarette in her mouth but didn't light it. She spoke around it and tidied away her tobacco.

"I yelled because I was surprised, and he yelled back. His was more like the noise you make when the gennie won't start, or you can't get a fire right. Then he lumbered off into the trees. Must have been six, maybe seven feet tall. Long arms, right down past his knees."

Bill mimicked the walk in a lope around the cabin, laughed, and tipped what was left in her cup back into the pot on the stove. She got her cigarette going. "But like I said, it was dark."

"You remember the Holly boys?" John asked. "They used to winter over every year until something started thumping the walls of their cabin at night."

"Well I remember but I don't know I believe them more than Teddy Wade."

"They found prints all around." John held his hands half a metre apart.

"They get a cast?" Laquita asked.

John and Bill looked at her.

"Look, this is a great way to pass the time," she said, "but—"

"I saw that man of yours not far from here," Bill said, pushing her palm at Laquita. "I was getting to it." She sat down again and puffed some smoke. "Old boy," she said. "*Chechako*."

Laquita gave her nothing.

"Struggled a bit in the snow but seemed comfortable enough under a heavy pack."

"What else?"

"Silver hair. Long silver hair, worn loose." She drew spread fingers down the sides of her head. "The wind was blowing his hood back all the time, so I saw it. He didn't see me, though. Probably just as well."

Laquita agreed but asked anyway, "Why?"

"The bushman left me alone. That time with the nets he might have even been playing, I don't know. But your man? He didn't carry a smell on him but there was something. You could feel it. Colder than the wind and snow, that one. Like something frozen about to crack, drop you in ice water. If he'd seen me see him, one of us would have shot the other, that's what I think. He looked old but then I ain't as quick as I used to be, either."

John nodded. "Killed Prait," he said.

"Shit. I liked Prait. He was always kind to my dogs."

The whole world was dying, one good person at a time. Laquita tried to stop it, to make the world better, but catching the bad guy who did the bad thing didn't make the bad thing go away and good people were left to suffer. If you even caught them at all. Muir had evaded capture for almost three years, giving them nothing but a grainy security video and a few unsubstantiated sightings. He wasn't a grizzly, wandering wherever and doing whatever he wanted. He was the bushman. Glimpsed, but never caught, on his way to becoming his own myth.

"Where was he headed, Bill? The man you saw."

"This way, most likely." Bill glanced at the spilled flour. "But I reckon somewhere else now."

"The boat lodge."

Bill nodded.

John said, "I'll take you in the morning."

No dreams startled her awake this time. The cold brought her gradually out of sleep. The wood-burning stove had died. John, a blanket up to his chin, slept in a nearby chair though there were plenty of beds in the cabin. Bill was stretched out in one of them, her pack and furs beside her on the floor. Laquita fidgeted, trying to redirect whatever trapped warmth she could find.

"What does 'ta gul' mean?" John asked.

Laquita rubbed her face. "You're awake."

John grunted.

"*Ta gueule*," she said. "It's French. Means 'shut up'."

"They speak French where you come from?"

"Some do, but not really. My grandmother was French, though. She said if I needed to say something bad I should say it in French."

It was quiet between them for a while. Laquita was just dozing when John spoke again.

"How do you know he's out here?"

"Mm?"

"All the way from New Orleans. How do you know?"

"I just know sometimes."

"Like magic?"

Laquita checked her watch. It was early. Or very late. "Do you believe in magic, John? Ghost bears? Bigfoot?"

John said nothing. She assumed he'd drifted back to sleep. It startled her when he said, "Sometimes I hear it. Smashing through the trees at night. I smell it sometimes, too. But I ain't never seen it, so I don't know."

"Do you think it was here?"

But this time John really was asleep, or he didn't want to answer.

Laquita listened to the wind outside, the occasional shiver of snow as it slumped from the warm roof, and strained to hear anything else that might hide behind the noise.

She spent the rest of the night waiting for day.

They found the boat lodge less than two hours into the afternoon. Bill had needed to get back to her dogs but she'd swapped coats with Laquita first. Laquita hadn't tried very hard to refuse. Bill's coat was a thick pelt one, heavier than her jacket but much warmer. "I'll want it back when you're done," Bill had said.

She pulled the hood back now for a closer look at the lodge.

"That'll go in breakup," John said, drawing her attention to a small fishing jetty. The river had swollen as it froze so that the boards seemed to sit directly on the ice. The boat lodge was different to the previous cabins, its logs positioned horizontally. There'd be kayaks inside too, Laquita supposed, and maybe even a fishing trap in the floor, depending if it projected over the river at the back. A lantern had been hung from one of the porch posts but a shelf of snow made it difficult to tell if it had been done recently.

"Is he in there?"

Laquita didn't know – not for sure – but she said, "Yeah." She reached into her coat but John put his hand on her arm before she could retrieve the gun.

"Remember the wolf," he said.

Laquita nodded. She thought it was his way of saying 'watch your back', but while she checked her weapon John stepped from the cover of the trees. She tried to grab him back without revealing herself as well, but he was already walking towards the lodge.

The wolf, she thought.

She used the tree cover to get around the side of the building, looking from the door to John to the door to the windows to John all the while.

"Hello?" John called.

This was stupid. Muir had already shot one man who probably did nothing but see him. John wasn't so much a distraction as a target.

The windows had shutters fixed over them, but Laquita watched them anyway. There was probably gap enough to see out from inside.

She hurried. She made a lot of noise, tramping through the brush, shaking snow from the branches she knocked, but she kept out of sight.

The front door opened. Laquita stopped where she was. The door opened into a dark interior, but she thought she saw a man there. There was a screen door, too, obscuring the figure into a shape of shadow among shadows.

John stopped where he was. He was right out in the open. "Cold out," he said.

The screen door opened with a metallic whine, springs already rusted or perhaps frozen. The door opened outward and kept Laquita's view obscured, but she had her gun up. The screen would stop mosquitoes maybe, but not a bullet.

John moved forward again, towards the cabin, pretending to assume he was welcome. He cast back his hood and began unfastening his pack, all so that shrugging his rifle from his shoulder would look casual too. He was in the middle of that when something caused him to stop suddenly and Laquita heard a single shot from the doorway.

She dropped to her knee and almost fired but the screen door had already slammed shut as Muir stepped back inside.

John had dropped his rifle. He cupped his stomach, looked into his palm, and then dropped to his knees. Laquita was ready to run to him but right then the screen door opened again and Muir stepped outside. He held a gun straight-armed, angled down at John, and walked towards him. He glanced left and right but his first few steps had already put Laquita beyond his peripheral vision. "You the one coming for me?" he called to John. "I know someone's coming for me."

John patted the snow for his rifle.

Laquita yelled. "Muir!"

She hadn't intended to warn him. She hadn't come all this way to read him his rights. But she wanted him to stop, and to turn. Not out of any sense of honour – she'd shoot him in the back if she had to – but because she didn't want him facing John.

He did turn. He crouched, but he turned.

Laquita fired. She fired four times. Muir fell onto his back. Laquita saw a rope of blood snake out from him to dash a long red line across the snow.

She hurried as fast as the snow allowed.

"Talk to me, John," she called.

He was still on his knees. He had his rifle now, but he was using it to keep himself upright.

Muir lay blinking. He was bleeding from his chest and neck. Laquita crouched and retrieved his gun. "You have the right to remain silent," she said, pocketing the weapon. His face was as pale as the snow around him, but she thought perhaps it always had been. His lips were bloody. Tiny bubbles popped between them. "Shh," Laquita told him. Just a man, dying in the snow.

His arm came up slowly. Laquita swatted it away, thinking it was a feeble last effort. A dead man's punch. But the fist she knocked away struck the snow bloody and dropped a knife.

"*Bordel de merde.*"

She stood and stepped away from Muir, cupping her body the same way she'd seen John do only a moment ago. Blood pooled in her hand.

Muir died with a smile.

"*Fils de pute.*"

She hoped Bill's coat was thick enough to have prevented the worst, but she couldn't tell. She couldn't feel it yet, either.

She pressed the wound and made her way to John.

"Let me see," she said.

She tried to kneel beside him but collapsed against him instead. The two of them fell sideways, John with a grunt of pain. Laquita sat and pulled him upright.

"You're going to be okay," she told him, then tugged his hands away from his stomach to see if she'd lied.

A light snow began to fall.

Laquita turned John to get to his pack. She pulled at the cords, fumbled at the pockets. When she found what she was looking for she said again, "You'll be okay," and pulled at her gloves with her teeth.

"*Ta... gueule,*" John said. Laquita laughed, then winced at the pain it brought to a wound she hadn't felt until now.

""*Ta gueule,*" she said back.

John said something else. It came out as an exhalation and a hiss.

"What was that?"

"*Checha...kos,*" he said, and closed his eyes.

Laquita followed the river. She moved slowly, leaning forward with each step, each foot making a post hole in snow that was deep on the open ice but free of obstacles. She dragged John roped to a kayak from the lodge, pulling it like a sled, breathing hard whenever a step or pull tugged at her clumsily stitched wound. She'd stitched John, too – just to slow the bleeding – but he needed better help than hers. She hoped the cold was buying them both time. Sometimes she thought it was getting dark and sometimes she thought it already was and had to shake her head against the snowfall to clear it. Sometimes she felt someone walking with her. She heard them in the trees. Sometimes she thought it was Muir, but Muir was dead. She'd made sure of it. Something else followed them, big as a bear but not a bear, best she could tell. A shape that disappeared whenever she turned her head to look.

She stumbled often. Sometimes she fell. Sometimes when she fell she stayed down for longer than she should because the body didn't always know how to tell the difference between what it wanted and what it needed.

The final time she fell she seemed to fall upwards. Something warm and rank smothered her. The dreamless dark came with a powerful stench.

Laquita woke in a comfortable bed, in a comfortable heat, to the aroma of baking bread. Her view was a horizontal log wall until she turned, groaning at the pain in her side.

"Easy."

Bill came to the bed. She looked small without her furs but far from frail. She wore jeans and a denim shirt rolled to her elbows. Faded tattoos lined her arms. She had a steaming bowl in one hand. She pulled up a chair with the other and sat.

"John," Laquita said.

"First thing you said last time you saw me." Bill offered her the bowl. "It's getting to hurt my feelings."

"He's been shot."

"He's been shot before. And stabbed. Hit by motorcycle too, once, though that one weren't his fault."

Laquita struggled to sit but Bill put a hand on her arm. "He's fine. Eat your oatmeal." She offered the food again.

The bowl felt wonderful in her hands. Warm. Its aroma was deep and sweet. Not like—

"What happened?"

"Yeah," said Bill. "We better talk about that."

"You found me?"

"*You* found *me*."

"You were still at the Hooper place?"

"No."

Laquita spooned up some oatmeal. It was too hot, but she tried anyway.

"You made it all the way back to my place," Bill said, "which is impressive. 'Specially as you've never been to my place. And those aren't easy miles." She smiled. "You're a tough *chechako*, but not that tough."

Bill waited for an explanation, but Laquita had nothing she wanted to say. She blew to cool her food.

"You don't remember?"

"A little."

"You were in and out of it, but you told me about John. I took the sled and the dogs sniffed him out on the river."

"And he's okay?"

Bill nodded. "He's okay. Well, he is what he is, but mostly that's okay."

Laquita closed her eyes and settled back against her pillow, bowl held against her chest.

"Hey. Don't sleep yet."

She hadn't planned to, but Bill's voice startled her from something close to it.

"They called Bruak," Bill said. "He's the closest we got to law in these parts."

Laquita remembered. "Trooper Bruak."

Bill shrugged. "Gunshot wounds are still reported, even in hospitals way out here."

"Hospital? That's good."

"John disagrees. Wouldn't surprise me if he turned up here to tell you in person."

"That'd be good, too."

Bill shook her head but smiled. "Little girl, I don't think you know him very well at all."

Laquita looked around the cabin. She saw shelves crammed full with supplies. Packets of dried noodles, mashed potato, powdered milk, eggs, cheese. She saw sacks of rice, flour, sugar, oatmeal, cans of coffee, cans of fruit, cans of vegetables.

"That's a lot of food."

"Out here you prepare for winter, recover from it, then do it all again. You looking for your gun? It's over there. With your jacket."

Bill started rolling a cigarette.

"Of course, I'm tempted to keep it – your jacket, not that pop gun – on account of mine stinks something awful."

Laquita remembered the dark she was carried in. The warm awful dark.

"Bill—"

"It's all right." Bill brought the cigarette to her mouth, licked it closed, and pretended to misunderstand Laquita's concern. "I gotta clean it anyway. It's got blood all over it. Now eat your oatmeal or I'll spoon it to you myself."

Laquita did as she was told, enjoying the heat of it in her mouth and stomach. "Why aren't I in hospital too?"

Bill puffed a cloud of smoke. "I don't know your story yet." She said it like the answer was obvious. "Thought you might want to get one straight before any law got involved."

Government busybodies, Laquita thought. She smiled, but it slipped away when Bill spoke again.

"I looked for that man of yours," she said. "After John. I went back and looked all over for him."

Laquita sat up, and never mind how it pulled her stitches. "But he's dead."

"I don't doubt it. He weren't where you said but a lot of the snow around there was red. And there were footprints."

"He was *dead*."

"Even if he weren't, I reckon he is now. Hey, come on." Bill eased her back to the pillows. "Don't worry," she said quietly, laying her down. "Prints weren't his."

John did come to Bill's cabin. By then Laquita was able to move around easily and had been in the process of learning how to skin a hare. They were outside at a table set up in the snow. Bill was hanging one of the stripped carcasses, stringing the bloody meat up a tree, when Laquita asked, "You not worried about the bushman, leaving that there?"

"He leaves me alone, just like he does you." Bill wiped her hands on her legs. "Or maybe it was that coat of mine kept you safe, eh?"

It was the closest they'd come to talking about it. It was close enough.

"John's here," Laquita said, and then Bill's dogs began to bark. Bill looked a question at her, but Laquita pretended not to see it, rubbing sweat from her forehead with the back of her wrist. Yanking the skin off a dead animal was surprisingly hard work.

Judging from the way he moved out of the trees, John was walking around sooner than he should have been. Bill's dogs continued to bark at the intrusion. They were roped up, but they pulled the lines taut trying to get him.

"They remember you," Bill said.

"Maybe they're just hungry," John said. He reached beneath his furs and withdrew some meat he'd kept warm there. He showed it to Bill who shrugged and nodded. John threw it to the animals, big hunks of meat still on the bone.

"Ain't poisoned, is it?" Bill asked.

John ignored the question and handed Bill a gift of her own as he walked past. A pouch of tobacco. Bill didn't seem to know how to look at it.

"Feeling okay?" Laquita asked. She scooped handfuls of snow and rubbed blood from her hands.

"About the usual." He stopped in front of her. Just two people who nearly died, looking at each other.

"Good to see you, podna," Laquita said. She offered her hand and John's swallowed it up in the shake.

"That like partner?"

"Close enough."

Afterwards he pointed to her waist. "Let's see."

"Show you mine, you show me yours?" But she had her clothing up to show him a ragged wound. "Bill neatened it up for me."

"Yeah," John said. "You can't sew to save your life."

"Saved yours, though," Bill said. "Waste of good thread you ask me." She held up the tobacco. "Thanks."

John nodded. He shrugged out of his pack. "Got something for you, too."

"Aw, John, you shouldn't have," Laquita said.

She saw a mass of silver hair and her first thought was a dark and ludicrous one, that he was handing her Muir's scalp. It wasn't hair, though. It was fur. It was another hat, only this one was—

"Got it from your wolf," John said.

He'd left the ears on it. She wasn't sure how she felt about that.

"Got you these, too." He dropped several teeth into her open hand. They shone against her skin, cleaned and polished. "Weren't no trouble," he said. "Just had to pick them up out of the snow."

Laquita continued to stare. Her palm was still lined with blood. She closed her hand into a fist, felt the teeth bite, then dropped them. They disappeared into the snow. Tiny holes soon to heal. "Trophies are for tourists," she said.

John nodded. "How are you sleeping?"

"Better."

"Your T and M report all done?"

She nodded.

"When you going back?" he asked.

She looked at him and then at Bill. She looked at the skinned hares and the dogs working at their bones. She looked at the fur hat in her hands. The sky. The trees.

"I don't know," she said.

Deep in the forest, something howled.

|The Castellmarch Man|

Atop Raiders Hill in Radnorshire stands a solitary stone that some believe resembles a weeping figure. According to folklore, the shadow it casts as the sun goes down points the way to a cave of hidden treasure, stolen goods hidden by thieves waiting for a safe time to sell. Whether the stone figure weeps because it was never able to find this bounty, or because it grieves some greater loss, nobody knows, though of course there are stories to accommodate both possibilities. There are certainly plenty of caves in the area and the hills and mountains make for rewarding hikes.

Geo-cache findings: a toy car, a single glove, and a tarnished silver ring.

The Hayward Stables guesthouse was a converted farmhouse with similarly renovated outbuildings, sturdy stone structures with heavy wooden mantles and beams. The door frames forced you to duck, and the sash windows rattled in their frames when the wind was high, but it was cosy. All of the rooms were tidy, with instantly forgettable décor. Upstairs was carpeted thick enough to muffle footsteps whereas downstairs was all stone floor. A wide parking area extended around the back, and further down the track was an old stable that had been converted into a large storage shed, or barn, Charlie supposed. In the year since his last visit very little about the place had changed. Even the weather was the same: rain, rain, and more rain.

The food, though. That was different. Then again, perhaps the food was exactly as it always had been, and he simply couldn't remember right; most food tasted bland to him these days, although he would have expected farmhouse fare to have been hearty and full of flavour, whatever his mood. The wine, of course, was fine. He'd worked his way through most of a bottle of red already. He'd probably order another.

It appeared there were only two other sets of guests staying at The Hayward Stables, judging by who had come to dinner. Maybe others had opted for bed and breakfast only (and maybe there was someone bedded down in the old stables – ha!). A large stone-floored dining room had been set with rows of mismatched tables and chairs, each piece of furniture up-cycled from something tatty to something deliberately dishevelled and shabby-chic. A young couple were trying to coax one child into eating and another into settling down, and they weren't doing a bad job. Another couple, middle-aged, sat only a table away from Charlie and bickered in hushed tones. The focus of their altercation was hidden beneath the noise of the nearby children and the persuasions of the parents, but the man seemed to be taking most of it, drinking his dark ale and listening, interjecting whenever moved by a particularly forceful point. The woman was a stern kind of beautiful, but maybe that was unfair. Maybe that was only because of her current mood: maybe she was usually more serene. Charlie used to get quite aroused whenever Lyndsey was angry, he didn't know why. He'd never told her that. Perhaps he should have.

Occasionally the husband caught sight of Charlie noticing and smiled politely, embarrassed by the quiet argument. They had bonded earlier over a complaint about the slow service, though neither party had voiced their concerns to anyone else but each other. While they'd waited for their food the man had joked, "Shame the stables are empty, I could eat a horse," and Charlie had laughed far too much. The man had noted the half empty wine bottle while Charlie raised a glass to toast his agreement, and to excuse his own reaction.

He pushed a piece of sausage around the gravy on his plate and loaded it with mashed potato but found he was no longer hungry. He never really had been. He laid the fork down just as the bickering woman wiped her mouth with a napkin she cast down like a gauntlet before excusing herself from the table. Charlie admired her legs briefly. The man made a half-hearted attempt to call her back, his volume restricted by public company. He looked around to check if they'd caused a scene. The young couple were far too busy with their own family, but Charlie had nothing better to do and he offered a tight-lipped smile in sympathy.

"She doesn't like the weather," the man explained.

Charlie looked at the window, but the curtains had been drawn against the dark. He knew it would be raining, though. Or had just been raining. Or was about to rain. It had been raining for days. Mostly only brief showers and a pathetic drizzle that was more like mist, hanging in the air, but it was all still rain just the same. "Welcome to Wales."

"Is it always like this then?"

"I'm not from here," Charlie said, and remembered the man in the barn, though he tried not to. "I think this is fairly typical weather, though, yeah."

"We're having a bit of a stay-cation," the husband said.

"Ah."

Charlie didn't care much for conversation, but the new silence between them felt uncomfortable so he said, "Well, there's plenty worth seeing around here. Lots of interesting places if you know where to look."

"What brings you here?"

My wife, Charlie thought.

"Treasure-hunting," he said. The man tilted his head for more, so Charlie added, "Geo-caching?"

"Sorry."

Charlie waved the apology away. "Bit of a hobby," he explained, and took another sip of wine.

It had begun as a joke, a nerdy pastime to get them both out of the house, away from the sofa and the TV. It gave them weekends of fresh air and exercise that was more fun than the gym. It gave them a chance to get to know each other again as they drove around the country, looking for geo-cache 'treasures'. Charlie told the man some of this.

"There's a website that provides coordinates for wherever you decide to explore, and a GPS will take you to each concealed geo-cache," he said, pausing to refill his glass. "Just a Tupperware tub or something, filled with an assortment of keepsakes. You take something, you leave something, you sign the notebook, and then you look for the next one."

"And this is a thing? People do this?"

Charlie nodded. "It's fun."

It had surprised Charlie to discover how much he enjoyed finding these secret places. Lyndsey had admitted the same, so it was to their mutual amusement that what had begun as a joke became something of a more serious pursuit, with weekly jaunts up and down the country. There were geo-caches hidden everywhere. They found them in trees, under hedgerows, submerged in ponds and rivers. They found them hidden behind road signs, tucked beneath old stone walls and concealed in ruined buildings. And as they searched, so they came to know hidden areas of the land, beautiful places off the beaten trail. They became tourists in their own backyard, learning more about their country. It always surprised Charlie just how much there was to discover. Every nook and cranny of Britain held a secret, it seemed.

"There are these clues," Charlie said. "Sometimes just coordinates to follow but sometimes something more cryptic. Those were Lyndsey's favourite. She liked to figure things out."

She had *me* all figured out.

"Lyndsey? That your wife?"

They both looked at the empty seat opposite Charlie. The plates were clean, cutlery still napkin-wrapped.

"Yeah. We came here this time last year. This is sort of an anniversary."

"Well, congratulations."

Charlie smiled a thank you into his wine, thinking, *not that kind of anniversary*. He tapped the wedding ring he still wore against the glass. He'd recently had it engraved with GPS coordinates. It represented their lives better than dates. The place where they met and the place where they parted suggested a journey that was both literal and metaphorical. Dates, he thought, would have seemed too much like an epitaph.

Charlie took a pouch of tobacco from the pocket of his chair-backed jacket and excused himself for a cigarette. He offered the pouch but was glad when the man declined. He didn't want to know him any better than he did already, and he'd shared too much about himself as it was. He left his wine and jacket to make it clear he was coming back, but he hoped the man would be gone by then.

The Church of Saint Brynach in west Dyfed, Wales, was founded in the 6ᵗʰ century. Its churchyard boasts the Nevern Cross, which dates back to the

10th century. Fashioned from dolerite, the cross stands 13 feet high and is beautifully carved, knotwork and ringwork and geometric patterns making it one of the most impressive carved crosses in Britain. The first cuckoo of the year is thought to land on this cross to announce the coming of spring. Also in this churchyard is 'The Bleeding Yew'. Its trunk bleeds a red resin believed to be the blood of a monk wrongfully hanged from its branches.

Geo-cache findings: a plastic bird, a colouring book of Celtic designs, and a packet of sweets (out of date).

It wasn't raining, but Charlie still sheltered beneath the small roof at the back of the guesthouse because the sky was thick with cloud. The moon appeared occasionally but only briefly. There was plenty of light, though, thanks to an automatic security bulb that had come on as Charlie stepped outside. It illuminated a vast puddled stretch of gravelled ground and four parked cars. One of them was a people-carrier which he guessed belonged to the young couple with kids, or maybe the owners of the guesthouse, though there was also a mud-splattered Land Rover that he thought might have belonged to them. The Audi was probably the bickering couple's car. The other vehicle was his. For a moment he thought there was someone sitting inside – on the passenger side, Lyndsey's side – but it was only the coat he'd draped over the seat. Not his new one, just his old waterproof, pale grey with bright orange reflective strips up the sides and arms, and absolutely hideous because those were the rules, according to Lyndsey, right up there with good hiking boots and a packet of mint cake. Every rambler, hiker, and apparently geo-cacher, had to have a vile waterproof jacket of clashing colours, preferably something that folded to the size of a handkerchief or packed itself away into its own pocket somehow. Lyndsey's had been orange and pink. It made her look like one of those sweets you used to be able to get from the corner shop, a rhubarb and custard. No, a fruit salad; rhubarb and custards were the other ones, the ones that lasted forever.

He rested the tobacco pouch on a nearby windowsill and set about rolling a cigarette. He tried not to look at the old stable but failed, glancing up at the dark shape of it several times between stages of the cigarette's construction. He would take another look inside before he left. He didn't particularly want to, but he was retracing his steps and the stable was a big part of that. Plus he needed to check if there was anybody in there.

He looked at the car again instead, hoping once more for that illusion of a passenger on Lyndsey's side, but the coat draped over the seat was just a coat.

Lyndsey didn't drive, but she was a fantastic navigator. Rather than rely on any conventional kind of sat-nav, Lyndsey used an app on her mobile phone with the volume down and provided her own range of voices, using outlandish, often terrible, accents, mimicking celebrities and sometimes people they both knew. Sometimes she made up characters, like Farmer Jones (*that be the wrong way, lad*) and Lady Wetherby (*oh, do be careful, driver*). She changed the voices whenever Charlie laughed. It was a game they had.

"Oh. No," she'd say, her voice overly robotic. "You do-not. Want. To-go. That. Way." Or she'd urge, "The other way, *the other way!*" in a voice filled with feigned panic, all the while calm as she looked out of the passenger window at whatever part of the countryside they were passing through.

"This is *not* the right way."

"It is."

"At the traffic lights, make a u-turn."

"There are no traffic lights."

"At the next junction, go off-road."

"In this car?"

"At the next dealership, purchase a new vehicle."

That's how she was.

"Warning: we are low on fuel."

"We're fine."

"Warning: we need coffee and chocolate or we will become annoying."

"*Become* annoying?"

"Advisory: coffee and chocolate will lead to sexual gratitude."

"That would be tempting if you weren't Stephen Hawking."

She'd laughed at that, loud and sudden and surprised, then covered her mouth with both hands. "Oh, that's wrong."

"I just don't find him attractive."

"You're not supposed to find *anyone* attractive."

"What about—"

"Anyone *else* attractive." Then, serious, "You do still find me attractive, right?"

Charlie smiled. He was standing outside, in the cold, smoking in full view of the stables that marked the beginning of the end, but he was also back in the car, back with Lyndsey who was asking, "Are we there yet?"

"Nearly."

"What about now?"

"Nearly."

"What about—"

"*Lynds...*"

He looked over at the converted stables.

It was a large but surprisingly squat building, with a sloping roof of corrugated metal. He remembered how it drummed with the rain. Inside was a vast open space. If there had ever been stalls for horses they were gone now. In fact, there was little to suggest they were ever stables at all, other than the name of the guesthouse, and he supposed that could have been a deliberate misnomer, something quaint and countrified to lure the tourists. The inside had smelled wet and warm, bales of summer-baked hay wrapped in plastic yet somehow releasing an aroma so that rain seemed to mix with sunshine. There was a metallic smell, too, and oil, from a vehicle that was not quite a tractor sitting guard in the open double doors, the tines of its threshing machinery like some medieval war machine to keep people out. It hadn't deterred them, though. If only it had.

Those doors were closed now, the machine tucked away inside, if it was there at all. Charlie exhaled a final stream of smoke with a sigh. If the fucking thing had been parked away properly in the first place, the giant doors shut, then they never would have gone inside. They'd have forgone the novelty of the setting and had sex back in their own room instead, only yards away.

Charlie dropped what remained of his cigarette and twisted it dead under his heel.

You look angry.

It sounded like Lyndsey's voice, but it was only in his head. Still, it made him smile. 'You look angry' had been one of their geo-cache clues last time they were in Wales. It had looked like a code at first – *Ydych yn edrych yn ddig* – but it wasn't long after crossing into Wales that they'd realised it was simply Welsh. *Ydych yn edrych yn ddig*, you look angry, became a game so that whenever one of them said it in the car, thinking aloud, trying to figure it out, the other would offer a reply. *It's just the way my face looks. You stole the covers last night. I'm trying to fart.*

Not all of the locations came with clues or riddles, but those that did were Lyndsey's favourites, and she never Googled the clues or read the message boards in the community forum, nothing like that. She never cheated, not when it came to geo-caching. They figured them out together, just like they did everything else.

'You look angry' was a clue for St Brynach Church.

"St Brynach Church, named after – *wow* – St Brynach," Lyndsey said. "Sixth century chapel, famous for the Nevern Cross or Great Cross of St Brynach, one of the finest in Wales, thirteen feet high..."

Lyndsey liked to research everywhere they went, but only after they'd arrived, to avoid what she called spoilers. While she read to him from her phone, Charlie used his to take pictures. He'd usually manage a few secret ones of Lyndsey before she spotted him, and then she'd strike ridiculous poses or give him the dreaded duck-face pout. At St Brynach's she hadn't noticed for ages, too busy searching among the gravestones, so after he'd taken a few shots of her bending over he turned the phone around for a secret selfie or two he'd send her later.

"You look angry."

As Charlie was contorting his face into an ugly sneer he'd assumed she'd caught him, but looking up, still sneering, he saw that she had her back to him among the graves. She patted one of them before turning to face him.

"You look angry," she said again. "Cross. Angry is cross. Get it? The Nevern Cross, probably. And you is probably yew tree. The one I told you about, the one that bleeds." She pointed and said, "*Yew* lead the way."

Charlie gave her one of his pity-smiles.

"Shut up, I'm hilarious."

Among the gravestones, Charlie said, "Honey, I love doing this with you, but I'm not digging up a grave. I've got my limits."

Yet here he was, a year later, digging up what should probably be left alone.

He contemplated another cigarette but it began to rain again, so he went back inside.

~

Dryburgh Abbey, in Scotland, stands as a remarkably complete set of ruins. It contains paintwork that dates back to its construction in 1150 and remains one of the most beautiful examples of Gothic architecture.

According to legend, a woman who lost her lover made a home in one of the vaults and swore never to look upon the sun again until her lover returned. Learning he had died, she only ever came out from the vault at night, living a half-life of loss and loneliness.

Geo-cache findings: a heart-shaped fridge magnet, a novelty pen, an ornate thimble.

~

Whatever the couple had been bickering about was either resolved or temporarily forgotten by the time Charlie returned to his room. He was reminded of how thin the walls were by the sounds of their passionate make-up sex. Or maybe it was angry sex. 'Fuck you' sex, Charlie thought, unamused by his own pun.

You look angry.

It sounded like good sex, whatever it was.

Charlie undressed and stretched out on his own bed. He matched his rhythm to the sounds from next door, masturbating to the squeak and creak of their bedsprings and looking at a photograph of Lyndsey he had on the bedside table. Eventually the woman's climax drew a scowling one from him and he was able, at last, to sleep.

~

Croagh Patrick is a holy mountain that rises 765 metres above sea level and overlooks Clew Bay in Ireland. It is believed that St Patrick made his way here from Aghagower and spent 40 nights on its summit praying and fasting and casting out demons. Time has altered the legend so that demons have become snakes instead.

 Geo-cache findings: none (not yet visited)

In the morning, Charlie skipped breakfast and went out to his car for the geo-cache he'd left on the back seat, a little of the secret life of Lyndsey and Charlie West. Deliberately awful poems Lyndsey used to leave for him around the house (*I love you like blue loves sky, oh me, oh my*). A strip of photo booth pictures, Lyndsey flashing her boobs (never breasts, *never* tits), pictures they used to keep on the fridge and had to remember to take down every time they had visitors (and forgetting on more than one occasion). A length of rope (look out for snakes!). He'd considered leaving his wedding ring too but he couldn't bring himself to do it, not yet. There was no comments book inside either because this would be a geo-cache he never registered online. If anyone ever found it, it would be the owners of The Hayward Stables during some clean up or sort out. Putting it here was entirely for his own benefit. Like flowers on a grave.

 The car was still wet from last night's rain. Puddles the size of small lakes blotted the gravelled drive and the early morning air held the smell of wet grass. Charlie took a deep breath of it and looked to the sky. Grey, but not raining, and somehow clean looking, as if grey was its usual colour and it had just needed the blue washing out.

 Charlie hadn't bothered to lock the car – there was nothing left he couldn't bear to lose – and he was glad not to ruin the peace of the country morning with the electronic blip-blip of central locking. He retrieved the container from the back seat and closed the door again, its soft thump the only sound to disturb the quiet except for the crunch and scrape of gravel underfoot as he made his way to the old stables that might never have been stables.

 The large doors were closed. Would they be locked, though? Were they more careful since the Castellmarch man? He doubted it. As he neared, Charlie looked out for a coil of chain wrapped around the handle grips or a large padlock clasped closed, or both, but there was no such thing. He tucked the Tupperware box under his arm, wedged high into his armpit, looked around for anyone who might see him, and gripped the door with both hands. It was a large one that slid across, essentially a moving wall more than a door, and he expected it to be heavy, but it moved easily and quietly, its bearings well-oiled. He opened it only enough to step inside and closed it again behind him.

For a moment it was pitch black dark. He heard birds waking up above him somewhere and smelled the damp sweet aroma of hay and feed and maybe manure, the sharp tang of petrol and machine oil, but he saw nothing. Eventually his eyes adjusted to the gloom, grey light filtering in through rusted holes in the metal walls and roof and through the sheets of newspaper that had been stuck over a large window. Most of the floor space had been taken up by a temporary holding pen made up of boards held between breezeblocks. There was no sign of any livestock, but as a veteran geo-cacher Charlie recognised the pellets of sheep droppings. At the back of the building, a stack of stored hay. That was where, a year ago, he and Lyndsey had enjoyed a private moment, a secret moment that turned out to be less secret than they had supposed. And over there, between the hay and a workbench cluttered with tools, that had been where the Castellmarch man had loitered. Unseen, at first, bedded down in a spill of hay and bundled blankets and tarp.

They'd been walking the grounds, exploring the fields just before dusk. It had been good to just walk together without searching for a geo-cache – there weren't any locations nearby, not then – and they had held hands and talked and made new promises to each other. To try harder. To do more fun stuff. She would be faithful, he would be more spontaneous. As they'd neared The Hayward Stables, Lyndsey had picked up the pace, claiming she wanted to get back before proper dark and the inevitable rain but walking with an urgency that suggested something else.

"You need to pee, don't you?"

"Maybe."

They only made it as far as the stables or barn or whatever the building was before Lyndsey had to relieve herself. She squatted behind a plastic rain barrel and a leaning stack of wooden pallets.

"Watch out for ropes," Charlie had warned.

Back when they'd first started geo-caching, one of the treasure boxes had been hidden among the roots of fallen tree. Lyndsey had crouched beside the trunk, reaching for an opening in the soil, but before she could finish a feeble joke about *rooting* around she'd leapt away with a scream of "Snake!" and the two of them had fled. The 'snake' turned out to be a length of dirty rope, some coiled excess from what had been used to secure the geo-cache container to the tree stump. Charlie had teased Lyndsey about it forever since. This new teasing as she peed saw her hand come up from behind the water barrel to give him the middle finger.

"You look angry," Charlie said. An old joke by then, but one they still used occasionally.

"There aren't any snakes in Wales," Lyndsey said, standing and pulling her jeans up with her.

"You're thinking of Ireland."

She'd put her hand to her chest in mock distress, gave him another one of her voices, temporarily Irish. "You mean there *are* snakes in Wales?"

"Baby," he'd said, "Wales has fucking *dragons*."

Worse than dragons.

While Lyndsey buttoned up, Charlie joked that she shouldn't bother. At least, it had started as a joke. But because she'd stopped to 'joke' back – "Oh yeah? Why's that?" – instead of simply dismissing his suggestion, he'd taken her by the hand and pulled her towards the open door. Her only protest had been an unconvincing, "We can't," but it turned out they could, and they did, rougher and wilder and louder than they had been in a long time. Proof, if any was needed, that they still had something. Reassurance, for Charlie, that she was still interested in him beyond the comfort and companionship of a long-term relationship. Reassurance for her, he supposed, that he could still be passionate and commanding.

Afterwards, panting from where she lay bent over a collapsed bale of hay, Lyndsey had expressed surprise and gratification with the exclamation, "*Fuck*."

"Again? Okay, five minutes."

She had made a pathetic backwards slap at him without looking, exhaling a laugh that had little sound as she tried to catch her breath, but Charlie had already stepped away from her to get dressed again. He swatted her behind, gently this time, and placed her clothes beside her. He kissed her back, and when she rolled over with an exaggerated sigh, he kissed her breasts until she sat up. They were criss-crossed with lines from where she'd been pressed against the hay and strands were stuck to her sweaty skin. He helped her brush them away until she brushed *him* away, slapping at his hands.

"If you want to help you can find my shoes."

They had been such a struggle to remove in the heat of the moment, stuck in her jeans, that Charlie had thrown them aside when they were finally off.

"Charlie?"

"Yeah, I'm looking."

He was peering into the shadows on the ground when Lyndsey called to him again, quieter this time, but with a new tone that made it sound more urgent; "*Char*lie." She had her t-shirt on but also held her arm across her chest while the other hand pushed her jumper and jeans into her lap, between her legs.

"Lynds?"

She didn't answer or turn to face him and finally Charlie saw what she was looking at. *Who* she was looking at.

The Castellmarch man.

He was wearing a hat, that fucking stupid hat with the flaps that came down over the ears. He was wearing an old army jacket, too, the type that was fashionable when Charlie was young if you wanted to prove how alternative or grungy you were. Army surplus with deep pockets, faded green (and if you were particularly rebellious or quirky, maybe you had a foreign flag stitched into the shoulder). His jeans were scruffy. Charlie couldn't see the man's boots properly but they were probably DMs.

"Oh, shit, sorry," Charlie said, "we just—"

"It was raining," Lyndsey said, slipping down from the hay bale to hide the lower half of her body. When that part of her was out of view she immediately stepped into her jeans, underwear be damned. It hadn't been raining, not quite, but it was now. It drummed loud against the roof.

The man exhaled forcefully from his mouth so that his lips trembled. Charlie couldn't tell if it was disbelief or amusement or anger or what.

"Sorry," Charlie said again, casting a quick look around again to ensure they had everything. He saw a pile of makeshift bedding, tucked away in the dark. A spill of belongings were spread across the ground nearby.

The man scratched at what he had of a beard and said, "Not from here." Charlie didn't know if he meant them or, judging by the rough bedding, himself.

"No, we're just… no. You? You staying here as well?"

Partly Charlie was trying to ascertain whether he and Lyndsey were in any kind of trouble. He was fairly certain the man was not one of the owners, and though there was a chance he was a farmhand or something, Charlie supposed the man was actually homeless, or a traveller, bedding down for a night out of the rain. Whatever and whoever he was, Charlie wanted to distract him from Lyndsey who was subtly trying to dress herself.

The man stamped one foot a couple of times and dragged it back across the floor as if trying to scrape something from his boot.

"I'm from *Castellmarch*. I *told* you."

Lyndsey shared a look with Charlie. It was a mildly judgemental look, as in she'd judged the man was mildly mental.

"I mean, I didn't tell you I was from Castellmarch," the man said, "just that I'm not from here. 'Not from here.' I said that."

"Right."

The man nodded. He looked at Lyndsey, dressing.

"So, is that in Wales then?" Charlie asked. "Castellmarch?"

"Castellmarch is in Abersoch, across the sea." He pointed in a direction that meant nothing to Charlie.

"Oh, right. Is it an island?"

The man laughed. "Abersoch's not an *island*." He looked at Lyndsey, who had just plucked items of underwear from the ground, bunching them into a tangle of lace and straps and bra cups which she tried to hold casually. He grinned at her as if they shared a private joke or secret intimacy. "He thinks Abersoch is an *island*."

"He's not very clever," Lyndsey said, with a quick smile.

"Hey," said Charlie, "I'm right here."

"It's not an island," the man explained. "It's across the bay."

"Okay."

"I'm going to Carreg Castle."

"Okay."

Lyndsey was looking for her shoes. Charlie made a show of helping her so that he was too busy for further conversation.

"How about some music?" the man asked. He reached down to the array of things scattered on and around his bed. Charlie expected a radio but the man produced a flute, no, a whistle, a recorder or something, but surely he wasn't going to—

The man began to play.

The look Lyndsey gave Charlie was loaded with amusement, a smile in her eyes that acknowledged just how strange all of this was turning out to be. They would have fun, later, talking about it, the look said. She'd probably add this man to her repertoire of sat-nav character voices, Charlie thought.

The whistling was shrill but the open space of the large building seemed to soften it a little, lending a haunting echo that wasn't exactly unpleasant within the drumming sound of rain. There was a melody, and the man played with a burst of enthusiasm that made it lively at first, but his joy dwindled quickly and he stopped as abruptly as he had began. "Do you know that song?"

Lyndsey shook her head. Charlie said, "No," and wondered if they'd been expected to sing along or dance or something. He wondered if they'd offended him somehow.

The man's scowl was only for his whistle, though. "That wasn't the song I meant to play," he said, pocketing the instrument. "I think it's broken."

Lyndsey laughed, partly in case it was a joke and partly because this was all just too weird. Charlie laughed a little with her, glad when the man smiled because it now it meant they were laughing with him instead of at him. Kind of.

The man withdrew a pouch of tobacco from his coat pocket. He offered it but they both shook their heads no.

"Don't smoke," Charlie told him.

"What are you looking for?"

Lyndsey said, "My shoes."

The man put his tobacco aside and crouched out of sight. When he stood again he had two hiking boots, one in each hand. He held them by his sides.

"Great," said Lyndsey, "Thanks."

The man made no move to offer them, though. "Want to hear a joke?" he said.

"We better get back inside," Lyndsey said. She reached for her shoes. The man made an underarm gesture with one of them. He did it a second time but didn't throw.

"Go on, then," Charlie said. He meant go on, throw the boots, but the man used it as an excuse to tell his joke, Lyndsey's boots held by his sides.

"Two men in a pub, right? One of them, he goes to find a table, see, and the other one gets the drinks in. 'Pint for me and my donkey.'"

Charlie nodded – clearly they had to listen to the joke as some part of an exchange – but when the man kept repeating the character's drink order, Charlie nodded again to hurry the man along.

"So this happens a few times, same one going to the bar and saying 'pint for me and my donkey', until eventually the other guy comes to the bar instead. Before he can order, the barman says, 'Your friend over there keeps calling you his donkey.' And the customer, he nods and says—"

Charlie knew the joke, he realised, but it had taken until now for him to remember the punch line. The man still surprised him, though.

"'Oh, *hee*-aw! *hee*-aw! *hee*-always calls me that!'"

The man brayed loud enough that each *hee*-aw! sounded like a scream, a shrill then guttural cry bouncing around in the confines of the barn. The sudden noise and volume startled both of them, as did the way the man thrust his head forward for each outburst, his lips peeled back against large slabs of teeth. Lyndsey had recoiled, pressing herself against a wall of stacked hay bales, wide-eyed. Charlie took her hand.

"Do you get it?" the man asked them, and without waiting for a response he said again, "He always calls me that. *Hee*-aw!" The final cry dissolved into laughter and Charlie laughed as well this time. Not at the joke, but in a kind of anxious release.

The man wiped tears from his eyes, still offering the occasional chuckle and sigh.

"Okay," Charlie said, "boots now, yeah?"

The man nodded. "You have a spirited filly," he said.

"Sorry, what?"

"Spirited," the man said. He looked at Lyndsey. "This filly likes a good ride."

"Hey," said Charlie, and, "Fuck," said Lyndsey.

The man laughed again. To Lyndsey he said, "Eager filly!" and to Charlie, "You ride her well," and then he tossed the boots. He threw them underarm, but he did it quick and Charlie had to twist and turn to try to catch them, missing both. Lyndsey gathered them up and pulled them on quick, laces loose, and Charlie turned her by the shoulders, guiding her outside and away, pushing her ahead of him. Behind them, the braying laughter of the man followed them out into the dark.

Charlie reported him to the owners. He did that much, at least. He gave them a slightly edited version of events in which he swapped post-coital surprise for seeing someone sneaking into the outbuilding and in the morning their breakfast was served with the reassurance that the man was gone. As to whether he'd been sent on right away or asked to leave that morning, the owners had been rather vague about that. 'It happens sometimes,' the wife had said, adding, 'we should really keep it locked, I suppose.'

Well, they still don't lock it, Charlie thought, and he was glad. He found a place behind the workbench where a metal brace and a supporting beam crossed (*x marks the spot*) and there, in a small nook close to the wall, he stowed his geo-cache of memories.

Sadie's Lane in Dorset, England, is reported to be one of the most haunted roads in the county. It came by its name in the early 18ᵗʰ century when a farm girl called Sadie Young allegedly rode her horse to its death as she raced to meet a lover who had abandoned her. Pitched from the fallen animal, Sadie was also killed and is said to haunt what is now a busy relief road. The location has since attracted several other ghosts, each of them linked to tales of heartbreak and loss. It is now a popular suicide spot.

Geo-cache findings: a selection of pressed flowers and a chess piece (rook)

Leaving the outbuilding, stepping from the dark into a morning still fresh and clean and grey, Charlie was greeted by last night's couple approaching their car (the Audi). The woman smiled, the kind of polite smile you give to strangers with whom you share a certain level of intimacy, like those in the same train carriage or a doctor's waiting room. If she'd known just how intimate they were, now, after last night, she probably wouldn't have smiled, Charlie thought. Or maybe she would. Maybe she was well aware of how loud they'd been. Today she was dressed in a jeans and jumper ensemble that was practical yet still somehow stylish, more town clothes than country. Charlie admired how the denim fit her.

"Beautiful, eh?" the husband said to Charlie. "That fresh country air."

Charlie nodded, more in hello than as an answer. "Morning," he said, stepping to his own car.

"Thought we might look for some of those interesting places you mentioned," the man said. He waved a folded leaflet to support his point. Charlie had seen a limited selection of them fanned out on a table in the dining room.

"Be sure to visit Carreg Castle," Charlie said, slipping the name in with little fanfare. The man opened up the leaflet to look but Charlie gave him directions anyway, hearing in his head one of Lyndsey's wonderful sat-nav voices in echo. "Just heading there myself, but I recommend you try it around sundown. It's a bit spooky, but beautiful. Romantic."

"Thanks," said the woman, and this time her smile was a little warmer.

"Yeah, appreciate it," said her husband.

Charlie prepared a cigarette, concentrating on the task until he heard the double thunk of car doors closing, then he watched them for a moment, a silent movie behind the windscreen. They seemed happy now, but then so did many couples. Anyone could look happy if they buried their secrets deep enough. Charlie watched them reverse out of the parking area. For a moment, when she turned around in her seat, the woman looked like Lyndsey. That quick profile and final look at Charlie that disappeared as they turned away and were gone.

Charlie smoked his cigarette. He didn't smoke in the car because Lyndsey wouldn't have liked it, but seeing her waterproof parcelled up into itself on the backseat he leaned in to retrieve it, careful to hold the roll-up outside the whole time. He turned the coat out, unzipped it open, and shook it into shape. He draped it over his on the passenger seat. From the corner of his eye perhaps it would seem as if she accompanied his drive. It was a pathetic hope, but strangely soothing.

"Okay," he said, finishing the cigarette, and though there was no one to say it to but himself, added, "let's go."

For a lot of the journey the roads passed through open countryside, fields dropping into valleys or climbing into hills, distant sheep scattered like chewed lumps of gum. Tiny towns or perhaps villages passed so quickly that moments later Charlie wondered at their existence. Eventually, though, the hills closed in and the road cut its way through trees and shadow. The lanes became choked with mud and vast puddles made sections into shallow rivers. The hedgerows pressed close, sometimes scraping the car on tight corners. Charlie tried to focus his attention on the road, assessing when to slow down, when to speed up, balancing the risks of soft ground and floods by fluctuating between two speeds in a sort of compromise against getting stuck and losing control. He rushed through puddles in a shushed-thunder of spray that drummed underneath the car and spread in sheets either side.

On the back seat, another geo-cache container rattled as it slid left and right with the corners and jumped with the bumps and dips of the road. There was only one item inside.

He'd been hiding geo-caches up and down the British Isles for most of the last six months, building up to this moment. Little boxes of their life together, here and there. Their old GPS from back before they simply used apps on their phones. A half-eaten mint cake, which neither of them liked because it made their teeth feel funny but which they bought anyway because it was one of the rules, like the hideous waterproofs. He wondered how many people had walked past them, these secret geo-caches, never knowing what was there, and he thought, *well, life's like that, isn't it?* Everybody has a story you don't get to hear. Even in a relationship, there were things you didn't learn until far down the line together, or things changed, and maybe you didn't always like what you found. Lyndsey had thought she knew all there was to know about Charlie, and he used to think the same of her. For him, that familiarity brought comfort. For her, it was different.

He slowed the car just as an oncoming vehicle turned into the road ahead, blocking the entire width. The driver made a token effort to move aside, but there was no way they were going to squeeze past each other. Charlie checked behind and manoeuvred the car backwards.

"Attention: this vehicle is reversing."

That's what Lyndsey would have said as Charlie manoeuvred the vehicle back. "*Bleep! Bleep!* Attention: this vehicle is reversing." Then the warning again. And then the bleeps. And then the warning again, and then the bleeps, until—

"Lynds."

Her name sounded lost with no one to answer it. Charlie looked at the empty seat beside him but the waterproof there remained simply a waterproof, hanging like a thin corpse. An empty shroud, trying too hard to be bright and cheerful.

The other car followed Charlie, keeping close as if Charlie might change his mind, pushing him back. As soon as there was room, it pulled out and passed. If there was a thank you, Charlie didn't see it.

"You're welcome."

He changed gears from reverse to first and the car rocked in place. That was all. For a moment he thought he was stuck – "Come *on*" – but all he'd done was stall it. Overcompensating with the revs, he sent a fantail of mud spraying behind as he pulled away again. Better to lose control than get stuck in place, he thought, hurrying towards something he'd never find with nothing left to lose but himself.

Carreg Cennen Castle can be found in the village of Trap about 4 miles from Llandeilo in Carmarthenshire, Wales. It stands on a limestone precipice and within its bowels there is a tunnel which leads to a well said to hold mystical healing properties, particularly regarding ear and eye complaints. Visitors to the castle often cast corks and bent pins into the water in order to be healed.

Geo-cache findings (four out of five caches): a novelty key ring, a decorative bookmark, a plastic toy knight, a packet of crayons, a rubber sheep, a deck of pornographic cards, a two-pound coin, 2 bottle openers, a candle.

The first time he'd seen Carreg Castle was between the stutters of the windscreen wipers, leaning forward to peer through the glass as if a few more inches would allow him to see it more clearly. Back then, the sun had barely been out all day and what there was of it was sinking behind the hill the castle stood upon, the sky taking on the deepening blue tones of early evening with some red shining behind and between the ruined walls. Part of the hill dropped away as a sheer cliff so that the castle walls on one edge seemed to merge seamlessly into the precipice.

"Spooky," said Lyndsey.

This time it looked postcard-picture-perfect. The sky had cleared by the time he'd reached the castle, the sun having burnt away the misty haze of the early hours to reveal a sharpening bright blue sky dotted with clouds that hung motionless in a panorama that was beautiful and all so completely wrong. It should have looked ugly. It should have been pissing down and miserable and the-end-of-the-world.

There had been a sequence of geo-caches here. It happened that way sometimes, especially with popular landmark locations. Clues to one revealed clues to another, and so on, giving you a good walk while building to what usually turned out to be an anti-climax. But then geo-caching was never really about what you found at the end. It was the journey, as clichéd as that seemed. The spending time together. It was learning more about your own country, the secret spectacles of home. Learning more about each other, and hoping you liked it.

They'd found the first geo-cache easily. Some of a stone wall had fallen and tucked amongst the rocks was an ice cream container bearing a strip of masking tape across its lid that declared, simply, 'geo-cache'. Inside they'd found yet another Welsh key ring (this time a flat rubber oval with Carreg Castle in bas-relief), a decorative bookmark (or quitter's strip, as Lyndsey used to call them), and a plastic toy. The toy was an armoured knight. He held a lance before him and his legs were unnaturally bowed, a half-circle scoop as if there had been a horse below him as well at some point. They took the horseless knight and left the key ring and bookmark, adding a yo-yo for whoever came next. Take something, leave something, move on. Another strip of masking tape inside the container provided a new clue and they followed it to the next location, and then again, and so on, until they were at the castle. It had become something of a silhouette in the fading light, and a cool evening breeze tousled Lyndsey's hair as she looked down at the glowing phone in her hand.

"We better get a move on if we want to get the last geo-cache. It's in the castle somewhere and it'll be closed soon."

The castle was privately owned but still open to the public. "It has a tea room and everything," Lyndsey told him, scrolling through information on her phone, offering Charlie the highlights. She gave him details about the accidental sale of the castle, gave him particulars of its history and structure, its six towers, the drawbridges, the chapel, all of it, speeding through centuries.

"It's mostly limestone here," she said, "and there's an underground tunnel that'll take us to where the last cache is, I think. '150 feet of tunnel leads you to a well, believed to hold mystical healing powers'. That's what it says. You throw corks or pins in and make a wish. It's particularly good at healing ear and eye complaints, apparently. Which is why I think the cache is there, because of the clue. 'You'll do well to keep your eyes open'. Which is a crap clue but it makes sense."

"Why corks and pins?"

She shrugged. "Doesn't say."

Charlie wondered at what else it didn't say as he made his way towards the castle again. As he walked among the shake holes, sunken depressions in the soil and cracked stone, he also wondered how Lyndsey made her decisions about what to share and what to not, and would she have left him anyway if it hadn't been for the Castellmarch man.

At the castle, Charlie descended into a gloom that suited his mood. The stone stairs were slippery with old rain and the castle's outer wall close beside him seemed like it was leaning, as if it wanted to push him over the edge. He imagined falling. He'd imagined it lots of times. But he didn't fall, and soon he was standing before a long narrow gash in the cliff face. Hardly any light penetrated the passageway, especially with his body blocking what there was of it, and he didn't have a phone this time to illuminate the way; he'd never replaced his, and the police still had Lyndsey's. Knowing how much darker it would become, he didn't bother waiting for his eyes to adjust and simply plunged right in.

"Here we go."

He was swallowed into nothing by the darkness. Arms out at his sides, he used the walls to guide him deeper. The stone was smooth and dry but very cold. He stooped, remembering how low the passageway became in places, and sometimes he was more comfortable turning sideways, but eventually he came to the standing pool of water where Lyndsey had joked about Gollum. She'd hissed "My *precious...*" into his ear in the dark.

"I expected an actual well."

Charlie backed up a few steps and sat. He was wearing his new coat, which was long enough to offer him some protection against the cold stone. In one of its deep pockets was the Tupperware geo-cache he'd brought, shallow but long, perfect for what it held. He checked his watch, its light casting an eerie green glow that only seemed to make the dark darker.

He was early.

He waited.

Charlie had shone the light of his phone around the perimeter of the pool that first time. There were shapes floating on the surface and gathered at the edges. Corks. Some of them had pins pushed through them. Back then he'd had to psych himself up to put his hand in the water, and he'd gasped at the temperature. This time he merely reached out and caressed the surface of the pool, making small waves in the darkness. He felt a cork or two against his palm. He had stabbed himself last time on pins at the bottom of the pool, reaching for a geo-cache they never found. He'd dropped his phone, swearing. For a moment the light had stayed on at the bottom of the pool, and he'd grabbed it up again quickly, as if speed could stop it from becoming *more* wet. Tried to shake it dry.

"What?" Lyndsey asked. "What?"

"Dropped my fucking phone."

"Yeah, but why?"

"Well I didn't mean to."

"I mean, did you hurt yourself? Did something bite you or something?"

There'd only been the brief sting of pins. "I'm okay."

"How's the phone?"

It was fine, until he pressed a button to check if it was fine, and then the screen went black and the torchlight went out.

"Shit."

"Well done."

"Ssh."

"You shush." Lyndsey had lit the tunnel with her phone instead but Charlie took it from her and plunged them back into the dark. He found Lyndsey's arm. Her hand. He pulled her close and found something else and she'd said, "Hey!"

"We'll have to grope our way out."

"Funny man."

And they had kissed. He remembered that very well. Sometimes, when he couldn't sleep, he'd close his eyes as tight as he could to replicate the utter darkness of that moment and he'd remember the kisses they'd shared under the castle, buried in its rock. He couldn't tell any more if they only felt like final kisses now, in retrospect, or if he'd known it even then.

"We should pick up some rice when we get out," Lyndsey said, breaking away. "For your phone."

"Does that actually work?"

He felt her shrug. "Saw it on Facebook so it must be true. Absorbs the water or something. You remember Jenny from—"

"Ssh."

"No, I'm telling you a fascinating story."

"I think someone else is here. Listen."

They strained their ears to hear. Charlie turned his head and, for some reason, opened his mouth. He found that helped sometimes. This time it did.

"Hear that?" he whispered.

"Yeah, someone's coming."

And yet neither of them felt relieved. Maybe because whoever was coming did so without a light.

As if they'd agreed it between them, neither of them called out or made any noise, and though Charlie had Lyndsey's phone he didn't even consider using its light. He backed away, deeper into the passageway, pulling Lyndsey with him, keeping close to the wall.

It was the Castellmarch man, of course. For a while he was only the scrape of footsteps, but somehow they'd known. Why else would they have remained so quiet? Why else had they tried to hide, when the normal thing to have done would have been to greet whoever else had come to this special place?

He was singing something softly to himself. Welsh words, unfamiliar, but Charlie thought he recognised the tune.

Lyndsey's breath was warm in Charlie's ear. Her mouth was so close that he felt her lips on him as she said, "It's him." He went to turn his head, to whisper back, but she held him still and said, lips to his ear, "It's the Castellmarch man."

The voice in the darkness with them was suddenly quiet, and though Charlie hadn't been able to follow the song properly he could still tell it had stopped mid-line.

"Somebody's there," said the man.

Lyndsey squeezed Charlie's arm tight but the two of them remained quiet. There was nothing to be afraid of, he thought. Not really.

"Who's there?" the voice called. "Why are you spying on me?"

They waited, silent, holding their breath and each other's hand.

"WHO'S SPYING ON ME?"

Charlie said, "We're *not* spying," and lit up the dark with Lyndsey's phone. Her grip on his arm tightened and they saw, together, the man crouching at the pool, that hat in his hands, and—

Charlie thought he saw... He thought, but he must have been wrong. He thought he saw the man's ears, long and pointed and furred, twitching at Charlie's voice. Horse's ears. Then everything was a chaos of movement and noise. The Castellmarch man leapt to his feet, literally bounding up and across at them on all fours. He knocked Charlie aside and into the wall, hitting him harder than he'd have thought possible for a man of such build. Charlie dropped the phone, but not into the pool this time. Its light stayed on, but the device was kicked several times in the to and fro of a scuffle. Lyndsey cried out, and swore, and Charlie yanked at her and pushed at the other, and they splashed through the shallows of icy water as the man cried out, "You saw me!" his voice bouncing around and back at them in the confines of the tunnel. "You *saw* me!"

Up close, Charlie saw the man definitely had horse ears. They stuck up from lank hair that swept from his head and down his back like a mane. He had one arm around Lyndsey from behind and then he leapt up so that he was on her back. Charlie tried to grab him, push him away, pull him down, and Lyndsey turned around, tried to run, tried to shake the man off. The Castellmarch man gripped her firm, though, fierce, his legs around her waist now. He reached down between her breasts with one hand, holding a bunch of her jumper in his fist, gripping at her ribs, and the other held a tangle of her hair, and he was laughing or he was screaming, it was hard to tell, all his noise coming out shrill and echoing back at them. His eyes were wide, and he frothed at the mouth, Charlie thought, and he rocked against Lyndsey's back, urging her on, pulling at her hair to guide her direction as she tried to run from him though he clung to her. Charlie saw her stagger the way they'd come and he pushed after them as the man's cries whinnied back and forth in the dark.

Near the entrance they became a hectic silhouette. Lyndsey was bent under the man's weight but still on her feet, ricocheting off the walls of the tunnel either side as the man held himself fast against her, upon her, one hand twisted in her hair and his groin rocking against her as if dry humping her back, playing giddy-up. In a panicked pirouette, Charlie saw his wife's head turn, saw her look at him a final time, the Castellmarch man leaning over with his cheek against hers and his ears, those stupid fucking twitching ears, and then the two of them were gone. They dropped away into open space and Charlie had to pull up hard to stop from following them over the edge and down.

Charlie had called out his anguish then, but now it was little more than a soft mewling sound in the dark as he remembered. Take something, leave something, move on, he thought. Lyndsey had been taken, he had been left behind, and if anyone had moved on then it wasn't him.

There had been no bodies down there, but in his dreams there were. Sometimes Lyndsey's, sometimes his own. Sometimes he saw her carried away, the Castellmarch man's bandy legs striding in great bounds. Sometimes it was Lyndsey who fled, carrying this strange man with her. The police found no trace of either person. They probably weren't even looking any more, but Charlie was. Leaving his geo-caches with clues only Lyndsey would understand, looking for her up and down the country. He wondered if she was looking for him. Just as he wondered, sometimes, about that final look she gave him. Sometimes he remembered fear. Other times, excitement. Occasionally what he saw, or thought he saw, was relief.

Charlie removed his wedding ring and, sitting on the ground, traced his finger over the engraving inside, the coordinates marking their life together. One of them was this one, Carreg Castle, where the water was said to hold mystical healing properties. The eyes and the ears and maybe, Charlie hoped, the heart.

He cast his ring into the water. There was barely any splash at all when really it should have thundered. Then, from his pocket, he took the final Tupperware container. He was wearing a new coat and the pockets were deep. From another he took the hat.

In that struggle a year ago he had torn the Castellmarch man's pocket and something had fallen from it. He had it now, in this final container. His wooden flute, or whistle, or recorder, whatever the fuck it was.

He took the instrument from its box and put it to his lips and played. It didn't take him long to get the tune right. Maybe it would call them back, isn't that how it worked in the old stories? Maybe *one* of them, at least, would come. Someone.

Anyone.

He played and he played until, finally, he thought he heard something. Voices, coming to him in the dark. He raised one of the flaps of the hat he'd put on and turned his ear to listen.

Yes. Voices. A man and a woman. He thought perhaps they were bickering, but that was okay. That might be better, actually.

He pocketed the whistle and the hat and stood. Take something, leave something, he thought. He pressed himself against one of the walls, hiding in the dark it made, and he waited.

In Abersoch there is a 17th century mansion that goes by the name of Castellmarch. According to legend it was once the home of one of King Arthur's knights, March Amheirchion, who had the ears of a horse. He kept

them hidden, but occasionally someone would discover his secret and March (whose name means horse in Welsh) would be forced to kill them. He hid the bodies in a nearby bed of reeds. His true nature was finally discovered when a boy made a flute from one of the reeds and the only song the flute could play was 'March Amheirchion has horse's ears'. Nobody knows what became of March Amheirchion, but it is believed he had several children and that his line continues to this day.

|The Final Girl's Daughter|

~

The truck was fucked, but Richard worked on it anyway. Sleeves rolled, oil up to his elbows, he cranked a wrench in the rusted engine block and swore at the part's stubbornness to come out. The open hood shielded him from the sun's glare, but it baked him from the waist up, and that didn't help his mood any. He always kept his overalls done up, though. As much a fuck you to Frank as anything. The garage was small, with room for only one vehicle at a time inside, and that was where Frank worked, where it was cool. Richard worked the ones waiting in the lot where it was bright and hot.

"Hey, Richie! How long you gonna be on that one?"

"Days," he yelled back. "Weeks, maybe."

He stepped out from the engine and straightened his back. Vertebrae didn't pop so much as grind.

Frank took off his cap and rubbed a hand over his scratchy head stubble. He turned to spit. "Say again?"

"Best to junk it," Richard said. "The old girl's done."

Frank let that hang between them for a moment. There was a radio on inside. Patsy Cline, singing about strange dreams with a voice like tin.

"You want me to tell Warren he needs a new truck?"

Richard didn't care enough to even shrug. "He's got us fixing something can't be fixed."

Frank was nodding, but he didn't mean it. "Uh-huh, uh-huh," he said. "But look. Right there, see what it says? It says repairs. So repair it."

Richard shook his head, muttered something not for Frank's hearing, and bent back into the engine. Damn thing was only held together with dirt, dust, rust, and promises.

"And Richie?"

"It'll get done quicker if you don't keep interrupting me."

"Yeah, and quicker than that if you didn't have visitors taking up working hours."

Again, Richard re-emerged from the truck's guts into bright light. This time when Frank took off his hat to spit, he didn't just turn his head but moved aside. There was a woman behind him in the shade of the shop.

She stepped out of the shadows and said, "Hey, Dick."

Richard wiped sweat from his brow, thinking maybe the heat had got to him, but when he put his arm back down she was still there.

"Never did like that nickname," he said.

"Okay," said Frank, sweeping his arms to usher the woman along, "there he is." To Richard he said, "Make it quick, *Dick*."

Richard acknowledged the command with a look but no nod. He started wiping his hands and arms with the rag from his back pocket, saw how it cleaned up his scars, and stopped. He limped towards her. She met him halfway to save him the bother.

"You look good," she said.

"You too, Sal."

"Then I guess that makes the both of us liars." She smiled, and the scar that slashed down across her lips made them pucker. She had another one running the length of her cheekbone. She wore her hair down despite the heat, but you could still see the scars on her neck and shoulders if you knew to look for them, and Richard looked.

Sally did the same. Richard had a scar that pulled his right eyelid down, and another striped his cheek, but it was his arm she checked when he offered his hand. She saw the lines across his forearm, the ones across his palm, but nothing new. Had he offered the left, she'd have seen different. Aborted wounds he lacked the courage to finish.

She took his hand and shook with, "A fucking handshake?" then pulled him in for a tight hug that surprised tears from him in being so fierce and so familiar. For a moment, dry cornfields burned around them, ashes floating high into the night sky.

He stepped back when she let go and took another look at her.

"My eyes are up here, Dick."

It was an old joke between them but carried new meaning now. Dust clung to where she'd sweated through a tank top that lay flat on her chest.

"Double mastectomy," she said.

"Shit, Sal."

She shrugged. "I'm alive."

Behind them, in the garage, Frank cleared his throat and spat something heavy. The radio's song was gone, replaced by the rise and fall of a preacher's voice suggesting they weren't in the panhandle of a Bible Belt state, or even the pan, but burning already in the fire.

"It's good to see you," Sally said.

"You, too."

He wondered if that also made them liars.

"Why are you here?" he asked.

Sally leaned on the truck though it must've been hot, even through denim. She pulled a packet of cigarettes from a pocket of her jeans and offered him one.

"Jesus, seriously?"

She shrugged again and put one to her mouth. She cupped a flame to it and exhaled her first breath of smoke saying, "Shit, Richard, you going to make me say it?"

"Say what?"

She bumped herself away from the truck with her behind and faced him again. She inhaled deeply from the cigarette and expelled the smoke as if it made her angry. "I'm going back," she said.

He didn't need to ask where, only why.

"Because I need to finish it. Properly, this time. Don't you want to finish it?"

Richard shook his head. She was asking more than one question. "I can't," he told her. "I'm sorry, Sal. I can't."

Sally nodded. She knew that already. "That's all right." She took a final hit from the cigarette and twisted it dead beneath her shoe. She still liked to wear sneakers, he noticed. Laces loose and tucked in beneath her feet.

"You wanna get a coffee or something?"

"That's all right," she said again. Before she turned to go she said, "It really was good to see you."

Richard nodded it back.

Sally slapped the truck beside them as she left. "Don't give up on her," she said, and, "You've always been good at fixing things."

Richard watched her go.

Frank watched her, too. "Okay, *Dick*, you heard the lady," he said when she was gone. He pointed at the truck. "Get it fixed."

The microwave hummed and Richard scraped old plates into the trash. Most nights he ate at Robsons but Frank had pissed him off even more than usual so he'd skipped the convenience of the diner to put some miles between them. Used to be he lived right above the shop, but when Bill passed, Frank moved himself in before the old man was even in the ground. Richard didn't mind all that much. He missed the cheap rent, but he missed the old grease-monkey more. How the man ended up with a son like Frank was something Richard never figured out.

You reap what you sow. What a load of horseshit.

His dinner pinged and he grabbed a clean fork. He tipped molten mac and cheese from the tray to his plate and took it to a ratty armchair he'd moved to the window so he could watch the street below. It wasn't all that interesting, but neither was the TV.

He pushed his pasta around with a slice of bread, soaking up pretend cheese, and he ate.

Things had been different once. With Sally, way back when, living in the city. They'd shared a place above a bowling alley, their evenings punctuated by the muted smash of pins and the noise of a rowdy crowd, but they'd been good enough years. As good as they could be. His dreams of playing football died right along with his knee and he forced himself to know engines instead. Sally found work in bar where nobody cared about her scars. They did all right. It wasn't their fault they didn't work out. Too much shared trauma meant it never went away for either of them. You could avoid mirrors all day long, but each was the other's echo. Sometimes there was comfort in that. The nights could be bad sometimes, but they had each other when the dark was too deep and the scythe came reaping.

I'm going back.

Richard forked more food to his mouth. It was still too hot, but the beer helped with that. He usually limited himself to one on a workday, but he knew with the first swallow he'd be drinking the rest of them tonight. Maybe even go get more.

I need to finish it.

He put his plate on the floor and finished his beer and set the empty bottle next to his plate. Sitting in his chair, he watched the people come and go on the street below and tried not to think about what his life had become.

You reap what you sow.

He was sitting with his hands upturned in his lap. He looked down at the palms where scars cut his lifelines into before and after.

Don't you want to finish it?

There was a shoebox in his wardrobe. He went to get it, and on the way back he grabbed another beer. He drank it and he opened the box.

Where someone else might keep a gun, Richard kept photographs. They did own a gun once, but Sally had come home one night to find him looking at it in a way she didn't like. Said it was a look she'd seen before. Richard didn't need to ask when. He gave her the gun, and never asked what she'd done with it.

He sifted through the photos with both hands like he was looking through a record store. Here was Sally at the bar, Sally squinting in the sun, Sally with her first car (and you bet he made sure that fucker always run). Time slipped through his shuffling fingers, all the way back to…

There.

It was an old photo. There were pinholes in the corners and a crease down the middle where the gloss had broken along a fold so that the photo carried its own kind of scars. It was the last picture of all of them together. They were leaning against the side of Ricky's RV.

And what does RV mean? It means Ricky's Vehicle, that's what it means, okay? Which means only Ricky drives said vehicle, okay? Just me. Capisce?

They'd all been more than happy to let him drive. It freed them up to goof around in the back, though they took turns sitting up front to keep Ricky company.

In the photo, Ricky was pushing his tongue into his bottom lip and he'd crossed his eyes, goofing around himself. He was wearing shorts he'd cut from an old pair of jeans, a button shirt with short sleeves, and a tie. Always a damn tie. He had his arm around Lauren.

Lauren's shorts were very short because she had great legs *and there's nothing wrong with knowing that*. She wore her bell-sleeved top tied high because she had a great midriff, too, and she knew. Sunglasses kept her hair back. Her hands were up making double peace signs.

Peace, too, from Debs, but only with one hand. The other held a lollipop in her mouth. She wore a flowered blouse like it was a dress and cowgirl boots she'd bought new.

Richard looked away from the photo, but he could still see it. He was next in line. Socks pulled high from hiking boots. Sport shorts. A football tee with the sleeves cut free, his arms crossed tense on his chest. That stupid grin on his stupid face.

And Sally, the reason for the grin. Both her arms around him.

He dropped the photo and Sally smiled up from what was left of his dinner. He rescued her from congealing mac and cheese and wiped the photograph clean.

He looked again and saw three dead friends.

Richard rubbed a fist across the picture, trying to smudge away what memory had made of them. He saw each of them posed in a bloody tableau and turned the picture and wiped it over the leg of his jeans, like the blood was on the picture. He didn't turn it back. He put it in the box and closed the lid over it. He shoved the box away.

He closed his eyes and finished his beer to the sound of crows erupting from rows of corn. Pieces of night on fire. When he slept, he ran through burning fields, ashes spiralling into the sky like feathers, and from somewhere behind came a whistling scythe to cut him down.

"When did you become such a lady's man, Dick?"

Richard was on a creeper under the same truck as the day before. He didn't bother to roll himself out. He shouted "What?" into the vehicle's chassis.

Frank kicked Richard's feet.

"I'm busy, Frank."

"Just get your ass out here."

Richard pushed off from the frame. He slid out from under the truck saying, "Stub axle's fucked as well." He sat up and winced into the bright sunlight.

Frank said, "Did I start a social club or something?"

"What?"

Frank pointed with a wrench. Richard looked, still squinting.

"Sal?"

She stepped closer as he stood. It was Sally in her twenties, young and scar-free. Except, of course, it wasn't.

"No," she said. "Do you know where she is? She come out here to talk to you?"

She looked just like her. Stood like her, too. Defiant. Her eyes were different, though.

"You know who I am?" she asked.

"I think so."

"Did you know about me before?"

Richard shook his head.

"Look," said Frank, "You can talk it all out on your own time. In case you haven't noticed, Richie, we got a lot of work to do around here."

Richard enjoyed how the woman looked at Frank. She did it with eyes like his, but the look was Sally's all the way through. Frank even took a step back.

Richard wiped his hands and tossed the rag. "I'm taking the rest of the day."

"You're what, now?"

For the first time in a long while, Richard straightened to his full height and Frank took another one of those backwards steps. He was used to seeing Richard bending over an engine or lying down beneath one, and he wasn't doing that anymore today.

"I'll be at Robsons," Richard said, jabbing a thumb like he was hitching to the diner across the yard. "I'm getting something to eat with my daughter and then maybe I'll come back, but maybe I won't. It depends on why she's here."

"Your daughter?"

Richard looked at her and she nodded confirmation.

"Hey, Pops."

⌒

The diner was empty. That was true almost any time of day, with just enough drop-ins trickling through to keep from closing down. Ginny was there, working the diner's lunch shift just as she always did. She said hello without prying into Richard's business, and Richard ordered his usual.

"And you, honey?"

"Just coffee."

Richard said, "You should eat something."

"Just coffee."

Ginny said, "We can do that."

They took a booth at the window. Richard dragged a tin circle ashtray to his side of the table and took a cigarette from the packet crushed in his shirt, all of it habit. He offered his daughter one and made to push the ashtray back, but she waved them away.

"I promised to quit."

Richard nodded, and put the cigarette to his mouth before realising who she'd likely promised and why. He put the cigarette back.

"She never told me," he said. "About you, I mean."

"It's all right. I'm not here for any of that. I had a dad for a while when it mattered, and he was pretty good."

"Good."

"She never married him or nothing."

"All right."

They looked at each other. Richard wondered what she saw.

"What about you?" she asked. "You married?"

"No."

"Girlfriend?"

"No."

There'd never been anybody else, not after Sally.

Richard turned the question back, rather than talk about that.

"What about you? Boyfriend?"

"Girlfriend."

"Serious?"

She shrugged. "To me. Hopefully to her, but you never really know, do you?"

Their coffee arrived. Richard drank some of his. He looked out the window and saw Frank go to a car pulling in, out of state plates, steam misting from beneath the hood.

"She talked about you sometimes. When things were bad."

He faced his daughter again.

"She said she wouldn't be here if not for you. I guess that's true for me, too."

She was leaving lipstick on her coffee cup. Sally used to do the same, but then so did a lot of women.

"She went back there, didn't she? To the farm."

Richard gave a nod. "That's what she said."

"Why didn't you go with her?"

"She didn't ask."

"What if she did ask?"

Richard shook his head. "Sally doesn't need someone like me."

"She used to. So what if she'd asked?"

"She didn't."

Showing up to see him, though. That had been her asking.

"She tell you about the cancer?"

He nodded. "I'm sorry."

"It's cool, she beat it. She's tough."

"She is."

"It was after the doctor told her, and through the… the treatments, she talked a lot about what happened to you. To both of you, and your friends. She never talked about all that before."

Richard's food arrived. They were both quiet while Ginny set the plate down and topped up their coffee.

"She used to make up all these stories about her scars when I was a kid, these far out stories, so when she told me about the farm I thought she was doing something like that again, but she wasn't."

"No."

"A fucking *scythe?*"

Richard nodded.

"That's fucked up."

"Yeah."

She pointed to his face. "And those scars?"

"Yeah."

"And the limp?"

He mimed a reaping motion. "Hooked in under the kneecap. Nearly pulled it out."

"Fuck."

"Yeah."

She pointed at one of his arms. "What about those?"

He held both arms up, not just the left, and turned his palms to her, shielding himself. "Defence wounds." He rested them on the table again. He didn't need to explain the scars across his wrist. They were defence wounds, too.

She looked away and Richard watched her watch Frank fixing the car just come in. Eventually, she said, "Is that why you became a mechanic?"

"Is what why I became a mechanic?"

"It's something Mom said, once. She thinks you became a mechanic so neither of you would ever break down again."

"We broke down plenty."

She looked back at him. "She also said you moved out here because this strip of road is close enough to where it all happened without being *too* close. You can keep an eye on things. Make sure it doesn't happen again."

Richard stared at his food. He wasn't going to eat it. He knew as he ordered he wouldn't eat.

"Where is she? Where's the farm? Mom never told me."

When Richard said nothing, she leaned across the table.

"You don't have to come with me," she said. "Just tell me where it is or draw me a map or something."

"It's gone."

"It's not."

"It was sold on."

"Maybe, but it's still there. Mom thought so, anyway, and I want to find her and I'm pretty sure she's there, so you need to tell me."

Richard watched Frank working the overheated car.

"She wanted to burn it all down to the ground," he said.

"Why didn't she?"

"Too busy saving me."

She nodded like she understood. "Well she doesn't need to do that now," she said.

"Then look for the smoke," Richard said. "Or follow the fire truck when it comes." He drank the last of his coffee as she collapsed back into her seat, hands at the table like she would shove it away if it wasn't attached to the floor.

"I'll find it anyway," she said.

"I know."

"I just wanted to save some time."

Richard looked out of another window, this one facing the road. He rubbed at his cheeks but didn't like the rasping sound his stubble made, so he stopped.

"Here," he said, and pushed his plate of food to her. "I need to pick up a few things, but then I'll take you."

He nodded at the plate as if eating was part of the deal, so she pulled it closer.

Richard stood. "I'll be right back." He left money on the table and limped out of the diner.

"Where are you going now?" Frank asked as Richard went to his truck.

Richard looked back and saw his daughter watching. She was eating.

"I have to go fix something," he said.

He gunned the engine over anything else Frank might say and drove away.

He'd never gone back but he knew the way.

At the side of the road, where Ricky's RV had died all those years ago, a wreath of fresh flowers wilted in the sun. They looked the same as the ones Debs used to wear in her hair sometimes. Richard slowed as he drove past, not wanting to drag the flowers after him in the wind he pulled behind.

The fucking radiator. Just the fucking radiator hose, that was all. An easy fix if you knew how, but they were just kids. They didn't know anything yet.

Richard checked the mirror. The road was long and empty behind him. Just his trail of dust, taking its time to resettle.

Out here, people either killed cattle or grew crops. He didn't need to see the corn coming to know he was close, though. He could already see the crows, circling. Dark fragments of a slow tornado, forming over where the farm would be.

Maybe someone there can help us.

The fence he'd been following fell away at his left. In the dirt of a turning was a faded sign. NO TRESPASSING. The chain that had blocked that way lay coiled beside it like a rusting snake.

Richard took the left turn and lurched onto uneven ground, bumping towards the house he knew waited at the end. Land they'd burnt down to stubble had been replanted and stalks of corn pressed in on either side. Richard remembered how it felt, running through the crops. How the plants lashed at him, whipped him, snagged his feet. He remembered the heat they'd held as they burned. He remembered the burst of crows like darkness exploding. The way he had screamed like he wouldn't stop.

He emerged from the crops to find the farm buildings sitting dark as tumours, house and barn both, but there was a car sitting in front and Richard shifted his focus to that. Sally was driving a Dodge these days. A Challenger. That was okay, the Challenger was reliable. Simple engine and transmission, sturdy running gear. Fast. She'd have problems with rust, but so did everyone.

He parked next to the Dodge. He looked inside and imagined Sally behind the wheel. He imagined himself beside her, too, and tried to imagine them laughing but there was something manic in the way he saw it. Hysterical. He closed his eyes on that.

He looked at the house.

It had swollen with age and grime and slumped under the combined shadows of the grain bin and barn. The roof had sunk in the middle as if too heavy. The porch leaned, sloping to the ground at one tumbled corner. It looked like the ground had once swallowed the place and was spitting it all back up. He'd expected to find the buildings bulldozed flat and the land absorbed into neighbouring farms. Instead, they lingered, rotten timbers black with damp and spores. The paint was peeling. The windows were boarded over.

Richard got out of the truck. He put his hand on the hood of the Dodge as if the heat might tell him how long it had been there. He limped to the steps of the porch. There was another NO TRESPASSING sign, this one nailed to the front door.

And forgive us our trespasses, as we forgive those who trespass against us.

Yeah. Right.

He looked around, like there might be someone watching. Someone waiting for him to go inside. He wasn't going to, though. She wouldn't be in the house.

She'd be in the barn.

Please! You don't have to do this!

Memory's echo, coming back for a different audience.

He wouldn't listen.

Richard went back to the truck. Most of his good tools he kept at the shop, but he had plenty of older ones with him and those he needed for his own vehicle. He took a tire iron. He hefted it. He swung it a couple of times.

He headed for the barn.

Like the house, the barn had fallen into a foul state of disrepair. It loomed over him as he approached, either a trick of light and shadow or a lean caused by the shifting weight of many years. There was another NO TRESPASSING sign on one of the doors. On the other one, DANGER.

Yeah, no shit, Richard thought. Where were you all those years ago?

One of the large doors had a smaller one set into it, slightly open. He pushed at it with his foot and it swung inward.

There had been screams in that darkness. He still heard them sometimes, nightmare-fresh, but here he could feel them, like vibrations trapped in the stale air. Seeds buried deep and sprouting into bigger horrors. The open door sent a wedge of light inside from behind him to fall on a section of earth floor. Death had soured the ground. The dirt looked almost as black as the dark around it. As if oil had been spilled here instead of blood.

He held the tire iron like it was a baseball bat and stepped over the threshold, into the gloom.

It smelled of hot dust inside. Dry soil. He could still smell the birds and their shit and their feathers, feathers that had once thickened the air and smothered the floor. As his eyes adjusted to the light, he saw there were still a few scattered feathers. Some had been trodden into broken shapes. The smaller ones had curled upon themselves like the desiccated bodies of dried flies.

Richard had run from this place, taking with him more scars than you could see on the outside. That reaping man had broken more than his bones and teeth, and what he'd done to Richard's friends had scraped him hollow. Bled him of all that was good and left him empty as a shucked husk.

"You reap what you sow."

He said it quietly, barely louder than his breathing, but the darkness took it and carried it and sent a scythe at him in reply. It came sweeping at Richard from the dark beside him. Memory or not, he leapt aside and stumbled and he swung the tire iron, wild and one-handed.

"Richard."

Sally stood poised to swing again, scythe high to one side.

Richard hobbled a few steps more away from her. He had one arm raised across his face, but he lowered it.

"Jesus, Dick. I thought you were him."

Richard said, "It's me."

"Your overalls look like dungarees and... I *heard* him."

"Me," he said again. "Reap what you sow."

Sally lowered the scythe. She held it across her body like cloakless Death.

"You came back."

Richard nodded.

"I knew you would. I waited for you."

Behind Sally was a wall for farming tools. A lot of them were gone now, but the hooks and pegs where they used to be remained. A wall of dots and outlines, constellations in the dark to mark the ways he and his friends had been hurt on the table below. The last time Richard had been here, Ricky had been laid out on that table, his eyes gone, and blood pooled in the sockets. His mouth a bloody cavity, broken open and stuffed with feathers. His hands, bound at the wrists with his own tie, gripping a cob of corn positioned to replace the flesh of his sex.

"Richard?"

The table was bare, but Richard still saw Ricky lying there. A phantom on the bloodstained woodgrain.

"Do you feel them?" Sally asked.

Lauren's legs had been cut from her torso, sawn off across the waist so she was two pieces. A grisly tableau: her stomach gaped open, and a nest made of her entrails was a home for dead crows. Another emerged from between her legs in a gruesome birth of blood and feathers.

Sally said, "I feel them all the time."

Debbie had been slumped in the wooden chair against the wall, her eyes as gone as Ricky's. A crow had been shoved down her throat and her hands bound at her mouth to keep it there, like she was trying to stop from spilling dark secrets.

"I see them," Richard said. He turned away from Debbie to face Sally instead. "Not as they were, but as he made them."

Sally's eyes were almost black, her pupils full in the dusky light. His would be the same. Like the darkness they'd seen was forever stuck there. It was like looking into twin eclipses and waiting for the brightness to come back, knowing it never could.

"Look," said Sally. "I want to show you something."

She put the scythe down and took his hand and led him deeper into the barn. There'd been a harvester in here before, making the large space small. Cadavers had been sprawled over the tines of the header reel, strangers reshaped and bound together by more than twine. Richard kept waiting for birds to burst from the dark, ready to duck as they swept at him before ascending to lofty corners in the rafters, but nothing came. There were still cages hanging from the beams up there, and broken ones on the floor. Cages made from bones and bent hanger wire, too small for their captives to do anything but fluster and caw. They were empty now. The crows that screamed and beat their wings were gone.

Sally pointed.

"Look," she said. "I brought him back."

He wanted to step back from what he saw but Sally kept a grip on his hand. For a moment it looked like a real man standing in the corner, but it was only clothes buttoned up and stuffed full over crossed poles. A baseball cap was tipped low over a faceless space that was a slack-hanging sack and shadow. Overalls fat with ears of corn, sleeves of a denim shirt rolled up from tool-handle arms markered REAP and SOW where tattoos would show. The curve of sickle blades where his hands should go.

"You didn't see the others," she said. "The ones in the field. Wasted things. Bones in clothes strung up like scarecrows, but the crows weren't scared. They'd fattened themselves on what he'd left them, feasting on the flesh he left to rot and drop in the sun."

"Sal..."

"Yeah," she said. "Yeah. I know."

She put both hands to her face and ran them down like she was wiping herself clean of what she'd seen. At her chin, her hands came together as if to pray, but only briefly.

"The dreams came back," Sally said. "Fields on fire. Birds the colour of cancer chasing me into the flames. My friends, *our* friends..." She didn't need to say because he knew.

"Screaming in the dark."

Sally nodded. "They're always screaming when I remember them because that's how I remember them most. It's like being haunted, only I'm doing it to them as well. They keep screaming because of me."

"Because of him," Richard said. He nodded at the effigy she'd made. A killer made from corn.

"Do you think he's waiting for us?"

"What?"

"Joseph Tillerman. Scarecrow Joe. Do you think he's waiting for us? In the long dark that comes after?"

"No."

She nodded. "Good," she said. "Good. Then I'm ready to go."

"All right," Richard said. "Then let's go."

But Sally's hand slipped from his because only Richard moved to leave.

"No," she said. "Not like that."

Richard reached for her again, but she only looked at the offered hand. At his wrist.

"I used to think it a weakness," she said.

Richard glanced at his scars, but he didn't hide them. He kept reaching for Sally.

"Now I see it as a strength," she said. "Choosing when to go. Choosing how."

"Sally—"

"You know, between them both, they got me. In the end. I never really escaped this place. I thought I did, for a while, with you, and even for a while after, but then – BAM! – cancer. And I'm telling you, Dick, there's no meaner killer. I thought I cut it out but it never went or it came back. Either way, I'm done. But I can't let it eat me, Richard. I've seen what that looks like. People looking like food for crows, pecked down to their bones."

"They might be able to—"

"No. Not this time. I can feel it. Like we both could feel it, remember?"

He remembered.

"I don't feel it anymore," he said. He lowered his hand and turned the scars away.

"No. I realise that now." She nodded. "That's good. You beat it."

"You can, too, Sal. You're a survivor."

She smiled at him, briefly, and for that moment it was like everything dark in that barn just beat its wings and left. "Yeah," she said. "I'm a survivor. But it's defined me my whole life and I'm more than that, aren't I? More than my traumas?"

"You've always been more than that to me."

"I know."

"And you're a mom, too."

She cried, then, suddenly and without warning. An eruption of tears like something had finally burst and she near collapsed with the force of it, except Richard was there to hold her up. As she had him, for so many years.

"She came looking for you."

"She's going to need you so much when I'm gone. She'll act like she doesn't, and that's my fault, but she will."

"Okay."

"I wanted to protect her, to *prepare* her, but now she hates the world and trusts no one in it, and that's my fault."

"No."

"She's tough, though. I mean, she's *hard*. I made her that way. You reap what you sow, I suppose."

"She's your daughter, that's all."

She nodded against him, then stepped away, wiping at her eyes. She said, "Fuck," to herself, and to Richard said, "Yeah. She's my daughter.

Now make her yours, at least for a while. Try to fix what I broke, okay. Like you did for me."

"What are you going to do?"

"I'm going to burn it all down."

"Let me help you."

She nodded. She smiled again. They doused the barn together, and when they were done Sally offered him a cigarette and he took one.

"You better smoke it outside," she said.

"You not having one?"

She shook her head and threw the pack to the scarecrow's lap.

"I quit."

From the back of her jeans, she drew a gun he recognised.

Whatever was left for them to say, they'd said already in different ways, including goodbye. They said it again, anyway.

Outside, in the light, Richard struck a flame to his cigarette and flinched when the gunshot came. A new scar for him to carry, to echo over and over in all the dark dreams to come. The cigarette fell from his mouth with his first sob, and he turned his back on the barn before he could see it burn.

Beyond the corn, a line of dust was rising from the unseen road. Richard waited, watching. He saw the corn stalks tremble, their tops waving with the movement of a vehicle passing through.

"Shit."

Richard went back to his truck and waited for her there.

She stared at him as she pulled up behind the vehicles. She was driving a Ford Maverick. The hood had been replaced with one she hadn't repainted to match, but it sounded like she kept good care of what was running beneath. She shut off the engine and slammed the door behind her when she exited.

"You forgot something," she said.

"Ginny give you directions?"

"Didn't ask. I waited and followed your dust from a way back." She nodded at the Dodge. "You speak to her? She all right?"

Richard couldn't answer.

"She in there?"

She started to walk towards the barn but then she saw the smoke and she asked again, "She in *there?*" and made as if to run in after her.

Richard stepped into her path. "No," he said. "She's gone."

She shoved him back, and he stumbled on his fucked-up leg, and she pushed him again as she said, "No she's not. She's *not*. Where is she?"

She drew a gun and pointed it at him.

He opened his arms to what she held and what she said. Admitting defeat was a crow he'd eaten long ago. So he stood like a scarecrow with his arms up, a strawman with no argument to make because life wasn't fair. You don't reap what you sow. People don't get what they deserve.

The barn was ablaze now, flames high and hot. He felt the heat of it at his back, as he always had.

"You left her."

He closed his eyes against the flash of a scythe he knew would come and waited for the crows to come calling.

Instead, he heard his daughter, sobbing as he had done. When he opened his eyes to look into hers he saw his own.

"She left me."

He walked to her with his arms still open and he held her, a loaded gun between them, and he asked, "What's your name?" but all she could do was cry. "What's your name?" he asked, in awe of all that Sally had given him and wondering if either of them deserved the other. "What's your name?"

Until eventually, she told him.

|The Whalers Song|

~

Sebjørn squinted against the pale light of the midnight sun. The sky was cloudless. There was no wind. Save for where it frothed against the hull of the *Höðr*, splitting around them into a wide V of wake, the sea was still, and vacant. It was so quiet that Sebjørn had become aware of the throbbing noise of the boat's engine, a sound so familiar that he was usually as ignorant of it as he was the pump-thump of his own heartbeat. The regularity of his breathing.

At the bow, Aaron leaned on the barrel of the harpoon cannon. He, too, searched the sea. He wore binoculars around his neck and occasionally he used them, but only briefly.

In the crow's nest, Sigved used his more frequently. He wore his bright orange waterproof, as if he'd seen rain the others were yet to notice. He wore the hood up, cords pulled so tight that it puckered around his face, and he held the binoculars at what little gap remained.

Brage and Nils – one port, one starboard – also looked to the water. Searching, like the others, for a plume of expelled spray. The run-off from an arching back. Maybe birds, sitting on the water, bobbing to eat krill.

There was nothing.

In the wheelhouse, Osvald held them steady. Grim-faced but fierce when others might be sullen. A suitable expression for a captain yet to catch his first whale of the season; of the thirty to forty they were set to catch this year, the crew of the *Höðr* had none.

Minke whales are the smallest of the baleen whales and can remain submerged for twenty minutes at a time. They barely breach when they come up for air, nor do they bring their flukes from the water when they dive. It makes them difficult to spot. For a species so apparently great in number – enough, at least, to be considered sustainable – they were proving to be frustratingly elusive this year.

Sebjørn checked his watch. Another day would soon be over. Another night. He clapped his gloved hands together a couple of times and rubbed them. Not because he was cold but because the gesture felt decisive. Come on now, he thought. Show us something. Give us something to take home.

Nils, standing close beside him, chose that moment to begin singing. Not a whaling song, but a traditional fishing song. His father, he'd said, had been a fisherman, but then every whaler was a fisherman in the winter.

The men on the *Höðr* knew the song.

Brage turned and smiled at Nils, smiled at Sebjørn, and added his deep voice to the chorus. Sebjørn mouthed the words as well, quietly at first but gaining enthusiasm with the others. Aaron, at the cannon, waved his arms to conduct an imagined orchestra and they sang of the rise and fall of the sea, of the catch and the haul, driven by a rhythm meant to ease hard work, though they had none.

A sudden whistle, brief and shrill, cut the song short. Sigved had the binoculars at his face but was holding them with only one hand; with the other he pointed.

There. A small cloud of spray. The mist of a blowhole, spouting. It settled quickly on such a windless day, drifting just enough to indicate a direction of movement.

Sebjørn offered Sigved a thumbs up. The man nodded, unclipping the radio from his belt and calling through to the captain, but Osvald was already steering the boat around. The men cheered as the vessel turned. This was it. At last, the thrill of the hunt.

There was another eruption of spray ahead and a dark shape emerged from the water before slipping back under.

There were two of them.

Aaron readied himself at the harpoon cannon. Brage took one of the rifles from the nearby rack. He wouldn't need it. The harpoon was grenade-tipped, designed to explode inside the whale's brain, and Aaron was a good shot.

The blast of the cannon shuddered through the deck. The *Höðr* was a small vessel and all of it trembled when the gunner fired. Sebjørn, resting against a rail, felt it thrumming as he watched nylon wire unravel behind the harpoon. Heard the wire hiss its sizzling echo to the sudden thunder that had launched it.

The whale turned and, with a final wave of fin, it rolled. Raised its side to the sky. Its pale underbelly.

Brage lowered the rifle.

"Eight meters," said Nils beside Sebjørn. Sebjørn nodded. Twenty six, twenty seven feet. Half the size of the *Höðr*. About average. But average was good. Small would have been good. Average was *very* good.

Sebjørn looked to the wheelhouse. Osvald, usually so serious, was smiling. Sebjørn was glad to see it.

A metallic whine from the winch signalled the men to their stations. The nylon cord yanked its slack out of the water, flinging seawater skyward as it pulled taut with the weight of their whale, and Sebjørn clapped his hands together.

"Let's get to work!"

The minke laid sprawled across the deck, a ragged pulp of meat and blubber where the harpoon had exploded close to the thorax. A good shot. Sebjørn inspected it briefly, nodded at Aaron, and with the others began to carve the animal into pieces.

They would strip several tonnes from the carcass, reducing it to a head and a tail with only bones in between. The tail had been nearly severed already in coming out of the sea, the winch pulling cord through flesh as the whale's own weight split skin and blubber and muscle down to the bone. The deck was awash with blood. The men were red to their elbows, rubber suits smeared about the chest and waist. Boots sliding in the mess that spread around them.

Sebjørn was in charge of the flensing. He carved blubber into thick strips, handing them to Nils to send below where Brage packed them in ice. Whale blubber was not like animal fat. It was not soft; cutting it demanded strength. Sebjørn was still strong. He enjoyed the work. It was greasy, stinking work, and he was slick with fat and fluids, but it was men's work and he was happy.

Sigved and Aaron followed Sebjørn's progress. They drew their knives through meat and muscle, laying each thick chunk on the deck ready to go below. They all worked in focussed silence, save for the grunts and exhalations of their exertions. There were plenty of songs they could have used to accompany, even ease, their efforts, but by some unspoken agreement they worked without them. As if a song would make this routine when the catch was far too special: they would honour it with quiet efficiency. There was chorus enough, anyway, from the birds that had appeared from nowhere, circling and diving and crying their impatience, calling at each other in battle over whatever scraps made it to the sea.

The heavy bulk before the men, thick under their hands and firm against their bodies, uncurled piece by piece until the body was an open wet cavity, red and white and steaming in the cold air. The grey-black whale, skin shining like an oil-slick, was swiftly becoming a length of bones. These would be thrown back to the sea; today's whaling was concerned only with the blubber and the meat beneath. The blubber would be rendered down to oil. The meat would be eaten.

Sebjørn cut away one of the fins, let it drop to the deck, and kicked it overboard. The sea had fed the whale, the whale would feed the sea. He cut into the sagging swell of whale belly and reached inside, pushing bones aside to locate the stomach. Cut it loose. He hefted it overboard like a shot-put, startling the birds with its heavy splash. For a moment it rose again, buoyant, but it wouldn't float for long. The birds were already pulling it to pieces, screeching their excitement, fighting. Tossing their heads back to swallow whatever chunks they managed to scavenge while smaller scraps sank for the fishes.

Behind Sebjørn, somebody swore. Somebody yelled. He turned to see Sigved throwing a punch at Nils, who sprawled across the whale carcass. Nils lashed out in return. Sigved turned the blow aside with an open hand but hissed in pain. Sebjørn yelled at both of them. One held the curved blade of a flensing knife, the other a metal hook for dragging slabs of butchered meat, but he stepped between them and shoved them apart. He didn't ask what the fight had been about because it didn't matter. Men would always fight.

Sigved snatched up one of the hoses and washed blood from his palm. A smile gaped there, filling with more blood as he flexed his fingers.

"Get it bandaged," Sebjørn said.

Sigved gestured with a quick jab of his head to where the meat was piling up beside Nils. "He's clumsy," he said. "And he's slow."

Nils was new. He had worked a couple of other boats previously but there was some truth to what Sigved said, Sebjørn had to admit.

"If we don't find another whale for a while you can take it out on each other then."

Sigved twisted a bandage around his hand. He nodded.

Sebjørn looked at Nils. The man was working his jaw, probing his cheek for loose teeth. "Fine by me."

"There's at least one more out there," Aaron said. "I saw it."

"Good," said Sigved, "because I've got more meat hanging between my legs than we'll get off of this one."

Aaron laughed. Sebjørn too, after a moment. Nils slammed his hook into another steak and dragged it away.

The radio at Sebjørn's belt crackle-spat to life and Osvald told him that the next man to strike another would be thrown overboard. Sebjørn acknowledged the statement and showed the men his radio as if the captain's words were still coming from it. The captain of a vessel was its law. Sebjørn looked to the wheelhouse but Osvald had already put them out of mind.

The *Höðr* carried them further north.

The men ate together in the cramped galley, bunched around a scarred table, hunched over their meals like hungry convicts. The room was warm and thick with the smell of whale meat fried in garlic and butter. The briny smell of drying clothes. The smell of hard work. And there was beer. They carried very little on board, but there was always something for celebrating the first catch. The men were loud with good humour. Laughing, shoving each other with boisterous banter. Drumming on the table. Around them, on the walls, on cupboard doors, were pages torn from magazines. Centrefolds. Celebrities in varying states of undress. The women had been renamed several times over. They had each been girlfriends, had each been wives. Many of them had been graffitied from boredom. Tattooed in pen, enhanced, made monstrous. Aaron, leaning in his chair, added a geyser gush to one of the ladies, swearing and shaking at the pen dying in his hand, but laughing with Brage's encouragement. Old men being boys. The captain always ate separate from the rest of the crew. It allowed them such freedoms.

Sebjørn shoved his plate aside as soon as his meal was done and grabbed for cigarettes that hadn't been in his shirt pocket for over a year. What he found there instead was the postcard he had replaced them with. He knew all of the words but he read them again anyway, faded though they were. On the other side, a familiar picture. The image cracked, white lines like scars where the card had folded. It was the Snøhuit facility where his son worked, flames spouting hundreds of feet into the air from the gas plant's chimney, higher than any of the mountains behind and casting a fiery glow over the town below. "There she blows!" his son had written across it. A joke, but also a sharp reminder of how times had changed.

"Hammerfest," Nils said, looking over from beside him.

Sebjørn nodded.

"Who do you know there?"

"My son," Sebjørn said, though he didn't really know the boy anymore. Didn't know the man. As a father he had always been more elusive than any whale.

"It is a good place," Nils said. He took another mouthful of beer.

It probably was. Anna had always said so, back when she used to try to make Sebjørn feel better. Hammerfest had been a dying town before the gas plant. Now it was not only rejuvenated but expanding. Yet it had been a fishing town once. Sebjørn couldn't help wishing it was still.

"He works there," Sebjørn told Nils, though the man had not asked. "My son."

He had gone away to school, and though he had returned he did not stay long. The young never did. They took work in the cities. Tourist jobs, and the oil industry. They left the island communities behind them. The fishing, the whaling. The winter seas and the challenging summers. When Sebjørn was a boy there were nearly two hundred whaling vessels working the waters off the north of Norway. He worked those same waters now on one of maybe twenty.

"Your son works at Snøhuit?" Nils asked. "Good! That's good!" He slapped at Sebjørn's arm a few times in celebration. "The world's cleanest petroleum project." Nils tried to explain how the company owning the plant separated carbon dioxide from the natural gas. How the carbon dioxide would be injected it into the seabed. Some way of helping with global warming. Sebjørn barely listened. He had heard it before.

"Why do you not work in the city?" he asked Nils. "You're young."

"My father."

It was answer enough. Nils's father had been on the *Lofotofangst*, lost last year. Sebjørn had already assumed it must have been something to do with that. Assumed that was why Osvald had hired someone so green. Only last month, the *Bjørn* had gone down with all hands, too. There had been experienced men on both of those vessels but it hadn't made any difference. The sea was like that sometimes.

"We never really got on," Nils said. Sebjørn thought that was probably true of most of the men here. Their own fathers. Their own sons. Nils grinned and said, "I never really liked whaling," and raised his bottle to toast the apology. The challenge.

Yes, he was like other sons.

"It is the same as farming," said Sigved. "They are like cows. It's like slaughtering cows."

Nils nodded. "Like cows, of course. Yes. Except people still eat beef."

"People still eat whale meat."

"People *buy* whale meat. It is tradition. They respect the tradition."

"*You* just ate whale meat," Sebjørn noted. In amusement, not to encourage argument. His own view depended on his mood. He was a fisherman, and whales drove the fish closer to shore. Made fishing easier. It was good to have them around. But they also ate the fish, and so he wasn't against culling them either. Sebjørn was a fisherman, but he was also a whaler. It only depended on the time of year. They were all of them hunters. Only the prey changed.

Aaron, who had been blowing a melody over the tops of beer bottles, joined in to say, "Sustainable." It was a word he liked to use.

Brage agreed. "Japan and Iceland do it, too."

"Last year we caught more whales than Japan and Iceland combined," Nils said.

"Didn't feel like it."

"And it's not even legal, not really. There are international treaties and—"

Sigved stood abruptly. He knocked the table hard enough that bottles bounced on their bases. "You don't understand," he said. "You're too young." He nudged Nils more than was necessary in leaving. Men like Sigved built their arguments on experience. Young men, like Nils, used statistics and what they'd read elsewhere.

Sebjørn looked again at the photo in his calloused hands and relished the day's ache in his arms, his back. His old bones. *There she blows!* He looked at that plume of fire. Looked at the buildings of the Snøhuit and the town around it. He tried to imagine working in such a place and was glad when he could not.

Sebjørn woke suddenly, thinking of the harpoon cannon. He could still feel its shudder through the boat.

Across from him, Nils stirred in his bunk. He turned to one elbow and rubbed at his face. He started to say something but there was another vibration, a thrumming through the boat from beneath.

Sebjørn leaned out to see Aaron nursing his head in the bunk below. "What was that? We shooting something?"

It wasn't the harpoon cannon. The reverberations were stronger.

Osvald appeared in the doorway. He held both sides of the frame for a moment – "Get up." – and was gone again. Sebjørn called after him but there was no answer to his question. He swung his legs out from the bunk, dropped to the floor, and staggered as the boat suddenly shifted. He fell into Aaron emerging from his own bunk and the two of them grabbed at each other and the bunks to stop from sprawling.

The vessel shifted again. A protracted list to starboard. It righted itself afterwards but was slow doing so.

"Something's wrong."

One of them said it. All of them knew it. Sebjørn pulled himself straight and used the momentum to hurry out to the passageway. The *Höðr* was sitting lower in the water. He could feel it. Could feel the sea pressing in on all sides. They were held in a grip of high water.

Brage was hurrying towards him.

"Where's the captain?"

But Brage pushed past. "We're abandoning ship," he said. Sebjørn grabbed him, caught a bunch of his clothing in his fist as the man pressed between him and the wall, but there was nothing else to say. The clothing in his grip told him everything; Brage was in his waterproofs. He had a life jacket hooked over his head. Sebjørn let him go.

"Come on," Sigved said, suddenly with them. He had his vest in one hand. Then he was gone, hurrying to the deck.

Aaron, pulling on his boots, asked, "What's happening?"

Sebjørn grabbed the handheld, but if Osvald had his radio he wasn't answering.

"All right," Sebjørn said, tossing the radio. He clapped his hands together once, twice. "Let's go."

They fell out of the room as the vessel plunged suddenly under them. The floor dropped away and came up again, pitching them against the wall. They rushed to the deck in a stumble, snatching life vests as they went.

It was bright outside. Calm. Boats could sink in any weather, yet Sebjørn thought there should be winds. High waves. The deck should be getting swamped again and again with crashing water. That was how it happened whenever he dreamed it. Instead, all was still. Brage and Sigved stood prepping the raft between them, taking a final moment to read through the instructions printed on its side. They could have been at the seaside or beside a swimming pool, preparing some novelty inflatable, though they stood to their ankles in seawater. A gentle wave of it washed over Sebjørn's feet.

He glanced at the wheelhouse.

"Where's the captain?"

Nobody answered. Brage or Sigved pulled the appropriate cord and together they threw the raft out to sea to inflate. They climbed over the gunwale and leapt one after the other without a backwards glance. There was no need to consider the necessary actions here. The *Höðr* was already lost.

Sebjørn called to Aaron. The man was patting at his pockets. Looking for something, or performing a mental checklist of all he carried. He looked at Sebjørn long enough to nod then made his way to the raft. Nils was looking around the deck, as amazed as Sebjørn at how it sat almost level with the sea. When it pitched backwards, all of them staggered with it, and then as it leaned to port they ricocheted off each other and fell that way, too. Clutched at the gunwales. Sebjørn hit them just as the boat righted itself again. Flipped over them with the sudden rise of the deck. Spun. Grabbed at something, anything, whatever he could. Caught his ankle on something hard that snapped a sharp pain into his brain. Maybe he felt water rushing in over him, but it might have been a moment of unconsciousness. Either way, when he shook the darkness off he was in the sea. His clothing had ballooned up around him. His vest was high around his neck, too loose on his body and too tight against his throat. He splashed and kicked in a circle to find everyone. A flash of bright pain lit up his ankle again but he saw the raft. Someone, Nils, was being hauled inside.

The *Höðr* was beside him. A protrusion of winch-arm and a wheelhouse roof and that was all. Strangely level, like a floor he could climb up onto, though it wouldn't be long before it sank completely. He wanted to get as far away from it as he could before that happened. He wanted to get into the raft. He twisted in the water to begin a strong, short, crawl.

He felt the pull of water. Movement on both sides as the sea tugged him back, pulled against him. He sensed something large behind him, displacing the water he moved in, and imagined the *Höðr* descending. For a moment he thought it moved beneath him, thought he saw its large dark shape in the water, and he grabbed at the air, desperate to pull himself away. His hand came down on the rubber of the raft. Then the others had him around the wrist, the forearm, under the armpit, and they hauled him in from the sea.

Dragging the life-raft ashore is difficult. Awkward. The men are exhausted. They splash through the shallows with their heads down, shoulders hunched against the wind as they stagger towards land. Wavelets froth onto a black shore salted white with ice and snow. Frozen sand cracks and scrunches tight under wet boots as they stumble inland. Raft bumping between them, they make puddles with each footprint they press into the beach. Churn its sand and snow into slush.

Sebjørn has no idea where they are.

Jan Mayen is far west. The Lofoten Islands are east, and closer to land. It is not Svalbard, nor anywhere near it. Osvald has taken the *Höðr* further out than is usual – he had admitted as much in the raft. They are well north of Norway, into the Arctic Circle. Stuck, now, on a barren spit of land they do not know.

The island is a sloping stretch of rock and black sand, lurching into a short chain of black mountains at the northern end. Sebjørn thinks of trolls and Valkyries and wonders where the hell they are. Remembers something his son told him once: in the last three decades, retreating sea ice has freed over a million square miles of ocean. That, he'd explained, was why whales were proving harder to find; global warming allowed them more space in which to disappear. He called this new space "the meltwaters". The Arctic was a ghost. A fading place that haunted the very ocean it created in its passing.

Osvald points, not looking to see which of his men pays attention. Assuming, correctly, that they all do.

White with ice, protruding from the snow-spotted sand, are rows upon rows of wooden racks. Cod-drying racks where loops of twine shine with icicles, some of them so thick and heavy it seems fish still hang there. Translucent. Ethereal. The ghosts of fish.

"Over there."

This time Osvald moves towards where he points. The men follow, dropping the raft, holding their wet bodies tight. Shivering as they make their way towards the leaning shape.

It's a boat. Turned over, propped into a makeshift shelter with poles from the nearby drying racks. Drifts of snow slope up the overturned hull. Curl around the prow and stern. The boat is half buried but still a serviceable windbreak.

Sebjørn runs his hands over the vessel. "Lichen," he says. It's been here for a while. It's wooden. It has been here for a *very* long while.

"We're looking at history," says Sigved. His bandaged hand is on one of the supporting poles. He's looking at where the tip has been forced into the wood of the leaning boat, and Sebjørn sees it isn't part of the drying racks at all. It's a harpoon. A rusting, metal-headed harpoon. The non-explosive kind. No, not a harpoon: a barbed lance. Whales were harpooned from small boats like this one only as a means of attaching the whalers to their catch. They would pull themselves closer, closer, as the animal tired itself fleeing, struggling, and when they were close enough they would stab it into submission with lances like these. Whale hunting has been part of Norwegian culture for centuries, but back in the beginning it had been far bloodier. Sebjørn shakes his head. How difficult it must have been, penetrating all that blubber with a lance. There were no grenade harpoons with their 80% IDR back then. No such thing as an instant death rate at all. Only stabbing and hacking until you found the right coil of arteries. Grinding the lance in widening circles as the sea spread red and the beast drowned in its own blood. Sebjørn imagines spouts of that blood gushing in a geyser spray. Falling as hot rain while the whale thrashes with its tail pounding, mouth snapping. Twisting and turning its body until finally—

"Listen."

Osvald has his head turned to a sound he's caught. The men are quiet with him, trying to hear it themselves. Sebjørn hears only the sea, sweeping down the shore. Raking over rocks.

Osvald shakes his head. "It's gone," he says. "The wind," he says.

But to Sebjørn he does not sound certain.

Not far from the boat, they find the rotten ruins of a building. It rises from amongst the rocks that curve with the cove behind the leaning boat. What is left of its wood is wet and soft. Inside, some collapsed roof, crusted with sand and shells. A shore station. More of the past. A remnant from when whalers would set anchor on an island like this, building a shelter to work from using materials from the ship. There they would wait, looking for whales from shore. Riding the waves out to fetch them, lance them, bring them back. Boil the meat and blubber down to bones. Barrel the oil for soap, paint, varnish. Store the bones for clothing, umbrellas. Ambergris for perfume.

Osvald stands where once there was a door, his head turned and tilted. He has been standing that way for long moments, the men gathered behind him. Eventually, Sebjørn speaks.

"Captain?"

Osvald raises his hand to silence him. The men look at each other. As if another one of them has spoken, Osvald hisses for shush. Says, "Quiet," and winces, as if regretting his own sound. He shakes his head as if to clear it and steps inside what little remains of the shore station. He looks around. He looks at the ground. He scuffs at something with his foot.

"Anything?"

He glances back at Sebjørn and shakes his head again, a silent answer as he listens. Snaps his attention left, then right. Stares at something he sees there instead.

The men wait. Some of them are shivering.

"We should shelter in the raft," Sebjørn says. "We could—"

In two, three strides, Osvald is back outside with them. He seizes Sebjørn by his life vest. Shakes him. "*Quiet.* I will tell you what must be done."

Sebjørn is a large man. He is bulkier still in his waterproof clothing and vest. Osvald is greyer with age but he is larger, and he carries the extra weight of his authority. Every man feels it.

He releases Sebjørn. Looks at each of the others. "Bring the raft here."

The men do as they are told and they do it in silence. The only sound between them is the heft of the wind. It comes to shore with more force than the waves, cutting over rock and casting sand at their skin in abrupt gusts. Sebjørn keeps his head down. He tries to hunch deeper into his coat. When he checks on the other men beside him he sees Brage pull hard at his hat, yanking it down to protect his ears. Fumbling at his coat's collar for the hood that is buttoned up inside.

Nils stops walking with them, so Sebjørn stops too and looks at him. He grabs his arm and pulls him forward but the man only stumbles. He points. When Sebjørn looks, he sees the other men have stopped as well. They are looking at the expanse of beach stretched out before them. They are looking at:

"Bones."

The beach is filled with them, scattered like strange seashells. Large lengths of rib protruding from the sand. Lines of broken spine. Scattered vertebrae. Irregular blocks of strewn bone. Giant skulls, half buried, sand spilling in neat slopes from the sockets and open mouths. Long frozen grins. Pale, ice-sheened baleen.

"There are so many," says Brage. He turns his whole body to look at the others, hood pulled down tight over his head with both hands.

"Yes."

So many. As many whales as Sebjørn has ever seen in his lifetime, it seems. Full skeletons, remarkably intact where they have come to rest, washed clean to bleached bone. Collapsed structures holding shape enough to show head, body, tail. A protrusion of fin. Ribs curving up in half-cages, or sitting in arched segments like giant bone-spiders. Too many for drift whales, Sebjørn feels. Surely this many would not simply wash ashore.

And there is so much more shore now. A vast spread of dark sand where moments ago there had been the frothy slush of a cold sea. The raft sits isolated on an open expanse of beach and bones while the tide washes out in retreat, far away. A quiet, passing, *hush*.

Sebjørn strains to hear it.

Husshhh.

A sudden gust of wind flings the sea at him. A fierce spray that stings his skin. Spits salt into his eyes. There has been no crash of wave to explain it, not that he has heard, yet the wind is wet and sharp. He winces into it and sees the blurs of his companions hunker down. Nils crouches. A trick of perspective makes him look like the eye of one of the skulls some way behind him. A foetal man against an elongated dome. A part-swallowed Jonah.

A stuttered shush draws Sebjørn to the life raft scudding across the sand. It comes to rest for a moment against a claw of ribs. At one end, a length of jaw, sharp and beak-like, angles up at the sky. The raft shudders to move again.

"Grab it."

He hurries the men from where they crouch and hunch their bodies. Only Sigved hesitates, his hood pulled down tight in fists that press against his face.

"Sigved!"

The man doesn't seem to hear, but he sees Sebjørn approaching and gets to his feet. He keeps his hands at his ears. The bandage on one of them has begun to unravel. A wet length of rag, dangling.

"Whale brains have a section we don't."

Sebjørn looks at Nils. He is staring into whalebone. "They have a section we can't even understand."

Sebjørn feels like he knew this. Perhaps his son had told him. His unfathomable son.

The raft rests against a skeleton far larger than the others, with a head at one end accounting for almost a third of its length. It does not have the baleen plates of a minke for filtering food. It's a toothed whale. The largest of its kind.

"Sperm whale," says Sigved. He is winding the bandage from his hand around his head instead. Over his ears.

Sperm whales have the largest brain of any animal, even the giant blue whale, but this fleshless head has been opened and emptied of everything. A man could stand inside the case where once there had been a brain and 500 gallons of thick, precious fluid. The first men to ever see it had thought of sperm. Sebjørn supposes they had been at sea for a while, without women. He wonders, if he put his ear to the skull, what would he hear? The ocean? Would it roar louder than the eerie whisper that currently hushed in with each wave? Or would it merely be the flush of his own blood, pulsing? His own heartbeat, a years-late echo of something dead.

We're looking at history, he remembers.

"The raft."

Between them, they prepare to carry it across the sand and snow. Sebjørn looks over the few supplies the others had thrown in with them. Amongst the plastic boxes and foil-wrapped bricks of food lies one of the rifles. Who had paused long enough on a sinking vessel to grab that? Still, he is glad to have it. Its presence reminds him of what they are, these men. That they are not helpless.

"Ssh!"

The men, reaching for handholds around the raft, rummaging at the few supplies within, pause in their actions. Frozen. Looking at Aaron.

"Did you hear that?" he asks.

The men have nothing for a reply, but they listen.

"The captain," Sebjørn says. Not because he thinks he heard him, but because he speaks his thoughts aloud and his thoughts are with Osvald.

Aaron nods. He hefts his side of the raft, and says, "Let's go."

They struggle the raft back to the ancient boat amongst the fishing racks. Back to where the shore station rots amongst the rocks. Of Osvald, though, there is no sign.

The captain is gone.

The photograph flutters in Sebjørn's hands. There are gaps between the boards of the ancient boat he shelters behind. He has not been reading the postcard, merely holding it while he thinks of Osvald. He is still missing. Tracks they'd found had led only to the sea, nowhere else. They'd followed them to the water's edge, and further still, into the shallows, as if the receding tide may have left some trace of them. But of course there was nothing.

A quick gust snatches at the place Sebjørn has never been, takes it from his hands, and casts it away down the beach. He grabs for it, stands in a hurry to chase it, but leaves it lost when he sees Sigved.

The man has been acting strange since the captain's disappearance. Talking to himself. Looking at places only he seems to see. Now he stands distant at the shoreline, waves lapping at his feet. His head is cocked to one side, bandage askew. Ear turned to the sea that hushes in. Hushes away.

Nils steps close to Sebjørn. "What is he doing?"

They watch as the tide washes out over the long skulls of whales. Each hollowed dome fills and empties with the waves, awash with ocean. Sigved stands amongst them. Head tilted, as if they have something to tell him. Some secret to whisper.

Sebjørn opens his mouth to call Sigved but the sound that comes to him on the wind quietens him. A piping noise, long and low. A melancholy melody sent to him through the bones. Whistling over them and through. One note. Two. Mournful, and haunting, beautiful and—

The raised voices of an argument pull Sebjørn back from his thoughts.

"Let me go!"

Brage is dragging at Aaron's sleeve. Yanking at his jacket. Aaron is pushing back. Shoving at Brage's chest. Kicking at his legs.

"Sebjørn," says Brage. "Help me."

"Help you what?"

But he goes to them. Puts his hands between them, tries to prise them apart. Brage shoves at Sebjørn to get his hands on Aaron again. The back of his jacket tears as the man turns away. "Let him go," Sebjørn warns.

Brage pulls so violently that he and Aaron fall. They topple some of the fishing trestles and the rifle that had been leaning against them. Sebjørn stumbles with them but keeps to his feet. He helps Brage to his then puts his body between him and Aaron. "What the hell are you doing?" He pushes him back a few steps.

But it isn't Brage who answers. It's Aaron. He's standing with the rifle cradled in his arms. "Don't you hear it?"

"Aaron…"

"Don't any of you hear it?"

Brage lunges at Aaron but Aaron sees it coming and strikes at him with the rifle. He has it turned, stock first, and he hits Brage in the chest. In the face.

Nils stands wide-eyed. Sebjørn glances for help from Sigved but the man has noticed nothing of this. He stands in the receding sea. Further out now, as if the tide has pulled him with each wave.

Brage grabs for Aaron again, this time for the rifle. Manages to get his large hands on the rifle butt. He pulls it to him, hand over hand, gathering it to him like rope, and Sebjørn sees what is about to happen a moment before it does. Too late to warn them. Too late to do anything. Brage pulls at the stock and Aaron pulls at the barrel and his head is flung back with a sudden spray of blood. A following crack of sound.

Sebjørn turns away from the sight of a man sprawled in the sand and watches Sigved wading deeper out to sea, too stunned to say or do anything to stop him.

∽

"Do you think the captain sent a signal in time?"

Nils is standing, looking down the beach when he asks. There is little to look at. The waves sweep in slowly, barely moving up the shore. Leaving more of it behind.

"Hmm?"

Sebjørn sits in the sand beside Aaron. The wind is making his ears ache. Constantly, now, he hears how it whistles through the bones. How it arcs over the turned boat and cuts between the soft boards of the collapsing shore station. The island is awash with the rise and fall of its music. The keening two-note call that threads through him, low and long.

"A distress signal," Nils says. "Do you think he got one out in time?"

"It's automatic."

The *Höðr*'s beacon would have activated as soon as the vessel took on water, broadcasting their position.

"How long before they find us?"

Sebjørn doesn't answer. After all, the *Lofotofangst* had the same equipment. The *Bjørn*, too.

"Sebjørn?"

"I don't know."

Aaron lies on his back on the beach, staring at the sky. Blood has pooled around his head, a crimson nimbus that refuses to soak into the wet sand.

"Sebjørn? Where's the rifle now?"

"Brage took it."

He can't remember if he knows that or not. Or if he knows where Brage has taken it, either. Can't think much of anything with that constant noise. The peep and elongated squeal. Regular enough it seems like song and frustrating in its patterned resounding. But beautiful, too.

Sebjørn looks back at where the raft sits, nestled between the fishless racks. A red light blinks from it. A white. Mostly they pulse out of time with each other but sometimes, briefly, there is synchronicity. A pattern that stretches out and comes back in and repeats.

"Do you think he'll come back?" Nils asks. Adding "Brage", because he could have meant somebody else. Anybody else but Aaron.

Sebjørn has no answer for him. He returns to staring out to sea. It has retreated further still, the shore expanding as the waterline recedes, and recedes, and recedes. And everywhere, all he sees are bones. Pale prisons curving from and on the dark sand. Giant skulls, scoured smooth by the sea, grinning their wide lines of baleen. Tails of spine behind pointing to where the sea retreats, retreats. And carried to him from between them, over and through them, comes that watery, drawn-out, sound of low notes.

Whale-song.

Sebjørn smiles. Of course it's watery. Water transmits sound far better than air. And then he thinks, we are 80% water. Something like that.

He slaps at his ears. Head bowed, he strikes himself a flurry of blows, as if he can knock the noise from his head. Muffle it with the singing sting of pain. Yet it is a smell that distracts him.

Smoke.

Beside the shelter of the overturned boat, a thick column of dark smoke rises from a fire where men warm themselves.

"Hey!"

Sebjørn scrambles in the sand to get up, clumsy with his injured ankle. He lopes towards the men in a limping stagger, dimly aware of Nils moving with him.

"*Hey!*"

The wind tears the smoke ragged, throws it around. Twists the black stink of it into a greasy coil that clings to the skin of the men gathered around the fire. They are not simply warming their hands by the flames. They are working with them.

"What are you doing?"

One of them holds something. He makes downward strokes with a blade.

"Captain? What are you doing?"

The man glances at Sebjørn through the smoke. His face is bloody. His forehead is dark with it. Hair sticks up in oily clumps. His beard is grimed. It isn't Osvald. It isn't anyone Sebjørn knows. None of them are. Each is filthy with the grime of their work, blood-streaked and soot-stained. They are dressed in simple clothes, all cloth and leather. One wears a coil of rope across his chest like a bandolier. Another carves at a slab of blubber with a rusted blade. He cuts it into sections like pages, each of them an inch or so thick. As Sebjørn watches, he fans them out and drops them into a pot that boils over the black fire. A glut of bubbling blubber, dense and popping, belching the heavy stench of melting meat juices. One of the men reaches into the pot, his gloves thick with grease. He retrieves crisp pieces from the oil, skims them from where they float, and casts them underneath into the flames. Fuel for the fire that renders the rest into something new.

"Sebjørn?"

We are looking at history.

Who said that?

As if suddenly aware that Sebjørn watches, each of the men looks up from their work. Together, they open their mouths wide.

Sebjørn slams his hands to his ears and crouches, turning away. He expects that drawn, hollow vowel sound, the two-note chorus of whale-song, to come from the mouths of those who once hunted them, and he turns from it quickly. Strikes the pot suspended over the fire. Nothing spills, though it falls to where there was once a fire and is gone, dispersed into absence like the wind-driven smoke. Like the men, too, gone with the song that retreats, retreats. Summoned away by the sounds of its own diminishing echo as it retreats. Retreats.

And repeats.

Sebjørn scoops up snow and sand with each hand and clutches them to his head. Packs ice coarse with grit into his ears to silence what he can't not hear. Handful after handful of sand, snow, stones. Forcing it in tight. But the song remains inside his head. He fights the pull of it, the rise and fall of its siren call, and shudders. Shivers. Spasms with the cold forever in his bones. And all the while his hands are at his ears, pressing them flat. Forcing a hush of blood that sounds like an empty ocean.

The hand on his shoulder startles him. He makes fists in reflex and so has no choice but to hear:

"What are you doing out here?"

He is crouching at the shoreline, Nils standing beside him. A wave laps over their feet. Sebjørn stands slowly and looks back at the long, long, expanse of beach behind. It stretches far away from him...

    ... away...

        ... away...

            right back to where an old boat leans out of the sand like a rotten loose tooth.

Nils reaches for Sebjørn –

"Come on, come with me."

– but Sebjørn steps away. He faces the darkening sea as a wave comes in, bringing with it more of the same music, and when it recedes it takes it away again. Leaves more shore behind. There are prints in the sand, impossible prints that have not been washed away. That lead into the sea and its music.

Nils positions himself in front of Sebjørn, holding his arms out as if to embrace him. Block him. He is speaking, but Sebjørn can't hear more than a muffle of noise because he has covered his ears as he walks with the receding tide. He does not stop walking, treading wet sand into gurgling puddles. A drowned man's splutter. Every step he takes is the sound of a throat closing with water as the sea draws back, and back still, and shows him the *Höðr*. The *Lofotofangst*. The *Bjørn*. Others. All of them beached and leaning vacant.

We are looking at history.

Sebjørn limps towards them, hands at his head like a marched prisoner. He thinks of the taut rope that tethers whalers to the whale. The tight line that tows one behind the other across the tops of white waves.

It's not just whales we're chasing, Sebjørn realises. It has never just been whales.

Suddenly the sea retreats from him no more. Where once there had been a growing expanse of shore comes a final surge and swell of surf as the ocean rushes in to meet him. It engulfs his knees, his thighs, climbs high up his vestless chest, and turns him about in its violent tide to show him a beach in illusory movement; the bones of whales rushing back into the swift encroaching sea.

And here are the whales now. Two of them. Three. Four of them. Five. They swim with him amongst them and draw him away, out to sea. Arcing slow curves as they appear, then submerge. Raising tails that make wide Vs in descent. Waves that haunt the minds of men in their beckoning.

On the diminishing shore, Nils struggles to free the raft that will save him, surrounded by whaling men. Sebjørn opens his mouth to call a warning but the water hushes him, rushing in with the roar of a whale exhaling as the island that had been slowly rising to heave itself free of the sea dives once more with a mountainous flip of its tail.

|Acknowledgements|

~

I need to say thanks to a few people regarding this book.

You, for example. Thanks for reading. I hope you enjoyed the stories. If you did, please spread the words.

Speaking of readers, Steven Dines, Mitch Larney, Ian Rogers, and Stephen Volk – you all took the time to read this when it was still becoming what it is today, and I really appreciate that, just as I appreciate every bit of feedback you gave along the way. Cheers, guys.

Stephen Volk gets a double thank you because he was kind enough to write the introduction, too. He also deserves thanks for buying the best cheese on writing weekends.

Steve Shaw, thanks for all you've done with this collection of sad little stories, and for all of your encouragement (and saint-like patience). Thanks for your editing skills (damn those em dashes!) and for the tremendous amount of work you put in with the cover design and entire look of this book as a gorgeous artefact in its own right. I love it.

Everyone who has ever taken my work – Andy Cox, Michael Kelly, Steve J Shaw, Mark Morris, Christopher M Jones, Anthony Cowin, and Ellen Datlow, amongst others – thanks. Every time you print or reprint a story I'm encouraged to write another one. So a lot of this is your fault.

And everyone who has ever reviewed my work, thanks. You're all stars. Reading it in the first place gets a big thank you anyway, but taking the time to write about it too? Thank you.

I'm winding up now, don't worry.

Very special thanks are due to my Sense4 who help keep me sane every Saturday by challenging my liver and my memory. May our undies always match. (Hashtag besties.)

And of course, thank you Jess, aka thespooktique.co.uk. Thanks for all the wax melts (never has horror smelled so good). And for all the beverages. And all the edits. And for being the best kind of distraction from everything I'm *supposed* to be doing. Most of all, thanks for reminding me to have fun once in a while. Add it to the list of reasons why I love you.

CPSIA information can be obtained
at www.ICGtesting.com
Printed in the USA
LVHW111832130622
721160LV00005B/41

9 781913 038762